Yulal
Lowen River
Montfar
Dulgaa
Plet
Chalda
W
E
S
Obesque
Valde
Trefair
Flum River
Dunsque
I0726265

To Buela
Enjoy a beautiful eternity

For we do not wrestle against flesh and blood, but against principalities, against powers, against the rulers of the darkness of this age, against spiritual hosts of wickedness in the heavenly places.

— EPHESIANS 6:12

PROLOGUE

The blood-red door on the right slammed shut as the first Reigner traded their heart away. The usual cool weather plummeted to a frigid chill. Damien frowned, crossing his arms over his chest as the crowd buzzed around him, thick with anticipation and desire. Something wasn't right.

As the thought flew through his mind, a guttural cackle erupted from between the two doors.

"You, stupid humans!" the vendor, Schism Breaker, laughed as his fingers elongated into midnight claws. His skin stretched as his limbs transformed him into a horrid creature with red eyes and decrepit wings. "It's time for a new reign in this dismal realm."

Before anyone could react, Schism attacked. Bodies flew through the market, striking buildings and crashing onto the cobblestone streets. Delectable pastries and shining trinkets plummeted to the ground as the crowd exploded into screams of terror and panic. People shoved against one another as the Traders scattered away from the popular vendor. Damien lifted his arms, ready to brace himself against the oncoming horde. He knew something like this would happen one day. Turning to his lady on his right, he placed a hand on her cheek, his forehead touching hers before he whispered, "Run."

With her eyes wide, she threw her thin arms around his neck. After squeezing him tight, she gathered up the fabric of her violet dress and joined the masses fleeing toward the white trees of Wintertide. Damien rushed behind her, elbowing the panicked people of Barracks out of the way. Relief lighted his chest as he turned quickly and watched her small form disappear between the trees of the surrounding forest, safe from the slaughter.

The cracking of bones snapped Damien's attention back to the market, and he veered left toward the blacksmith's forge. He needed something to defend himself, and Gladio always had new weapons ready for Heart Reign.

Streams of people swarmed around him, toppling over one another as they screamed and pointed. Damien spun around. This time he did panic. The odor of decaying flesh plunged through the air as a flood of sickly-looking beasts poured through the red doors. Their elongated limbs and gray skin were grotesque. Long, ebony claws dug into the ground as the monsters preyed on his people.

Bile rose to the back of Damien's throat as he watched a creature impale Brit Hocking, the clock master. Blood dribbled from the puncture wounds, pooling at the monster's feet. With a flick of its wrist, the creature flung Brit away and leaned over the blood, sucking the red aura from it until the pool was dull and gray. Damien brought a hand to his mouth and bit his fist to prevent his scream. What were those things? Creatures from the shadows? But why were they here?

Forcing himself to move, Damien clambered his way through the frantic people, commanding them to hide or escape into Wintertide.

Leaping over the fallen displays of the once-jovial festival, he arrived at the forge. Damien froze as he saw the blacksmith's apprentice, Silas, bending over Gladio's portly body. The old blacksmith's vibrant, olive-toned skin was dull and lifeless.

"What happened to him?" Damien gasped, barreling toward the apprentice. He fisted Silas's shirt in his hands before slamming him against the wall.

Silas stared back at Damien, his face blank, but he lifted his hands in surrender. "I—" he began before wrenching out of Damien's grasp and retreating from the forge.

"Wait!" Damien cried, regretting his hasty accusation. "Wait, I need your—"

Silas's blond locks melded into the chaos, and Damien lowered his hand. It was too late. He was already gone.

Sorrow weighted Damien's shoulders as he turned back to the deceased blacksmith. He closed Gladio's eyes, then covered him in a canvas. How could Silas leave his master in such a dishonorable way?

Anger churned his stomach as he ran to the opposite end of the forge. Damien's gaze landed on a wall of gleaming knives. Silas may flee from a fight, but he, Damien, never would.

He ripped knives off the wall, not caring about their size or jewels. The screams of the massacre outside sent his hands in a fury as he strapped the various blades onto his belt.

Rushing out of the forge, Damien darted through the streets, the icy air dense with the metallic stench of blood. Gripping a knife in each hand, Damien lunged at a gray creature chasing young Willy Travis. The poor child was only seven.

He stabbed the knives in the creature's back and arm before retracting them. The monster moaned, grabbing Willy's leg. Willy whimpered, covering his face as Damien impaled a knife in the creature's head and stomach repeatedly until the beast's limbs went limp. It fell forward, squashing little Willy. Damien heaved as he pulled Willy out from beneath the monster. Thankfully, the boy had nothing more than a few scratches.

"Run to Wintertide and hide," he commanded.

With tears rolling down his plump, red cheeks, Willy nodded and took off.

Deep moans ricocheted off the broken displays as the creatures ravaged the market. Damien's knees quivered, but he forced his legs to move. He wouldn't allow these monsters to kill the people who had helped him when his father wouldn't. Though it had taken him several tries to kill one beast, he was ready to destroy the rest.

Damien hurried to the center of the market, daggers still in each hand, and tackled the first monster he saw. He pierced the knives anywhere he saw gray skin. Sweat dripped down his temples, and his arms strained after multiple strikes, but he wouldn't stop until each creature was dead.

Snatching one of the knives off his belt, Damien flung it at a monster dragging Old Man Chank through the crowd. The bronze hilt protruded between the soulless black eyes of the creature, and it crumpled to the ground. Old Man Chank almost fainted but was caught by Chandra Dunkis, one of the seamstresses from the market. The two scrambled toward the white birch trees of Wintertide.

Wiping the sweat from his brow, Damien narrowed his gaze as he scanned the chaos. Dread coiled around him as Headmaster Clive was captured by two monsters and dragged from the market. He anticipated the headmaster's demise, but the creatures didn't kill him. What did they want with him?

Damien turned, ready to save the headmaster, when he noticed an angel in the crowd. Blonde waves flowed from her head as she glided through the panic. He couldn't take his eyes off her.

"What do we have here?" Her voice danced over him like freshly fallen snow. She lifted a hand, and the monster to his right ceased its attack. "A hero among the cowards?"

"I'm no hero," Damien replied.

The curvaceous woman raised her hand again, and another creature next to her stopped, as well. Though it still moaned and swiped the air, it didn't attack. Damien cocked his head to the side, waiting.

"If you're not a hero, then what are you?" She licked her crimson lips sensuously.

He held his knives pointedly at the woman. "Nothing you would like, madam."

The woman placed a hand on her chest and let out a sultry laugh, sending Damien's nerves on end. Yes, his judgment about this one had been correct.

The woman stroked the yellow stone on her necklace. A staticky sound popped before she pointed her slender finger at him. An electric-blue light zinged through her skin.

Damien held his stance and waited for the blow. But when nothing happened, he gave an impish smirk.

"Interesting," the woman mused, studying her fingertips. "I can't harm you."

"Don't you hate it when that happens?"

The woman pursed her lips, the playful tone of her voice fleeing as she tapped her small chin. "There must be something else."

Her gaze darted behind Damien, and a vicious grin split her face. "Find the females," she commanded, with a flick of her wrist. A group of monsters groaned, stretching their sewn lips before sprinting into Wintertide.

"No!" Damien screamed, launching after the group of monsters before his legs were swept out from under him. Groaning, he quickly spun over his shoulder and lodged his dagger in the face of the creature. It hissed. Black blood dripped from the wound onto Damien's face. Damien threw the monster off and started running, only to be hit by more creatures.

Damien stabbed and punched as many as he could, but they kept coming. He had to stop the beasts. He couldn't let the creatures find them.

With a yell, Damien simultaneously pierced two monsters in the backs of their heads before breaking free of the pack. His feet flew across the snowy ground, trying to catch up with the first group of monsters, but it was too late. The woman had pointed the creatures straight in the direction of the people he valued most dear. High-pitched screams echoed against the gray cloud. Each familiar shriek shattered his soul, and Damien cried out in anguish. He fell to his knees, allowing the monsters to pile on top of him. He sobbed as the creatures killed them, one by one. And he would be next.

CHAPTER 1

As I left the white door's warmth, the cool breeze slapped me in the face, and I welcomed it as an old friend. Goosebumps popped on my arms, although I rubbed them furiously. The dress Sana had given me was beautiful, but the fabric was a terrible defense against the chill. I shivered as the wind beat against my exposed neck, blowing my short locks from their braids.

Home. I could hardly wait to find Nana and Silas and tell them everything that had happened. I could practically see them as I opened my eyes, expecting their blank faces to greet me. But as I scanned the horizon, my heart dropped.

Dark, filthy ice coated the field before the market. While there had always been ice in Barracks, it had never been dirty. A thick, muddied coating covered the trees, as well. The sky was dense with charcoal clouds. Grabbing the strap of my satchel, I searched around. Where was everyone? Worry rose in my chest. This was not the Barracks I had left.

I stepped onto the mud-streaked ice, my foot sliding across the fickle foundation. Catching myself before I fell, I unwrapped Lyle's sweater from the bundle and yanked it over my head. The warmth of it cocooned my skin, reminding me of what I had been through and what I had overcome.

I placed the additional shirt and pants Sana had given me in my satchel before turning to James, who had his hands fisted on his hips, staring blankly ahead. His gaze was heavy, drinking in the icy land; the downturn of his lips deepened.

"It wasn't always like this," I started to explain.

"I know," James replied gruffly, covering his mouth as he gave a raspy cough before cutting his eyes to me. "It was my home, too."

"Oh." I had wondered which Land he was the Magister of.

"We should probably take a look around," he continued. His fingers adjusted the pack on his shoulder before he trudged through the thick snow.

Brushing the stray curls from my forehead, I followed. The layer of ice on top of the snow crunched beneath our feet, echoing against the eerie silence.

Every few steps, James's head rotated from left to right as he analyzed the state of his former home. Barracks was probably still a fruitful land of happiness and warmth when he was here last.

Taking a few long strides, I caught up to him. He took a deep breath, allowing the air to trickle slowly from his mouth and form a thin cloud.

"So, a Magister?" I asked, hoping to distract him from the cold wasteland.

James grunted as he rubbed his chin, keeping his ice-blue eyes forward.

The wind howled, and I wrapped my arms around my stomach. Had the weather gotten worse since I had left? How long had I been gone?

The question sent uneasy tingles through my veins before James responded.

"It's a position of honor bestowed upon those who have mastered the way of the Mender." He tapped his chest, where the mark of the Mender was carved.

"Is that what that extra mark means? That you're a Magister?"

He nodded, keeping his attention on the icy plain. "Eman is an ancient creature, knowledgeable in the oldest of magics. When darkness first descended from Regno, he chose one Magister from each of the Lands to protect and defend them. I was the Magister for Barracks."

I sucked in a breath as my foot sunk into thick mud from melted ice. Luckily, I had changed into my boots before leaving Ramni, but the beautiful dress was now ruined from the sludge.

Yanking the hem out of the muck, I turned back to James. Should I ask how Ophidian infiltrated Barracks so easily? Luckily, James explained without much prompting.

His thick fingers tightened around his pack. "It was my job to protect the people. And I failed," he whispered so quietly, I barely heard it.

I studied James's downcast gaze. I could almost see the guilt layered on his shoulders. How long had James been carrying that burden? Dropping the hem back into the mud, I stopped.

"Yes, you did," I said. He winced at my words. "But that's in the past now," I continued, remembering what Eman had told me before. "Everything that happened in the past can't be changed. What matters is what we do now." Pulling out the sword, I offered him the gilded hilt, imitating Eman. "This time, together, we won't fail. I promise to fight for Decim. Can you promise to me, even in the face of failure, that you'll stand by me? To unite the Twelve Magisters and defeat Ophidian?"

Like James, fear and anxiety had crippled me for years. Every pang of loneliness from not having parents had tormented me. Each wave of abandonment from losing Lyle had tortured my soul. And, while sorrow and pain would always be with me, I wouldn't let them control me ever again. I wasn't about to let regret define James's life, either. We wouldn't be fighting the coming battle alone. Together, we'd be stronger. Together, we would win.

James eyed me carefully, his gaze darting from my face to the sword as he ran a hand through his graying hair. With a resolute snort, he gave a nod before extending his hand toward the hilt. As soon as his large fingers encased my own, a line of white light wrapped around our hands, twisting in on itself until an intricate knot formed. A surge of cold power rushed from our grip and into my heart. I stepped back, feeling the power solidify in my chest. When the knot tightened, the light dissipated from the air, sprinkling to the ice below.

"An iuram," James coughed with fascination, staring down at our hands. "It's been many years since I've seen one made."

"Eman showed me," I replied, placing a hand on my chest. James's power circled around my heart, empowering and protecting it.

"It's a powerful oath," James continued, flexing his fingers. "Not many can bind another to an iuram without the use of strong power." The final light faded, and we broke apart.

"I am bound by my oath to you, Bellata," James said, lowering to one knee. "You are the prophesized warrior that will save Decim, and I will fight with you until the end."

I bent my fingers a few times, the cool power rushing through my blood. I reached my hand out to James, not wanting him to treat me as his superior. James smirked before grasping my hand and standing. He brushed the grime off his slacks, and we continued to the market.

A fierce wind erupted, spewing debris against our already frozen faces. We both held up our arms as shields. Hunching forward, we marched through the slick terrain, fighting the strong gusts with each step. I didn't remember the air being so thick or demanding.

As we reached the market entrance, my eyes widened despite the wind, taking in the scene. Displays were knocked over, broken beyond repair with holes torn through their fabric roofs. Countless items were sprawled, tattered, and broken along the street. The old clock tower that hadn't told time in years had fallen into a pile of rubble. Pieces of its stone pillar were scattered through the market, buried beneath the snow.

The air smelled of ice, but a repulsive stench hid beneath it. I wrinkled my nose.

"What happened here?"

James shook his head, his eyes narrowed as he continued to scan the market. "Nothing good."

I took a step to investigate when something soft squished beneath my foot. A rotting odor secreted from the now smashed fruit. Covering my nose in disgust, I wiped it off my boot in a nearby snowbank.

As I scanned the area, I spied several footprints still imprinted in the ice. They were smeared and pointed away from the market as if people were running frantically. The eerie quiet crept across my skin, raising the hairs on the back of my neck. The destroyed displays and rotting food were disturbing enough, but where was everyone?

A door slammed at the far end of the market, and I jumped. Was there someone else here? Hope rose in my chest as I gathered my dress and bolted toward it, dodging the wooden boards and shattered glass across my path. The door slammed again, and I spun to the left, stomping through the ice until Doctor Magnum's office came into view. The memory of Doctor Magnum's Extraction tool flew into my mind. Shaking my head, I placed a hand over my heart, assuring it that it would never be extracted like my last one.

Maneuvering around a barrel splattered with colorful paints, I made my way to the door. Disappointment drowned my hope, as I found the culprit to be the wind.

Testing the rusted knob, I tiptoed into the familiar office, gently shutting the door behind me. The legs of the patients' chairs were broken off or missing entirely. Strands of shredded newspaper were spread all over the floor, muddied and crumpled. My shoulders fell as I remembered how tidy Doctor Magnum had kept everything. At least the sterile scent of the office kept the stench from outside away.

When I turned to leave, a glint of color beneath a sheet of newspaper caught my eye. Pulling the sword from the ring of the satchel, I dragged its tip along the page and gasped. Large, blotched letters scrawled across it: Run. The end of the *n* whipped to the right as if the person writing it had been yanked away before they could finish.

Crouching down, I traced the letters, the dark substance flaking off on my chilled fingertips. It'd been dry for a while. A nauseating knot twisted in the back of my throat. There was no way this dull red-brown was cherry filling.

I focused on the letters and traced them once more. "What happened to you, Doctor Magnum?"

Moving more of the newspapers out of the way, I found my answer. Five long claw marks were etched into the stone floor. I sucked in a sharp breath.

Standing abruptly, I hurried out of Doctor Magnum's office. James lifted a log out of the path, then wiped his brow and stared in the direction of Nana's house.

"James," I said. "Ophidian was here. Or at least the siti were."

James nodded thoughtfully as he crossed his arms over his chest, not adverting his gaze from Nana's house. I followed his line of sight, confusion threading through my thoughts. Had he known Nana?

"Is there someone you'd like to see?" I asked, my intrigue of the Magister growing.

"There's someone I've been wanting to see for a long time," he replied hoarsely. Tugging on his pack, James marched over the broken displays of Heart Reign toward my grandmother's house.

Excitement bubbled in my chest as I bounded through the debris to catch up with him. The memory of Nana's journal and the man who had returned her extracted heart resurfaced in my thoughts. Could James be him?

Small flakes of snow spiraled around us as we stopped in front of the old house. It had aged since I was here last. Shingles from the roof scattered the icy ground, and the shutters were askew or missing. A black shutter from the top window swung by a single hinge, a shuddersome squeak escaping from the rusted metal as the wind rustled by. I clasped my hands in front of me, praying that my fears were unfounded.

James didn't move. He opened his mouth, but no words came out, not even a cough or wheeze.

I placed a hand on his shoulder before sliding past him and up the wooden stairs, enjoying the familiarity of their creaking. The rickety steps creaked again as James followed.

Once we reached the porch, we both stood outside the wooden door. A giant claw mark had slashed through it, leaving five long gaps in the wood.

Lifting the sword, I pressed the tip against the weathered boards. The door slowly swung in, sending all my senses on alert.

The floorboards groaned beneath my steps as I scanned Nana's house. Splintered pieces of wood from her bookshelf covered the ground, and shards of glass from the shattered windows gleamed on top of broken furniture. Claw marks punctured everything. My new heart ached at the sight. If this was what the siti had done to the house, what had they done to Nana and Silas?

James wandered through the rooms as if in a daze, picking up things and turning them right-side up. A few canned jars seemed out of place on the windowsill, but I continued searching, letting James have this time to himself.

A rustling came from Nana's living room, and I plastered my back against the wall. Fear froze my muscles as my heart hammered in my chest. Someone else was here.

James stopped moving, too. As did the rustling. As softly as I could, I tiptoed toward the living room.

My breathing became quiet, my pulse quieter. The only sound was the roll of the saliva running down my throat as I swallowed my nerves. The rustling sounded once more, only to stop again when I did. I'd learned how the siti attacked. This was no siti.

Bracing myself against the wall, I closed my eyes and focused. Ophidian could have created any number of creatures to stay in Barracks. Eman had said the Beast could make more. I had already witnessed the power of the siti, phagos, and malum. I didn't want to meet any more.

Or I could be paranoid, and it could be a small animal searching for food. Either way, I was going to find out.

Taking a deep breath, I tightened my grip around the hilt of the sword. In one solid move, I lunged, swinging my sword wide, only to hear the clanging of metal against metal.

My eyes flew open as my sword clashed against Nana's long, iron fire poker. I followed the line of the iron to the hand holding it, then up the black sweater to the ferocious face staring back at me. I gasped as the hand released the poker, sending it to the ground with a clang.

CHAPTER 2

"Addie?" Silas asked, his jaw gaping as his warm chestnut eyes roved over my face in disbelief.

Before I could respond, two strong arms wrapped around me so tightly I could barely breathe. Smoke and cedarwood enveloped my nose as Silas crushed me against his chest. The sword dropped from my grip as my body turned rigid against his. Was Silas real?

He lowered his hands too soon, furrowing his brows. I realized my muscles were tense—ready to bolt.

"Addie," he breathed again, steadying me as he took a step away.

I blinked at him, confusion and turmoil overwhelming my thoughts. Steady Silas had a crooked smile on his lips: the beautiful crooked smile I had seen in Ophidian's Realm. But there, it wasn't real. Was it real here? Even if it wasn't, it was the most amazing thing I had ever seen.

"I thought I lost you," he said softly, still examining me.

My heart tore between the Choices and the present. Too many emotions and thoughts swirled inside of me. It was better not to speak. I shook my head, sending my short dark curls sprawling.

His grin faltered, but he didn't move from his position. "What happened to your hair?"

I tucked a strand behind my ear, focusing on the muddied hem of my dress. I couldn't tell Silas of the shame I held from Ophidian's Realm. From every door, I had received a mark, a scar of what happened there. Though not all of them could be physically seen, they were all still fresh and easily torn open. I had cut my hair to be rid of my greed, but the burns on my skin, though healed, were still aflame beneath my skin, reminding me of that horrid blue door.

"I know it looks bad," I finally said, refusing to meet his gaze as the memories of the beautiful blonde woman he had danced with whipped through my mind. Reaching up, I grasped a short curl and twirled it around my finger.

Silas took a cautious step forward as if I were a frightened animal and would run at any sudden movement. "No, it looks beautiful. You always look beautiful."

My pulse elevated at his words, and I took in his soft gaze. Was this all a dream, another trick? Steady Silas would never be so forward and say things like this.

I tried to conjure some sort of response when Silas slowly reached for my hand, untangling my finger from my hair. I didn't stop him as he lifted it to his lips. I worried that his touch would singe my flesh, but it didn't. Instead, a soft, warm flutter danced on my skin and into my heart, wrapping it with comfort and peace.

For a moment, the memories fled, allowing me to study Silas as he released my hand. His tall stature and strong muscles. His handsome face and tousled golden locks. I let out a small gasp as I finally saw three red lines etched from his forehead down to his neck. I recognized the brand of the siti, but how Silas managed to survive, I had no idea.

My heart tugged toward him, and I took a step closer. "Silas, what happened?"

Before he could respond, the mechanical sound of wheels along the old wooden floor rolled toward us.

"Addie?" a withered voice asked.

I spun around, my eyes locking onto Nana. Her white hair was thinner than it had ever been, revealing the pale skin of her scalp. Her arms and legs were corpselike. So frail, they would probably break with any movement. My heart almost cracked at the sight because I knew it was my fault.

A fresh batch of tears welled in my eyes, and I rushed toward her. She extended her trembling arms with a weak smile, beckoning me closer.

"I'm so sorry, Nana," I cried as I fell to the ground, clutching her old, tattered skirt. A musky scent ballooned from the fabric.

"Shhh, child. There's nothing to apologize for." She stroked my hair as if I were a carefree child once more.

Closing my eyes, I relished the closeness until I remembered why I had left Barracks in the first place. Releasing my grip on her skirt, I whispered, "I found Lyle."

Nana's hand paused as she gasped.

Heavy steps pounded against the creaking wood and into the living room. I glanced over my shoulder to find James standing in the doorway. He nervously rubbed his jaw as if he were scared to come closer. A cry of shock, pain, and relief shot from Nana's mouth, making me jump. Tears streamed down her wrinkles, as a haggard sob broke from her lips. I moved out of the way as James knelt before her. He took her hands in his and bowed his head.

"Anna." He kissed her old hands. "Will you ever forgive me?" His shoulders shuddered with each word.

Nana, too overcome by emotion, laid a delicate hand on James's head before lifting it. She placed a tender kiss on his forehead, and James wrapped his arms gently but tightly around her.

I turned away from the tender embrace, fiddling with the ends of Lyle's sweater. Was James the man from Nana's journal? He had to be.

"Addie," James said, wiping his eyes on his plaid shirt sleeve before standing. Though his voice was hoarse, his face was bright and alive. "Eman thought it best not to give you too much information at once."

"But" —Nana cut in softly, taking James's thick hand in

her own thin one— "James is my husband. He's your grandfather."

"Really?" I beamed, my gaze darting between the pair. "How long have you known we're related?"

"The first time I saw you in the Sixth Choice, I hoped that one of my kin hadn't been sucked into Ophidian's lies," James explained. "But after I saw how you defeated the Choice and stood up to the Beast, I knew you were my granddaughter. Eman confirmed it when we arrived in Ramni."

I remembered when James had saved me from the light wall in the Sixth Choice, then again when he battled Schism and cloaked us from Ophidian when we were flee-ing. My grandfather, all this time. Though I wish he would've told me sooner, I easily accepted James. The pieces of my family were starting to come together again.

I jumped toward James and flung my arms around him. Burrowing into his flannel shirt, I breathed in pine and ice. I peered up at him with a grin and asked, "Does this mean I can call you Paw Paw now?"

His body went stiff beneath my hug, and he coughed twice before patting my back. "James is fine."

Releasing him from my grasp, I chuckled. "Sounds good."

A hand lightly touched my shoulder, and I glanced over to Silas. Placing his hands in his pockets, he jerked his head toward the kitchen. Turning back to Nana and James, Nana gave me a delicate smile of encouragement. I tilted my head to the side. First Silas, now Nana. There were so many new and beautiful smiles to admire.

As I followed Silas, my boots brushed the tip of the sword. The mark of the Mender glimmered as I stooped down to retrieve it before entering the kitchen.

Silas's back faced me as his hands gripped the edge of the sink. A line of tension ran through his broad shoulders, and I paused in the threshold. My fingers flittered with nerves as I gripped them around the hilt. Why was I so nervous?

His shoulders rose and fell before he faced me. Those warm chestnut eyes stirred with questions as they focused on me before moving to the floor. Silas rubbed the back of his neck, his throat bobbing before he spoke.

"It's been so long, Addie," he said quietly. "I thought—" He ran a hand through his hair. It was thick, much longer than how I remembered. And it matched the light-blond hairs growing on his jawline. Silas was even more handsome with a beard. How had I not noticed before? "I thought you were dead."

My breath hitched. If only he could understand how close I had been to dying. I licked my lips, dreading my next question, but I had to ask. "How long?"

"Over a year."

"What?" I found the nearest unbroken chair and collapsed into it before I could faint.

A year? It was only days to me. How could I have been gone over a year? I leaned my head on my hand as my mind raced back to the ruins of the market. Something must have happened after I left.

"You didn't know?" Silas asked, pulling a clawed stool up to the table.

I shook my head and placed the sword on the table where the shined metal winked at me. Eman was right. Time did flow differently between our realms. *A lot* differently.

Yanking my satchel off my shoulder, I placed it in my lap and hugged it. "I had to go. I had to know what happened to Lyle. I had to see if there was a way to save him."

Silas balled his hand into a fist on the table. "And you did? You found Lyle?" I nodded. "Where is he?"

"With Em—" I stopped, realizing Silas wouldn't recognize the name. "With the Mender." I pointed to the mark on the sword. "He's real, Silas. Just like the stories said. Everything, the good and the evil. It's all real."

Silas leaned back, and his muscles relaxed as if relieved. "That's great, Addie." He started to reach out to me, but stopped, noticing me tense at the movement. Recoiling, he asked, "Is Lyle okay? Is he safe?"

I nodded, deciding not to mention my brother's unraveling before I left. I sent a prayer to the Heavens, hoping he was healing well in Ramni.

"He's safe. The Mender will take care of him."

"What about you?" Silas watched me intensely, his brows puckered with concern. "Who's going to take care of you?"

I drummed my fingers along the sword. "I'm not alone, so I'll be okay."

Resting on the table, Silas placed a hand under his chin and studied my face before he grinned. My stomach flipped. I loved his smile.

"Plus" —I grasped the hilt and held up the blade— "I've learned I'm a pretty good swordswoman."

Silas laughed, and my heart swelled with adoration. It was deep and soothing, full of life and joy. I couldn't help but laugh, as well. But when his gaze found the sword, his lips faded into their familiar stern line. He held his hand out, and I placed the weapon in it, curious about his sudden change.

"Silas, what is it?"

As soon as the hilt touched his skin, a golden glow lined the blade. Silas's arm trembled as he grasped the hilt, flecks of gilded light adjoining over his fingers. I gaped at the sight, yet Silas was completely unfazed as he brought the sword to eye level.

"I don't know," he confessed. "I feel like I've seen this sword before. Like from a dream."

As I clamped my lips shut, a thump rammed against my chest. I jumped in surprise, but Silas didn't notice, still entranced by the sword. The thump came again, and I glanced down to find the satchel moving.

Opening the flap, I reached in until my hand rested on the tiny purple bag Eman had given me. I waited a moment longer, and the thump vibrated against my fingertips.

I cupped the purple bag in my palm while Eman's words swirled in my mind: *You will know what to do with it when the right time comes.* The thumping increased.

"Silas," I started, staring at the small sack. He tore his attention away from the sword. "I think this is for you."

Silas held his hand steady as I placed the pouch on his palm. His long fingers carefully drew the gold cord, unfolding the pleats along the top. Bringing the bag to his chest, he peered inside, and his brows rose. I gripped the edge of the table, bursting with anticipation.

"Addie," he whispered, not taking his gaze off whatever was in the bag. "How did you find this?"

I was about to take the pouch myself when he placed his hand inside.

"What is it?" I asked, trying to contain my overflowing curiosity.

Extending his arm across the table, Silas opened his hand. I brought my hands to my mouth, stifling a gasp.

Beating steadily against his palm lay the severed half of a bright red heart.

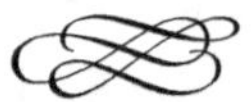

CHAPTER 3

The half-heart brightened, beating triumphantly in Silas's palm. Lowering my hands, I gawked at the life force, unable to pull away from its mesmerizing glow. The pieces of information floating in my mind clicked together. I reared back, finally connecting every-thing. This heart had finally returned to its owner.

"You're—" I stammered.

"I couldn't tell you," Silas said, cutting me off as he cradled the gift from Eman to his chest. His expression flickered through several emotions. "I-I didn't remember everything—anything. I still don't. But now with this—" He peered down at his half-heart. "Some of my memories are coming back." Silas raised his head. "I've always known you were an important part of my life. Whenever I was with you, everything seemed right."

I gaped. The story Claire had told me was true. And out of everyone, it was him. The young blacksmith who had survived the Seven Choices was real and was currently standing in the middle of Nana's half-destroyed kitchen. It was Silas all along. Silas and the young blacksmith were one and the same.

My gaze drifted to the sword on the table. This entire time, I'd been wielding Silas's sword. The one *he* had made. The one the stranger had enchanted for him. The wheels turned in my head. No, it wasn't a stranger who enchanted it for him. How could I be so blind? Only one man could enchant a sword with the mark of the Mender.

Then, I remembered my promise. How I had sworn I would find the blacksmith and return what he had lost. Burying my face into my hands, I shook my head in disbelief. My grandfather *and* the young blacksmith, all on the same day.

Once I regained my composure, Silas gently lowered his half-heart back into the purple bag before handling the sword. His hands carefully caressed the blade as if it were a rare treasure. As he tilted his head, the tips of his hair curled, brushing against the new beard accentuating his strong jaw. A rosy pink tinted his cheeks as he brought the hilt close to his face. I didn't remember Silas ever looking flushed. My neck grew hot, and I quickly glanced down to my hands. How long had I been staring at him? Coughing, I adverted my attention to the sword, not its creator.

I ran my finger through my hair, trying to smooth the windblown tangles. "You know the Mender? Eman?"

Silas nodded slowly, his gaze shifting from the sword to me.

Eman said that the sword, an alme, would be limited in my hands because it wasn't mine. Only in the hands of its true master would its full power be unleashed. Watching how the sword pulsed and glowed under Silas's touch, there was no doubt about it. It was his.

"If that sword really is yours, why did it work for me?"

Like a fog lifting from a meadow, confusion vanished from Silas's face, replaced by unwavering resolve. Setting the sword aside, he gripped the purple bag, never once breaking eye contact with me. My mended heart beat recklessly against my ribcage as I sat, paralyzed by those piercing, chestnut eyes. Never had I seen them so alive.

Hesitantly, Silas leaned across the table and reached for my hand. I tensed before his tough, calloused fingers softly grasped mine. A ribbon of peace hugged my anxious heart once more, reassuring me that this Silas was real.

Carefully unfolding my fingers one-by-one, Silas placed the purple bag on my palm. It was light, like mine had been, but heavy at the same time. Opening the mouth of the bag, I peeked inside. There was strength and depth to his heart that drew me in. It pulsated with vigor, but its red hue seemed strangely dim. Still, after holding the power of my own life force, I had no doubt Silas's held the same, if not more.

Silas took a shallow breath before saying, "My heart always has and always will belong to you."

My knee hit the leg of the table as my eyes snapped to his, jaw dropping open.

The half-heart beat excitedly in my hands, satisfied

with my reaction. Closing my mouth, I cleared my throat and tried to ignore the pleased grin on Silas's face.

"I never thought I would make you speechless twice in one conversation."

Heat flittered through my body, a new sensation that my heart seemed determined to give me around Silas. I was sure I was as red as cherry filling.

Silas brought a hand to his mouth, trying to hide his broadening smile. "That reaction is new."

"So is that," I countered, pointing to his lips.

He lowered his hands and beamed. A giggle escaped my throat, and I almost felt at home.

I peeled open my fingers, and the red hue spilled out, the steady beating warming my palms. I grazed the heart with my thumb, and it shuddered. No wonder Ophidian wanted it so badly. Even with only half of Silas's heart, the Beast had built an army of terrifying monsters. If Ophidian got his hands on the remaining half, there was no telling how powerful he'd become.

My thoughts raced, and I jerked my head up. Ophidian. He was still out there, hunting for not only my heart but Silas's, as well. If he'd attacked Barracks once already, I had no doubt that he'd do it again.

"Silas, we can't stay here, not for long. Ophidian's hunting for me, for you. If he finds us…"

Silas's eyes widened, then narrowed. "Ophidian," he muttered, his lips turning downward. Since when had they been so pink and inviting?

I shook my head. Now wasn't the time to get distracted.

Still cupping my hands around his heart, I asked, "What happened after I left?"

Silas clenched his fist once more, beating it against the clawed table. "As soon as you jumped through, Schism changed. It was horrifying. I've never seen something so human turn so … monstrous."

My mind flashed back to the first time I had seen Schism's true form in Ira's Vindicae. I shuddered, remembering those horrifying claws tearing into my legs, tossing me like a ragdoll. It was a miracle I even survived that fight with him. If it hadn't been for Silas's sword and Claire's healing salve, I would definitely be dead right now.

"Other creatures poured through the red doors," Silas continued, flattening his palm on the table. "So many people gone."

Ice ran down my spine, and I clutched his half-heart to my chest. "What do you mean 'gone'? Schism didn't kill them?"

Silas glowered at the floor. "Oh, he killed some, but not all of them. The ones that were 'deemed worthy,' as he said, were taken."

"Taken?" Fear sliced through me as I remembered Claire, taken from everything because her mother had traded her away. Another face, Governor Willow's, transforming into a siti, followed the thought. "Didn't a trade have to be made?"

Silas's face turned cold, his eyes like stone. "The days of fair trading are over."

I shrank back, realizing the severity of what lay ahead. "What about Doctor Magnum?"

After searching through his office, the chance of his survival was slim. But I didn't want him dead. Certainly, by extracting hearts, he had given Ophidian everything he wanted and more. But at the same time, instead of turning my heart over to Governor Willow, the doctor had told me to run.

"I don't know if he's dead or alive," Silas explained. "When everything started, Schism and his monsters killed and took so many. I don't know why. The only thing I do know is everyone's gone."

Swallowing my fear, I nodded. "How did you and Nana escape?"

Silas rubbed the back of his neck. "As soon as Schism attacked, I ran here to find her. I didn't know what to do or where we could go, but I had to keep her safe. I was all she had left."

Guilt piled on my shoulders. I wasn't thinking about Nana, or Barracks, or anyone else when I ran through Schism's door. If she had died while I was gone, I wasn't sure what I'd do.

Silas's voice softened. "I'm not trying to make you feel guilty. I'm just trying to be honest. Who else would think of her? Protect her?"

He was right. If it weren't for Silas, what would Schism have done to Nana? Especially after discovering her connection not only to Lyle and me, but also to James, as well.

"After I got here," Silas continued. "We packed everything we could and locked ourselves in the cellar." He stood and began pacing. "We were doing okay, and I would search the market for more supplies when we ran out. I always went in the morning because the monsters scour the market every afternoon."

I squeezed my eyes shut. "The siti are horrid creatures."

"You know what they're called?"

I peeked down at the glowing heart, still in my hands. "Ophidian's Realm is full of them."

"You fought them?" Silas asked, his tone heavy with skepticism.

He doesn't believe you, a new voice slithered through my thoughts, and I paused. The voice didn't sound like Eman. More like my own, just a little deeper and smoother. I pursed my lips. Maybe it was just another side-effect of having a mended heart.

"Of course, I fought them," I replied, lifting my chin. "How else would I be here?"

"I'm not sure—"

He still sees weak, pitiful Addie. That's all you'll ever be to him. A poor little girl who needs his protection.

"I'm capable of taking care of myself, Silas," I huffed, shoving the bag and his severed heart across the table.

"Addie," he began in an apologetic tone, but a shriek from the doorway silenced him.

We both shot up, but I snatched the sword before Silas could and started toward the noise.

"Addie!" Silas exclaimed, reaching out to stop me.

I dodged out of his grasp and lurched toward the door, unleashing the sword.

CHAPTER 4

James threw up his hands, and I lowered the blade, immediately regretting my paranoia.

"Don't worry, Addie. It's just me," he said softly. Concern glinted in his ice-blue eyes as he spoke.

"Sorry," I breathed, placing the sword on the table. Silas scanned me, then the sword. I spun away from his penetrating stare, taking in a deep breath to calm my racing pulse as James and Nana shuffled into the kitchen.

James carefully maneuvered Nana's wheelchair to the table, its wheels emitting the shriek from before. Once she was settled, Nana reached out to me, and I squeezed one of her hands. Her once hollow eyes were now filled with abundant joy.

"Addie," James said. "Ophidian is searching for you as we speak. Your Nana has told me about how the siti roam the market every afternoon for food. Though this old house kept her and Silas safe, it's not going to hold up once the siti know you're here." He placed his hand on the adjacent wall, giving it a tender pat as if thanking the house. "It won't take them long to find us. Your heart carries a strong aura, one they can smell from miles away. The sooner we leave Barracks, the better."

"Right." I stood and carefully paced the kitchen. Broken bowls and plates decorated the counters and floor. "We should probably gather whatever supplies we can from here before moving on."

"You should stay here with Nana, sir," Silas said quickly, fumbling with a pack as he awkwardly swung it over his shoulder. "We have some food left in the cellar, but it's not a lot. As for Addie and me—" He glanced over at me.

My fingers paused over a cracked red bowl, and I peered over my shoulder. "Yes?"

"We have a second stash of food at your house," Silas continued, gesturing toward my old house. "And, I was wondering, if you wanted to, you could come with me..." he trailed off.

Home: the prison I had condemned myself to for so many years. Something about the word chilled my bones. If I wanted to be strong, I had to face it once and for all.

"Sure, I can come," I tried to say as casually as possible. "I should probably change first, though." I motioned to my mud-stained dress.

"It looks great on you," Silas said, before snapping his lips shut, his cheeks oddly red.

James shot him a look, and Silas gave a nervous laugh before shuffling away from my grandfather.

I touched James on the arm. "Sana packed me an extra outfit. I'll change real quick, then we'll head over."

Silas assessed my dress once more, sending tingles through my body before he grabbed his half-heart and placed it back in the purple bag. Once he secured his heart in his pack, he started for the sword but stopped, his hand hovering over the weapon.

"Go ahead." I reluctantly waved to the sword. "It's yours."

Silas didn't hesitate before latching onto the hilt and heading out of the kitchen.

My shoulders sagged as I watched him go.

"Be careful," James said, keeping one hand on Nana's shoulder. "It won't be long before the siti return to hunt."

I gave him a nod and hurried up the stairs. I quickly changed out of the muddy dress and slipped into dark pants and Lyle's sweater once more. The thick fibers instantly warmed my skin, and I felt like myself again. I neatly folded the dress and left it in Nana's room before tightening the laces on my boots and heading downstairs.

Nana and James greeted me at the doorway while Silas stood next to the clawed door, his hand ready on the rusted knob.

"We'll be waiting for you," Nana said as she grasped James's hand. "Hurry back."

James shifted his attention from Silas to the loving face

of Nana. His stern lips softened as he leaned down and placed a kiss on her frail cheek.

I smiled at their sweet relationship before I found my gaze drifting to Silas. The same warmth from earlier bloomed through my body. Though I wanted to welcome this budding love, I had to ignore it. Now wasn't the time for intense emotions.

Silently, Silas and I walked down the steps of Nana's house toward my own. We were halfway between the two when Silas said, "You walked down the steps and all this way without clutching your hands once."

I forced a laugh but couldn't control the snarky comment that followed. "The people of Barracks are hardly anything for me to fear anymore. I've seen evil far worse than them."

Focusing my gaze ahead, I enjoyed Silas admiring my tall stance and confident walk. I had stared evil in the eye and almost died. But I had also seen life, and because of that, I was standing strong today.

"I apologize for letting you go," Silas whispered as we stepped up the stairs of my home, the creaks of the rotting wood wailing against our feet. "Letting you go through with it, all of it."

"Why didn't you try to stop me then?" I asked, not giving him a chance to respond before trekking through the chaos.

My home had deteriorated more in the last year than it ever had while I lived in it. The front door was gone, leaving a perfect view of the siti destruction inside.

"I—" he began, but when I waited for his reply, he slammed his lips shut, as if he were unable to explain.

After a moment, I lifted my shoulders, dismissing the topic. "I'm going to go upstairs and see if there's anything left. Can you check the kitchen?"

Silas's throat bobbed, and he gave a silent nod before heading to the adjacent room.

Cold air seeped into my home from the shattered windows. I rubbed my hands together for warmth. Mounds of snow and ice piled around the old wooden floor and layered on the pieces of Lyle's dismantled clock. His wooden chess set was completely destroyed, as well. It pained me to see the destruction of his things after I had tried so hard to preserve them. The chair I used to sit on had multiple gashes in it, the stuffing protruding through the lining. Numerous siti claw marks branded each of the walls surrounding my former home.

Placing my hand on the curling wallpaper, I took the stairs one at a time, the burdens of my former life rising. The steps moaned as I cautiously placed my weight on each board. The splintered wood would probably hold, but I wasn't sure.

How many times had I rushed up these stairs in terror of the realm around me? The memories were so distant now, like a dream. As I made it to the top of the cracked staircase, it was like I was a stranger in my own home. Was it my home anymore? I wasn't sure if I wanted to come back to Barracks.

The door to my bedroom hung by a hinge, a gaping

hole where the knob used to be. I paused. Did the siti destroy all the houses in Barracks?

Squaring my shoulders, I pushed through the broken door. My hand fell to my side as I took in the wreckage. My small space was destroyed. My clothes, my bed, everything was ripped to shreds. Pages from one of my favorite books were torn through by a siti claw, the paper scattered like snow. Rage burbling, I flipped through the tattered text, but I pushed it away, trying not to let my anger take hold of me again.

Biting my tongue, I dropped the book and started to search for anything we could use on our journey.

While I rifled through old shredded blankets, my mind filtered through everything. Silas was the young blacksmith. That meant he had given up half of his heart for me. But did that mean I had to give my heart to him? I did care for Silas; in fact, I might even call this emotion love. But with everything on my plate, from prophecies to journeys, I didn't think I could handle love right now.

After searching through the tattered fabric, I found a woolen blanket that would suffice. Folding it, I stuffed it in the satchel. As I exited my room, I bent down and snatched a tangle of string peeking out from the head of a dismembered doll. I threaded my finger through my short curls. Did my mother ever cut her hair short?

The thought startled me. Ever since Lyle had said he knew something about our parents, my mind kept drifting back to them. I twisted the string around the bundle and tied it into a knot. What were they like? Would we get along if they were still around? The cool air tickled my bare neck as I returned to the hallway, praying for more answers about our mother and father soon.

I stepped on the first stair when the sight of Lyle's bedroom caught my eye. The door had been torn off and thrown to the end of the hallway, leaving everything in his room exposed.

I raced over before freezing in the threshold. The destruction of my room was tame compared to Lyle's. Not only were all his clothes shredded, but his bed was split down the middle, the stuffing puffed out along the tear. Tufts of stuffing and fabric were strewn across the floor as if the monsters were searching for something. Either that or the siti had been fascinated by mattress stuffing.

Deciding it was probably the former, I stalked closer to examine the scene. Everything under Lyle's bed was now unmasked by the torn mattress. Crystals, springs, and other unique things I had never seen were sprawled out along the floor's wooden planks. My breath hitched as I recognized my father's handwriting on a shredded piece of paper. I bent down and grasped it. The ink had been smudged, making the words illegible, but I was sure this was from him. Just like the note he had given Lyle that said to take care of me.

Standing, I held the piece to my chest. I hoped Lyle was healing well. I'd lost too much of my family already.

Folding the paper, I placed it in my satchel before turning my attention to Lyle's bed. Using my foot, I moved several of the broken items to the side. As I kicked over a ripped pillow, something in my satchel jerked. I peeled back the flap, and my hand touched the glowing binding of the book from Eman. But when I tried to open it, the text jerked out of my hands and dove beneath the remnants of Lyle's bed.

Was the book looking for something? I didn't know magical texts could search for anything. Lying on my stomach, I followed the book under the bed. After elbowing away miscellaneous treasures, I spied two identical glowing items coated in snowy stuffing.

Another book? My curiosity spun as I stretched my hand forward. Without much effort, the two books flew to my fingertips. I grasped them tightly and slid out from under the bed.

"Are you okay? I heard a noise." Silas stood in the doorway, his messy hair standing straight on his head as he clutched a bulging sack. Placing the sack down, he glanced around Lyle's room before focusing on the books. "What are those?"

"This is from Eman," I said, holding up the brown book that was meant to direct me to the Twelve Magisters.

"And that?" He motioned to the other object.

I turned it on its side. "I think it's a book, too."

Silas held out his hand, and I dropped the book from Lyle's bed into it. The glow brightened as soon as it touched his fingers.

There was something about this book that was familiar. While I studied the glowing text, a forgotten memory shot through my mind.

"*Don't go where you're not supposed to, Addie,*" *Lyle said, staring down at me, his eyes glowering with warning.*

I looked up at him with a big grin, standing on my tiptoes to appear taller than my short, childish height.

"*I mean it,*" *Lyle shot an icy glare at me through his spectacles before turning.* "*When I come back after work, I'll show you what I traded for, okay?*"

I huffed, folding my arms across my chest as I returned to my flat-footed height. "*Okay, Lyle.*"

The intensity melted from Lyle's face, and he chuckled, ruffling my already wild hair before walking through the door.

I stood on the porch, waving until I was sure he was long gone to the market before darting up the stairs. With a devious grin, I sped into his room. I didn't have school that day, so what else was I going to do? The various items from all his trades were too tempting to resist. So, I didn't.

With a laugh, I sprang onto his bed, admiring all the trinkets Lyle had laid at its foot. A stack of sparkling rocks, all different colors, stood tall. Every time I would knock them over, they would rearrange themselves again. My young self laughed with delight, remembering Lyle had said these rocks were from the caves of Dunsque.

Once I had finished with the rocks, I moved to the next item: a small, blue puffball.

I crouched over the puff, waiting for it to do something. When it didn't, I poked the puffball, causing it to double in size. Grinning, I poked the ball again. The puff was now the size of one of Lyle's books. Poke. The puff encased Lyle's entire room.

I kicked my feet in the air, laughing wildly until I realized I didn't know how to make the puff return to its original size. I poked it once more, but it only grew bigger. Sighing, I knew I was going to be caught.

As I rolled from beneath the puff, my foot landed on something hard. When I glanced down, I saw the corner of a gray rectangle sticking out from beneath Lyle's bed. Curious, I reached down to grab it, but it jumped away.

I dove after it but the smell of sweat, dirt, and who knew what else bowled me over, and I quickly sprang back. Gasping for air, I sat next to the bed, peering at the gray rectangle. Carefully, I extended my hand, and the item flew forward, smacking into my palm.

I placed the bland, simple rectangle on the floor and studied it. Warmth flowed beneath my fingertips as I walked my fingers across the cover. Its gray color shifted into a pale yellow before it flipped open, revealing it was a book. Crouching on my hands and knees, I examined the pages. Dark words scrawled across the pages in a tongue I didn't understand.

Soon, a series of circles and triangles spun together to form what looked like a sun. I watched in fascination as the words and shapes danced together. The bright pages so completely absorbed my attention, I never heard the whistling coming down the path. By the time the front door opened, it was too late.

The giant blue puff receded with a burst of air as Lyle slammed the door open. With my hand on the pale-yellow book, I was caught. I quickly shut it and slid it under his bed.

"What did I tell you?" Lyle said in a low, clipped voice. He *was furious, his shoulders rigid and tense as all the kindness and joy left his eyes, replaced with darkness I had never seen.*

"Addie, are you all right?" Silas asked, his face concerned as his strong fingers grasped my shoulder.

Blinking, I gave my head a quick shake before nodding. I eyed the book, expecting it to change to the pale yellow I remembered. But instead, it twisted into a shade of dark green. We watched the color change as a gold line traced itself into a shape on the front. Before it had a chance to complete, a deep moan stretched through my hollow home. My gaze shot to the window. The sun was getting lower. Hadn't Nana said something about the siti coming out in the afternoon?

Without another thought, Silas threw the book in my bag and grabbed my hand, squeezing my fingers together as we raced down the stairs. My pulse thundered as I clasped Eman's book to my chest. We barreled down the front steps and across the barren land to Nana's home. The moaning rumbled again, this time louder as it echoed around the snowy plain.

Rushing up to Nana's porch, we found James standing in the entrance, cradling Nana in his arms. She was now wrapped in a torn quilt. On the floor next to them was a bag of supplies. Nana clutched the quilt close, her limbs trembling.

"You heard it, too," James grunted, holding her tightly. We both nodded as we entered and closed the door shut.

The moans drew closer. Silas whipped to the front

door, his eyes boring into the wood. "We need to go. Here
—" He opened his pack and thrust the purple bag at me.

"But—"

"No, Addie," he said, placing it into my palm before wrapping his hands around my own. "Like I said before, my heart has always been yours. It'll be safe with you."

I blinked at our hands. Why would it be safe with me? "Silas, I—"

The noise from before was now only a few feet away, a deep moaning that I had only heard in the depths of the shadows. The blood drained from my face.

Raising the blade with the skill of a master swordsman, Silas strode toward the clawed door.

"They're back."

CHAPTER 5

*A*nxiety cinched my breath as I clenched the small purple sack.

How will you defend yourself against the siti without your *sword?* the condescending voice from before asked.

The voice was right. I loved that Silas had given me his heart, but he had taken away my defense, my protection. I glowered at the small bag. His gift couldn't protect me from the siti.

"Ready?" Silas said, his eyes sparkling with confidence. I clenched the strap of my satchel, mustering a wary smile. Silas's lips thinned, seeing right through the façade. "I know you've faced worse than this. You survived Ophidian's Realm, didn't you? One thing I remember is that place is hell. If you got out of there in one piece, I know you can face this, too."

My insides fluttered at his compliment. Ophidian's

Realm *was* hell. But when I first entered it, I wasn't sure what to expect. Now that I did, I was more terrified than before.

"Wait right here," Silas said before darting to the living room. In a few moments, he returned with Nana's fire poker. "Here," he thrust the rusted metal rod at me. "We can do this."

Placing the purple bag and Eman's book in my satchel, I gripped the cold iron and mumbled a heartless thank you. Gritty metal scratched my fingers as dark red chunks of iron flaked off and fell to the ground. I poked the pointed end into the floorboard. A chunk of the tip snapped off. My confidence wavered. How was this going to protect me? I eyed the sword again. The fire poker was nothing compared to the sword. Now that I held the iron rod, I couldn't believe the sword hadn't severed the fire poker in half before.

The frigid chill circled around us as Silas opened the door. James gently seated Nana right inside the doorway before a deathly weapon formed in his grasp. As the light solidified into metal, an axe with a steel hook curling off the adjacent end appeared.

"The fun's just starting, kids," he chuckled, a spark of amusement in his eyes as he rotated the weapon between his palms.

The moaning of the siti vibrated through the air as we gathered onto Nana's porch. The thick stench of rotting flesh infected the crisp air. Did Ophidian let the siti roam free, or did he allow his second in command to control them? As soon as the thought crossed my mind, a plume of black smoke billowed before us, and I sucked in a breath.

I did my best to shed the emotion from my face. But as I stared into the cool eyes of Schism, panic topped the fear already burrowing inside. Before, he could only harm me. But now my family was in danger.

The siti roamed along the stone path, their long, gray forms stretching as they crawled back and forth. Their black claws scraped against the ice, and my old wounds flared up. Hordes of siti flanked Schism on both sides, watching and waiting for his command to attack. Their thin lips stretched against the black cords sewing their mouths shut. The hairs on my neck rose with anticipation.

"It's been too long, little Addie."

Focusing back on Schism, I noted what had happened to him since the Seventh Choice. The arm I had severed was replaced by a long, black limb, like shined ebony. This time, however, his other arm was identical. Two false hands and forearms had been repaired with stone all the way up to the elbow. Ophidian's blow to him in Ofavemore had caused more damage than I thought. But it was his face that rattled my core. Though his features appeared the same as before, it was as if they had been carved from black marble, adding a menacing layer to his beautiful appearance.

"It has," I replied coolly, lifting my chin as I took a step forward. There was no reason to endanger everyone. I was the one Schism wanted.

Silas tensed in my periphery, one hand tightening around the sword, the other snapping out in front of me. I stumbled back before finding my balance.

The sword glowed a glittering gold, beaming brighter as Silas leveled a scowl at Schism. I expected its cooling power to rush through my heart, but it wasn't there. Now that the alme had reconnected with its master, I could no longer feel its power.

All this time, the sword was yours, and now it's gone.

I wrung my hands around the fire poker, despising the pitiful weapon to defend myself while Silas had a magnificent alme. Why couldn't the sword have been mine?

"Now, now," James said, twirling his weapon. "There's no need to start anything."

Schism scoffed, and Silas crossed in front of me, positioning himself between Ophidian's commander and me.

"Is this your protection?" Schism guffawed. "A lowly town boy and an old man?"

Before I could respond, Silas pointed the sword at Schism. "What do you want?" His face was stern. His once warm eyes hardened like his blade as they bore into Schism.

James stretched his shoulders before tightening his grip on his weapon. "You really want to do this the hard way, don't you?"

Schism ignored both of them, keeping his glower locked on me. "What are we to do, little Addie? There you are, bearing not only a brand-new heart but the other half of my lord's. While I'm here, completely heartless." He motioned to himself.

"That heart doesn't belong to him, or to you," I said, shouldering up to Silas. I held out the fire poker, ready to pierce him through. Or watch it shatter to pieces. Still, whether I lost or won, I wasn't about to go down without a fight. I was no longer a burden. I was strong and could protect myself.

"Oh, yes, my dear, sweet little Addie, I'm afraid to say it is *his* heart now." Schism waved and gave a dramatic bow as if it were Heart Reign again. "Once any heart fuses with my lord's, it becomes bound to him, permanently."

The memory of Ophidian yanking the two halves of the black and red heart out of his chest entered my mind. How long had Silas's heart been fueling Ophidian? The unsynchronized beat of the two hearts thumped through my thoughts, and an uneasiness crept under my skin. After all this time, Silas's heart *still* hadn't fused perfectly with Ophidian's. But if the Beast got both halves … I shook my head. I wouldn't allow that to happen.

"You're wrong. No matter what he tries, that heart will always stay true to its real master," Silas growled.

His half-heart pulsed rapidly inside the satchel. I didn't dare open it, fearful Schism would take it, but in my periphery, small specs of ruby light escaped from inside my bag. I subtly tugged the flap down, snuffing the hue from sight.

The sword glowed with the same brilliant light. Not

like how it had glowed for me; this light was gold, brighter, and purer.

The glow encased the blade, sending droplets of radiance into the afternoon sky. It was as if the sword was aflame with gilded fire. Its heat blazed so intensely, I had to stumble away. Shielding my eyes, I realized Silas now stood in a halo of golden beams, his skin shimmering like the morning sun. Soft gasps came from behind me, and I turned to check on James and Nana. James crouched next to Nana, hugging her to his chest as he grasped his weapon, both of their mouths agape.

"It can't be," Schism squeaked like a terrified rat, backing away. He tripped on one of the siti and flailed, landing on his backside.

Short, quick moans escaped from the siti's woven lips as they scurried away, fleeing toward the trees of Wintertide. Soon, Schism was all alone, the solitary obstacle in our path.

"It's—it's impossible." Schism cowered. He held up his ebony arms, trying to block the light.

I stood, transfixed on Silas as Schism writhed.

After he took a final step, Silas stopped. Pointing the blade at Schism's throat, he boomed, "Tell your master I'm coming for my heart."

My skin tingled at Silas's voice. It was no longer his soft, soothing tone, but hard, commanding, and powerful.

Schism snarled once before scrambling out of the glowing light. As soon as he scampered into the shadows, the cracking of bones erupted from his back. His dark, decrepit wings sprouted from his shoulder blades.

"This isn't over," he growled. Beating his wings, Schism took off into the evening sky.

As soon as Schism was gone, the rays around Silas disappeared. He slammed to his knees before falling prostrate to the ground. Without hesitation, I threw the fire poker to the side and rushed down the stairs.

"Silas?" I knelt down and flipped him over, brushing the filthy snow away from his face. He was still breathing but didn't respond. I ran my fingers along his scars when James wailed.

Spinning around, I gasped as James fell to his knees with Nana in his arms, tears rolling down his face.

"What happened?" I cried.

"I don't know," James sobbed. "She's ice cold. I can't … she's not responding." He gently cupped her face. "Anna? Anna, can you hear me?"

Breaking from Silas's side, I barreled up the stairs to Nana's. Her body was even more frail and thin than a few moments ago. Fresh tears misted my eyes as I pushed away the thin strands of her white hair from her face. Her skin was cold as death.

"Nana," I whispered. One of her eyes cracked open, searching for me.

"Addie," she wheezed, extending a trembling hand. "You came back. I'm so … so … happy you came back."

"Of course, I came back," I answered, my voice wavering. Why was this happening? I had only just found Lyle and returned to Silas. Was Nana getting sick? Would I lose her?

Pain jabbed my chest, and I clutched my hand over my new heart, fighting back a scream. A sharp snap whipped between my ears, a crack ripping through my heart. I pawed at the spot, desperate to apply pressure, anything to soothe the sting.

Not even a day old and you already damaged your new heart. Are you sure you're worthy of it?

I shook the slithering voice away. Then, my satchel quivered.

The book. *Eman.*

Yanking the flap back, I plunged my hand between the various items until my fingers gripped the binding of Eman's book. The book was meant to direct me when he couldn't. Praying through the pain, I hoped he was right.

As I peeled the cover open, the binding perfectly balanced itself atop my fingertips. Then, an invisible quill scrawled in blue ink:

Bring her to me.

I had just enough time to read it before the text disappeared, replaced with a map. A conglomerate of houses appeared, surrounded by a thick forest of trees. Bringing the map closer, I noted that the houses were the same as those surrounding the market. The quill sketched a solitary house at the edge of the trees. I glanced at Nana's house before referencing the map again. That had to be Nana's. And if that were true, then this was a map of Barracks, and the forest was Wintertide.

Rotating the map, I traced the trees with my finger. The page ended at the edge of Wintertide. I tapped the artfully drawn forest. There were more Lands beyond Barracks. Why did the map end there?

"James, what does this mean?" I pushed the pages toward him.

James leaned over and scanned the map while rubbing his hand across his chin. "It's a map telling you where to go next."

"But it stops at the edge of Wintertide."

James tucked a lock of Nana's snowy hair behind her ear before securing the quilt around her. "Then we go to the edge of Wintertide. Eman must be guiding us to the doorway back to Ramni. He'll be able to help Anna and Silas."

"You're right." I shoved the book back in the satchel. "We should probably get moving before the siti return."

"Agreed," James replied. He scooped Nana up in his arms and stood. Her head lolled to the side, limp. Gingerly, I helped James adjust her head, so she rested against his chest in the crook of his arm.

As I hurried back to Silas, I inspected the surrounding trees and the barren market. We were at least fifty yards from Wintertide, and there was nothing that indicated a way to Ramni. I pulled at my thoughts, trying to remember what Eman had said before we had left: *The door will always open, you only need knock.*

I made a mental note to inform Eman to be a little more specific about which door to knock on.

Creaks and snaps echoed from Wintertide, and I halted. The siti had hidden within its trees. Were they returning to finish us off?

After no other sound emerged, I carefully crept toward Silas, praying the monsters wouldn't appear.

Before I reached Silas, his hand moved to his forehead, and he groaned.

"Silas," I breathed. Kneeling down, I laid my hand on his cheek, my fingers running over the raised skin of his facial scars.

"What happened?" He rolled onto his side and tried to sit up.

I stood and offered him my hand. He locked his fingers with mine, and, leaning back, I pulled him up. After a few wobbly attempts, he managed to stand, but he didn't release my hand.

Moaning drifted through the air, and Silas tightened his grip. Although the siti didn't sound near, I didn't want to take any chances.

"I'll explain later," I said, gently shaking his hand away and motioning him to follow James and me. "We need to go."

Silas reached for my hand again but hesitated and tucked his hand in his pocket. "Right. Those creatures will be back."

I sprinted toward Wintertide with James right behind me, carrying Nana against his chest. A darker gray coated the sky in a foreboding patch of fog. The sun must be setting. If the siti came back while it was night, we were done for.

"Come on," I yelled over my shoulder. But as I focused back on Wintertide, the crunch of our footsteps faded away, replaced with the strange ticking of a clock.

CHAPTER 6

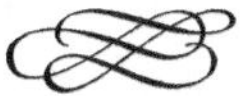

I spun around, nearly losing my balance as Silas collided with my front. His hands grabbed my shoulders, steadying me. That ticking—where was it coming from?

"Do you hear that?" I asked, twisting my head around. Wisps of hair escaped from the string as I searched.

An eerie silence filled the air as the wind vanished around us. No birds chirping. No branches swayed in the breeze. No snow falling. Everything had come to a dead stop as we stood at the edge of Wintertide. As did the ticking.

"Hear what?" Silas questioned as he peered around my shoulders into the trees.

"I—" The moaning returned, closer this time. The branches of the white-barked forest shuttered.

I clutched Silas's arms. Was the noise coming from inside? Was there a safe path? Where do we go from here?

"Addie," Silas said, cupping my face. "It's okay. We'll be okay."

My pulse leveled, and I stepped away, feeling foolish. "Right, of course."

Taking a few steps to the left, Silas held the hilt of the sword, his knuckles turning white. "Shouldn't we head south? The siti have been staying to the north. Are you sure this is the right way?"

Is it the right way? Are you sure?

Tucking the stray hairs behind my ears, I flipped the map open. The picture hadn't changed, but I was sure we were still headed in the right direction.

"This is still the right way," I said as Silas hovered over my shoulder. As he leaned toward the map, his arm brushed against mine. My breath hitched, and I closed the book to check on Nana.

"How is she?" I asked James, sweeping my fingers across Nana's cheek.

"She's stable," James replied. "Do what you need to do, Addie. If anyone can get us back to Ramni, it's you."

"Ramni?" Silas questioned.

"It's the only place that can heal Nana," I explained.

A low moaning rumbled from my right, so loudly, snow and icicles fell from the trees. I tensed, holding the book up like a weapon.

After a few minutes, the noise quieted. Relief itched at the back of my thoughts until the familiar scratching of razor claws scraped against tree trunks. I backed away as a long-limbed figure sauntered its way out of the trees, impaling the white birch with its midnight black claws. Spirals of bark spun to the ground, surrounding the trunk of the once beautiful tree. A cold sweat dripped from my brow.

"Silas," I whispered, beckoning him away from the edge of the forest.

"I know."

Silas planted his feet, widening his stance as he leveled his sword at the siti. The weapon immediately gleamed. Silas's shoulders rose as the golden power soaked into his arm. Though he was shaking, the glow seeped steadily into his hand, coating his body with glittering light.

"When I say run, you run," he commanded.

Is he in charge now?

The group of gray siti from Schism's entourage crawled out of the forest, their leathery skin a stark contrast to the white birch bark. The tips of their black claws sunk through the thick ice, plunging into the frozen crystals as a small pack surrounded us. Moans tumbled from their sewn lips as they focused on trapping their prey.

Fear heightened my senses as I heard every step, saw every breath of our predators. These monsters were once human. A tremor skittered through my bones at the thought.

The siti continued their slow crawl out of Wintertide as if they were taunting, playing with us before they attacked.

Placing the book in my satchel, I readied my stance to

attack as the siti circled us completely. There was no point in going back to Barracks; there was nothing left. Our only option was to continue into Wintertide and hope the door to Ramni was in there. And that meant we had to get through the siti.

"Addie, did you hear me?" Silas demanded. "You run."

I stood straighter and glared defiantly at him. "No. I'm not running."

Silas spun toward me so fast, I didn't have time to react. He wrapped one arm around my shoulders and crushed me into his chest, sending my stomach into a spiral as I breathed in his earthy scent.

"Stubborn girl," he whispered in my ear, his warm breath tickling the nape of my neck. "I can't lose you again."

I placed my hand on his chest, gently pushing off from him. "You don't have to. I'm not that same little girl anymore, Silas."

"I know," he said, kissing the top of my head before releasing me. He pointed his sword at the encroaching siti, and his warmth left my skin, replaced by the bitter cold. Shivering, I yanked Lyle's sleeves over my palms.

One siti leapt forward, claws extended. I screamed, ducking down, but Silas surged into action. Lunging, he wielded his sword with expert precision, as if he'd been fighting his entire life. With one swipe, he took off the siti's head, pushing me behind him. Black blood spurted through the air before the siti's body plummeted with a sickening thud.

As if the death of their comrade was the signal to attack, the siti lurched forward. Their claws reached out, blindly swiping at any part of our bodies they could reach. James fought them off as best he could, one arm holding Nana.

"James!" I cried, tugging Nana from him. "I'll hold her."

James awkwardly lobbed off a siti's arm with his axe before handing Nana off to me. "Thank you, Addie." He spun back around and jumped into the wall of siti.

I held Nana tightly, hating how useless I was. How helpless I had always been. And here I was again. No power, no weapon.

Useless burden.

"Addie!" Silas yelled, plunging his sword into the face of a siti. Hissing slithered from its sewn mouth as black blood spewed from the wound. "Run, Addie! Please, run!"

His plea brought me back to Doctor Magnum's office a year ago. The words that led me to Ophidian's Realm and the Seven Choices—that led me to Claire, Lyle, and Eman.

"Watch yourself!" James called, but he was too late.

One siti swiped at Silas, its claws slicing a deep gash across his chest. Pieces of his black sweater curled to the ground as bright red blood dripped onto the ice.

"Silas!" I cried.

I waited for the panic to claw at my throat, for rage to burble in my chest, but they never came. I had to do something to help. But without the sword, what could I do?

Frustrated, I balled my hand into a fist, then flinched.

A bright glowing orange illuminated my fingers. Brilliant flames flickered off their tips, begging to be released. Life and power surged through my veins, more than ever before. Was this the power of the Bellata? Had it been inside me all this time?

A frail hand laid on my arm. "Go," Nana croaked, her lids still shut. "Go, Addie." Her skin was turning blue. I had to hurry.

Placing her down gently, I positioned my hands toward the siti, mimicking how I had seen James command his power in Ofavemore. My fingers shook as orange light streamed from my palms. The light twisted and turned, surrounding the creatures until it tightened. Shrieks rose from the horrible monsters until the light suffocated their noise. Like a raging river, refreshing energy flowed through my veins and out my hands while simultaneously leaving my heart. My knees shook as my body weakened from the purge of power.

I held on for as long as I could before a hand grasped my wrist. I forced my gaze to James. Black droplets of siti blood marked his face and neck.

"Stop now, or you won't return," he said hoarsely, worry flooding his eyes.

"How?" I cried. The power was draining out so quickly, I couldn't stop it.

"Command it. You control your power." He gripped my wrist tighter.

Focusing on my hands, I willed the power back to me.

It was wild and free, not willing to be tamed. I tried again, more firmly this time, and the light slowly dwindled.

"Good," James exhaled as he loosened his grip.

After the light receded, I placed a hand over my heart. It thrashed against my ribcage, readying to explode. Sucking in the frigid air, I focused back on the siti.

Long, gray limbs draped over one another as the siti bodies laid motionless on the snowy ground. Yet as I watched their chests still moving, my shoulders fell. After all that work, I had only knocked them unconscious.

"You did well, Addie," James said with a quick pat on my shoulder before heading to Nana. He whispered something in her ear and scooped her up once more, his axe nowhere in sight. "We need to leave while we still can."

I brought my palm up to my face, scrutinizing the cold, red flesh before following James. Had I stored all the power inside of me? How could I unleash it again?

Underneath a pile of lifeless siti, a tuft of blond hair poked through gangly gray limbs. Silas. With a grunt, I shoved the siti off him, and he hungrily gasped for air.

After he coughed a few times, Silas smiled up at me. "That's new, too."

Snorting, I offered him my hand. He grabbed it firmly and stood.

"Silas," I said as he brushed the ice and snow off his worn pants. "Your wound. It's healed."

I cocked my head, as I trailed my fingers along the rip in Silas's sweater. Nothing but Silas's milky skin showed through. What had happened to the giant gash? Had the power of the sword healed him?

Silas's breaths turned heavy, and the half-heart in my satchel rammed against my side. Realizing what I was doing, I jerked my hand away.

"Sorry," I breathed.

"Don't worry about it," he replied, his voice husky. Clearing his throat, he bent down and grabbed the sword. "Maybe the wound healed because of this."

"All right, kids," James said, joining us. "We better get going. Addie, do we continue through the forest?"

Pulling my gaze from Silas, I addressed the map. It had shifted, drawing rows and rows of trees. Snapping the cover shut, I replied, "Yes, the map now shows the entire forest."

Staring through the endless rows of trees before me, I took a deep breath, then plunged into their depths.

Thin trunks of birch trees filled the frigid forest, obstructing any distinct trail. But as we approached their bare limbs, the trees folded out of the way, creating a path for us to follow. I had always read stories about Winter-tide being enchanted but never realized they were true.

Silence blanketed the forest, just like the market and my house.

Tick, tock.

Tick, tock.

Once again, the ticking softly tapped the back of my ears. I paused, searching for the source. But before I could look any further, the ticking vanished beneath the sound of James's and Silas's footsteps, crunching through the icy foliage.

None of us spoke as we anticipated another attack. The cracking of bark bounced against the branches as the next trees rolled enough away to let us through.

I stayed alert, looking in all directions as we continued. But after wading through the endless rows of tree trunks, I calmed my steps, keeping my attention focused on the white bark ahead.

Just then, a cloaked figure dashed across our path. The cloak billowed behind the figure as it sped through a pair of trees thirty feet ahead. In an instant, the dark green cloak was gone.

The book wriggled in my hands. The map had redrawn itself again, and, if I read it correctly, it wanted us to follow the strange figure.

"Come on," I whispered to the others as I took the lead. Maybe this mysterious figure could help us.

I took quick steps, holding the book just below my eyes so I could track the figure. But when I tried to find them again, they were gone. I started through the next section of trees when the tip of a blade prodded my side.

"Lonely damsel traipsing about the woods?" a sardonic male voice asked.

My gaze slid to the side, trying to discover the identity of my captor. But the hood of his cloak shrouded everything except the long, thick beard cascading from his chin.

"I'm not alone," I replied with cool confidence.

"No, she's not," Silas said, he and James with Nana appearing between the snow-covered trees.

The man growled as he turned toward them. "Ah, the valiant hero come to save his beloved?" He grabbed my arm and wrenched it behind my back. Eman's book fell from my grasp. Bursts of white light exploded in my vision as the cold point of his dagger rested against my throat. "You're too late, hero."

He yanked me backward a few steps, and before anyone could stop him, the man whipped around and sprinted through the forest, dragging me behind him.

"Wait!" I cried, my muscles straining to match his long gait. "Where are we going? Where are you taking me?"

"Quiet, Adelaide! They'll hear us," the man hushed, tugging me down behind a giant trunk.

I wrenched out of his grasp and massaged my shoulder. How did he know my name? Was he someone from Barracks? The demand for an explanation rose in the back of my throat when the man brought a finger to his lips before pointing to the worn bark.

I followed the direction of his finger and bit back a gasp. The trees of Wintertide had been cleared. Not moved, but cut down, leaving a large, open circle filled with cages. Dozens of square, iron cages filled with people.

Placing my hand on the trunk, I swallowed hard. Though a year had passed, I could still recognize some of the local vendors that had participated in Heart Reign each year. Lady

Truosh, who was always squeaky clean, was now seated on the dirt, her face and hands covered in filth. I remembered Old Man Chank and his long, black beard. But now it hung in scraggles from his chin, as if it had been haphazardly cut.

The groups in the cages were quiet. Some were munching on rations of bread, while others sat with their legs crisscrossed, and heads bowed, as if praying.

"Who did this?" I whispered. "How long have these people been here?"

The stranger reached beneath his cloak and fisted a jeweled dagger. "Too long. Help me free them, and I'll help you with anything you want."

The rough voice held a twang of familiarity. Trying to get a better look, I leaned in and spotted dark waves beneath his hood. "Who are you?"

Before he could answer, the stranger wrapped his arm around me, smashing me against his hard chest. He whipped his cloak around us.

"Hey, what are you—"

"Quiet!" he hushed again, his breath blowing the stray curls along my cheek. Ice and iron wafted into my nose as I quieted my breathing. After a few moments, he threw the cloak off. "Don't speak, just look."

Scooching to the other side of the trunk, I peeked around, and my heart dropped to my stomach. Surrounding one of the cages was my worst nightmare from Ophidian's Realm: malum. Three of them focused on the furthest cage from us, their red eyes swirling. Why were the malum here? What did Ophidian want with these people?

The malum hovered around the cage, their black forms twisting like smoke beneath them. As if in a daze, the once somber people inside began to rise, staring blankly at one another until a man with thinning red hair punched his neighbor in the jaw. I brought a hand to my mouth as a full-out brawl started in the cage. The group of thirty people continued thrashing and beating one another senseless. They snarled and growled, attacking one another until there wasn't a single body that moved. Those in the surrounding prisons fled from the wild cage, backing into the farthest corners of their cells. Curling my hand into a fist, I turned away as Lady Truosh fell to the ground. What Claire had said was true. The malum could change a heart from good to bad.

A shimmer of yellow light glimmered from the corner of my eye, and a beautiful woman with long golden waves materialized from the woods. I did a double-take, my inner voice screaming in horror. Her tall, voluptuous figure was wrapped in a snug, black coat that grazed the tips of her black boots. A silver necklace with the yellow stone glinted around her neck as she stalked to the cages.

That woman was the one I saw with Silas in the Seven Choices. The air escaped my lungs. How was she real?

Her lips twisted in satisfaction as the malum moved to corrupt the next cage of people. I gritted my teeth. Beautiful or not, it was clear she sided with Ophidian.

As my gaze ran along the line of the cages, my heart

jolted at something I hadn't noticed before. Or rather someone.

In the cage closest to us, rocking back and forth, sat a man hugging his knees to his chest, with a long white braid cascading down his back. Doctor Magnum.

CHAPTER 7

Retreating around the trunk, I knelt in front of the bearded stranger. "How do we save them?"

I couldn't let these people, especially Doctor Magnum, be killed. My own father was taken from me; I wouldn't allow the same thing to happen to Claire.

He twisted a thin blade between his fingers. "We need to distract those creatures long enough, so I can get the locks off the cages."

I peered over my shoulder, watching the malum float to the next cage. We had to hurry. "Then what?"

A scowl curled the man's lips. "What else is there?"

"Where do all the people go? How do we keep them from being captured again?"

The man angled his head before turning toward the sound of snapping branches. He growled.

"Stay here." He yanked his hood down further before

taking quick, silent leaps in the direction we had come from.

I quieted my breathing and focused back on the cages. Those people weren't just any people. I grew up with them. They thought I was a burden to Lyle and accused me of ruining the best trade of his life. They called me a leper; they destroyed my home. But no one deserved to be at the mercy of the malum.

My throat thickened as I recognized more of the prisoners. Headmaster Clive's balding head contrasted with the auburn ringlets of Nelly Shone, the baker. Though my former teacher hadn't been correct about Ophidian, I didn't want this to be his end.

Who wasn't in the cages were the members of The Reliance, Eman's followers. I searched through the faces, trying to find the man with the woolen cap from my Heart Reign, but he was nowhere to be found.

As my sight reached the furthest cage, a twinkling just beyond it caught my eye. I pressed my palms against my knees as tiny sparkles of light gathered in an arch formation. Past the malum and through the cages lay a door made of shimmering white wood. The door to Ramni.

Running a hand over my hair, I huffed in frustration. To get to the door, I would have to fight through the malum. Eman had said to bring Nana to him, but maybe I had found a way to save the prisoners, too.

Swift footsteps glided across the ice before the bearded man returned, followed by Silas, James, and Nana. James quickly eased Nana to the forest floor, trying to position her as comfortably as possible against a trunk nearby. Her skin was almost translucent, her chest barely moving.

After tightening the quilt around Nana's shivering form, James stood, offering Eman's book to me. As I took it from his grasp, he started to speak when the hooded man gave a motion of silence. Any sound could alert the monsters to our location.

After securing the book in my satchel, I motioned for Silas and James to come closer before pointing to the cages. They peeked around the trunk, and their eyes widened in horror. James surveyed the area before he locked his gaze on the white door.

The bearded man crouched down next to me, drawing back his cloak and unveiling several daggers and knives attached to his belt. Picking two, he gripped one in each hand.

"I know how to save the people once you free them," I said.

He brought one of the knives to his face, inspecting it as he snorted. "And how's that?"

"There's a door that will transport us to another realm, one of healing for these people." I wasn't sure whether this man would go on blind faith that there was a door on the other side of the cages.

"White, shimmering?" he grunted while straightening the other knives on his belt.

I paused, surprised. "Yes, behind the cages."

"I don't see any door," Silas added, one hand gripped

around the hilt of the sword, the other balled in a fist. "Addie, who is this guy? Why are we helping him?"

"We need to help save these people."

Silas pointed to my dying grandmother. "But what about Nana? She's our main priority." Silas flicked a hand at the stranger. "Let him figure out his own problems."

"Silas," I chided in a hushed tone. "These are our people. We can't just let them die."

"They've never cared about you before. They would've let you die."

He's right, you know.

I flinched at the truth. Silas was right. These people had never cared about what happened to me. I had hated them and everything else in Barracks. But I was different now. I didn't want to be friends with any of those people, but it wasn't right to let them die.

"I'm helping save these people," I said with finality. Ignoring Silas's mumbles, I directed my attention to the man. "What do you need us to do?"

A sly smile crept over his bearded lips. "A distraction."

"I can help with that," James volunteered. A spark of white light emitted from his palms, causing the axe with the hook to appear in his hands.

I blinked at the weapon. It must be James's alme.

Without warning, James gave a battle cry and ran toward the malum.

"Is that what you had in mind?" I asked.

"It works." The stranger shrugged before launching into a sprint.

The cloaked man threw one of his knives as he ran toward the malum but missed his mark. Quickly, he reached for another knife on his belt and threw again, this time striking a malum at least forty yards away. How had he hit it from that distance? Who was this man? He soon joined James in combat against the malum, using his two knives to swipe and jab.

The shocked and hopeful cries of the people bounded through the forest as James and the man fiercely attacked the malum, successfully leading the monsters away from the cages.

I itched to join in, but what could I use? Back at the house, I had been in such a rush to save Nana that I had forgotten the fire poker. Turning, I saw Silas rubbing his temples, a disgruntled look contorting his features.

"What's wrong?" I asked, still not pleased with his earlier suggestion of leaving the people at the mercy of the malum.

"I-I don't know," he said, squeezing his eyes shut. His whole body tensed as if in pain. When he opened them, he caught me ogling the sword. "Here." He handed me the gilded hilt. "Help them."

I didn't need him to tell me twice. Grabbing the weapon, I headed toward the cages. Everything slowed around me, the screams fading into the backdrop of my mind. The cold of Barracks left my skin. Nothing but the wild beating of my heart filled my ears.

Screaming a battle cry of rage and sorrow, I attacked as the soft ticking clicked once more.

Death consumed the air as I passed the first cage of the malum's victims. My heart cried out at the loss of innocent lives.

I sped by the blonde woman, expecting her to stop me, but she didn't. Instead, she stood with her arms folded in front of her, watching us through narrowed lids.

James sparred against two of the malum while the bearded man stationed himself in front of the first cage. As he fumbled for the lock, another malum drew close. Before the monster could attack, I rushed at it, not hesitating to impale its red eye.

The malum screeched, falling forward as black blood dribbled onto the snow.

The bearded man fiddled with the lock, using one of his many knives as a key. In a matter of seconds, it clicked, and the door flew open. With her ringlets bouncing, Nelly Shone was one of the first to pour out of the cages. The rest followed, frantic.

"This was your part, remember?" the man yelled before running to the next cage, his dark cloak billowing behind him.

As if in response, Eman's words appeared in my thoughts: *The door will always open, all you need is to knock.*

Swerving through the panicked group, I planted myself in front of the door to Ramni. I knocked three times. The white wood shimmered before the door swung open. Swirling lights of blue, pink, and orange twinkled, welcoming me back.

"Over here!" I shouted, waving my arms above my

head. A few people froze, their eyes darting from me to the door, unsure. "Please, trust me." I motioned to the door.

Before they could decide, streaks of blue lightning zinged through the sky. The people screamed and ran, fortunately toward the open door. The light zapped again, followed by more screams.

I ushered the people through the door, trying to count heads as they blurred past. By the size of the crowd, the hooded man had unlocked almost all the cages.

"Hurry, please," I said as I stood on my tiptoes, trying to find James, Silas, and the bearded man in the crowd.

Soon, James appeared. He and Silas ran side by side, clutching Nana's frail figure between them. They paused at the door just before a bolt of lightning struck behind them.

"Go!" I yelled. Standing guard, I raised the sword, ready to defend my family. It wasn't my alme, but it was the only weapon I had.

The light churned behind me, assuring me they had gotten through.

I started lowering the sword when a strong hand gripped my shoulder. Snapping my fingers back around the hilt, I reared my elbow back.

A grunt sounded as I whipped around, holding the sword steady.

"What are you doing?" Silas wheezed, one hand on his stomach as he leaned forward. He coughed. "You need to leave."

I winced, wanting to offer an apology before a bolt of lightning cracked behind me. I jumped forward, and Silas caught me before we both turned and faced the beautiful woman stalking toward the final cage. Lifting her hand, she rubbed her fingers across the yellow gem at her throat. A bolt of blue soared from her fingertips, barely missing the cloaked man as he wrestled with the last lock.

"I'll be fine, Silas." I tore away from him. "You need to go."

Without hearing his reply, I dashed toward the woman. Her pleased look from before had disappeared, replaced with one of repulsion.

Pleadings from those inside the last cage ricocheted off the iron bars as I passed by. Without any concern for the lightning-wielding woman, the cloaked man continued wriggling his knife in the lock.

"Are you all right?" I yelled over my shoulder, lunging away from another lightning strike. Shards of ice cut into my cheek as I flattened myself to the ground. Warm droplets of blood oozed down my neck.

"Why wouldn't I be?" he barked, scowling at the lock. "Aren't you supposed to be saving people?"

Growling, I wiped the blood off my face and neck and stood. I swiveled my head, trying to find the blonde woman when I spotted her pointing to the door to Ramni. The malum floated toward it, their red eyes humming. My boots slid across the ice as I bounded after them. When I was almost near, blue lightning struck in front of my footsteps.

The blonde woman shot an icy glare at me, her fingers pulsing with cerulean static. "I was wondering when we'd meet." Steadying her hand, she paused, her eyes darting behind me. A look of panic crossed her features before she quickly covered them with a sly grin.

"Leave her be," Silas commanded, standing beside me. Though he didn't wield the sword, his presence commanded power.

The woman bristled as the static dissipated from her hand. "No matter." She smoothed the black leather fabric of her coat and fluffed her blonde waves. "My pets can have the fun until it's my turn." Lifting her slender arm, she pointed her blue lightning at the ground and disappeared, leaving a new group of malum to consume us.

Spinning around, I faced the last cage. Men, women, and children stared wide-eyed at Silas and me, recognizing our identities. Their cries grew silent as they waited.

"We don't have any more time," I told the bearded man before lifting the sword. He barely had enough time to scamper out of the way before I slammed the blade against the lock. Metal clanged against metal, sending sparks flying. But the lock didn't break.

Although they didn't draw near, the heat from the malum burned my back, making each swing of the sword more agonizing than the last. I tried again and again to break the lock, each time with more force and frustration. Sweat dripped down my neck as my hands glowed a bright orange, but none of the power went into the sword.

Suddenly, a strong arm wrapped around my waist, yanking the sword out of my hands. Before I could comprehend the action, I was tossed to the side. A loud clash bounded against the trees, and the prisoners screamed. Terror suffocated my throat before I found Silas gripping the sword, the iron lock disintegrating. The people kicked open the bars and rushed out in a frenzy toward the white door, trampling the bearded man in their escape.

The malum immediately soared over to us. Their dark claws were sharper than the siti's, resembling talons as they sliced through the now empty cages. Rods of iron clanged against one another as they rolled across the ice.

Without a word, Silas yanked me up and retreated to the open, white door. Though it was only a few feet away, the malum bore down on us.

You don't have to run, the same slithery voice encouraged in my mind. *Or help these people. What have they ever done for you?*

The malum's power clouded my thoughts of what was right and what I had to do.

But I was mended.

My heart let out a beat, and the temptations from the malum fled my mind.

"Wait." I stopped, turning back to the fallen, bearded man. "We can't leave him."

"Yes, we can," Silas snapped, tightening his hold on my hand.

Jerking out of his grasp, I ran back to the bearded man. I bent down and slung one of his arms over my shoulders, doing my best to hoist him up.

Wielding his sword, Silas made a final lunge at the malum, slicing the tips off one of their claws. The creature howled and reared its arm back, hissing at the glowing weapon. Silas slashed the sword through the air again, forcing the malum to retreat. Once they had fled to the woods, Silas sprinted back to me. Without a word, he grabbed the man's other arm, and we ran toward the door.

We jumped through the bright light, and the screeching of the malum faded into the distance. I lost my grip on the bearded man, and he tumbled out of my grasp. Flailing my arms, I tried to find him before my head hit a hard surface, turning my vision black.

CHAPTER 8

Soft footsteps awakened me from a dreamless sleep. I struggled to lift my head, but the throbbing in my skull was so great, I stopped trying. A large, round bump had formed on my forehead. Jolts of pain raced down my skull as I poked it. I sucked in a sharp breath. So that was the source of the throbbing. Luckily, the ticking had stopped. I couldn't imagine both the throbbing and the annoying tick-tock noise swirling through my mind. When I opened an eye, a smiling face with bronzed skin and bright green eyes peered down at me.

"Welcome back, Bellata," Sana said in her light, cheery voice.

I managed a weak smile and tried to sit up again. Dizziness washed over me, and I flopped back onto the soft pillow. Overhead, a series of silver leaves from the branches of the surrounding trees wove together in an ornate and symmetrical pattern. I sighed. For once, I wished I could come to Ramni and enjoy its splendor without an injury.

"Here. Drink this. It will help with the bump and the drain of power." Sana handed me a warm wooden cup. Her thick black braid coiled around her arm.

Wrapping both hands around the cup, I held it up, allowing the lavender-scented steam to coat my face. In a few sips, I finished the herbal tea before the door to my room slammed open.

"Where is she?" a female voice demanded.

Yelping, I dropped the cup and shrank under the covers. I peeked out to see Sana's eyes sparkling with amusement as she placed the bundle of my clothes at the base of the bed. The healer tiptoed away, leaving me with no defense at all. The covers were soon ripped off, and I was immediately thankful for the long, cream gown I was wearing.

"Do you know how long you've been gone?" Claire demanded, glaring down her freckled nose at me.

The soothing lavender tea worked its way through my body, and I was able to sit up and assess Claire. Her hair was still white with the same brown streak. But instead of being braided as it had been before, it was tied up into her usual messy bun on top of her head. A branch slowly crept up from the ground toward her tousled strands.

I kept an eye on it, curious. "Well, for me, it was only a few minutes, maybe hours."

Claire gripped the branch and growled at it. The poor

foliage shriveled and shrank back into the dirt. "At least six months, Addie! Six months of stupid trees trying to fix my hair, putting idiotic little flowers in it!" She groaned, slumping down on the bed.

I watched her for a moment before letting out a loud laugh. And soon, Claire was laughing, too.

Once our laughter had died down, I sat up and asked, "Are you sure, Claire? Six months in only a few hours?" How much time was I losing to unite all the Magisters?

Claire crossed her arms over her chest. "Of course, I'm sure." She then broke her glare and focused on her tapping toes. Her hands dropped to her lap, and she nervously twisted her fingers.

"What's going on, Claire?"

After a few moments of silence, she sighed and finally said, "Eman will be able to explain it better than I can. I'm sure he'll tell you soon enough."

I bent my knees and hugged them to my chest. Why wasn't Claire telling me what was going on?

She doesn't trust you.

Could that be true?

"Well," Claire said, her face lighting up as she slapped her hands against her thighs. "I didn't come here to depress you. Lyle wants to see you."

At the promise of seeing Lyle, I noticed the stack of clothes at the end of the bed. The baby blue wool had been folded into a perfect square. Bouncing forward, I tugged it from the pile, sending the other items tumbling to the floor. I rubbed the soft blue fibers between my palms, noticing that any rips or tears had been mended by Sana's diligent hands. It looked brand new. I hugged the sweater. I needed to see Lyle soon. I needed some proof, some evidence that after everything I went through in Ophidian's Realm for him, he was okay.

Still, the horrid image of the malum in Wintertide flashed through my mind. While I was safe in Ramni, Ophidian's monsters were hard at work, destroying our realm. As much as I longed to spend days with Lyle, my iuram, my oath, to Eman was greater.

"Where is he?" I asked, laying the sweater back on the bed. I pressed my palms against the sheets and rose to my feet. The silky fabric of the gown tumbled to the floor. Leaves sprouted from the ground, binding themselves around my feet into a soft pair of slippers.

"He's with Eman," Claire said, scowling at the leaves before she stood. "He, at least, has gotten better since you left. Every day Eman helps him. He'll be done soon. And when he is, I'll tell him to come find you."

"Thank you," I said, noticing how Claire's face lit up at Lyle's name. But, before I could ask any prying questions, she cut me off.

"Oh, and some guy you brought with you wanted to see you as soon as you got up."

My heart swelled. "Silas." He made it through. And if he made it through, the bearded man from the woods must have, as well. I needed to find out who he was.

"Yeah, tall with blond hair that looks like a mess?" Claire asked. I clasped my hands in front of me and nodded with a grin. Claire cocked her hip to the side. "He wouldn't leave your side until Eman asked to speak to him. That was the last time I saw him."

"Thank you, Claire," I said, running my hands down the gown's soft fabric. She shrugged nonchalantly, but the corner of her lips twitched, showing she was pleased.

I glanced down at the bundle of clothes that were now sprawled on the ground. Along with Lyle's sweater, my dark pants, shirt, and boots were all cleaned and mended. I reached for the sweater, yearning to wrap myself in its warmth and protection. Scooping up the rest of the pile, I padded to the corner of the room where a wooden dressing screen stood.

Once changed, I laid the dress Sana had given me and the delicate leaf slippers on the bed. I straightened my sweater and patted down the frizz in my curls, wishing I had another string. The frightened twig from before tapped my shoulder before offering me a spool of twine.

"Thank you," I said before taking the spool. It gave a bow and offered a thorn for me to use. Cutting off a strand, I hoisted my wild hair back and knotted it with the twine.

I motioned to my hair, then clothes and spun around, waiting for Claire's assessment and approval. Her hazel eyes scanned my appearance before giving me a nod and a satisfied smirk. I adjusted Lyle's sweater once more and tucked my stray hairs behind my ears before Claire let out a huff and strode toward the open door without me.

Taking a few large steps, I caught up with her and said,

"And when we have a moment, I want to know about you and Lyle." I wriggled my brows and gave her a wink. Her cheeks reddened. Before she could reprimand me, I dashed through the door and down the hallway.

The arched trees wove throughout one another, forming the long hall I had traveled down before. Though their bark was still bright and beautiful, it seemed like their glow had dimmed. In fact, the flowers weren't dancing like they had the last time I was here, and the butterflies were nowhere to be found.

As I began my search for Lyle, I debated hunting for the library. I really wanted to do more research on the Twelve Magisters. Plus, if I was going to find Lyle anywhere, it would be with his nose in a book. And, there was a pretty good chance I might run into Silas along the way, too.

With a skip in my step, I set off, following what I thought was the fastest route to the library. However, after a few turns here and there, I became lost. With another right turn, I paused, tapping my foot. This hallway didn't look familiar, either. Retracing my steps, I tried a different route, but once again, I got lost. I didn't think I was this terrible with directions. Scratching my cheek, I rounded another corner and found myself at the beginning of the Windows of Light. Excited to have some extra time to snoop, I crept up to the first window, remembering how stunning each one was. The image was so clear and crisp, like I could jump through each of them into a different realm.

But as I studied them closely, I saw that there was something wrong. The window that had held the beautiful starry night before was now only a darkened sky. The twinkling stars had vanished. Biting my lip, I moved to the next window. The crystal waves that had once held bright-colored fish were empty, the waters stagnant, refusing to move in any direction. What had happened?

I reached the window that held the castle of Lignum. The glowing lights in the picture had dimmed to a cool blue. A soft violet hue peeked out from each of the windows in the castle. At least Lignum was the same as before.

There was something about the spacious wooden castle that enchanted me. I took a step closer to study the beautifully carved structure. The trees stood tall, creating the strong walls and towers of the castle that was the home of the Rexus. My mind rolled over the title—Rexus. He was another mystery in my pot of prophecies to unfold. I leaned in closer. The carvings on the towers spiraled around the base, detailing various flowers and plants that I had only seen in Ramni. Why would the Rexus ever want to leave this beautiful place?

As I padded to the next window, my blood ran cold. The frame holding the Shadow realm wasn't empty but filled with thousands of siti lined next to one another like pieces on a chessboard. Unease dried my throat as I took a step closer. There weren't only siti in the frame, but malum behind them, hovering beside one another in the same manner, as if positioning for a war.

A large, black door laid on the opposite end of the army of siti and malum. In front of it stood the Beast's second in command, Schism. Though his skin was still obsidian, he wore new clothes: a uniform of black slacks and a black jacket with silver serpents sliding down his sleeves and pants. A thick, black whip coiled around his fist as he snarled at the siti closest to him.

I blinked at the window. Was this Ophidian's army? Did Eman realize that the Shadow realm was hosting them? How soon would they get here?

My pulse quickened as a beam of light flashed, and the woman with blonde hair appeared next to Schism. Though I couldn't hear what they were saying, I was sure there were a few rude remarks shared, judging by the bared teeth they gave one another.

Yet as I stepped closer, the woman spun to me, and I stilled. I lurched away from the frame, hoping to become invisible as she snarled and lifted her hand. A blue bolt of energy shot into the window, shattering the image from the inside.

I wasn't sure how long I stood there until a cough from my left took me by surprise. When I turned, Eman greeted me with a gentle smile. Arm extended, he beckoned me to come.

CHAPTER 9

"Welcome back," Eman said, his gaze drifting from me to the Windows of Light. A slight sorrow lingered behind his gentle smile.

"Eman," I said before pointing to the shattered window. "Ophidian, the army." I grabbed my ponytail. "The window, it's gone! You can't see them anymore." I continued to babble until he lifted a hand, silencing me.

"Worry not, Bellata. Everything you've seen, I have seen, as well. Come." He extended his hand further. "We have much to do."

I reached out and took his large hand. It was warm and welcoming but powerful. I could barely cup my small hand around his thick fingers. The strength of the magic swirling beneath his olive-toned skin radiated heat from his palm. But there was something else intertwined with his power: a weariness I hadn't realized Eman had.

Holding my hand firm, Eman led me back down the

hall of the Windows of Light, only glancing at the other frames over his shoulder as we passed.

Once we entered the main hallway, Eman led me to his mending room. The rectangular table where he had mended my heart had been pushed to the side, stacks of books and scrolls sprawled across it. Three empty chairs formed a circle in the center of the room. Eman released my hand and collapsed into one of the wooden chairs. Letting out a heavy sigh, he rubbed his eyes with his thumb and index finger.

Concern washed over me, but I shrank back, fumbling with the hem of Lyle's sweater. What could *I* do to comfort the Mender himself?

His shirt was wrinkled, with one side untucked. The suspenders on his slacks were slightly askew, running across the middle of his chest instead of the sides. As he glanced up, strands of his long, dark hair fell from their ponytail, barely concealing the shadows layered beneath his eyes. His face still held youth, but his molasses eyes had lost much of their glow, heavy with grief.

"Eman," I said, finally mustering the courage to speak. "What's wrong? What's happened?"

He blinked at a spot on the floor before straightening in his chair. "Nothing that can't be undone, Addie."

He didn't answer your question.

I ran my tongue across my teeth, debating if I should even reply. Everything Eman said had a double meaning to it, a hidden code for me to figure out. Avoiding my question was perfectly normal for him. Still, part of me wished he wasn't so cryptic.

Eman rose from his seat. He cleared his throat and righted his suspenders as if casting off the sorrow he'd been carrying. "First things first, I'm glad you got my message. Your grandmother is doing well."

I searched around the room, expecting to find Nana. "Where is she? Can I see her?"

Eman chuckled. "All in good time, Addie. There are a few things we need to discuss first."

I held my breath. Finally, some answers.

Eman motioned for me to sit in one of the empty chairs before striding to the back room. Was someone else joining us? I was the only other one here. Who was the other chair for?

"We were meant to have one more with us," Eman called.

My mind raced, hoping it was my brother. "What happened to Lyle?"

"Lyle is fine, young Bellata. He is not the one I'm worried about." Eman motioned to the chair again. "Please."

I quickly took a seat, fiddling with the sleeves of Lyle's sweater as a wave of loneliness weighed my shoulders. Where was Silas? Lyle? Nana? When could I be with them again? Why was Eman keeping me from them?

"While you were recovering," Eman began, resting his elbows on his knees. "I discussed a few things with your friend." His eyes glinted with amusement. "Who is, in fact, my friend, as well."

"Did you already know?" I butted in, remembering Silas's pure half-heart beating in my hands. "Did you know Silas was the blacksmith?"

Eman settled back in his chair. "I cannot always reveal what I know when you want to know it. Time has to line up correctly."

I bit my lip, focusing my gaze on my lap as I smoothed out the wrinkles in my pants. That didn't answer my question, but I wouldn't press any further.

"I can only tell you that change is coming for you and those you love."

My hands paused as I thought back to Silas's reaction to the bearded man, and how he initially didn't want to help him. Steady Silas had always helped when he could. Was this new Silas not as kind? But then again, Silas did help free all those people from the cage, and he gave me the sword to use.

I laid my elbows on the arms of the chair. "So, if Silas is changing, is he going to be all right? I mean, in Wintertide he wasn't himself. Is something wrong with him?"

"Something is not right," Eman replied, his brow wrinkling.

My chest squeezed with worry. If something was wrong with Silas, could I make it right? Could any of us help him?

Eman lifted my satchel that had been hanging on the

back of his chair. He raised a brow. That was when I remembered the gray book I'd found in Lyle's room.

Eman nodded as he rifled through the satchel, pulling out the thin, rectangular text.

"Now, where did you find this?"

He held the strange book in one hand. Surrounded by the glory of Ramni, the binding was insignificant and dull. But as Eman studied the cover, he cradled it as if it were the most precious thing in the world.

"I found it in Barracks," I said, breaking his trance from the text.

"Where?" His voice was stern, a demanding tone I had never heard before.

"Um—I—uh . . ." I stammered. Should I rat Lyle out? Surprisingly, another voice answered for me.

"It was back in Barracks. In Addie's house," Silas answered from the entrance of the room.

I glanced over my shoulder, and my insides twisted. Silas stood with his hands in his pockets, his feet rooted beyond the threshold as if he were unsure of whether he was allowed to enter. He rubbed the back of his neck, causing drops of water to roll off his hair to the ground. I took in his tousled wet locks and new, clean clothes, surmising that he had just bathed. The thought of Silas taking a bath heated my ears, and I quickly squashed the thought, turning back at Eman.

Eman narrowed his eyes slightly, studying Silas before motioning to the vacant seat. "You may join us if you are well, Silas."

Silas nodded before sitting in the chair beside me. An aroma of cedarwood wafted from his cleansed skin. His eyes bore into me, and I swallowed, watching his gaze roam up and down my face. I offered a quick smile before adverting my gaze to the stack of books in the corner. My heart pounded at his attention, but I couldn't allow myself to be distracted.

Eman scrutinized Silas. "How are you healing?"

Silas brought a hand to his chest. "Well. It feels amazing to have my heart again, even if it's only half."

Silas had been mended by Eman, just like me. Hopefully, that meant that the change happening to him was a positive one.

Eman gave a stiff nod before focusing back on the book. "Now, where in Addie's house was this book?"

I took a breath, calming my pulse. "Lyle's room."

Eman's eyes grew dark, then softened. "I see."

He placed the book on his lap before carefully opening the cover. Instead of the yellow light I saw as a child, or the green color we saw when Silas touched it, thick, black liquid poured from the pages. Heart-wrenching screams bellowed from the open text. I covered my ears, desperate to silence the frightening noise. Beside me, Silas had doubled over, his face buried in his knees as he pressed his palms tightly against his ears. With a grunt, Eman slammed the book shut.

"What was that?" Silas asked, shaking as he tried to sit up straight.

"A curse has been placed on this text," Eman replied

gruffly before rising from his chair, taking the book with him.

"But it didn't do that before," I said. Eman paused mid-step, giving me a glance. "I mean when I opened it. It turned yellow."

"Have you held this before?" he asked Silas. Silas bobbed his head. "And?"

"It turned green and began writing something, but we didn't have a chance to find out what it was before the siti attacked."

Eman's lips thinned, and he placed the book on a square table in the back before facing us once more. "The book is cursed to transform into what the reader desires it to be. That way, the true information it holds is never revealed. He picked up his chisel from the table and passed it between his hands a few times before pointing it at me. "For Addie, it turned to light: a symbol of happiness and restoration. Something she has often yearned for since childhood."

I gripped the arms of the chair, remembering the bottle of happiness I gave my hair for. Flicking a loose strand out of my eyes, I nodded.

Callused fingers brushed against my knuckles, and I fixated on Silas's hand on my own.

Eman pointed the chisel to Silas next. "For Silas, it changed to green: the color of life and growth. Something you've always yearned for as well—a life to call your own and someone to grow with you through it."

His strokes stopped, and he pulled his hand away. I

gaped at him. Silas had always cared for my needs, but never once had he told me about his dreams or desires. Then again, I'd never asked.

Guilt tightened my chest. All this time, he'd listened to my fears, dreams, and desires, and I'd never returned the favor. I balled my hand into a fist, frustrated with my past and my terrible, needy self.

His touch returned, and my skin tingled from the heat of his hand.

"I wouldn't have chosen differently," he said. "I enjoyed every moment with you, even if I couldn't express it."

I took a shallow breath of surprise, my heart thumping.

Silas's gaze lingered on me as if I were a rare jewel. Small lines of concern rimmed his eyes. "But what does that mean for you, Eman?"

Eman looked beyond our heads. "It showed me sorrow and death. Because that is what the future holds."

"What?" I said, the blood draining from my face as I remembered the countless rows of malum and siti in Ophidian's army, waiting to strike. "You desire sorrow and …" I couldn't bring myself to finish the question.

"It is a strange desire," he agreed.

"That can't be right." I shook my head. "I'm supposed to gather the Twelve Magisters, and with them, *we're* going to defeat Ophidian." I pointed back and forth between us. I couldn't have failed already; the journey had just begun.

"You've done nothing wrong, Bellata," Eman said, gripping the chisel. "This is something I've known and wanted for some time."

Silas slid to the edge of his seat. "Is there any way to remove the curse from the book to show us what it really is?"

Eman slumped back down into his chair, his arms dangling like broken branches. "The only person who can lift the curse is the one who cast it."

I peered around Eman to the book on the table. How had something cursed ended up in Lyle's room?

More secrets, the slithering voice hissed.

If the book was cursed, Lyle could have been protecting me from it. Same with his choice to go through Schism's doors. If he had told me beforehand, I would have tried harder to stop him. He had his reasons. He needed to keep me safe.

But you're not a little girl anymore. Do you really need them to protect you?

I banished the tempting thought. No, the last time we met, Lyle told me he had things he wanted to tell me. And, once he had the chance, I was certain he'd tell me everything. No more secrets.

My toes tapped against the floor as I rubbed the arms of the chair. Where was Lyle? I figured he would have shown up by now. I really wanted to talk to him, especially to find out if he'd learned anything more about our parents.

"How are we going to figure out who cursed it?" I asked.

"Well" —Eman tapped his chisel on the palm of his hand— "there's one of two things we can do. We can wait until the curse wears off, which, seeing how it's been hidden for all these years and is still strong, that probably isn't the best course. Or, I can trace the magic back to its owner. It will take time, but that's the best option."

"Tracing the magic sounds like a good idea," Silas offered.

"It's settled, then," Eman agreed, completely ignoring the book. "Now, are you ready to see your friends?"

"Friends?" I asked.

Eman gave me a pointed look as he placed the chisel on his mending table. "You do know you brought more people into Ramni than just yourselves, don't you?"

My mind shot back to Barracks. The cages. The people. It was as if months had passed since our battle, even though it had only been an hour or two. My lips parted as I remembered everything and everyone.

"I'm sorry for all the people I brought to Ramni without permission," I said in a hurry. Eman didn't respond, so I continued. "There were cages and malum and this blonde woman." I shook my head. "I didn't know what else to do."

"It's all right, Addie," Eman replied with a chuckle. "Ramni is meant for all who need healing."

My shoulders relaxed as Eman stood abruptly, tucking in his shirt. Re-tying his thick strands, he faced Silas and me, a mischievous twinkle lurking behind his eyes. "Do you not remember who *else* you brought with you?"

I bit my lip. The bearded man. Was he someone important? He had to be. I glanced at Silas to see if he had come to the same conclusion, but he only shrugged.

Eman chuckled. "I suppose we should go meet him then."

Eman exited his mending room toward the main hallway. Shooting up from my chair, I waved to Silas. "Come on."

We strolled silently through the hallway until we approached the division of the four corridors. Stopping, Eman placed his hand on the smooth bark of the two trees adjacent to him. The trees shuddered and twisted, cracking as they rolled away from one another, creating a new wooden door.

"Whoa," Silas said, lifting his hands as a shield as he took a step back.

"Come." Eman beckoned us through.

As we crossed the threshold, I gasped. Like the hallway before, tan trees arched over one another, creating a long corridor. Yet this area was large and spacious. Different plants of all sizes grew along the upper branches. Vines and branches cascaded from the high ceiling to where even the smallest person could touch the leaves growing from them. Reaching out, I gently rubbed one of the leaves between my fingers, recognizing it as linkslock, the herb that had healed me during my mending.

A series of beds lined the walls, most filled with victims of the malum attack in Barracks. I instantly noticed Headmaster Clive's balding head. Though his arm had been wrapped in bandages, he chuckled at something another man said.

Little balls of light fluttered around the occupied beds, providing drinks and food to each of the injured. And directing the lights was Sana. Upon noticing Eman, she flushed, then ushered us over.

"Just in time," she said, flipping her long, ebony braid over her shoulder. "Anna is waking up."

I held my breath, expecting to find my old, frail Nana, moments from death. But as I followed Sana's motion, I blinked rapidly, not understanding who was before me. In the bed lay a woman much younger than Nana. Years younger. Her long, dark strands sprawled around the bed, curling at the ends. Her skin was flawless, and her hands folded neatly over her stomach as if she were royalty.

I shook my head, turning back to Sana. "There must be some mistake. This—"

"Addie?" Nana's rich, soothing voice stopped me before I could finish. Hope hugged my heart. The younger woman carefully pushed herself up, staring at me with tears in her cinnamon eyes. I recognized those eyes. And the slight pinch in her nose. Was this really Nana?

The woman's tears vanished, and she furrowed her brows, shaking a finger at me. "Adelaide Tye, you get over her and give your nana a hug, or so help me, I will get out of this bed and give you a beating."

My jaw dropped to the floor, and Silas burst out laughing. Before I could react, he jogged over to Nana's bed and scooped her up in a huge hug.

"Isn't it great to feel again?" Silas's face lit up like the orbs assisting the patients. "It's good to see you looking so well, Nana."

Nana playfully swatted Silas on the arm. "Don't butter me up, young man. I don't know what's going on, but I know that grin of yours means nothing good."

Silas held back another laugh before gesturing for me to come closer.

I took a step, then studied her again. "Nana?"

"Of course! Who did you think it was?" The woman pursed her lips, just like Nana's grimace. Familiarity tugged me closer, and I immediately fell on Nana's lap. The floral scent of geraniums wafted from the lilac-colored gown. I pressed my face against Nana's legs, draping my arms around her sturdy, warm body.

"I thought you were gone, and it was all my fault."

"Shhh …" Nana stroked my head. "Stop blaming yourself for everything, child. Life happens, you just have to do your best to endure it." She lifted my chin. "And look, here we are, together again."

Wrinkles creased the sides of her eyes as a beautiful smile full of small, pearl teeth appeared.

For the next few moments, Silas and I caught Nana up on everything that happened since I had returned from Ophidian's Realm. She nodded here and there but continued to watch Silas with a strange intensity. I glanced between them, not understanding what she was seeing, but wishing I could. Silas laughed and used exaggerated hand gestures while recounting our events. He was kind and jovial, an exact contrast to how he had acted in Wintertide.

"Addie," Nana said, interrupting my thoughts. "I do have to tell you how lucky I was to have Silas when those beasts attacked."

Silas's cheeks flushed as he rubbed the back of his neck. "There's really no need—"

"Quiet, young man," Nana chastised, her voice stern.

Silas immediately shut his mouth, but a grin played on his lips.

"Now," Nana continued. "I knew you were going to do something crazy on your Heart Reign. A grandma just knows." She held up a hand, silencing me before I could respond. "I didn't know that those terrible beasts were going to ravage our Land." Nana laid a hand on her chest. "I don't believe I'll ever forget the screams of our people."

My heart sank. Because I had jumped through Schism's door, I had caused all the suffering in Barracks.

"I was wheeling away from the door when those creatures burst into my home, moaning and destroying everything. I didn't know what I was going to do. How could I kill them?" She reached over and grabbed Silas's hand, giving it a squeeze with a proud smile. "But I didn't have to worry because this amazing young man came to my rescue." Nana gave Silas's hand a pat.

Silas's face was now scarlet.

"I'm sure you would've found some way to fend them off," Silas said, covering her hand with his own, his red blush fading into an adorable pink.

"I don't think so," Nana said, shaking her head before giving Silas's hand another squeeze. "Thank you, Silas. I wouldn't be here without you."

I wanted to jump over Nana, wrap my arms around Silas, and kiss him. Who else would have been so selfless to protect and care for Nana? I scooched toward him when Nana turned her head and tapped her chin.

"Speaking of 'here,' where am I? And what happened to James?"

With a laugh, Silas and I explained how we arrived in Ramni and that James was probably recuperating from the battle with the malum and would be here soon. Once we finished, Nana asked Silas how he was coping with his half-heart. They started to discuss their new emotions while I strode over to Eman, who was whispering with Sana at the front of the room. As soon as they saw me, they ended their conversation and gave me simultaneous smiles. I slowed my steps, taking in their forced grins. What were they talking about that I couldn't hear?

"Thank you for everything," I said.

They both nodded, replacing their painted smiles with genuine ones.

"Eman." I turned to the heartmender. "I have a question."

"Ask away, Bellata."

I chewed the inside of my cheek. "What was wrong with Nana? What happened to her?"

"I need to attend to my patients." Sana excused herself with a bow and pranced back to the lights, which had begun to cluster around another patient.

As soon as she was out of earshot, Eman said, "As you know, your grandmother traded her heart at her Heart Reign for wealth and beauty."

I nodded, remembering Nana's journal I had read the night before my Heart Reign.

"But after that, she met James and fell in love; thus, her original heart returned to her body."

Pursing my lips, I scratched my neck, waiting for further information.

"Your grandmother traded her *physical* heart for wealth and beauty," Eman continued, "but her heart that held her essence—her emotions, thoughts, and memories—is the one she gave to James. Though they're two separate things, they're still connected."

I rocked up and down on the balls of my feet, crossing my arms over my chest as I worked through Eman's explanation. "That's why Nana could feel again when James was around but also reacted when her traded physical heart was in danger?"

"Exactly," Eman confirmed.

Nana's delicate laugh chimed through the healing

room. A nearby vine sprouted vibrant orange flowers in response.

Eman clipped one of the flowers and handed it to me. "Your grandmother's love for James was so strong, it brought her physical heart back from her first trade."

I took the flower as the elegant script of Nana's journal entered my thoughts. I was shocked to discover a heart could be returned after being traded away. Placing my hand on my chest, I paused as a steady pulse greeted my fingertips. "But why did I gain a new heart, and Nana got her original heart?"

Eman knelt in front of a large herb bush with thin, pointed leaves. "While your grandmother *traded* her physical heart away, you *gave* your physical heart away." Carefully, he snapped off one of the outer branches. "When Anna gave her love to James, her emotional heart attached to him, allowing her physical heart to return. Whereas you gave your love *and* your physical heart to Claire and Lyle. Your sacrifice for them was so great, a new, pure heart was formed."

I chewed my lip and stared at the long, orange petals of the flower. "So, when Traders trade their hearts, they're really trading their physical *and* emotional heart away." I twirled the stem between my fingers. "The two can be separated, as in Nana's case, but are usually connected. That's why a Trader's emotions disappear after Heart Reign."

"Correct." Eman snipped a few more sprigs, then stood. "Your grandmother had her original heart extracted once more after that. She and James were already married when Anna traded her physical heart a second time to a vendor of wealth. And the vendor did with it what all vendors and merchants do—they trade it. In this case, the vendor traded it at Perda Forum."

"What?" I asked, a swirl of questions emerging in my thoughts. Could you trade your heart twice? I remembered Governor Willow said the vendors traded hearts to Ophidian, but what was Perda Forum?

"Perda Forum," James said, standing in the doorway. His voice was no longer hoarse and rough as it had been in the Seven Choices. Stepping into the healing room, James grasped a bouquet of bluebells that twinkled as he strode toward Nana. "The Market of Thieves."

Eman moved aside, allowing James to pass. Falling to one knee, he presented the bouquet to Nana with a dashing grin. Nana brought both of her hands to her lips before giving him a kiss. I had never seen her eyes light up like that. They stroked each other's hands and talked to each other so gently.

Without prompting, my gaze found Silas watching them, too. His attention latched onto me, sending my nerves in a frenzy. Focusing on the flower, I inhaled its sweet honey scent, breaking away from Silas's penetrating stare. I turned back to Eman, whose eyes were lit with a twinkle of mischief.

"Why would they do that?" I asked, absentmindedly checking my hair and clothes.

Eman pulled a piece of twine from his pocket and

secured it around the herbs. "The merchants and vendors find no value in a heart once traded away too often. So, they trade it to Perda Forum, in exchange for admittance."

"Admittance to what?"

"To walk freely through the Forum." Eman's eyes grew hard as he tied the bundle to an overhanging branch. The pleasing aroma of rosemary fluttered around us. "Perda Forum is one of the most violent places in the Twelve Lands. Without payment or protection, you will lose your life the moment you step in."

I brought the flower to my chest, sending a quick prayer to the Heavens that I would never have to go there. "But what do the people in Perda Forum *do* with the hearts once they get them?"

Eman shook his head. "I would rather not share that evil with you today, Bellata."

More secrets.

What secrets? I asked the slippery voice, but it didn't reply.

I shuddered. What could the thieves have done to allow Nana's life to be minutes from ending?

I glanced back at Nana and James. My grandfather had his arm wrapped securely around my grandmother as if he would never let her go. Across from them, Silas sat with his elbows on his knees, chatting with my grandparents. My family. I would treasure this moment forever.

But as soon as I thought that, the happiness vanished. Sadness darkened my thoughts, and my shoulders sagged. Three pieces were missing: my mom, dad, and Lyle.

Thankfully, Lyle was safe here in Ramni, but I still hadn't seen him. And I hadn't forgotten what he had said before I left to return to Barracks—that our parents had been murdered. Who would have done such a thing? Were my parents somehow connected to Eman? Were they enemies of Ophidian, too?

"What matters now," Eman said, breaking through my thoughts. "Is that we got your grandmother's physical heart back, and she's healing well."

Pressing my luck, I interrupted Eman before he could change the subject. "But *how* did you get her heart back?"

Mischief sparked Eman's eyes. "I have friends."

Placing the flower behind my ear, I asked, "You have friends that are thieves?"

"I have a friend among the thieves," he clarified.

How could a thief do good? Does Eman know what he's doing?

I quirked a brow at him, causing the heartmender to chuckle. Would I ever figure him out?

The peaked door opened once again, and Claire sauntered in with her messy bun and elegant gown.

"So, this is where everyone went." She placed her hands on her hips and plastered a triumphant grin on her face as she headed toward us.

Fear stifled my words, and I looked to Eman for guidance. I hadn't told Claire that I had brought Doctor Magnum, her father, to Ramni. Though Doctor Magnum was covered in bandages and sleeping, Claire would definitely recognize him if she saw him up close.

"Claire will understand, Addie," he encouraged, gently pressing me forward.

"Claire," I started. "There's something you should know." Before I could continue, she peered over my shoulder. Her eyes widened in shock, then darkened in fury.

Shoving past me, Claire stalked up to the bed where the light clusters were floating, but her father was in the bed behind her, not the one she was scowling at. All went silent as we waited for her to speak.

Claire sucked in a deep breath and pointed her finger. "Why, in all that is good in this realm, would you bring this idiot here?"

The lights finally disappeared, revealing the patient's face.

"Oh, no." I squeezed my eyes shut, huffing in frustration. So, that's why the bearded man looked so familiar.

The man laid on the bed with combed chestnut locks and a trimmed, sleek beard. He glared up at us with giant, green eyes, a scowl forming on the lips that had once enticed so many women.

Crossing his long, muscular arms over his chest, he asked, "Where in the realms am I?"

A light chuckle came from James as Claire snatched up a pan from the table, ready to strike. Eman plucked it from her hands and nudged me forward. My heels dug into the ground before I stood at the edge of the bed. Stifling my indignation, I said, "I didn't expect to see you again, Lord Farmount."

CHAPTER 11

"And I didn't expect to see you again either, Adelaide," Lord Farmount growled. "Imagine my surprise to find you traipsing through Wintertide." He sat up in the recovery bed, his once sultry eyes harder than stone as he took in the faces around him. "Not hiding away anymore, are we?"

Silas jerked me back from the bed and crossed his arms in front of his chest. "Don't speak to her like that," he snarled through clenched teeth.

Lord Farmount snorted, rolling his eyes before inspecting his fingernails. "Stand down, hero. I don't want your pet."

Now you're something to be owned?

Irritation flared through my chest, and I grabbed Silas's arm, moving him out of the way. I glowered at the lord, ready to make him apologize when I stopped, bracing my hand against my heart. I willed the rapid beating to slow. Why was I wasting my energy over something stupid from the mouth of *Lord Farmount?* It wasn't a stretch for Farmount to call me a pet. To him, women were like jewels or houses; the more he owned, the better he looked. There was no point in arguing with a man who'd never viewed me as more than someone's possession.

Still, I had to say I understood why he was always listed as one of the top trades for Heart Reign in *The Barracks Conversations.* He was tall, dark, and handsome—chiseled with lean muscle and strong, angular features. Yet, despite being handsome and his deep emerald eyes, the spark of life was gone.

The door of the healing chamber suddenly slammed open. We all turned to find Lyle, his shoulders heaving as he rushed in.

I brought a hand to my lips and started toward him. Before I could speak, Lyle gathered me up in his arms, squeezing me until I couldn't breathe.

"Y-you're stronger," I wheezed, returning his hug. As I burrowed my face in his shoulder, the woodsy scent of parchment drifted from his clothes.

Once he released me, I analyzed him thoroughly. Lyle looked like an entirely different person from the broken being I had left behind. His body was fuller, and his skin was rosy and healthy. Thick, dark curls grew past his ears and swooped behind his spectacles. With a flick of his neck, the curls bounced out of his bright eyes. Was this what our father looked like at Lyle's age? Or did he look more like our mother?

"Now that we're all present," Eman interjected, bringing his hands together, "the time has come for you to continue your journey."

"All present?" Claire asked, scrunching her freckled nose in reference to Lord Farmount.

"Yes." Eman snapped his fingers, causing enough chairs to sprout out of the ground.

"Eman, what's going on?" Lyle asked, adjusting his spectacles, before reaching a hand toward Claire. She quickly laced her fingers through his, cuddling into his side. I glanced at their hands, then gave her a wink. She stuck out her tongue before snapping back to attention.

The heartmender motioned us all to sit before beginning. "I'm glad we could all meet together one last time before you return to your journey."

"We're going so soon?" I blurted, sitting on the edge of my chair. I thought I would have more time to spend with Lyle this time. And now with Nana being here, too …

"Ophidian is growing restless," Eman explained. "As some of you know, his army is preparing to strike Decim with full force. I have a barrier keeping his army confined in the Shadow realm, but it won't last. If we don't gather the Magisters soon, there will be no hope left for Decim."

Eman placed a hand on Silas's chair. "We've had much time to talk since you arrived here. I think it would be best if you accompanied Bellata on this journey."

Silas's form relaxed. "Thank you, Eman."

I was thankful for Silas being with me. He had always

been my security blanket, and I wanted him by my side. But we were both different since the last time we were together. His half-heart had changed him. Everything had been mostly good: his confidence, his smile. But I still wasn't sure about his actions in Wintertide.

And my time in Ophidian's Realm had changed me, too. We were two completely different people now and had to relearn everything about each other.

"I hate to cut your reunion with your wife short"— Eman turned to James— "but Decim still needs you to assist in gathering the Magisters."

James nodded firmly but briefly lowered his eyes. "I made an iuram to my granddaughter. I would not soon break it. It would be an honor to stay by her side."

Eman laid a hand on his Magister's shoulder. "I know you will do your best, Dimitte. Your wife will be under the care of Sana, who, as you know, is my most trusted Healer." He motioned to Sana, who bowed her head in agreement.

"I will make sure she is in perfect condition when you return," Sana confirmed.

"Thank you," James murmured, clutching Nana's hand in his.

Eman moved to Claire, who was gnawing at her bottom lip. She kept her eyes on Lyle's and her hands still knitted together.

Eman chuckled as he addressed her. "Lost in the darkness, but always finding the light." Claire squished her brows together, accentuating the wrinkle between them, but she didn't stop chewing. "You are also a gifted Healer. You will accompany Bellata, as well. She will no doubt need your assistance again."

"What?" Claire asked, staring wide-eyed with her mouth agape. "But you said I couldn't go last time without knowing where my heart is."

"That's precisely why you can go," Eman replied. "I know where your heart is."

I almost jumped out of my seat. After Claire's heart had been extracted by her father to protect it from Ophidian, it seemed like it would never be found. Claire herself had spent countless years hunting for it while she worked as Ophidian's slave. And Eman had found it at last. But how and where?

Then it hit me. Something he had said earlier: a friend among the thieves.

As soon as the thought crossed my mind, Eman winked at me and turned to Claire. "There's no need to worry, Claire. You will be reunited with your heart in due time."

A giddiness bounced in my chest with the addition of Claire to our group. Not only was she a healer, but she was also my friend. Hopefully, I'd be able to explain about Doctor Magnum and that he would be waiting for her when we returned to Ramni.

Eman snapped his fingers, and the gray book from Lyle's room appeared in his hands. Clasping the text, he analyzed the book. After a few moments of silence, he strode to Lyle, who swallowed and tapped his fingers on his thigh.

"Lyle and I will work on tracing the last power used on this book while you are gathering the Twelve."

Keeping his gaze lowered, Lyle said, "I don't know much about curses yet, Eman. I'm still very weak."

Eman shook his head, disagreeing with the statement. "You have more strength than you know. I also need an assistant to make sure the trace is done correctly."

I watched Lyle out of the corner of my eye. He adjusted his spectacles before tapping his fingers on his thigh once more. Claire bent her head toward him and whispered something I couldn't decipher. Lyle hissed back a response. This went on for a few moments until Lyle let out a reluctant sigh and nodded at Eman.

"We know for certain Ophidian is still in possession of your heart, so it would be better for you to stay here." Snapping his fingers, the heartmender caused several bags, stuffed to capacity, to appear at his feet. After motioning to the bags, he addressed the rest of us. "I've gathered everything you'll need for your journey. The sooner you return to your realm, the better." He hurried to the edge of the room.

Lyle and Claire murmured to one another as Sana began explaining to James how she would continue to help Nana. I glanced over at Silas, who, considering the harsh furrow of his brow, seemed to be lost in thought.

"You okay?" I asked, standing next to him.

Silas blinked a few times, ran a hand through his hair,

then managed a small smile. "Yeah, I'm okay. Are you okay? I mean, with all of this?"

I lifted my hands and shrugged. "I don't think I have much of a choice."

"You always have a choice, Addie," he said, touching the flower behind my ear. "You know that." His fingers trailed along the stem, and I had to lock my knees to keep them from buckling.

Ever since Silas came into my life, he firmly believed in everyone making their own choices. He never forced me to make a decision I didn't want to make. And even though he hated Heart Reign and everything to do with it, he always supported me in making my own trade. My own choice.

Before I could respond, Eman called him over, and Silas's shoulders locked back, stiff as a board. Silas woodenly marched to Eman, each step heavier than the last. For the first time, I realized that, just like Claire, Silas's choices had been taken from him.

The room grew somber as I reflected on what little information I had about Silas from the blacksmith's story. His parents never loved him, and the only man to take care of him, beat him. Then, with the discovery of his pure heart, Silas's life changed again, and he had to leave his home. Another choice he didn't make. And then there was the choice that Ophidian made for him by taking his heart. The only choice he did make was to leave half of his heart with Ophidian to save the woman who he would give it to.

After everything Silas had gone through, the one choice he had made was to save me. Before Lyle traded his heart to Ophidian, he asked Silas to take care of me while he was gone. And even though I shut him out at first, Silas diligently watched over me.

I traced my hand where his fingers had just been. New Silas, old Silas, weren't they one and the same? The same flame of desire welled in my chest, and I wanted to do nothing but wrap my arms around him and tell him how much I cared for him.

But I couldn't. Not yet.

I couldn't allow him to take on any more of my problems and responsibilities. *I* chose to jump through Schism's doors and fight through Ophidian's Realm. *I* chose to make the oath to bring the Twelve Magisters together. If I allowed Silas further in, he would bear those burdens, as well.

Silas peered at me over his shoulder, his eyes full of adoration, as if I were a long-lost treasure. My insides jumbled together at the sight, and I had to turn away, deciding to make another choice. I would protect Silas, no matter the cost. I would get the other half of his heart back from the Beast, even if it killed me.

After handing Silas his sword, along with a conveniently matching sheath, Eman headed over, picking up the gray book and passing it to Lyle. He whispered a series of words to Lyle before striding back to the bags for our journey. Lyle's shoulders sagged as he shuffled over to me.

"Guess this is good-bye again, huh?" he asked, giving my shoulder a playful nudge.

"Not good-bye," I replied, swallowing the knot in my throat. "Just see you later."

I wrapped my arms around his neck, praying Ramni would continue to keep him safe. We soon broke apart, and Lyle sniffed. Removing his spectacles, he rubbed his eyes with the sleeve of his shirt.

"So much pollen with all these plants." He coughed.

I laughed, and he grinned. Before he turned to exit the room, he glanced at Claire, who adjusted her messy bun before hurrying to his side.

"Where are you going?" I asked, noticing the wild grin on Lyle's face as Claire tugged him toward the doorway.

Claire flicked her hand in the air. "I'll be back before we leave." With one last yank, they were gone.

"Addie," Eman said, pulling my attention away from the new couple. "I've packed your bag with some additional items." He handed me the satchel, which was a lot heavier than before.

"Thank you," I said, securing it across my chest.

"You will also need this." He handed me the brown book.

It was our map, our compass—the whole reason why we made it here safely in the first place.

"You *will* need this, Addie," Eman emphasized. "Without it, you'll never know how to win the favor of the Twelve Magisters."

I clutched the book to my chest. "Win their favor? I thought I had to gather them together."

James appeared beside me and clapped a hand on my shoulder. "The Magisters won't come freely nor willingly unless you convince them to come to your aid. We are a strong and stubborn group of people." He shrugged, giving me an apologetic look.

I glanced down at the book. "So, this will help me convince them to come with me?"

"Yes," they both agreed when Silas came up beside me. I could almost hear him saying, "You have a choice, Addie. You don't have to do this." And he was right. I did have a choice. And I had already made it.

Grasping the book, I stuffed it in my already bulging sack. "We better get going."

Silas dipped his head as he tied his sword to his belt.

"What about me?" Lord Farmount grumbled, standing from the hospital bed. He shoved the light orbs out of the way. "I'm not staying in this flowery place." His green eyes surveyed all of us through narrowed lids.

I turned to Eman.

"Unlike the rest of you," the heartmender started, "Lord Farmount has successfully survived off the land since Ophidian's attack on Barracks. You will need his survival expertise during your journey."

I pressed my lips together to prevent the groan that wanted to escape.

"No," Silas cut in with a harsh tone. He extended his arm as if blocking Lord Farmount from joining.

"Silas," I gasped and looked to Eman. Did he just say *no* to the man who mended his heart?

Before Eman could respond, a coat of red slid over my vision, and a snide comment formed on my tongue. Eman may not defend himself, but I would. Who did Silas think he was? Hot fury boiled in my chest, and I bit my tongue. The red dissipated from my sight. Closing my eyes, I sucked in a breath. What was the matter with me?

"It's all right, Addie." Eman lifted a hand, but the kind smile from before was gone.

I released the breath and faced Lord Farmount. Gone were the frocks and frills he used to wear. Instead, dark slacks and a thick, leather vest with a tattered white shirt took their place. A dark green cloak hung from his shoulders and was swept back, revealing the knives he'd used earlier. His jaw flexed, and I drew away. What had happened to the petty, arrogant lord to make him change so much?

I gave him a pointed look. "You better not be any trouble."

Silas grunted, tightening his grip on his sword but said nothing.

Lord Farmount straightened to his full height, and I resisted shrinking back. Had he always been that tall?

"Stay out of my way, and I'll stay out of yours."

The room quieted before Eman clapped his hands together once again.

"Now that that's settled, it's time for us to say farewell once more. Come." Eman glided past us. James gave Nana one last kiss before joining Eman. With a sneer, Lord Farmount went, too. I started toward the others until Silas stopped me.

"Why did you let him come?" he asked, placing his hands on my shoulders as he spun me to face him.

My body was aware of every place his hands touched.

Though I wanted to stay close, I gently pulled away. "Silas, how could you say no to Eman? He mended your heart. He saved you. *I* didn't allow Lord Farmount to come, Eman said he needed to come. But I do think the lord is with us for a reason. You saw how he helped free all those people in the cages. And without him, we would've never found the door back here."

Silas ground his teeth. "As long as he behaves."

I squeezed his hand. "I'm sure it will be fine."

Silas didn't look convinced as he shoved his hands in his pockets and joined the others. As I watched him stalk out of the room, I ran my hands through my hair. Silas, Claire, James, Lord Farmount, and me, trying to save our realm from evil incarnate. What could go wrong?

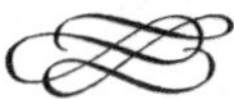

The shimmering door swirled with pink and gold spirals, a contrast to the darkness growing in Decim and the Shadow realm. Eman and I stood before the door, watching the lights spin.

"The door will deposit you at the edge of Wintertide, facing the Shalley Mountains," he explained. "From there, the book will tell you which direction to go."

The last time I had traveled through this door, I saw the destruction of my home. What would be waiting for me this time?

Clutching the hem of Lyle's sweater, I ran my fingers over the worn fibers. Although I had come so far, my worries were still pertinent. Could I really do this?

Is everything okay? Eman asked in my mind, and I jumped, forgetting he could hear my thoughts. Was his voice the one I had been hearing all this time? He gently placed his hand on my shoulder. Eman couldn't have said all those things before, could he?

I'm scared.

Eman lightly tapped my shoulder. *You are more powerful than you believe.*

I bobbed my head to avoid any further conversation. Everyone kept saying that. But I had only just learned of my power when we fought against the siti. And even then, it wasn't that strong.

Don't give up so easily.

With a twang of irritation, I scowled back at him. *Give up? I jumped through Schism's doors, fought through the Seven Choices, and endured the mending of a new heart. I've done everything but give up.*

Eman tapped my wrist, and I followed his gaze. My hands were lit with the same orange glow as before. My body tensed, and the glow faded. I extended my fingers to release the rest of the sparks of light. Eman gave my head a pat and strode toward James and Silas, his shoulders straight and tall, a sense of satisfaction rolling off him.

Before I could follow, Silas strolled up to me, rubbing the back of his neck as an uneasy smile crept across his lips.

"What?" I snapped, still irritated about my conversation with Eman.

He dropped his hand and took a step back. "Nothing." He quickly averted his gaze.

Breathe, Eman's voice said.

I poured my irritation into my grip as I strangled the satchel strap.

Silas lifted his shoulders. "I haven't felt anything in a long time, much less battled monsters." He looked down at the sword hanging from his belt. "I guess I'm a little nervous."

My irritation fled at his sincere tone. I took in his tapping fingers on the sword and the unsure look on his face. Silas was adorable when he was nervous.

Struggling to keep my grin from spreading too wide, I said, "You're nervous? The young blacksmith, who battled his way through the Seven Choices and almost defeated Ophidian, is nervous?" A pink tint bloomed across Silas's cheeks. That was even more adorable. "We'll be okay."

Silas stepped forward and took my hand. The rough patches of his skin pressed against my own as our fingers intertwined. My insides stirred at his touch.

"Silas—"

He pressed a finger to his lips. "Shh, follow me."

While Eman was still speaking with James, Silas tugged me away from the door to a tall willow tree nearby. The thin, green leaves swayed around us, creating a blanket of privacy, something we hadn't had since I returned from Ophidian's Realm.

My body tensed. What was he doing?

"I know we'll be okay," Silas said softly, caressing my cheek with his knuckles. My flesh tingled where his skin touched mine. "Because you've become so strong." His hand paused, gently stroking my jawline. "I've known for a while that you're not that scared little girl anymore."

My heart rammed inside my chest. I licked my lips, trying to form words, but none came out. Focusing on Silas, I watched his throat bob. Silas's eyes traveled down to my lips, his breath wavering. Blood rushed between my ears as he leaned forward, the beat of his half-heart in perfect rhythm with my own. I tilted my chin up, wanting to taste Silas's lips—the real Silas, not the one from Ophidian's Realm. Our lips were almost touching when a sharp pain shot through my arm as if my bones were being crushed together.

Icicles shot through my veins as I saw Silas's fingers locked around my wrist. Panicking, I tried to pry their firm grip from my arm.

"Silas," I said, clawing at his hand. "What are you doing?"

He didn't respond as his pupils expanded.

"Silas," I said again, yanking my wrist away as fear lodged in my throat. "Let go of me."

Silas immediately released me with force, and I stumbled back. The orange flower fluttered from my hair, wilting as it hit the ground. Red marks branded my wrist from where his fingers had clenched it. The memories of the scorch marks from the Fourth Choice shot through my mind, and I shook my head, trying to push them away. My skin still burned.

"Addie," Silas whispered, blinking down at his hand in disbelief. "I don't know what happened."

I backed away from him, clutching my arm to my chest. Eman had said something wasn't right with Silas, but I never expected this.

"Addie," Eman called from the doorway.

I jumped at Eman's voice, guilt thickening my unease. Did Eman know what had just happened?

Silas's back faced me, and his head bowed while he pressed his hands against his temples. I wanted to help, but fear convinced me otherwise. I turned away from Silas and hurried toward the others.

Claire and Lyle finally rejoined us, their hair more tousled than before, and both of their faces were flushed. Claire stood beside James and Lord Farmount, all three of them clad in clothes for Barracks' icy wrath. Claire tightened her messy bun as I rushed out from beneath the tree.

I muscled my way between Claire and James, comforted by their presence as I hid my wrist behind my back.

Did Eman choose correctly when picking Silas for this journey?

"Everything okay?" Lyle whispered in my ear.

"Mhmm," I replied, quickly yanking my sleeve down before folding my arms over my chest. Were these thoughts my own? I couldn't decipher all the voices ranting in my brain. But I didn't disagree with it.

Silas stumbled out from the leaves of the willow tree, rubbing his forehead as if he had been struck. I ran my eyes up and down his dark blue sweater and tan slacks, but nothing seemed out of place or different. When his gaze met mine, I quickly turned away.

Eman knocked on the door to Decim, bringing our attention back to him and the long journey ahead. The swirling door opened inward. Sparks of colored light flurried through the white, foggy air. "There is a darkness that has been infiltrating the Twelve Lands for much time, and it has finally reached them all. You will witness things you never thought you would see. Bloodshed and disease are just a few of the many horrors you will encounter."

My mouth went dry. I had never been beyond Barracks' borders. Realizing that the other Lands would be ravaged with evil made me fear for my safety and those I was bringing with me. Would we all return from this journey?

Taking a breath, I adjusted my pack and pushed my fear away. I had made an oath that I would bring the Twelve Magisters together. Once I gathered the Magisters, we would defeat Ophidian.

"Bellata," Eman said, drawing my attention away from my thoughts. His shoulders drooped, lines of weariness appearing around his usually bright brown eyes.

Guard your heart.

I stilled. So, he did know.

I'll try, I responded as I headed toward the door. I couldn't think about *anything* else except uniting the Magisters.

"Be smart, Addie," Lyle said, giving me another hug.

"I will." I returned his embrace. Lyle ruffled my hair

like when we were young before facing Claire. A more intimate expression covered his face as he held her close.

The spinning lights danced all around, inviting me into their bright embrace once more. I took a step forward, placing one foot in the warm, feathery air. Before I immersed myself completely, I glanced over my shoulder at Eman.

"You better be here when I get back."

He inclined his head but didn't smile. "You will never be alone."

The exhaustion and misery filling his gaze made his words hard to believe, but I nodded regardless. Turning back to the open doorway, I plunged into the light, unsure of what awaited me on the other side.

CHAPTER 13

I braced myself for the harsh slap of the cold, but it was as if thousands of needles plunged into my skin. The air had gotten more deadly.

Wrapping my arms around my stomach, I shuffled away from the doorway and waited for the others. Within moments, Silas, Claire, Lord Farmount, and James walked through, all stiffening at the bitter atmosphere.

"Where are we?" Claire asked, pulling on thick mittens as she shivered.

We scanned the trees surrounding us. The snowcapped peaks of the Shalleys pointed through the tall trees of the forest.

"We're still in Wintertide," Silas replied, suddenly by my side.

I tensed before taking a few steps away from him.

Silence coated the air, lifting the hairs on the back of my neck. Silas must have felt it, too, by the way his stance stiffened, and his head twisted back and forth, searching. He placed a finger to his lips as he walked out in front. But when I began to follow, he held up a hand, directing me to stay where I was.

Is Silas in charge now?

"I thought you were the leader," Claire said as she rubbed her hands together. I only huffed and rolled my eyes in response.

Silas soon disappeared into the trees. After a few moments without his return, I pulled on my own mittens and played with the strap of the satchel. James tensed at every sound. His fists balled at his sides as he searched the trees to his right. Next to him, Claire had her arms tucked tightly to her chest, her weight shifted to one side as she watched the smoke-colored clouds rolling across the sky. That was when I noticed Lord Farmount was gone.

Panic clenched my gut, and I whipped around. It had only been a few minutes. Had he left already?

Appearing on my left side, two hardened emerald eyes glared back at me. I stumbled back with a yelp before Lord Farmount clamped a large, gloved hand over my mouth.

Claire and James stared, wide-eyed, as footsteps sounded in the forest. I stifled a whimper, praying the malum and siti were long gone from Wintertide.

"Hush, Adelaide," Lord Farmount scolded me. A smokey aura surrounded his thick, leather gloves. "How will we evade the creatures if you tell them where we are?"

I ripped his hand from my mouth. "I wouldn't have made a sound if you hadn't tried to scare me."

Lord Farmount snorted. "If that scared you, you shouldn't be here."

He flipped his cloak over his shoulder before stalking toward the trees. Though he had scared me, I relaxed as I watched him crouch down and survey the ground. Carefully, he unsheathed a dagger and shaved pieces of wood from various surrounding trees. They floated to the ground in perfect sheets.

Impressive, isn't he?

The thought startled me, and I realized I was still staring at Lord Farmount when the heavy footsteps crunched from the forest again. I quickly broke my gaze from the lord. A figure with a head of golden hair broke through the iced trees.

"What was that?" Silas scowled, brandishing his sword.

"L-lord Idiot was being st-stupid," Claire replied through her chattering teeth.

Lord Farmount growled something, but he continued slicing the branches, so his words were muffled.

"What'd you find?" I asked, trying to turn Silas's attention elsewhere. The last thing we needed right now was a fight. "Are we where Eman said?"

"Yes," Silas replied, ignoring Lord Farmount. "We're about a hundred yards from the edge of Wintertide and the beginning of the Shalleys. There doesn't seem to be any creatures in the forest." He looked up at the sky, then into the trees. "I suggest we get moving."

"How do we know where to go?" Claire asked, rubbing her arms.

"The book," James replied, his hands snug in his pockets. "Eman gave *Addie* the book so she could lead us to where we need to go." He sent Silas a frown before motioning to my satchel.

I nodded quickly, reaching into my satchel and pulling out the brown text.

Using my teeth, I pulled my mitten off and caressed the worn leather binding. The power of the pages surged through my veins, sending a bolt of energy to my heart. Sucking in a sharp breath, I opened the cover. Silas and Claire crowded around me while Lord Farmount continued his work. James gave a firm nod and stayed where he was, scanning the trees around us as he rubbed his chin.

The invisible quill drew on the pages as it had when Eman first showed it to me. The curved shape of Barracks was drawn with the trees of Wintertide surrounding it. Soon, the tips of the Shalleys formed, accentuating the valley where the Flum River flowed. The river extended off the edge of the top of the page.

"Is that it?" Silas asked. His face was so close, his warm breath danced against my cheek.

I wanted to back away, but my heart still fluttered, keeping me close to him.

"I guess so," I managed to reply.

"But we already know we're at the edge of Wintertide," Claire exclaimed, pointing to the trees on the page. "Why isn't it telling us something more useful? Like what's ahead or where we're going?"

"It tells you what you need to know at the present. No more, no less," James answered.

Peering at the map again, I watched the blue ink forming the Flum River shift back and forth as if it were an actual river. The soft trickling of water filled my ears. A lightness filled my chest, and my legs had me taking off before I could stop myself.

"Addie, where are you going?" Silas called.

"Come on," I responded, too curious to stop.

The snapping of branches echoed behind me as I bounded through the trees. Every few feet, I glanced at the opened text, making sure I was still on the right path. Excitement pumped through my veins as the sound of churning water grew louder with each step. The faster I ran, the more the river in the book glowed.

The energy was pulsing so quickly from the book in my hands, I couldn't stop. I ran, my pulse pounding with the flow of the river, until I found it.

The water shimmered as it gushed down its path. I took a step closer to the edge, peering into its crystal-clear depths, straight to the bottom of the stream's light-brown foundation.

The Flum River flowed from the Shalleys into the center of Barracks, providing us with the water we needed to survive. But it was always dark and lifeless—nothing like the water before me.

As I referenced the book once more, the map shifted, removing the previous section of Barracks and adding more of the river with the Shalleys surrounding it. Noting the change, I brought it closer to my face as the lines criss-crossed over the pages.

I placed my hand on the map, remembering what Eman had said. Although he couldn't be here with me, he was still guiding me in the right direction. I laid the open pages on the ground and crouched near the river. The water was so beautiful and clean. Rolling up the sleeves of Lyle's sweater, I plunged my fingertips into the diamond ripples.

A jolt of power rushed through my arm, and I quickly yanked my hand out, examining my fingers. That was new. Holding my breath, I watched, transfixed, as tiny orange flames sparked off my fingertips again. Footsteps crunched through the ice behind me, and I stood, frantically shaking out my hand before drying it on my pants.

Soon, Silas, Claire, James, and Lord Farmount barreled out of the woods, panting for breath.

"Wow, I knew you were fast, but I didn't know you were that fast," Silas breathed, resting his hands on his knees as he caught his breath.

"You should've seen her in Ophidian's Realm," Claire said with a laugh.

"I'm sure she was fantastic," Lord Farmount replied monotonously. My excitement drained from his sarcasm.

Claire shot him a pointed glare. "What's your problem?"

Lord Farmount gave her no answer as he stalked to the edge of the river and knelt down. I couldn't help but watch as he rolled up his sleeves and removed his glove to allow the cool waves to flow through his bare fingertips.

It seems you two are more alike than you thought.

"We're being followed," Lord Farmount said before flicking the water from his fingers.

He turned to me, and I realized I was staring at him. Again. Why did I keep doing that?

Because he's nice to look at.

"We need to keep moving." Lord Farmount picked up some more sticks along the path before trekking down the river.

"Followed?" Claire questioned, looking from Lord Farmount to me. "By who?"

"Don't listen to him," Silas interjected. "He doesn't know."

"Well, I think—" James began before Silas cut in.

"So, this is where the book led you?" Silas asked.

I watched Lord Farmount pause further down the river and dip his hands in the water again. Were his skills that good? I searched all around, trying to find any hint of someone following us, but nothing stood out to me.

"Yes," I replied and bent down to pick up the text from the cold ground. Lifting the pages toward Silas, I said, "The book shows me what I need to know when I need to know it, as James said." James gave a grunt of approval before I continued. "It was leading me to the river. Once I got here, the map changed." I pointed to the mountains across the page and the river flowing between them.

Silas hummed as he looked at the map. "We follow the river."

"Right." I pushed my sleeve back down before pulling the map away, not wanting to give Silas the chance to take charge again.

Within a few steps, the beginnings of the Shalleys came into view—the dark, dense floor of the forest shifting into the mountains' tan, hard ground.

Silas's footsteps caught up to me, adjusting their stride to match my own. I noticed him in my peripheral vision but said nothing. The quick steps of Claire and steady gait of James soon followed. When I glanced over my shoulder, I was surprised to find Lord Farmount gliding behind James, his steps silent.

Claire asked James about the healing properties of his Magister's power, and I eavesdropped until Silas spoke.

"I want to apologize," he said.

I pressed my lips into a line and waited.

"I don't know what happened back in Ramni, but I shouldn't have reacted that way." He craned his neck and mumbled something to himself before continuing. "I shouldn't have even tried to…" He stopped, clamping his mouth shut.

I whipped my attention to him. "Tried to what?"

Silas's throat bobbed as he swallowed. "You know."

His cheeks turned pink and adorable from embarrassment, and I found myself falling for Silas all over again. "Why shouldn't you have tried to kiss me?"

Silas swallowed again before focusing on his feet. "I've never been sure about how you feel about me. Before, I was some strange guy bringing you food and coming into your house. Now, I'm …" he trailed off again, studying his hands as if remembering his actions under the willow tree. "I don't know what I am."

My throat constricted as I glanced at the map to make sure we were heading in the right direction. Silas had gone through a lot of changes within a short amount of time. He had been without a heart and emotions for years, and within a few hours, he regained half of his heart and was helping protect Decim from the Beast who had taunted him years ago. It must be hard.

"It wasn't that bad," I mumbled, tugging my ear, softening to him.

Silas perked up. "What?"

"You coming over every day." I scratched my cheek as his chestnut eyes glistened with delight. I held his gaze for a moment before tearing my gaze away. I had to focus.

"I would have done the same thing all over again if I had to."

Are you sure Silas means that? the voice interjected before I could answer. *If he did, why did he try to hurt you?*

"Come on, kids. Let's save it for another time when we don't have to save the realms," Claire interrupted, flinging her hand in the air.

I jumped away from Silas, then hurried a few paces ahead to give us some distance.

"Ridiculous," Lord Farmount sneered, appearing silently by my side. The scrape of metal vibrated off the trees as Silas pointed his sword at Lord Farmount's chest.

"If we offend you so much, why are you here?" Silas growled with a deep voice that wasn't his own.

The edges of the sword glowed dark crimson as Silas's grip tightened around it, his knuckles white. His shoulders tensed as he leaned forward, ready to attack.

My gut turned to stone as I recognized the same look Silas had from the willow tree. What was wrong with him?

"Silas," I said before two daggers appeared in each of Lord Farmount's hands.

"Why are *you* here, hero?" Lord Farmount taunted, clutching both of his daggers, readying to throw them. "You've been absent for years. Why start caring now?"

The glow of Silas's sword dimmed, but his position didn't waver. His eyes glassed over. They darted between Lord Farmount and me, a battle raging behind them.

Was he thinking that something was going on between Lord Farmount and me? I moved far away from the lord, and Silas lowered his sword, the glow dissipating from its blade. His glassy eyes never left Lord Farmount.

James stepped between the two men and shoved them away from each other. "There's a more serious matter than who is the stronger man right now. If you two were smart, you would stop this nonsense so Addie can think clearly and not be distracted by idiocy."

Claire applauded James. "Well said."

Silas crushed his eyes shut and shook his head. When he opened them again, they were back to their warm chestnut color. Straightening, Silas secured his sword in its sheath once more. The muscle in his jaw twitched as he held out his hand to Lord Farmount, offering peace. Lord Farmount's gaze cut to me before he secured his weapons. He glanced down at Silas's offered hand before crossing both arms over his chest.

James lifted his hands in surrender and turned to me. "It's getting late. We need to find a place to make camp. We don't want to be exposed in the mountains at night."

Nodding, I studied the map, hoping to find such a place. As I scanned the page, a ticking pulsed in the back of my mind. It wasn't painful, only annoying as I tried to concentrate on the text. The map grew fuzzy as the ticking continued. Bringing the book closer to my face, I focused on the mountains. A series of caves were drawn, from what I could decipher—about a mile into the Shalleys.

I let out a breath and lowered the text. *Thank you*, I thought to Eman, but only silence answered. In its place, the ticking continued.

Blinking a few times, I tried to find the direction we were to go in, but the ticking grew worse, making my vision hazy.

"Here." I offered James the pages. "There are caves up

ahead. We should reach them right before nightfall if we hurry."

James hesitantly took the book. "You would tell me if something was bothering you, right?"

Would you?

I can't, James, because I'm not sure what it is. "Of course," I lied.

He nodded once more before treading into the mountains. "Let's get going."

Claire followed him; her neck craned as she admired the mountains. Lord Farmount followed, giving me a once-over before he joined them. I found myself checking my appearance before I stopped and dropped my hand back to my side. Silas motioned for me to go ahead as he took the rear of our group. His lips were pulled tight as he kept his attention focused on the mountains ahead.

I wanted to approach him, but I wasn't sure what to say. There was one thing I did realize, though: whatever was wrong with Silas was getting worse.

CHAPTER 14

The frigid air finally settled into a cool but comfortable temperature as we marched deeper into the mountains, the high peaks of stone blocking the wind's wrath. We trekked through the Shalleys, scattering pebbles with each step. It was oddly quiet, the range void of any life. Up ahead, James and Claire discussed the creation of the mountains and how some peaks were rounded and others pointed. I was glad that they were getting along. Behind them, Lord Farmount lagged with his hood hiding his features.

Silas eventually made his way next to me. We walked side by side for a while, neither of us saying a word.

I had so many questions I wanted to ask him, but I found myself hesitating, afraid to ask.

You were never afraid of talking with the old Silas.

The old Silas would always give me a calm, but truthful answer. But now, I was scared that anything I said would cause this Silas to do something rash, maybe even hurt someone. I ached for my Silas. What had happened to the jovial Silas from the healing room? I wanted more than anything to break through this new Silas and find him again.

The sky fully darkened. The brightness of the moon shined upon the dirt, leading us along our lonesome path. As our feet stepped in time with one another, I focused on the path in front. Twice now, Silas had reacted violently to trivial things. I agreed that Lord Farmount was rude, but Steady Silas had never been so rash. And I still couldn't figure out what had happened under the willow tree. Were these the effects of his heart?

Was the real Silas prone to starting fights so quickly?

These questions spiraled through my thoughts like leaves in an autumn wind until we reached the cave's opening.

As Silas and I approached, a bright-orange glow from a fire pooled out into the evening, greeting us to our home for the night. James, Claire, and Lord Farmount had already entered and had quickly gotten to work on getting a fire going. My mind thought back to Lord Farmount, cutting branches from the tree for the roaring flames.

Eman was right about the lord, but was he right about choosing Silas?

The crackling of the flames invited us to accept its warmth. My feet throbbed, and my head might explode from all the unanswered questions piling up. I needed to rest.

But as I headed in, Silas grabbed my hand. I jerked away, immediately wrenching myself free. I wouldn't allow him to trap me again. Not like the Fourth Choice, even if that wasn't the real Silas.

Silas's mouth hung open, his hand still extended from where he had grasped mine.

Lowering it slowly, he hung his head. "I'm sorry, Addie."

I cradled my wrist, trying to erase the memories of the burns from the Fourth Choice and the harsh grip from before.

He brought his hand to his head while pinching his eyes shut. "I don't know what's happening to me. These voices … I'm so confused."

I dropped my wrist to my side. "What voices? What are they saying?" Was Silas hearing the same voice as me? "What's happening, Silas? What's wrong?"

Silas kept his eyes shut. "They're saying terrible things. Things I know aren't true, but I just don't know …" He slammed his palm against his forehead, reminding me of Lyle when I had left him in Ramni the first time. This couldn't be Ophidian, could it? How could Ophidian get inside Silas's head? Surely he wasn't that powerful.

"I know," I replied, wanting to reach out to him and hold him close, but my feet refused to move. "There's a lot that's happened in a very short amount of time."

Silas opened his eyes and lowered his hand. The intensity in his gaze left me speechless. Swallowing, he took a step toward me, his voice low. "Addie, I need you to know that I've always been yours."

My pulse thrummed, and I lowered my gaze. He was so certain.

I fidgeted with the ends of Lyle's sweater, the image of my brother and Claire holding hands entering my thoughts. What would Lyle do in this situation? Did he and Claire have problems before their relationship budded? Or did it work out effortlessly?

"I decided to give my heart to you a long time ago," Silas continued, taking another step closer. "But I need you to know that you don't have to choose me."

I pinched the hem between my fingers. Of course, Claire and Lyle had problems. They were both perfectly stubborn, and that's why they were amazing together.

Silas took another step. My body was keenly aware of his tall stature and broad shoulders within arm's reach.

"I don't know what your old heart felt for me," he confessed. "And I know from your hold on my heart, how this new one feels." Silas caressed my face. The calluses from his fingertips were softer than feathers as they held my cheek. My eyelids fluttered closed, relishing his touch. "But you've never said how you feel."

The warmth of his touch erased the horrors of the Fourth Choice. My new heart held more emotions for Silas than my old heart ever did. If I cared for the old Silas, couldn't I care for this one, as well?

I laced my fingers through his, drawing him closer. Without hesitation, Silas brought his warm lips down upon mine, kissing me softly. My heart raged with emotion, beating so hard it hurt. His lips were soft and inviting, not demanding and hard as siti Silas. I yearned to be closer to him. I tied my arms around his neck, crushing him against me. His strong hands gripped my waist, gliding up my spine. A shiver ran through my body. I wanted more and more of him, but after a moment, he pulled away. I flushed, realizing how quickly I had gotten lost in the moment.

"Are you guys going to come in or not?" Claire called, a snicker following her question.

Silas let out a breathy chuckle as he stroked my cheek once more. I never wanted his fingers to leave my skin.

"We better go inside," I said, reluctantly releasing him.

Silas gave me his crooked grin before leaning in and giving me another kiss. My heart soared.

Standing straight, Silas coughed before offering his hand to me. I couldn't keep the smile off my face as I laced my fingers through his.

When we entered our home for the night, Lord Farmount sat stoking the fire in the middle of the cave with James next to him. Though the fire was already large, James rubbed his hands together, allowing streams of white light to pour from his palms to further ignite it. The flames burst forth, doubling in size.

Lord Farmount jerked away from the growing fire, but once he noticed us all watching, he scoffed and stalked to the back of the cave.

James chuckled as he continued to feed the flames with pieces of wood until it was big enough to warm us all.

Though we were all exhausted by the day's events, no one was able to sleep. I took a seat next to James with Silas settling next to me.

James handed the book back to me as he retreated from the fire. "Is it saying anything new?" He held out the bundle of twigs to Silas.

When I opened the pages, they were blank.

"They've been that way since we got here." James nodded at the text. "I wasn't sure if you would see something different."

My heart warmed at James's faith in me, but if the pages had been blank since we arrived, that probably meant that we wouldn't need the map again until tomorrow. I started to close the cover, then stopped as new words formed.

Probar se Duodecim forti resurge

I waited as the translation read: "A warrior will rise to prove herself to the Twelve."

James read the words over my shoulder. "I don't need to tell you what that means, do I?"

I shook my head warily.

"For what it's worth"—he gave my shoulder a small nudge with his own—"you've already proven yourself to me."

As soon as he finished his sentence, the words on the

page changed. The word Twelve disappeared and was replaced by an Eleven.

"Whoa," I said, running my finger along the words.

James laughed. "It won't be as easy with the others, trust me."

"That's unfortunate," I replied, securing the book in my satchel.

Claire crouched next to Silas and offered him a small metal cup. "You need to drink this."

Silas quirked a brow at the cup, then at Claire. "Why?"

"Because I want to poison you." She rolled her eyes. "It's an herbal blend from Sana's garden that will help your body adjust to having a heart again. Lyle and I both had to drink it for a while after Addie placed her heart in us." She pushed the cup toward him until he took it.

Silas swirled the liquid around. "Well, I trust Addie, and she trusts you, so, here goes nothing." Taking a breath, he gulped the liquid down in one swig before handing the cup back to Claire.

"Oops, I think I mixed up my herbs, and that was my blend for trapping and killing rodents." Claire whisked the cup from his hands.

Silas's face paled. "What?"

"I'm joking," Claire chuckled as she sat next to me. "Or am I?"

"Claire," I scolded but laughed at Silas's wide eyes. I linked my arm through his. "She's not going to poison you."

"Not yet, anyway." She gave Silas a toothy grin, and he inched away from her.

James and Claire both laughed as I tried to contain my laughter.

"The last time I was in a cave," Claire said, untying the twine that held her hair. Thick white strands spiraled around her shoulders as she massaged her scalp. "You broke me out of my cell." The light of the fire flickered against her snow-white hair, making it glow orange and yellow.

I brought out a bag of dried meat Eman had packed and nibbled on a piece before handing the rest to James. "The last time *I* was in a cave, you helped me save Lyle."

Her smile faltered slightly upon the mention of him. Did she miss him as much as I did?

"I hate caves," Lord Farmount grunted, his back still turned toward us. Though he tried to hide it, his shoulders were tense, and his head kept jerking back and forth, scanning the cave as if he were frightened.

Silas chuckled under his breath.

"What about you?" Claire asked, pointing a strip of jerky at Silas.

"What?" he asked.

She motioned with her hand, leaning forward. "The last time you were in a cave …"

"How do you know this isn't my first time?" he asked, his lips twitching as he tossed more sticks into the fire.

"Do I need to actually mix up my herbs next time?" Claire threatened.

"Okay, okay." He put his hands up in surrender. "The last time I was in a cave, I had fought through the Seven Choices and was ready to kill Ophidian."

Claire spit out the tea she had just drunk. "What?"

"Are you serious?" I asked at the same time, the food in my hand dropping to the ground.

We waited for Silas's response until James slapped his knee. "I think he wins!" he said with a chuckle. It was contagious enough to cause laughter to erupt in all of us.

As soon as it died down, everyone shuffled around, choosing their places to rest for the night. I grabbed my blanket from my satchel and spread it across my legs. Taking a few hard jars from my bag, I started to relax when something fast flew in my periphery, and a sharp point pricked my neck. I jolted up, lifting my hand to swat away whatever hit me. In the glint of the flames, drops of blood trickled down my fingertips.

My vision spun through the darkening cave. Lord Farmount was rolled on his side, unconscious, and only inches away from the fire. James had fallen backwards, and Claire was slumped on top of him.

"Addie," Silas mumbled, falling to the ground. I lunged to catch him before he hit the hard wall. Clutching his head in my lap, I searched around the cave. Who could have done this so quickly? So stealthily?

A large figure, cloaked in a gray robe, materialized out of the shadows.

"Who are you?" I demanded, gently laying Silas on the

ground before I stood, sounding more courageous than I was. "What do you want?"

"We've been waiting a long time for you, Bellata," a deep, raspy voice replied. Before I could respond, another prick burned my neck, forcing me into the depths of darkness.

153

CHAPTER 15

$\mathcal{I}$t was as if a thousand boulders had smashed my skull. I tried to lift my hand to rub the pulsating spot, but my arms wouldn't move. Pins and needles pierced my skin as blood rushed down my veins. A strong cord secured my wrists together above my head. Grunting, I twisted them, attempting to stretch out the cord and escape, but it only tightened. Once my eyes fully adjusted, I tried to stand and found another cord biting into my ankles. I strained to pull my feet apart, but the cord was the same as the one on my wrists: the more I struggled, the more it tightened.

"Struggling is pointless," the same raspy voice from before said. A softer tone lay beneath the hoarse voice, but I couldn't assume my captor was kind.

"I figured that much out, thanks," I muttered.

A dark abyss surrounded me on all sides, obstructing my vision. Where was everyone? What if something bad had happened to them? What if it was Ophidian? Had he taken them?

"Who are you?" My voice wavered at the end.

The figure stalked toward me, a ball of white light hovering from his fingertips. The gray cloak and darkness of the cave shaded his face from the light.

"Come," he said. "Our time is limited."

Grabbing my ankles, the man cut the cord holding my feet together. He then sliced through the air, and my arms fell. Warm blood sped back into my fingertips as he yanked me up from the cold ground. He latched another rope, like a leash, around the cords still binding my wrists.

I yanked at the bondage before searching for an escape.

"There is none," he said without turning around. He moved down the long, stone tunnel, tugging at the leash.

Digging my heels into the ground, I glared at him. "Where are my friends? What did you do to them?"

His heavy footsteps ceased. The ball of light on the man's other large palm transferred to his thick, tanned fingertips. He then pressed his fingers to the cave wall. Rays of light scattered through the wall like spiderwebs before the stone wailed, its cracks echoing off the neighboring walls. A moment passed, and one last crack burst across the cavern.

I dodged a chunk of rock that barely missed my head and held my bound arms up, shielding myself from any more falling debris. Pieces of stone nicked and scraped against my hands. Fortunately, the larger rocks landed elsewhere. Once the dust settled, I saw that the stone in front of us had shattered.

Beyond the rubble, a new tunnel appeared in the center of the broken rock. The man continued through, giving me a good yank on the leash. I scrambled after him, nearly losing my balance on the uneven ground.

How deep were we in the mountain? And where did it lead?

As we continued down the dark corridor, flashes of light glinted off the man's large fingertips. It was like the magic I had seen James perform, but slightly different. James's light was a steady stream, resembling a river. This light was like sunlight bouncing off water, a reflection. That meant only one thing then: I'd found another Magister.

Excitement flitted through me, but I stayed alert. If this man was a Magister, why was he holding me captive?

In moments, small shimmers on the walls sparkled into radiant jewels and gems, shining against the Magister's light. Distracted by the twinkling surrounding us, I ran straight into the man's back.

Stepping back, I rubbed my nose and asked, "Where are we?"

The man turned, illuminating his hand fully, and I shut my lids. Not only was the light blazing, but the reflection off the gems magnified it so brightly, it burned my eyes. I waited a few seconds before opening them again.

The Magister's power revealed his stout physique

beneath the gray cloak. With the light illuminating the tunnel, I could see dark green leaves embroidered into the ash-colored fabric.

The man held his arm high, allowing the light to leave his palm. It formed a small sphere in the air and floated above our heads, lighting the wide stone tunnel surrounding us. I gasped as the cave walls sparkled with a rainbow of jewels and gems. Shades of purple, blue, and orange decorated the brown rock wall.

The Magister removed his hood, revealing a large, burly man with a mass of black curls tied into a bun. Dark red splotches covered his forehead and cheeks, only allowing small bits of his olive-toned skin to show. The rest of his face was hidden behind a neatly trimmed beard that grew from his cheeks and chin.

"I am Neural, the Magister of this Land," the man said in a booming voice. "I apologize for the bindings. But we can't let you get away." Spreading his arms wide, he grinned. "Welcome to Dunsque."

The cave was empty save for us. "Where is everyone?" I asked.

Neural lowered his arms, his shoulders drooping as pain shadowed his features. "That is why you are here."

He snapped his fingers, and the sphere bobbed higher, reminding me of Sana's healing orbs in Ramni. The crystals twinkled brighter as another figure emerged from an adjacent corridor. Like Neural, this figure wore a cloak. Only theirs was dark green with gray leaves, the exact opposite.

As the new person approached, he yanked off the hood, revealing a tall, slender man with long, blond hair tied back into a simple ponytail. His skin was a creamy white but was covered in the same blotches as Neural.

"Is this her?" the man asked, raising a brow as he peered down his long nose at me. His voice was deep and rasped, like Neural's—the only similarity they seemed to have.

"This is Divad," Neural said, ignoring his comrade's question.

"I thought there was only one Magister per Land," I commented.

"There is," Divad snapped, causing white light to pop from his fingertips. "Because of the morb, we had to join forces. I'm the Magister of Trefair."

"The morb?"

Divad scoffed and swatted his hand at me. "How can this be the Bellata? She's too young and ignorant."

My toes curled in my boots as I tried to control my tongue. Irritation ignited under my skin, warming my palms as I glared at the pasty Magister. "I don't know where I am or what's going on, but I do know that you still haven't told me where my friends are."

Divad clenched his jaw, showing his long, white teeth below his curled upper lip. He opened his mouth to rebuttal with a nasty remark, but stopped, his eyes drifting to my hands. Orange sparks of light crackled off my fingertips.

"She is the one," Neural said, grinning at me before shooting a smirk that said, "I told you so" to Divad.

Divad worked his jaw, then bowed. "You were right, my friend."

Neural hummed happily to himself as he cut the bindings off my arms. "Come, I will take you to your friends, and we will explain everything."

I rubbed my wrists as I followed the two Magisters. We hurried through the tunnel until we reached an area lined with sparkling emerald jewels. Floating in the air, the light of the orb reflected off the different shades of green. It was a breathtaking sight, but the eerie silence that barricaded us kept my senses on guard.

The cave walls widened until we were in a cavern like the one in Ophidian's Realm: Ofavemore. But while that one was deadly, this one was beautiful. Octagonal gems and spherical jewels of all different shapes, sizes, and colors sparkled as many glowing orbs lit the open space. Soft whispers echoed against the walls. The ceiling couldn't be seen from where we were standing, but I could see the floor very well.

Hundreds of people stood, sat, or laid upon the ground. Those lying on the ground were wrapped in red cloaks. They hardly made a sound as we crept by. Like Neural and Divad, their skin was covered in red blotches. Some skin tones were lighter than others, but the shapes of the splotches were all the same: a filled red circle, smeared out around the edges. Every so often, one of them would let out a breath or sigh, but, other than that, the cavern was silent.

"What happened to them?" I whispered, trying not to disturb the stillness.

"The morb," Divad replied less harshly than before. "Or, at least, that's what we call it."

"It's a disease that plagued Dunsque years ago," Neural continued, his eyes downcast. "It has since spread throughout our caves and into those of Trefair. Those that wear red cloaks tell us who are infected with the morb. All of those infected have also had their hearts extracted."

My stomach lurched. "What?"

Neural let out a defeated sigh. "When the morb first infected my people, we noticed that the red clusters appeared on the skin above the infected's heart. The disease takes the blood, or the life, out of a body. That's why so many of the infected are pale, and their marks are bright red."

I looked down at my own skin before folding my arms over my chest. Was I already infected?

Neural brushed a curl out of his eyes. "A traveling doctor from another realm said the same disease infected his home. He told us that if we extracted the heart of those infected, they would be healed. He showed us how."

I pursed my lips. A traveling doctor?

"But it didn't work," I surmised, my shoulders deflating as I took in the abundance of red cloaks covering the cavern floor.

"The disease only grew more rampant as we extracted

hearts, becoming impossible to contain in Dunsque," Neural confessed, motioning to Divad, who was surveying the cavern.

"At the first cases of the morb, I contacted Neural," Divad explained, his frown deepening. "Through many hours of research and experimentation on ourselves, we discovered that a sleeping draught prevented the morb from spreading as quickly." Divad's sharp eyes filled with regret. "Unfortunately, many have been under the draught for so long, the moment we'd wake them, the morb would consume their bodies, instantly killing them."

"Which is why we decided to group our people together," Neural added. "We could tend to those who were still conscious but also look over those that were not."

"And two Magisters are better than one, right?" Divad asked gruffly. "We were chosen to protect them," he said to no one, his face somber. "But they're dying, and there's nothing we can do."

"There is something we must confess," Neural said, standing beside me, wringing his hands. "As we said before, the disease spreads quickly to all who enter our caves."

He extended his hand and pointed to a far area of the cavern where I spotted Silas, James, Claire, and Lord Farmount. My breath caught, fear creeping into my heart when I saw only Silas and James seated upright. Claire and Lord Farmount laid motionless beside them, cloaked in red. I started toward them before Neural reached out and grabbed my arm.

"We injected each of you with the sleeping draught, hoping the morb hadn't reached you yet." Neural held out a tiny green dart with a black tip.

I rubbed my neck where it had hit before. "Yes, I remember. Thank you."

Neural nodded and motioned to Silas and James at the back of the large cavern, leaning against the wall. James had his hand over Claire's forehead while Silas sat next to him, his head bowed. I bolted over.

"Addie." Silas stood, wrapping his arms around me. His strong embrace soothed my worries. As I pressed into him, his half-heart thumped against my cheek. "We were so worried." He looked down at me, his eyes swimming with questions.

I rocked back, dread twisting my stomach into knots. Silas wasn't nearly as covered as some of the others, but splotches were forming on his neck. When I took his hand in mine, I saw another red mark forming.

"I met the Magisters of Dunsque and Trefair," I explained. I gently ran the pads of my fingers over the splotch, studying the mark. "What happened?"

Silas sucked in a breath, keeping his focus on our hands. "All we remember is being around the fire, then blacking out before waking up here." He watched my reaction as he said, "We don't know how long it's been, but judging by Farmount and Claire, we don't have much time."

I peered over Silas's shoulder to find Lord Farmount's body sprawled along the cold stone floor. His skin was so covered in dark red marks, I could barely recognize him. When I saw Claire next to him, my heart wrenched. Her face and hands were almost entirely red.

Squeezing Silas's hand, I let go and moved to James's side. James sat next to Lord Farmount, eyeing him closely before he rifled through Claire's satchel on the ground. He pulled out a vial filled with purple leaves and placed them on the lord's forehead.

"I'm glad you found us," James said when I approached. I laid my hand on his back, noticing he only had one red patch on his arm.

"How is he?" I settled beside him before studying Lord Farmount. His eyes were closed, his chest barely moving. Placing a hand on the lord's arm, I bowed my head. After leading them here, I couldn't lose them. They were my responsibility.

"Not good," James said, returning the vial to Claire's satchel. He ran a hand through his speckled light-brown hair. "It seems the disease affects each person at a different speed. While Silas and I have barely any markings, Claire and Farmount are becoming more covered as we speak."

As if in response, a new splotch made a home on Claire's forehead.

"Why is it affecting you less?" I questioned.

James lit his hand with white light, then extended his fingers, allowing the light to fade into the air. "I think it has to do with the mark of the Mender. That's why you, me, and Silas all woke up from the sleeping draught."

"But Claire ..."

"Doesn't have his mark," James interjected. "You gave her half of your heart so that she could survive. Eman can't mend your heart within her. And Farmount is completely exposed."

Biting my lip, I scanned the citizens of Dunsque and Trefair. There were too many red cloaks filling the cavern. If James's assumption was true, then what Eman had said was also true: the mark of the Mender was disappearing from our realm, leaving the people of Decim vulnerable and unprotected against Ophidian's darkness.

"Ah, so you were telling the truth," Divad said, towering over James and me with a smug grin. James rolled his shoulders as he stood. The air weighed with tension as the two Magisters faced one another.

"You must forgive my remarks from when I first saw you again, Dimitte," Divad sneered, his long ponytail swishing behind him. "The last time we heard from you, you were selling your allegiance to our enemy."

James's hands balled into fists, white light lining them as he held them at his sides. The muscle in his neck corded as he clenched his jaw. Yet, just as I thought he would make a stand, he released the light and hung his head. Divad's grin turned vicious at the reaction, and his hands popped with white light.

Heat swirled around my fingers as my nose flared. I stood between the two Magisters, lifting my chin as I glowered at Divad. James had suffered in Ophidian's Realm, and when he could've escaped, he stayed to help

Lyle and me. I wouldn't allow anyone to talk to my family like that.

The Magister's smug expression faded into one of annoyance until he relented and retreated a few steps.

Snorting, I placed my hands on my hips. "Now, Neural said I was here because of the sick, but how can I help?"

Divad flicked an invisible speck of dust off his shoulder. "Neural believes in the prophecies of old, one of which claims a great warrior will come and save our lands from the darkness."

While I was thankful for Neural's faith in me, panic thundered through my veins. "Did he happen to mention how to save them?" I asked warily.

Divad lifted his shoulders. "If we knew that, we wouldn't need your help."

"But I don't have any medical knowledge." I gestured to Claire's motionless body. "She would know what to do better than me."

"Addie." James touched my shoulder. "Remember, you're not alone. Eman knew what you had to do and has prepared you for it. If Claire was meant to save these people, Eman would have given the task to her. But he gave it to you."

I swallowed my fear and nodded, remembering what Eman had given me in Ramni. Reaching into my satchel, I grabbed the brown book.

"Apparently, Eman thinks you're the prophesied one, too," Divad said, pointing to the book. "Not many are allowed to take his books outside of Ramni."

The book from Lyle's room shot through my mind. If it was also a text from Eman's library, how had it traveled from Ramni to Barracks?

"As you probably know by now," James explained stiffly, regaining his confidence, "Divad has been mended by Eman and healed by the realm of Ramni."

Divad flipped his cloak over his shoulder and bowed. "I must return to my people," he said as he straightened. He cast a snide smile at James. "Don't go wandering off, Dimitte."

James muttered a few choice words as I shuffled back to Silas.

"Let's hope you have an answer," I said to the book. Settling next to Silas, I noted that the splotches on Claire had doubled. The skin surrounding the red spots was beginning to pale, making the red stand out more.

"Are you okay?" I asked Silas as he absentmindedly rubbed his own blotched hands.

"I'm just praying we figure this out, and fast."

Anxiety tightened my chest as the splotches spread to his forearms. Crisscrossing my legs, I opened the pages, laying the book flat on my lap. I had to figure this out.

Will you figure it out in time?

"What does it say?" Silas asked.

I peered down, my heart dropping. "It's not saying anything."

There were no words that greeted me, no cryptic sayings. Only a red page.

"What do you mean?" Silas leaned over, his shoulder

rubbing mine. I didn't move away. The smell of cedarwood wafted between us, and I forced myself to focus on what Silas was saying. "Has it always been that color?"

Diverting my attention to the book, I shook my head. "No. I'm not sure what it means."

I thumbed through the other pages to find them all turning the same shade of red. Closing the book, I looked up. A field of red cloaks laid out in front of me. Red pages and red cloaks. Was there a connection?

Suddenly, an image came into my mind; an image of something else that was red. Something that had haunted me for years.

I quickly stood and turned to Silas. "Are you well enough?"

He raised a brow. "For what?"

I extended my hand to him. "To follow me."

He gave me his crooked grin as he grasped my hand. "Always."

"Come on," I said, pulling him up. "I think I know how to stop this."

We wove through the crowd of people, leaving James to tend to Claire and Lord Farmount. We stopped beside Neural, who was using his magic on a young woman and her baby.

"You will be well soon," he said gently, placing a hand on the baby's smooth forehead. He stood to face Silas and me, sorrow replacing the hopefulness he held moments before. Neural led us away from the young woman before speaking.

"I pray you have an idea, Bellata. Time is running out."

I clutched the book to my chest. "You said the disease came to Dunsque and spread to Trefair a few years ago." He nodded in confirmation. "How many years ago, exactly?"

"Eight," Divad said from behind us. "Eight years since this disease has ravaged our people."

"Eight years since Schism," Silas said, following my train of thought.

Neural took a deep breath, stroking his beard. "The doors."

I hugged the book tighter. For once, I wanted to be wrong. But it looked like I'd have to face those horrid doors again. "Where?"

Neural cast a hesitant glance at Divad.

"We must show them, Neural," Divad said. "It's our only hope."

Turning back to us, Neural took a deep breath, igniting his hand with light once more. "Come. I'll show you where this evil began."

CHAPTER 16

Silas and I rushed to keep up with Neural's rapid pace through a tunnel lined with crimson crystals. Divad followed behind us, his steps so light I almost forgot he was there. With each step away from the cavern, the crystals dimmed, shifting from bright red, to dark ruby, to brown, then black.

The light from Neural's palm dwindled as we trekked further and further into the tunnel. Sweat beaded on his brow as he tried to ignite it to a brighter light, but it only faded into a small glow. Eventually, he couldn't light it at all, and we were enveloped by darkness.

A low moaning and scratching echoed ahead of us, and my heart stopped, halting every cell in my body. The memory of the siti's claws ripping my flesh churned my stomach.

The scratch of Silas's sword against its sheath rang throughout the tunnel. I clutched the book to my chest and my fingers immediately heated. When I looked down, I saw the pages glowing. Lifting it above my head, I watched as the book shone brightly, lighting the tunnel once more. Ebony crystals stood out against the tan walls, blemishing the once beautiful gems.

As I moved the book to light the rest of the tunnel, a siti clawed at me, and I screamed. It moaned loudly as its large black eyes bore into mine. Thick obsidian claws reached out, scratching at the air as if they were ready to attack. Was this where Ophidian wanted to unleash his army from the Shadow realm? Did the black door I saw in Ramni lead to Dunsque?

"No need to fear, Bellata. They cannot harm you," Neural said, taking a slow, cautious step toward the creatures.

There were several siti packed tightly together, moaning and scratching. Although they continued to reach for us, they were fixed in their position like boards nailed together. Around them, a swirling gray mist flowed, creating a barrier.

"We thought this was the source of the disease, as well," Divad commented, fixated on the siti. "We've done all we can to prevent the monsters from taking any more of our people, but we still can't figure out how to destroy them."

"'Any more'?" Silas asked.

Neural sighed as he rubbed his eyes. He looked more worn and tired with each moment that passed. "These monsters came through our tunnels before the morb. After we had slain many of them, our people became infected with the disease." He straightened his cloak and squared his shoulders before he shook his fist at the siti. "First, the beasts, then the morb, then that 'doctor.' What more destruction can these cursed doors bring?"

"Is this where the doors are?" I asked.

"The creatures had to get here somehow," Divad explained, matching his comrade's glare. "We saw the doors when they first appeared, but since the monsters have grown to so many, no one has been able to get close enough to see if they're still there."

I chewed on my lower lip. They weren't sure the doors were there? Was I wrong? Was this a dead end? Doubt magnified my failure before the text moved beneath my fingertips. The glowing book shook, beckoning me to open it. Grasping the cover, I flipped open the pages. The red stain had been washed away, allowing a passage to appear on the cream-colored page:

Destroy the doors, and the sickness will flee
Then you will prove yourself worthy

Annoyed, I pinched the bridge of my nose. While I was pleased the book was now speaking in my own tongue, it was definitely a message from Eman. It told me what I needed to do, but not how to do it.

"Destroy them, how?" Silas asked, reading over my shoulder.

I shrugged, not willing to close the cover, hoping the

book would give further information. But the letters dissolved until a blank page stared back at me.

Grunting, I slammed the pages shut and scrubbed my face with my hand. There had to be a connection between the phrase and the previous red page. Well, the doors were red. But then there were the siti. The only way to get to the doors, *if* they were there, was to get rid of the siti.

Are you strong enough to kill them all?

Would Eman ask me that question? Or was there someone else infiltrating my thoughts?

I glanced at Neural, who was leaning against the cave wall, wiping the sweat from his brow. It amazed me that he hadn't died from the disease yet. I assumed being a Magister had protected him, but since he had been exposed to it for so long, the morb had probably weakened his power. Divad sat on the ground with his head in his hands. He looked exhausted as well, but not as bad as Neural.

Then there was Silas and me. Silas had his sword and could probably take down a good amount of siti. But all I had was this book. If I really tried, I could whack a siti with it, but that probably wouldn't work too well with a greater number of monsters.

My heart pulsed with the solution. We didn't need to kill all the siti, just enough so we could destroy the doors. Once the doors were gone, no more siti would come through. Between the four of us, there was a chance it would work.

A confident, clear voice spoke in my thoughts, confirming the idea. *You are more powerful than you believe.*

I recognized that voice.

The black gems on the wall winked back at me. Something within me understood that these jewels hadn't always been shadowed, but bright and beautiful. Pressing my palm against one of the jewels, I dipped my head. Like the people in Barracks in the cages, the people of Dunsque and Trefair had been overtaken by shadows and darkness, and it was my responsibility to free them.

With a fire burning in my heart, I lifted my head and turned to Neural. "Can you remove the barrier?"

He straightened from his hunched position. "What?"

"Can you remove the barrier?"

Neural bunched his brows. "Well, yes. But I don't see why I would want to."

"The siti got here through the doors. We had similar doors back in Barracks. I'm guessing it's how Ophidian collects people from each of the Twelve Lands."

"Collects people?" Silas and Neural asked simultaneously while Divad considered my words. He nodded along, but a tight expression contorted his face.

"For us to destroy the doors," I continued, "we need to get rid of the siti, which would require the barrier to be removed."

Neural paused for a moment and scratched his chin. Acceptance rolled over his features as he fully understood my words.

Divad came up beside him, brushing the dirt from his

cloak. "We don't have much of a choice. Time's running out, and it has been for a while."

Divad's mention of time reminded me of the constant ticking invading my thoughts. Why did it keep starting and stopping? Was there a pattern I was missing?

"Okay, Bellata. I will put my faith in you," Neural declared. Rubbing his palms together, he directed them at the gray mist. The Magister's reflective light poured out in a steady stream, covering the wall of gray smoke. The mist swirled into a spiral as the light and smoke receded beneath his skin.

"Addie," Silas said, his attention on the moaning siti. "Once we get to the doors, do you know how to destroy them?"

"No," I said truthfully, avoiding his gaze.

Silas flinched. "What?"

"Not yet, anyway," I gave him a weary smile.

Silas sighed, rubbing the back of his neck before he gripped his sword with both hands. He mumbled something under his breath that I was glad I didn't hear.

Within a few moments, the last of the gray mist entered Neural's palms, and he stumbled back before falling to the ground.

With the barrier gone, the moans of the siti ricocheted off the stone walls, rattling into my bones. A dark wave of monsters raced toward us, eager for destruction. Pointed claws scratched along the hard ground, icing my bones. My hands trembled as the siti came right at us. Without the sword, I had no idea what to do or how to react.

A beam of white light from behind us cut them off, and the siti shrieked and hissed.

"Go!" Divad yelled, forming two scimitars out of light. Launching them forward, he impaled the first few siti as they attempted to slice Neural with their claws. Divad's long, blond locks whipped behind him as he used both swords to maim and stab the monsters. "I'll hold them off! Destroy the doors!"

Before I could think, Silas grabbed my hand, and we ran through the mob of siti. They swiped at our limbs as we sprinted past, their long claws tearing into our clothes before piercing our flesh. My calf tore open, and I bit back my cry. I needed to focus. I had to get to those doors.

Silas stabbed a siti in the forehead, black blood painting his blade. As the monster writhed on the ground, Silas pulled me over its body. Another siti lunged at me, and I smacked it with the glowing book, rendering the monster unconscious.

We ran down the tunnel, the light of the book illuminating our way through the abyss of siti. The pain in my calf amplified with each step I took, blood coating my pant leg. My lungs squeezed as I tried to suck in more air. Finally, the light reflected off what we were searching for: two blood-red doors, exact replicas of the ones in Barracks.

"Schism," I growled, his name tasting like poison on my lips.

"Okay." Silas lowered his sword and circled the doors. "What now?"

All siti had retreated to the opposite end of the tunnel, leaving the area around the doors barren. The clangs of Divad's scimitars echoed down the tunnel, along with the moaning of the siti.

At their groans, Silas whipped around, leveling his sword in one fluid movement. I dodged out of the way before stepping up to the doors. There were no scratches or markings on them. No chipped paint or splinters. I kept my hands clenched around the book, not daring to touch the cursed doors.

"I don't know," I said quickly, trying to push out the moaning from behind us. I wasn't sure of how many siti had been locked behind the barrier, but Divad probably couldn't hold them for long. I opened the book again, ignoring the red splotches forming on my hands. I didn't have time to think about dying. "It said, 'Destroy the doors, and the sickness will flee,' but it doesn't say how."

Silas jogged over to me, squinted at the book, then glanced up. The moaning bounded closer. Holding the blade steady, he stood guard between the growing groans and me. "I'll hold them off while you figure it out. You can do it, Addie. I know you can."

His words rejuvenated my spirit, and a new burst of strength flowed through me. I tapped my fingers on the blank page. How was I supposed to destroy the doors? I squeezed my lids shut. Think, Addie.

The disease came eight years ago when Schism first came to Barracks. It affected everyone, but not at the same rate. Those with the mark of the Mender had more time. Those without it were doomed.

I threaded my fingers through my hair. But what could destroy the doors? It couldn't be something as simple as literally destroying them, could it? And the red page. Did that have something to do with it?

"Addie!" Silas yelled.

My eyes snapped open, and I jumped out of the way before a siti claw nearly sliced me in half. In one swipe, Silas's sword cut through its arm. In another, he severed its head. The metal of the sword glowed crimson as Silas paused to breathe. Black blood splattered his clothes, and his chest heaved while a spark of excitement glinted in his eyes. "Anything?"

Scrunching my nose, I watched the siti head roll away. "Not yet."

"Keep trying," he said before running into the horde of oncoming siti.

I took another breath and pinched my eyes shut again.

Tick.

Tock.

Tick.

Tock.

"No, not now," I groaned. Dropping the book, I pushed my palms against my temples, trying to cease the pounding clock. Instead, I focused on the moaning siti.

Ophidian created the malum and the phagos. Both creatures were far more powerful than the siti, and each could easily corrupt and destroy both Dunsque and

Trefair. Why the siti? Did the morb have to do with them? And red? The cloaks, the pages, the doors, and now Silas's sword? How did it all connect? *Did* it all connect?

A memory instantly resurfaced in my mind of my first encounter with the siti. They had surrounded me, torn my thigh open. It was bleeding profusely. I couldn't run anymore. But then Claire saved me.

"What were those things?" I asked.

Claire crouched down and began gathering her broken bowl. "Siti."

"What?"

"Siti, or Life Parchers. They feed on all life that enters this realm. They were once humans, but now ..."

Alarm ran through me as I remembered the life force I had stupidly carried straight into this realm.

Claire watched me suspiciously at first, then her eyes widened. "That's why they were after you ... No one ever gets past that wretch at the gates with their heart. I could practically feel the life coming out of you when I carried you here."

My eyes flew open, the ticking gone. "Life Parchers."

"What?" Silas yelled above the chaos as he ran his sword through another monster.

"That's what the siti are," I yelled above the wails. "They feed on the life of those who enter Ophidian's Realm. They attack the Traders, draining them of their lives to survive. When they were barricaded, they had no other way to feed. The siti used the morb to slowly suck the life out of the people of Dunsque and Trefair like Neural said." I bounced on my toes.

"Not to take away from your triumphant conclusion," Silas said as he stabbed another siti in the forehead, "but how does that destroy the doors?"

A sharp pain pierced my shoulder. This time I cried out, wrenching away from the siti as I clutched the wound. Silas rushed over, cutting the siti down the middle before I could blink. His eyes filled with worry as he carefully peeled my hand away to inspect the wound

"This needs to be bandaged as soon as possible."

I winced as he turned my shoulder before I noticed my hand. Bright-red blood from my wound coated my palm and fingers.

"Blood," I whispered. As the thick droplets rolled down my wrist, I finally understood what I needed to do. I hurried back to the doors.

"What?" Silas asked, taking quick, long strides to catch up to me.

"Blood, Silas. It's what gives us life," I explained. "It's what the siti crave. They slice through their victims to parch the life out of them just like the morb sucks the blood out of its victims."

He studied the blood dripping from my hand. "Blood is going to destroy the doors?"

The scarlet shade of his sword caught my eye, and an idea sprouted in my mind. I stretched out my blood-stained hand. "Give me your sword."

Silas tightened his grip on the hilt. "Not until you tell me what's going on."

The doors creaked open. More siti were coming.

"Silas, please! Trust me!"

He hesitated, keeping the sword close to his side.

"Please," I whispered, his distrust slicing through me like a knife.

Forcing his arm forward, Silas handed me the sword. "Don't be stupid, Addie."

I let out a relieved laugh. "You sound like Claire."

Taking the sword, I carefully ran my bloodied hand along the blade. The crimson light shone brighter as my blood coated the metal. More wails escaped from the doors. Wincing, I dipped my fingers in my bleeding wound and painted more blood on the sword, until there was no silver left.

Lightheaded from the pain and blood loss, I reached out to Silas. "I need your help."

He quickly grabbed my arm, his distrust lessening as he held me close.

"You lead, I'll follow," he said in my ear, sending shivers racing down my neck.

I pressed into him, thankful I wasn't alone.

A siti stomped out of the pit of the red doors. It was bigger than the others and didn't have a cord sewing its mouth shut. I couldn't stop my knees from shaking. The new siti's mouth opened in a snarl, revealing several rows of jagged, yellow teeth, almost as if it were a siti-phagos hybrid. My thoughts froze, my limbs with them.

"Addie, you can do this," Silas whispered as he tightened his arm around my waist.

You are more powerful than you believe, Eman's gentle voice encouraged me again in my mind.

With a deep breath, I raised Silas's and my hands and rammed the blade through the siti-hybrid's face before it could take another step. It wailed a deep, guttural scream, then fell to the floor, black blood oozing from its forehead.

Before any more creatures could enter, we took the sword and plunged it through the keyhole on the first red door. The door let out a loud, piercing cry as if it were in pain. I winced when the high-pitched sound vibrated against the cave walls but continued to the second door. With one last push, Silas and I stabbed the sword into the crimson frame.

A large crack sounded from the doors. Silas spun me around, tightening his arms around my waist as he shielded me with his body. As soon as we turned, the doors exploded into pieces, thrusting us to the hard ground.

I tumbled from Silas's grip, stars appearing in my sight as pain shot from my leg and shoulder. Lifting my face from the dirt, I found that the siti bodies had disappeared, leaving nothing but pools of black blood.

CHAPTER 17

"Are you okay?" Silas asked, stroking my forehead.

"I think so," I replied, testing out my limbs. Pain simultaneously jolted from my arm and my leg. I sucked in a breath, blinking back the tears.

"We need to get you to Claire," he said as he stood, sheathing his sword, which had now returned to its original silver. Silas wiped the siti blood off his hands and onto his pants, then held his somewhat clean hand out to me. I placed the book in my satchel and grasped Silas's rough palm. He easily hauled me up as if he hadn't just battled a dozen monsters.

"Easy," he cautioned, encouraging me to place my weight on him as I stood. Silas held me tight to his side as we limped back.

I glanced over at him. Save for the previous siti scars

on his face, not a single scratch marked his skin. "How are you doing?"

Silas gave a light chuckle, nudging me with his shoulder. "I'm fine. How are you?"

"No, I mean, are you hurt? Is the disease gone?"

He studied his hand where the red splotches had been. "I'm not hurt. At least, I don't have any injuries I'm aware of. As for the disease"—he held up his hand to my face with a crooked grin—"I'm cured. Nice work, Bellata."

The crystals around us shined a rich red as they faded back to their original color. Thick black poison oozed from the walls, steaming once it hit the ground. The cave was soon lit with the gems' miraculous light, leading us back to the Magisters.

"You did it!" Neural laughed, picking me up and swinging me around.

I yelped before he let me go, gently placing me next to Silas.

"I apologize, Bellata. I haven't felt this strong in years." His voice had lost its rasp, holding a warm, smooth tone. Neural's face was completely void of patches, revealing high cheekbones and flawless olive skin.

"I must say, I'm impressed," Divad added, gliding up behind him, a smile creeping to his otherwise straight lips. Though his green cloak was completely drenched in black blood, the Magister's creamy complexion was no longer plagued. Divad grimaced at the stains on his cloak. "Those creatures don't go down easily."

"Come!" Neural shouted, running down the tunnel like a child. "Let us see the others!"

"You must forgive his overexcitement," Divad said, returning to his controlled demeanor as he sheathed his two swords. "Neural has always loved his people more than himself. It was one of the reasons he was chosen to become one of the Twelve."

We hurried after him as best as we could and were soon greeted by the sounds of laughter vibrating throughout the caverns. My chest was light, full of happiness and warmth. I couldn't believe I figured out how to destroy the doors. Maybe I was better at being the Bellata than I thought.

Before we followed Neural further into the cavern, Divad held up a hand.

"There is one thing you must know before you continue your journey," he said, lowering his hand. "Not all of the Twelve Lands are like Dunsque and Trefair. While we've had an alliance, others have had a long period of battle. Prepare yourself; the coming Lands will not be as kind."

My excitement dulled. I had to stay focused on the task ahead and couldn't get distracted by the first victory.

Silas pulled me closer. "Thank you for the warning."

Bowing, Divad extended his arm, motioning for us to continue past him.

Laughter, hugs, and tears of joy streamed down the faces of the citizens of Dunsque and Trefair as they rejoiced, thanking the Heavens for their cure. Thousands of empty red cloaks scattered the ground, no longer needed.

Is this what all of Decim would be like if we defeated Ophidian?

If.

I ignored the comment.

"Getting beat up again?"

Claire stood across from me, leaning to one side as she fisted her hands on her hips. Not a single splotch plagued her beautiful bronze skin.

"I told you I needed you to stick around to heal me," I replied, my lips twitching. Silas released me, and I showed her the wounds on my calf and shoulder.

Claire instructed me to sit. While she coated my wounds with her healing salve, Neural and Divad approached us. Divad held both his scimitars while Neural grasped a golden spear.

"Bellata," Neural said, his voice booming over the chatter of the crowd. A little girl with charcoal ringlets and a wide grin stood beside him, gripping his hand tightly. Behind them, Divad stood with James and Lord Farmount, both healed of the morb.

Neural bowed his head. "How can we ever thank you?"

The coolness of the salve danced through my muscles, healing my wounds.

"The only thing I can ask for in return is your allegiance," I said, standing. "Darkness has descended on Decim, and we must defeat it. We need all Twelve of the

Magisters to fight alongside Eman in order to save our realm from Ophidian."

Neural gave a hard nod, releasing the girl's hand before striding toward me. Divad followed, and both Magisters knelt. They raised their weapons to the Heavens and said, "We, Neural Barringer, Magister of Dunsque, and Divad Miscure, Magister of Trefair, swear on our almes to fight with you until there is no life left within us."

The blades and spear glowed white. The magic of the iuram reached out to me, and I grasped each weapon. Hot, pulsating power flowed from their weapons into my heart, solidifying the oath. We were another step closer to defeating Ophidian.

Adrenaline tingled through my body as my heart pulsed with delight. Three of the twelve Magisters had allied with me.

"Now, there isn't much time," Neural said. "You must continue your journey. Come, we will give you any supplies we can provide." He quickly turned, his cloak flowing through the air as his spear evaporated out of sight.

After Neural had packed us with additional rations and some of Dunsque's prized jewels, he and Divad led us through another tunnel that took us outside.

"Thank you again, Bellata." Neural squashed me against his chest. "I don't know how many able bodies we can round up, considering we lost so many to the morb," he explained, releasing me from his tight grip. "But we will do the best we can."

"Thank you, Neural."

While Neural offered more jewels, in my peripheral vision, I caught Divad take Silas off to the side. With my curiosity piqued, I strained to hear their discussion, but the distance was too great.

Silas wants to know everything about you but has secret conversations with Magisters?

My jaw tightened before I joined the others.

At the opening of the cave, Claire pointed at the height of the sun. "How much longer are we going to stay here?"

"I'm sure they'll be done soon," James comforted her. Claire scoffed, rolling her eyes.

Lord Farmount was the farthest one away, standing outside the cave near the cliff's edge. His back was to us as he faced the Shalley Mountains. It was the first time he had been uncharacteristically quiet, and then I remembered what he had said by the river. Were we really being followed?

Silas and Divad returned to where Neural and I stood.

"Ready?" Silas asked as he sauntered toward me. One hand was placed on the sword's hilt while the other's thumb hooked casually in his pocket. I sucked in my lips, trying to keep my jaw from dropping as I memorized every feature on him. I didn't remember Silas being so handsome and confident.

"Yes," I breathed, turning away so he wouldn't notice my embarrassment.

He angled his head. "Are you okay?"

Not trusting my words, I nodded and hurried to the mouth of the cave.

"Finally!" Claire said, throwing her hands up. "I lived in the darkness for too many years. I'm ready to get out into the light again." She joined Lord Farmount outside, followed by James. Silas went next. Before I left, I turned to face the two Magisters one last time.

"We will be there when you need us," Divad said firmly, placing a fist over his mended heart before he bowed.

"How will you know when I need you?"

A ball of light popped from his fingertips, and the sparks immediately spun toward me. The strength of the power raced through my heart. Divad closed his palm and placed his hand by his side, dissolving the light.

"We are connected by our iuram. Until we fulfill our oath or die, we will be connected to you."

Neural gave me a reassuring smile and led me to everyone else. "Be careful, Bellata."

As we strode away from the Magisters, our group was quiet. Whether from exhaustion or astonishment, I wasn't sure. Although my lips were silent, my thoughts were whirring, unable to forget Divad's warning: the coming Lands would not be as kind.

CHAPTER 18

As soon as I forgot about it, the ticking returned. But this time it was different. Its ring was louder and faster than before. Was it warning me of something coming? The loud tick-tock blurred my vision, elevating my anxiety as I tried to focus on not falling off the side of the mountain. Ahead, Silas led the group. His shoulders were hunched, and his strides were long and hard. Something was bothering him. It had to be what Divad had said to him.

The ticking rattled through my mind, and my foot slipped. I saw the bottom of the mountain coming into view before I was jerked back.

"Keep your head, Adelaide," Lord Farmount scolded, clenching my forearm. He didn't release me until I found my footing.

"Thank you," I said, scurrying past the edge and onto safer ground.

Just then, a bolt of blue light shot the rock beside us, shattering it to pieces.

"Duck!" Silas yelled before we all dove to the ground.

Lord Farmount breathed softly beside me; his arm wrapped protectively around my shoulders as we waited. Shards of gravel bit into my face as we pushed ourselves into the ground. I risked a glance at Claire and James, who were huddled in the dirt, but I couldn't find Silas.

Tendrils of terror punctured my thoughts, and I lifted my head higher, trying to find him.

"Keep your head down," Lord Farmount hissed, pressing his arm into my shoulder blades.

I wriggled out of his grasp. "I can't see Silas. I need to make sure he's okay."

Shimmying on the ground, I made it behind another boulder. I squinted, peeking around it. A body with a head of blond hair was curled on the ground, motionless. The pebbles surrounding me scattered beneath my boot as I jumped up and sprinted to Silas. His hand clutched his left arm as his body convulsed violently. Who had struck him? And why?

"Silas, Silas look at me," I said as I knelt beside him, holding his face in my hands. Though my vision was still blurred, that blue lightning looked exactly like the blonde woman's from the cages in Barracks.

Silas turned his head toward me, his pupils dilating, expanding until his irises were consumed by black. Was he going to lash out again?

"A-A-Ad—" he stammered.

Lightning burned the ground next to me, and I screamed, lunging out of the way. I glanced over my shoulder. Standing on the landing not forty yards away was the blonde woman from Ophidian's Realm.

James ran and stood between the woman and us, gripping his axe. In a few moments, she sent another bolt, and he deflected it.

"Can we move him?" James asked.

I placed my hands on the sides of Silas's face. "I'm here, Silas." My pulse thundered between my ears. "Can you move?"

Slowly, Silas moved his hand away from his arm. The heat from the lightning singed away the sleeve of his sweater, revealing a large, white scar carved into his skin. Running from his shoulder all the way to his fingertips, it was as if the actual bolt had lodged itself into Silas's arm. Sparks of blue scattered off his arm as another bolt crackled above.

Static clung to the air around us as the woman unleashed a rain of lightning. James shielded us from as many bolts as he could, but there were too many.

"We need to get out of here!" Claire yelled, darting away from the lightning. A large bolt hit right where she had been, and she screamed, dashing to my side.

"Run!" I told her, motioning to James. "We'll be right behind you."

Claire quickly grabbed James's arm before they fled from the lightning.

"Silas." I gently shook him, trying to get a response.

"Silas, I'm going to try to carry you, okay? I don't know if I can lift you alone. Can you walk? I need you to help me. You're going to be okay." His eyes rolled back as his body continued to jerk.

Adrenaline pumped through my veins as I slung his uninjured arm around my neck. I stumbled under Silas's weight when he let out a groan. Turning, I found Lord Farmount grasping Silas's waist and slinging his other arm around his own neck. Why was he helping me?

"I told you we were being followed," Lord Farmount muttered. He glanced at me and scowled. "What? It looked like you needed a hand."

The air grew heavy, charged with another lightning storm. The bolts danced around us, practically singeing our feet as we ran. The ticking grew louder in my mind, pulsating with vigor. My vision blurred around the edges, making it nearly impossible to see. Panic lodged in my chest as I gasped for air. What was happening to me? Had time run out? Had I already failed?

The sound of rushing water flowed from just ahead. The Flum River. I remembered reading a report from *The Barracks Conversation* of a man that had been struck by lightning while swimming. His lifeless body was found, floating in the murky water. An electric bolt snapped at my heels. Lightning and water never mixed well, so, maybe, if we could make it across, the blonde woman wouldn't be able to follow us.

As we neared the river, Claire and James stood at its

edge, staring at the harsh, choppy waves. The waters had elevated, gushing faster and deadlier than before.

"Any ideas of how to cross?" I asked.

Claire shook her head. "I was hoping you would know."

Another bolt struck a few meters away. I bit my nails, trying to think of a solution when a cold power tugged at my heart.

"Take Silas." I motioned to Claire before I reached into the satchel and grabbed Eman's book. My vision immediately cleared as I opened the glowing pages. A new text emerged on the page.

All that glitters is not gold
Give, and the river will do as it is told

I gritted my teeth, vowing to demand a book from Eman that was more straight forward. A streak of blue flashed next to me, and I jumped away.

Slamming the book shut, I pressed it against my forehead and shut my eyes, trying to ignore the insistent ticking piercing my brain. Give. Give what? What did I have to give?

I breathed deeply as another bolt zapped, causing Lord Farmount to let out a string of curses.

"He's okay," Claire deadpanned.

Ignoring the comment, I opened my eyes and searched through my satchel. There had to be something to help us in there. As I moved aside another bottle of Claire's green salve, something twinkled. Next to a bundle of linkslock was the bag full of crystals Neural had given us from the Dunsque caves.

"'All that glitters is not gold,'" I mumbled before taking out a ruby.

We didn't have any gold, just jewels. Hoping the ruby was enough, I sent a quick prayer to the Heavens before tossing the glittering crystal into the churning rapids. The waters immediately calmed, and square, gray stones rose from the surface. The stones connected to one another, forming a bridge.

I dropped my hands to my sides, still clutching the book. It worked.

Another bolt landed too close to James.

"Get across!" I yelled. Claire and Lord Farmount darted across, carrying Silas between them. James ran to follow but stopped halfway.

"Hurry, Addie!" he yelled. His eyes were wild as he looked over my shoulder. The bolts were hitting closer.

I started toward the river's edge but stopped. My heart pulsed, recognizing a strong power behind me. Balling my hands into fists, I turned and faced the blonde woman from the Seven Choices.

CHAPTER 19

"*A*ddie!" James screamed again, but my boiling blood muted his words.

I focused on the woman in front of me. How did she find us?

An arrogant grin split her red lips as she twirled a bolt of lightning between her slender fingers.

"Did you miss me?" she purred, her voice smooth as silk. "I know *someone* who did." She flicked her blue eyes in Silas's direction as she toyed with the yellow gem around her throat.

Silas dancing with this woman, holding her close, flashed in my memory. A growl rumbled in my throat, but I swallowed it.

No, it wasn't real.

Are you sure?

Another memory, the one where Silas and this woman had a happy life together, stabbed my heart.

It wasn't real.

Positive?

But *this* woman was real. Did that mean other things in the Seven Choices were real, too? Did Silas have a relationship with her? An image of Silas embracing this woman and kissing her created an emerald shade over my vision. I blinked it away, squashing the jealousy. Focus, Addie.

My chest warmed, my fingers twitching as I took a step closer. "Leave us alone."

Blue sparks rattled off the woman's fingertips as she pointed her black nails at me. "I don't answer to you, Bellata." Her lips curled in disgust as she flung her bolt at me.

I ducked out of the way, and the bolt impaled the ground, leaving a gaping hole. I didn't have a chance to get far before another bolt stung my foot, melting my boot's side.

Burnt rubber pierced my nose. Through the hole, I could see that my foot hadn't been too badly injured. My hands heated, and my fingers gleamed with the same orange glow as before. I thrust them at the woman before running toward the river.

The jewel from Dunsque must have had a time limit because the waters of the Flum were no longer serene, but fierce and wild.

A high-pitched screech erupted from the woman before more bolts crackled, their heat radiating against my back. I prayed Lyle's sweater hadn't been burned.

Lunging, I landed on the first stone of the bridge, but it started to sink.

Scrambling, I raced across the other stones that swayed in the raging waters. Another blue bolt hit the waves next to me, and the river reacted—a large wave filled with the crackling electric power. A whirlpool spiraled before rising up, hovering over the blonde woman.

I leapt off the final stone and crashed face-first into the gravelly shore. Spitting out sand and pebbles, I turned and watched the wave rise higher and higher, before crashing into the woman. Her screams became garbled by the suffocating water, and the current washed her down the river, away from us.

My muscles melted in relief, and I rolled on my back, thanking the Heavens I was still alive.

"Addie, come quick!"

Claire and James tended to Silas's motionless body while Lord Farmount stood close by. I jumped up, ignoring the stabbing pain in my chest and rushed over. There were no longer blue sparks radiating off the scar on Silas's arm, but his skin had started to turn a deathly white, like the victims of the morb.

"He just stopped shaking," Claire said. "His pulse is slowing. I don't know …" The wrinkle between her brows deepened as she examined the woman's brand on Silas's arm. "I can probably relieve the burning, but I'm not sure what else to do."

I grabbed my satchel and rummaged through it,

remembering the additional supplies Eman had packed. I shoved various jars around. I had no idea what any of these were or how to use them.

James bent down and pressed two fingers on the white scar. Silas's arm jerked as he wailed.

I furiously dumped everything out of my satchel. Tinctures and herbs scattered along the ground, rolling as I spread them out.

"What do these do?" I asked, holding out one jar filled with small orange berries and another filled with dried pink petals. "Will they help?"

"He needs salebra," James said, standing. "It's red and looks like crushed leaves."

I threw jars out of the way, trying to find the right one.

"Silas's pulse has slowed," James continued calmly. "If it doesn't return to normal soon, his heart will stop altogether."

"What?" Claire and I gasped. James nodded quickly and motioned to Claire's satchel before he rolled up his sleeves. "It's probably with Claire's things. She's our healer."

I buried my nails in my palms as I watched Claire rummage through her bag. I prayed to the Heavens Eman had packed us what we needed, until she held out a clear bottle filled with red flakes.

"What are you going to do with it?" Claire questioned as she handed it to James, appearing more fascinated by the medicinal practice than the fact that Silas's heart wasn't beating.

"He needs to save Silas with it," I snapped.

"Calm down, Addie," Claire bit back.

James closed Claire's hands around the bottle. "I'm not going to do anything. You are."

"What?" Claire and I shrieked.

James nodded. "Claire, Eman made *you* the healer, not me." He turned to me. "Silas will be fine, Addie. His story doesn't end here."

I jerked back, surprised at his words.

"Get water from the river. Quickly," he instructed Claire, holding out a metal cup.

Claire jumped up and sprinted to the river's edge before returning with a full cup of water.

"Now, open the bottle and place three leaves in your palm." Claire obeyed. "Crush them until they are a fine powder," James instructed.

When the salebra was a fine dust, Claire lifted her head, her brows rising.

"Wait, I remember this. Sana taught me about this herb back in Ramni." She angled her head toward James. "Thanks for the help, 'Grandpa.'"

James grunted, then grinned as he stepped out of the way.

Claire dipped two of her fingers in the water, carefully dripping three drops onto the powder in her palm. A purple smoke rose from the red powder with a hiss.

"Addie, take the rest of his shirt off," Claire said.

I quickly peeled the remnants of Silas's scorched sweater over his head, exposing his translucent skin. Dark veins pulsed beneath the surface. His brows were bunched tight, as if he was still being struck by the bolts that branded his body. Claire cleared her throat, and I scurried out of the way, backing into Lord Farmount's chest. His hand came down on my shoulder, and I turned to see his lips downturned as he watched Claire work.

In one fluid motion, Claire rubbed the paste between her hands, then slammed them onto Silas's chest. Silas's body jolted as a red light glowed under his skin.

"What's happening?" I cried, clutching Lord Farmount's arm. The lord winced but gently placed his gloved hand over mine.

Claire slammed her hands into Silas's chest again. Another red light illuminated his veins. Claire waited a few moments, analyzing Silas's body through narrowed lids. Nothing happened. Dread crept under my skin as we waited. Lord Farmount grunted but cleared his throat to cover it as he peeled my fingers from his arm. He threaded his gloved fingers through mine and held my hand.

Silas let out a deep gasp, his back arching off the ground. Then he relaxed, his chest rising and falling in a peaceful rhythm.

Claire waited a few moments before she lifted her arms in the air. "He's alive!" After brushing her hands together, she returned the salebra to her bag. "I guess all those months with those annoying plants paid off after all." She pulled out a roll of bandages and secured them around Silas's arm.

"Great work," James said, clapping her on the back.

I quickly threw myself on top of Silas, not caring that he was still injured. I couldn't imagine him not being in my life. He groaned but managed to wrap his warm arm around my back.

"What happened?" he asked warily.

Tears streamed down my face as I breathed in his earthy scent. Resting my head on his chest, I watched the rosy color return to his skin while listening to the steady beat of his half-heart.

"I thought I lost you."

"It's a good thing Grandpa helped me remember what to do, or you would've been a goner," Claire said from behind us.

James chuckled from where he was washing his hands in the river. I sat up and placed an arm under Silas's back, easing him into a sitting position.

"Thank you, Claire and James," Silas said, glancing up at them. He placed his hand on his adjacent bicep, squeezing it as he winced. "I owe you two my life,"

"Claire did it all." James gestured to our healer before scanning the river. He studied the rippling waves. I followed his line of sight, expecting to find the blonde woman waiting for us. But only the sparkling water winked back.

"Who was she?" I asked.

With a huff, James sat down next to Silas. He unbuttoned his shirt, revealing a second one underneath, before holding out the green and black plaid.

"Thank you," Silas said and took it, taking care to mind his injured arm.

Not willing to meet my gaze, James said, "Her name is Dacenda. She's been with Ophidian for many years." He cast a glance at me, opening his mouth to say more, but clamped his lips shut.

He's hiding something.

I studied the concern in his ice-blue eyes. "James, what's wrong?" Was he hiding something about Silas and Dacenda? Did they really have a relationship?

Rubbing his hand over his scruffy chin, James stood abruptly. "Farmount was right. We were being followed." He glanced over to where the lord was standing at the edge of the river, filling up a leather sack with water. "We can't stay out here tonight. We're completely exposed. And now that Dacenda knows where you are, we'll have the malum tracking us wherever we go." James motioned to Silas. "You need to rest and not put any additional stress on your heart."

Standing, I laid the pages of the book flat and waited. The invisible quill returned, sketching the Flum River on the outer edge of the page before drawing trees.

"It looks like there's a small forest not far from here," I said, turning to Silas. Though he was upright, his skin was still incredibly pale, and dark rings layered his eyes. My heart wrenched as I stretched out my hand. "Do you think you can make it?"

Silas gave me a weak smile in response. He grabbed my hand and stood slowly, trying not to let out a painful groan, but failed. I kept my hold on him until James gently separated our palms.

"Addie, you need to lead the way," James said, walking next to Silas. "I'll make sure Silas is fine."

I bit my lip, glancing between the two of them.

"I'll be fine, Addie," Silas said, trying to cover his weary face with a grin. "We'll only be a few feet behind."

"Okay." I hesitated before brushing a strand of his hair out of his eyes. "But if you're tired or need to rest, you better tell me."

"Come on," Claire groaned, taking me by the arm. "I don't want to be here when Blondie comes back."

CHAPTER 20

As Claire and I led the group, Silas and James followed, softly murmuring behind us. It took every ounce of self-control I had not to slow down to listen. First Divad, now James? What were they all talking about? Wasn't *I* the Bellata?

More secrets.

Trying to tame my curiosity, I attempted to start a conversation with Claire and Lord Farmount.

"So, how are you guys doing?"

Claire knotted her fingers in her hair as she twisted the snowy strands into a perfect braid. She flicked it behind her back. "I'm too tired to talk." Giving me a half-apologetic shrug, she purposefully lagged behind.

Lord Farmount kept his face forward and said nothing.

Taking my chances, I turned to the lord. "I haven't said thank you yet, Lord Farmount."

He gave me a sidelong glance, then turned his face up front once more. "For what?"

"For trying to warn us about Dacenda and for helping me with Silas." I couldn't help being excited to have someone to distract me from my own thoughts. "And for helping save all those people in Barracks. You didn't have to do that."

And for holding my hand when I was terrified for Silas, I wanted to add.

He kept his face forward as he fiddled with the ends of the knives on his belt. "No, I didn't. I got trampled in Wintertide, remember?" He snorted. "But you also didn't have to risk your life to save everyone in Barracks and Dunsque, did you?"

I hesitated. "No, I guess not."

"So, why did you?"

I started. No one had asked me that. "Because I was supposed to." I reached down and trailed my fingers along the map. "Because they needed me."

Lord Farmount said nothing before grabbing one of his knives and twirling it between his fingers as we walked. He was silent for a few moments longer before asking, "What if they don't need you? What if they don't want you?"

Good questions.

I watched him flip the knife in the air and catch it. There was no way this was the same man who had invited me to join his harem over a year ago. "What do you mean?"

He pointed the blade ahead. "Let's say this next Land is like Dunsque and Trefair, where something terrible has happened." He waved the knife around before pointing it at me. "What if they don't want your help? What will you do then?"

I stopped, taking in the tops of a cluster of oak trees rustling in the evening breeze. What *would* I do? I had never considered that the Magisters wouldn't want my help.

The lord turned and quirked a brow.

Lowering the map, I stared down at my melted boot. "I don't know."

Lord Farmount's laugh startled me, and I jerked my head up.

"At least you're honest." He waved his hand with another chuckle. "Come on."

He has a great smile, doesn't he?

I hurried beside him. "What would you do?" The question sprang from my lips, surprising me. I didn't want my conversation with Lord Farmount to end.

He pointed the tip of his knife to his chest, his emerald eyes wide in mock surprise. "Me? Adelaide, you have me all wrong if you think I would help all those people. I would leave the first chance I got."

"You helped all the people of Barracks, and you warned us about being followed, *and* you helped Silas." I leaned over and nudged his shoulder. "That sounds like helping to me."

Lord Farmount grunted as he secured his knife back on his belt. "I'll make sure not to next time."

We strode side by side in silence until a new question tumbled from my mouth: "Lord Farmount, what did you trade your heart for?"

The lord kicked a rock, sending it rolling to the right. "Why do you want to know?"

"You still have all of your emotions, but no heart."

He growled, toeing another stone. "Can a man not feel when he wants?"

"You know what I mean, Lord Farmount."

"You don't have to keep calling me that."

I pushed a stone toward him with the side of my foot, noting he had ignored another one of my comments. "What?"

His lips quirked at the offered pebble. "Lord Farmount."

"Isn't that your name?" I asked drily.

"I think we're past formalities by now," he said flatly. He held out his hand. "Damien."

As we approached the edge of the trees, we slowed down, allowing Claire, James, and Silas to catch up. I grasped his hand. "It's nice to meet you, Damien."

Damien shook my hand before crossing his arms over his chest. "You as well, Adelaide."

The sun started to set, painting an array of pinks, purples, and oranges across the sky. If we weren't trying to hide from a madwoman with malum, I might have enjoyed it.

As Silas and James shuffled near, Silas eyed Damien with suspicion, noting how close the lord and I were standing. Guilt spun inside me.

"We need to find shelter," I said, avoiding Silas. "We don't have much daylight left."

"I'll collect branches for a fire," Damien offered. A softened expression rolled over his face before he disappeared into the trees.

"Claire and I will join you," James called after him. Not allowing any opposition, James motioned to Claire, then stalked through the trees.

Claire let out an exaggerated sigh. "My feet are screaming at me to stop. I just want to lay down."

"The sooner you get firewood, the sooner you'll rest," James called from the forest, causing me to snicker as Claire stomped through the trees.

As soon as they were out of sight, Silas's hand gripped my own and spun me around. Before I could react, his lips landed on mine. A cool sensation passed through my body before it ignited every cell. His strong arms wrapped around my waist, holding me close. My chest warmed, my desire for him growing as I draped my arms around his neck and ran my fingers through his thick hair.

After a few moments, we broke apart, and Silas pressed his forehead against mine.

"I thought you were injured," I said, between breaths, trying to rein in my excitement. "What was that for?"

"Just clarifying," he said.

I brushed my lips against his cheek. "Clarifying what?"

Silas shuddered under the kiss before stepping away. He grabbed my hand, interlocking our fingers. "We should probably start looking for shelter. Claire will punish us both if she doesn't have somewhere to sleep."

Laughing, I followed him into the trees.

Fallen branches and foliage crackled beneath our feet as we searched through the forest. Eman's book had led us here, so there had to be shelter somewhere.

Craning our necks, we discovered a cleaned-out area surrounded by thick trees. It was as if someone had molded the trees into a dome-like shape specifically for us.

Silas and I removed the remaining brush before we heard the others.

Throwing her branches to the ground, Claire flopped to the dirt. "It feels like we've been walking for years. My blisters have blisters." She took off her boots and rubbed her feet.

"Stop complaining," Damien said, placing his branches next to hers before he began tenting them for a fire. "It hasn't been that long."

"Says the guy who complains about everything," Claire scoffed. She took out the metal cup, herbs, and a flask of water.

Damien finished tenting the sticks with a growl.

"Addie"—Claire turned to ignore him—"make sure Silas drinks his tea." She took a small, yellow sack out of her satchel. Opening the pleats, Claire swallowed the whole bag of nuts and berries before laying down and lacing her fingers behind her head. She then stretched out her long legs, crossed her ankles, and closed her eyes. Her breaths soon deepened into a sweet slumber.

In a huff, Damien relocated to the opposite side of the shelter, analyzing the trees first before finally settling on the ground.

"They're perfect company," James grumbled, following behind them as he rubbed his palms together. White light soon emerged, igniting the wood. "When one's not complaining, the other is. If you're real lucky, they'll both start complaining at the same time."

I burst out laughing, never having seen James so frustrated before. James peered up at me, exhaustion rimming the new wrinkles around his eyes.

"You're amazing to have dealt with both of them," I chuckled, sitting down next to him.

The warmth of the flames seeped through the fibers of Lyle's old sweater. I pulled my knees to my chest and wrapped my arms around them, attempting to hold in the heat as long as I could.

Leaning back, James cracked his neck before scrubbing his hands over his face. I glanced over at him, now noticing his age. Though he physically didn't look any older, the shadows growing under his eyes said the opposite.

"You doing okay?" I asked.

"Don't worry about me," he replied gruffly. He plucked a few pieces of dried meat from his satchel before yawning.

"Why don't you rest," Silas suggested, taking a seat next to me. "Addie and I will keep a lookout for anything."

James chewed slowly, watching us suspiciously before giving in. "All right, but wake me if you see or hear anything. Understand?"

We nodded obediently.

Satisfied, James slumped to the area between Claire and Damien and laid down.

Once I saw the steady breathing of his chest, I couldn't contain my anticipation any longer. Scooting closer to Silas, I whispered, "What were you guys talking about earlier?"

Stoking the fire, Silas raised his brows, a flicker of mischief gleaming in his eyes. "Stuff."

Taking the bait, I moved closer to him until our knees touched. "What kind of stuff?"

He waited a moment until his lips curled.

I crossed my arms over my chest. "Are you going to tell me or not?

Silas laughed. "There were some things I wanted to ask him, and some things he wanted to tell me, that's all."

"The same things Divad wanted to tell you, too?"

He worked his jaw, keeping his attention on the fire. "Sometimes, I wish you weren't so curious."

With questions overflowing, I wanted to drill him for further information. But when I saw his stooped posture and distant look, my chest ached, heavy with grief. I had seen that look before; it was the same one Eman had. It was as if Silas had to carry a thousand burdens, and I couldn't lift one for him.

More secrets.

"Silas," I said, placing my hand on his arm. "I understand that you want to keep this to yourself, but it's clearly bothering you. What's wrong?"

Avoiding eye contact, Silas poked the fire once more before answering. "There's just a lot I forgot while I was in Barracks." He gave me a weary smile as if his troubles were nothing.

"I know there's something you're not telling me," I began to say, but Silas cut me off.

"I know there are things you haven't told me, either." His voice was sharper than the blade he carried.

I pulled my hand back at the harsh tone. Steady Silas had never spoken to me like that.

He's not Steady Silas anymore.

Silas's fingers gripped tightly around the stick he was holding. His breathing became heavy as his eyes darkened.

I scampered away from him. Why did these episodes keep happening?

After a few moments, the muscles in his back relaxed, and his hand with the stick fell to his side. Silas's throat bobbed, and he sniffed as if he were trying to hold back tears.

Keeping my distance, I decided to try a calmer approach. "Ophidian's Realm was hell."

Silas slowly turned toward me, a dark fog covering his

eyes. The hairs on my neck stood on end as fear punctured my thoughts. What was happening to him? He resembled Claire when Ophidian took over her body in the Seven Choices. Is that what was happening to Silas?

I wrapped my arms around my stomach and stared into the fire. "If it wasn't for Claire and Eman, I would be dead."

Focusing on me, Silas's chestnut irises reappeared, the fog lifting. Good, my new approach was working.

"I made it through the first few doors with only physical injuries," I continued. "But I left the Fourth Choice completely broken."

Silas's eyes fully cleared, and he blinked, closing the gap between us. "What happened?"

My neck grew hot, and I started drawing in the dirt, trying to hide my embarrassment. "You were there," I said, creating a lonely stick figure in the earth. "Well, it wasn't you. But I didn't know that until after."

"Until after what?"

I wanted to crawl inside my sweater and never come out. "Me and you, well, not you, but the creature that looked like you were ... closer than we've ever physically been." I risked a look at Silas to find him staring at me with raised brows. "But I took care of it," I said quickly, glancing toward the dancing flames again. "And then my heart broke, literally."

Silas was silent before asking, "How did you take care of it?"

I rubbed my neck, trying not to remember the pain I

endured during that door. Taking the stick Silas had used, I poked it into the fire.

"You were very demanding," I said quietly. "And were going to make me do something I didn't want to do. At that point, I knew it wasn't you, so I took care of it."

"How?"

I turned away, not wanting to see his response. "I killed you."

For several minutes, only the sound of crackling flames stifled the silence. Then, Silas asked, "Really?"

The genuine shock in his voice took me aback, and I whipped my head around. Staring back at me were two clear, focused eyes, not filled with revulsion or horror, but utter surprise and possibly admiration. Why wasn't he horrified?

"Yes, really," I spat, pressing my palms against my knees. "But I almost killed myself in the process."

"Whoa, whoa." Silas put his hands up in surrender, trying to hold back a laugh. "Calm down." He studied my palms, which were glowing orange again.

Seeing them glow orange made me angrier. Couldn't I feel without there being a consequence?

"Addie," Silas said gently, grasping one of my hands. The orange light rolled between his fingers but didn't harm him. He carefully caressed the top of my hand with his thumb until the light disappeared, and I found myself leaning into his side. "You did what you had to do. And obviously, you were right, because here I am. Alive." He motioned to himself with his adorable crooked smile.

I pursed my lips, trying to stop my grin, but it didn't work.

"Ah, there she is." Silas's face grew serious. "I know that was hard for you, but think about it this way: if you hadn't killed 'me' then, you wouldn't have gotten through the last Choices to get to Lyle. Sometimes a sacrifice has to be made for a better outcome."

More secrets.

I studied his solemn expression closely, and although I nodded in agreement, I couldn't help but think he was talking about something else.

Silas stroked my hand, sending chills up my arm. "Why don't you get some rest? I'll keep watch for a while, then wake the lord," he said, motioning toward snoring Damien.

I chuckled and squeezed his hand before grabbing my blanket and a bag of dried berries out of my satchel. Standing, I padded to the vacant area next to James.

As I munched on the berries, I wrapped my blanket around myself and laid on the cool ground. My mind replayed my conversation with Silas, and I realized he hadn't told me anything at all. I ran a hand along my hair as I stared up into the trees. Maybe now that I shared some of what I went through, Silas would share more with me. My heart gave a thud, hoping it was true.

As my eyelids fluttered closed, the point of a blade pricked my spine.

CHAPTER 21

I opened my mouth to scream, but a gloved hand clamped over my lips.

"Make the slightest sound, and I'll kill you all," a commanding voice whispered in my ear.

The tip of the blade dug deeper into my lower back, and I bit my tongue, restraining my cry. This couldn't be a Magister like in the caves before, could it? We weren't anywhere close to the next Land. I tried to calm the racing palpitations thundering in my chest.

"Very good," the voice continued, removing his hand. "Now, grab your bag and follow me."

I instantly felt the presence behind me leave, expecting to hear the twigs' rustling, but nothing stirred. I obeyed and stood, my knees trembling as I shuffled toward the fire where Silas and my satchel were. Hearing my steps, Silas blinked up at me, gripping the metal cup in his hand.

"Hey," he said with a soft smile, drowsiness touching his eyes before taking another sip of the tea. "Can't sleep?"

I mustered the best grin I could, but it fell short. My fingers twitched at my sides. Instead of answering, I nodded and reached for my satchel. Silas watched my shaking hands as I slung the strap over my shoulder.

"Going somewhere?"

"Um," I said, wishing he would just let me take my bag and leave. I didn't want to lie. But I would rather lie than find Silas dead.

"I have some … feminine things I need to take care of," I blurted out, watching his face turn from suspicion to embarrassment.

Silas rubbed the back of his neck and focused on the flames. "Oh, right, sorry."

If I wasn't lying right to his face, I would've laughed.

Clutching the satchel to my chest, I spun around and rushed into the trees, praying I didn't walk straight into the tip of a sword. After I few more steps, the deep voice spoke behind me.

"That took longer than expected."

"I didn't know there was a time limit." Snapping my lips shut, I closed my eyes and scrunched my shoulders, bracing myself for a quick kill. But to my surprise, a chuckle responded instead.

"Yes, I heard you had a mouth on you. Luckily, I came prepared for that."

The scraping of metal echoed off the trees, and I

stilled. I couldn't find the owner of the voice, but he had to be nearby.

The icy tip of a dagger pricked the skin at my throat as I searched the darkness. Moonlight glinted off a harsh, black blade. The hilt was black, as well, but lined with shined bronze. A black-gloved hand extended out of the darkness, not revealing more than an arm covered in gray material.

"Don't speak. Only nod," he commanded sternly. "Understand?"

Carefully, I nodded. The gloved hand slowly moved the dagger away from my throat before returning with an empty, open palm. "The crystals."

My skin tingled from where the blade had just been. "What?" I asked, gambling he wouldn't act on his threats.

"The crystals from the caves."

Pressing my luck, I asked, "Why do you want them?"

Before I could react, the fingers quickly locked around the dagger, and the blade pressed into my throat again. I winced as a small slice broke my skin, a thin trickle of blood dribbling down my neck.

"You sure do ask a lot of questions for someone whose life is on the line."

I stood like a statue, waiting. After a few moments, the hand faced open once more. "The crystals."

Without questioning again, I rummaged through the satchel, surprised to see that the book wasn't glowing as it usually did when I was in danger. Moving it aside, I found the blue leather pouch holding the crystals from Neural.

My stomach twisted as I grabbed the pouch and placed it in the gloved hand, praying we wouldn't need them anymore. The gloved fingers firmly grasped the pouch before slinking back into the shadows. Only a slight rustling of leaves sounded, suggesting the thief's departure.

I leaned against a nearby tree, my head sagging between my shoulders as I let out a shaky breath.

"We will meet again soon, Bellata." The voice carried through the leaves, echoing until it was only a whisper.

I whipped around but was only greeted by the sound of ticking fading into the dark forest.

I forced my wobbling legs to walk back to camp and quietly emerged from the trees. Silas was right where I left him by the fire, enchanted by its roaring flames. Thank the Heavens he didn't try to come check on me. Quietly, I laid on the ground, clutching the satchel to my chest, wondering how a thief in the night knew who I was.

~

Morning dawned, and the sun radiated on my skin, warming it from the coolness of night. As I cracked open an eye, James hurried past me. I opened the other and started to rise, letting out a groan, when my muscles refused to move. Grunting, I flung my arm from its place beneath me, a tingling sensation rushing through my veins as the blood returned. Carefully stretching, I realized I had curled my whole body around the satchel, protecting it just in case the thief returned.

"Hey," Silas said too cheerily as he approached.

I growled.

"Still not a morning person?" he asked with a laugh.

"Obviously, you still are," I grumbled back at him.

Black rings laid heavily under his bright eyes as if he hadn't slept in weeks. And though he smiled down at me, it seemed strained.

What is he hiding from you?

Silas chuckled again, extending his hand to me. Grumbling under my breath, I took it and stood, loving being so close to him, but hating the pain shooting down my spine. I let out another groan, shoving my fists into my lower back until it snapped like a twig breaking in half. Warm relief immediately quenched my sore back.

"I'm surprised you're not in two pieces," Silas said, grimacing at the sound.

Straightening, I grinned as I rolled up the sleeves to Lyle's sweater. The morning was pleasant and sunny, and I wanted to enjoy it. As I moved to the other sleeve, I wondered if I should tell everyone about the crystals and the thief. I thought back to how Eman's book hadn't glowed. Shrugging, I pushed the thief from my mind. If the book didn't find him dangerous, then I wouldn't either.

Now, who's keeping secrets?

As if in response to my decision, my satchel shuffled on the ground. Snatching it up, I grabbed the book. The pages fluttered with excitement as my hands folded open its cover. The invisible quill sketched the edge of the trees we were in. The map moved further west, showing a small village not far from where we were. At the top of the page, the lines stopped, indicating our next destination.

Still laying on the ground, Claire let out a loud yawn, stretching her lean arms above her head before flinging one over her eyes. "Where to now, oh, great leader?"

"Here," I said, offering the map to her.

She lifted her arm and squinted at the pages. When she couldn't read it from her position on the ground, Claire sat up, scrunching her freckled nose as she leaned in to study the page.

"Where's that?" Silas asked as he gathered our supplies.

"I don't know," I responded.

"Are we going to walk there?" Claire whined as she stood, undoing her long braid before whipping her hair up into its usually messy bun.

"I'm sure it's not too far," James encouraged, giving Claire a quick pat on the shoulder as he strapped on his bag.

"There's no other way to get there," Damien retorted at the same time, securing his pack across his chest. His emerald eyes scanned my face, and I found myself reaching to smooth my tangled curls again.

"Thank you, Grandpa," Claire said, cramming her vials of herbs into her bag. She slung it over her shoulder. "Unfortunately, the lord is right." She gave him a mock bow. "We must not dawdle for his majesty's sake."

I bit my lip, stifling my laughter. Damien mumbled a few curses under his breath and stalked away.

Once we erased all traces of our night in the forest, we followed the book to the next village. My legs ached with each step, but my mind was on full alert. If a thief in the night found me, that meant word was getting out about us. And if that were true, it was only a matter of time before Dacenda, or worse, Ophidian, came after us again.

Time is ticking.

As we breached the edge of the forest, our group came to a standstill in awe of the scene before us. A beautiful breeze twirled around us and onto the soft plains. Tall, yellow-green grass swayed in the delicate wind. It was so different from Barracks, so gentle and welcoming.

Soon, all grumblings from the hard night on the ground vanished as the sun kissed our faces. We threw jokes at each other as we waded into the plains. Even Damien offered a riddle or two.

My chest lightened as I admired everyone's cheerful faces. I couldn't remember the last time I watched the light sparkle across the grass or dance upon the dew-covered leaves. Maybe, one day, the old Barracks would return, and there would be warmth and happiness again. Maybe I would even consider returning there.

As we continued across the grassy plain in good spirits, a village made of gray stone cottages and thatched roofs came into view. Men and women roamed around their homes, running errands as average townsfolk.

"Welcome!" a cheery voice yelled as soon as we entered.

Everyone jumped. We all turned toward the portly man whose grin was a bit too wide.

"Welcome!" he repeated, skipping toward us. Silas tightened his grip around the sword but waited to unsheathe it.

As the man approached, he suddenly jerked to the right and hopped in a different direction.

"Welcome!" he shouted to another person walking by.

Goosebumps prickled my skin as we watched the man shouting at anything that crossed his path.

"That was weird," Claire said as she inched closer to James. She surveyed a group of children barking and running in circles like they were dogs chasing their tails. "Let's hurry up and find the Magister so we can get out of here."

"They have to be around here somewhere," I replied, taking slow, cautious steps through the village.

We passed a woman with mousey brown hair sitting among chickens with a bag of feed. Everything looked normal until she folded her arms to mimic wings and started pecking at the ground. As we hurried by, the chicken woman clucked at us, jabbing at Damien's foot with a wooden stake. He jerked away, grabbing two knives from his belt and pointing them at the woman before retreating.

"They know we don't belong," he hissed as he sheathed

his knives and started to strut like the chicken lady. "Try to blend in."

Claire's eyes went wide as she looked from me to Silas. "What does he expect us to do? Act crazy?" Silas and I shared a look. Claire's lips parted in disbelief. "You can't be serious."

I scratched my cheek. "It's not a bad idea."

Claire huffed but started jumping up and down, saying, "Hi!" to everyone. Silas spun around and walked backwards while I hopped on the ground like a frog.

"This is ridiculous," Silas murmured as we moved along.

Keeping my distance from a lady talking to a tree, I glanced around to find James. I hoped these odd people hadn't done something to him.

A few men and women stood around a well in the center of the village. They hastily waved their hands as they spoke, engrossed in their conversation. But as we drew near, I heard not one conversation, but several with the same lines being repeated.

"Nice weather we're having. Nice weather we're having. Nice weather we're having."

"And she had six eggs. Six! And she had six eggs. Six! And she had six eggs. Six!"

"I don't know. He doesn't seem like good folk. I don't know. He doesn't seem like good folk. I don't know. He doesn't seem like good folk."

Silas grabbed my wrist, pulling me up before leading

me in a far circle around the people; the others were not far behind.

"Addie, this place is really creeping me out." He monitored each person of the village. "Any idea where the Magister would be?"

Reaching into my satchel, I grasped the book once more, hoping for a new destination. But as I opened the cover, the same map laid flat before me.

"It hasn't drawn anything different," I said, rifling through the pages. "Just the same map."

The warm breeze blew by again, pushing my hair in my face. As I tucked it around my ear, I paused. The chattering and clucking had vanished, but the silence spoke volumes. An uneasy sensation crept up my neck, and I forced my gaze up. With unnaturally round eyes and gaping mouths, the villagers had surrounded us.

CHAPTER 22

"I told you to blend in," Damien scolded, slowly moving until he stood next to Claire, knives grasped in each hand.

"Are they going to eat us?" Claire whispered, backing up behind Damien.

White foam bubbled from the townspeople's lips, pouring out of their mouths, and sizzling once it reached the ground.

"It's as if they've lost their sanity. Addie," Silas said out of the corner of his mouth. "Ideas?"

Before I could think, the people charged. All I had time to yell was, "Run!"

We set off in different directions. Snarls and growls erupted from the rabid people as they split and chased after us. Panic clawed my throat when I barely escaped the grasp of the "Welcome!" man. Damien ran by with feroc-

226

ity, trying to lose the chicken woman, and Silas and Claire were fending off the people from the well.

"Help!" Claire cried, using her satchel to whack the man who had been talking about eggs.

"We don't want to hurt them," Silas said, untying his sheathed sword from his belt and using it to push back the howling children nipping at his heels. "They probably aren't aware of what's happening."

Claire smacked the egg man in the face with her bag, and he spun to the ground. "I'll hurt him if he tries to bite me again."

"Claire, look out!" Damien cried as the chicken lady launched herself at Claire.

Claire's high-pitched shriek pierced the air before Damien interceded. The chicken lady clamped down on his forearm, foam bubbling from her lips as she sank her teeth into Damien's forearm.

"Get off of him!" I yelled.

The village people had surrounded my friends. I had to do something. I sprinted to the well, when a hand grabbed my own, yanking me into one of the cottages.

I screamed as the door slammed behind me. I didn't want one of those things to bite me. Spinning around, I held up my fists, ready to attack whatever lunatic had grabbed me. But the familiar face of James greeted me.

"James," I breathed.

"I think I know where the Magister is," James said, searching around the cottage. The wooden floor was scattered with yellow, gray, and white papers. But that didn't distract me from the floor-to-ceiling bookshelves that lined the walls. Each book was perfectly intact and arranged by color. In front of them was a rainbow of plush chairs.

"Where? We don't even know where we are."

"We're in Valde," James replied. "Asenav should be around here somewhere."

Before I could reply, a crash came from upstairs. James grabbed my hand, pulling me back against the door as he stood in front of me. Slow, even steps padded down the wooden stairwell as elegant golden slippers came into view.

Holding my breath, I gazed at a woman cloaked in a dark-blue robe lined with golden leaves. Her hair was wild with blonde curls bouncing around her head like a halo. Although her pupils were large, there was no foam falling from her lips. Yet.

"Dimitte," she said cheerily with an elegant smile. "What are you doing here?"

James took a step forward. "Asenav," he breathed with relief. "We need your help."

The Magister furrowed her thin brows, then replied, "Dimitte, what are you doing here?"

The same eerie feeling crept up my spine as cold sweat dripped down my temple.

The Magister's face contorted in pain. "Dimitte, what are yo—" She let out a scream, bending forward, and I jumped back. Panting, she glanced up, her face in pain. "The doors. Destroy the doors." She screamed again before she snapped straight. The cheery look came back to her face as she said, "Dimitte, what are you doing here?"

An aura from the upper level of the cottage tugged at my heart. Cautiously, I followed the pull and crept to the stairs, aware of Asenav watching me. Her pupils dilated before returning to normal size.

"The ticking. It won't stop," she said in a panicked voice. She took a step toward me. "Don't you hear it? Don't you hear the ticking?" She placed her palms on her temples, folding forward once more. "Tick. Tick. Tick. Tick." She focused on me, with tears in her dark-blue eyes. "Make it stop. Please, make it stop."

I took a step back, my thoughts reeling at her words. The strength and pain of the clock in my head was merciless. I hated that someone else was suffering from it, too.

"I will," I replied, trying not to worry about whether the ticking would make me turn rabid, too.

I took another step, and Asenav's stance turned predator, her wide eyes focused on me. Her pupils dilated again, and foam trickled out of her mouth.

"Addie," James said slowly, white light forming on his palms. "Run."

Without hesitating, I raced up the stairs, the snarls of Asenav roaring behind me. Reaching the top step, I paused as a harsh pain jolted through my heart. I slammed into the wall. Groaning, I struggled against the heavy pressure weighing me down, my back creaking as if it would snap. Finally, I collapsed to my knees, my head throbbing.

Straining to open my eyes, I saw a flash of red and hissed. It was those doors. Again. Another jolt seared my heart. I thrashed about, desperate to make the pain stop. A crash thundered from downstairs, warning me I was losing time.

Digging my nails into the palms of my hand, I dug into the satchel, grasping the book, my only hope. But as I opened the pages, I found them blank.

"Addie!" James yelled up the stairs as quick, efficient footsteps bounced upon the wood.

As I glanced over my shoulder, I gasped. Asenav towered above me, her beautiful face contorted into a snarl. In one hand, she brandished a deadly mace. Foam bubbled around her mouth as she growled.

There was no escape. I dragged my body upright, trapped between the madwoman and the doors. Then, the ticking returned.

Asenav lunged at me. Hurling my body to the right, I barely avoided losing my head. Of course, with the horrible throbbing from the ticking, part of me wished for anything to stop the pain.

The doors screeched open, the force of the shockwave driving both of us to the floorboards. Asenav writhed, screaming like a mindless animal. Crawling away from her, I fought to think straight.

This was just like the morb. An illness, probably from the doors. This couldn't be Asenav, not the *real* Asenav. As she threw back her head and howled, I felt sick. It was as if she had lost sight of who she was, losing all sanity.

'Lost their sanity,' I thought, remembering what Silas had said. But what would make her remember who she was?

From downstairs, I could hear James struggling. More of the rabid must have invaded the home. I coughed and pulled myself back to my feet. If I didn't do something soon, I could lose James and the others.

Just like I almost lost Lyle.

Lyle. Rubbing my fingers across the loose threads of the sleeves, I glanced at the sweater. Seeing Asenav so helpless, so weak, was just like witnessing Lyle losing all his memories. Losing his sanity.

Then, it hit me. Memories. Memories were the threads that stitched our lives together. That connected us to each other. And, as memories unraveled, so did the very fabric of our minds.

I studied the sleeves. Lyle's sweater had been with me through so much: loneliness, fear, heartbreak. But it always reminded me of why I was suffering: to bring back what I had lost.

My heart let out an assured beat, much louder than the ticking.

My memories would save Asenav. Just like my memories tied to the sweater had saved me and kept me going. But what was I meant to *do* with Lyle's sweater?

Bellata, a soothing female voice entered my thoughts. *Can you hear me?*

I turned, trying to concentrate despite the continuous waves of pain.

I know this is hard to believe, but I'm right over there. The thought guided me toward Asenav, who was howling and foaming on the ground.

Confusion and shock entered my thoughts, and the voice chuckled. *Yes, not the best first impression, I know. But hear me, Bellata. I had a moment of weakness while trying to discover how to destroy the doors. I had lost my faith in Eman, thus losing my identity and my purpose. The foul Beast knew I was weak, and before I could vanquish these doors, he struck me rabid.*

I tried to nod but instead coiled into a ball as the ticking rose in volume. Still, Asenav's voice echoed, clearing the storms in my skull.

But I did find what is needed to destroy the doors. Someone must sacrifice a most precious memory. If you are to save us, you must make that sacrifice.

What? I replied, finally able to think clearly enough to respond.

Your sweater, you said it was what helped you remember your purpose in Ophidian's Realm, did you not? she asked, matter-of-factly.

Yes, but how did—

Details for later, she waved a thought-spoken hand in my mind.

I can't, I replied, struggling against the pain waves. *Why should I have to give up Lyle? It doesn't make sense. He's all I have.*

Then we are all lost, her gentle voice replied.

The presence of Asenav's voice receded from my mind.

The moment it vanished, rabid Asenav's attention locked on me. Fighting against her thrashing limbs, she reached for her mace and began crawling in my direction with a murderous gleam in her eyes.

Scrambling backwards, I searched for something to defend myself. Was sacrificing Lyle's sweater really the only way?

Splinters of wood spewed around me as the mace landed inches from my face. Pulse racing, I realized I had no other choice.

Rolling toward the doors, I sat up and yanked off Lyle's sweater, the protection of it vanishing from my being.

A plank of wood flew through the air, knocking me back down. Asenav had quite the arm for a scholar.

I balled Lyle's sweater under my arm and dragged my body to the doors. Their blood-red wood pulsated with power as they opened simultaneously, releasing wave after wave of pain, like a violent wind. It poisoned the minds of everyone in this land.

It wasn't fair that I had to give up Lyle's sweater, but it also wasn't fair for these people to be tormented by Ophidian. I clutched the sweater to my chest. The soft, worn fibers brushed against my skin as I remembered him wearing it one last time.

"Thank you," I said, tears welling up in my eyes as I threw it through the closing doors.

The snap of the seal resonated throughout the room, which drew eerily silent. I waited, stifling my sobs, hoping my sacrifice wasn't wasted, when the doors exploded, knocking everything away. I lay stunned for several seconds.

The ticking stopped.

With a few heavy breaths, I uncurled myself, wiping the tears from my cheeks. Sitting up, I couldn't believe what I saw. There, resting between two mounds of red dust, lay a single golden leaf.

CHAPTER 23

e all packed tightly together in Asenav's reading room. But even with so many bodies close together, I felt cold and naked without Lyle's sweater. What mattered was that my friends were safe, and the Magister was back in her right mind. But without the sword and now the sweater, I couldn't help but realize just how defenseless I really was.

I rubbed my hands over my thin, long-sleeved shirt, hoping Lyle would forgive me for sacrificing his sweater. I sent a prayer to the Heavens, hoping he was still safe in Ramni.

"If everyone would've listened to me, this wouldn't have happened," Damien spat as he clutched his bloodied wrist where the chicken lady had bitten him.

"Let me see," Asenav said, reaching her petite hand out to the lord.

He quickly snatched his wrist away with a growl. "I've

235

already had enough encounters with magical blonde-haired women, thanks."

"Damien," I hissed, giving Asenav an apologetic look.

"Damien?" Silas questioned with a frown, casting a glance between Damien and me.

Asenav clasped her hands in front of her, giving Damien a gentle smile. "There's no need to fear, but I will help the others first."

Asenav quickly passed out bandages and a healing salve to patch up the cuts and scrapes the others had received from their encounters with the townspeople. Thankfully, no one other than Damien had been severely injured.

"Now," Asenav said, standing before Damien once more. She fluffed her wild blonde curls before giving him an expectant look. He let out a frustrated sigh and reluctantly held out his wrist to her. She grinned. "Try not to move. This will sting quite a bit."

Damien winced, then gritted his teeth as Asenav took hold of his arm.

Asenav closed her eyes as she titled her head back. A swirling glow lined her hands. A small trickle of white light escaped from her fingertips and slid across the oozing red cut on Damien's arm. He curled his fingers before relaxing them. Asenav guided him to a plush purple chair in the corner of the room where the light continued to swirl around his arm. We all gathered around with curiosity.

"What happened to him?" Claire asked as she sat next

to him. She leaned toward the cut on his arm, her lips downturned.

Asenav went to her shelves and pulled out a green book. Standing behind Claire, she opened the text and pointed down to one of the pages before handing it over. "He was bitten by one of the rabid. Luckily, because of the Bellata, my people are rabid no more. But if bitten by one, it is deadly."

"That would've been nice to know earlier," Damien said, his words beginning to slur.

"Shh," Asenav said, placing her hand on his forehead. Damien's lids fluttered closed, and he slumped into the chair, asleep.

Claire grasped the book and read the print, her brows furrowing as she turned to the next page.

"He has the worst luck," Silas said, shaking his head.

Asenav turned her scrutinizing gaze on him. Silas stiffened as the Magister analyzed him thoroughly.

"Interesting," she said, focusing on me, then Silas again. "Very interesting."

"He's also not protected," James added, securing a bandage around his knee.

Claire glanced up from the book. "Not protected by what?"

James placed a hand over his chest. "Eman. When Eman mends your heart, you're sealed with his mark, protected from evil. Things can still happen to you, but you won't be severely affected by them."

Claire laid the book flat on her lap and placed a hand

on her own chest. "But I'm not protected by Eman. Addie placed her heart in me."

"Yes," James nodded. "Addie's heart can protect you from minor things, but I do worry about the Lands we'll encounter next."

Claire turned back to Damien while I waited, curious for further explanation, but James didn't continue. Instead, he hobbled toward Asenav, who had begun organizing the yellow papers that had been scattered on the ground.

"It's so good to see you again, Dimitte." Asenav beamed as she neatly stacked the papers and laid them on a nearby table before grabbing his hands. "I thought for sure we had lost you to the darkness."

"Don't worry, Asenav, I'm here to stay," James said, patting her hands before slowly kneeling to pick up more papers.

"Oh, don't worry about those," the Magister said. She swept her hand in the air, and the papers quickly floated before filing themselves into the floor-to-ceiling bookcases lining the back wall.

Asenav ran her thin fingers along the color-coordinated book spines, then directed her attention to me. "How have you come to make this young lady's acquaintance, Dimitte?" Her dark-blue eyes scanned me up and down like I was an ancient document being analyzed for the first time.

James chuckled. "Asenav, you and I both know you already know."

She flicked a hand at him. "Oh, humor me."

James shuffled to a bright-orange chair and motioned to me with a grin. "This is my granddaughter."

Asenav clasped her hands to her chest and gasped in playful surprise. "Your granddaughter is the Bellata? How fascinating!"

The Magister circled me, her blue cloak swishing with her confident strides. The golden leaves embroidering the edges shimmered like the morning sun as I stood still, waiting until her analysis was complete.

Once Asenav finished, she held her hands in front. "Yes, quite fascinating indeed." She turned back to James. "I assume you've already passed through Dunsque?" James nodded. "How was Neural?"

"He and Divad joined forces to save their people," I cut in.

"Ah, she speaks! Very good, very good." Asenav patted down her thick mane before adjusting her cloak. "So, Divad needed assistance? I'm glad he gave up his pighead-edness enough to save his people. Sometimes the bad does bring good. Did he believe you were the Bellata?"

I thought back to the battle with the siti and all of Divad's snide remarks. "He was reluctant at first, but he came around after Silas and I destroyed the doors."

Asenav laughed angelically as she pulled a thick, yellow book from the shelf. She turned back to James. "I like your granddaughter very much, Dimitte. Even more so since she saved my people."

Asenav motioned for Silas and me to sit in the other

colorful chairs next to Damien's. The light still coated the lord's arm, but a look of contentment bathed his features as he leaned back with his eyes shut.

"Well, Bellata," Asenav said. "I can't thank you enough for your assistance." She put up a hand. "And you need not ask. Before you continue your journey, I will summon my mace and make my iuram with you. I'm sure there are still a few Valdeaens left strong enough to fight for Eman."

I settled into my chair, thankful I didn't have to beg for her help.

"It's been many years since my people turned rabid. This is just one of the villages that was affected. There are many more. We lost so many those first years." Asenav held the worn leather-bound book in her lap, stroking its binding. "I was able to save the rest of us by splitting up the people, making them believe there were only a few people in each village so they could do little harm. But once I began to see the signs in myself, I couldn't save any more of them."

Asenav shut her eyes and took a moment before opening them once more. "I know Ophidian sent the doors and the rabid. What is even more horrible was that I isolated myself from my people, allowing the Beast's forces to further pull them into darkness."

"What do you mean?" Silas asked.

"A traveling doctor came to one of my people's villages, saying the cure for becoming rabid was extracting the heart." Asenav glowered at the door to her home as if the doctor were right outside.

Another traveling doctor? Just like Dunsque and Trefair. It was too coincidental not to be the work of Schism and Ophidian.

James drummed his fingers on the arm of his chair, probably having the same thought as me.

Asenav laid her hand on the text. "I don't know how many lost their hearts to that 'doctor,' but I do know that more of my people became rabid after having their hearts extracted." She delicately placed a finger to her temple with a sigh. "By the time I found out, it was too late. The effects of being rabid had started to consume me. There was nothing left I could do but wait." Asenav crossed one slender leg over the other before cradling her book like a child. "What a terrible curse the rabid were. To know so much, then to forget it all in an instant was torture. I know the rabid were sent specifically for me."

James leaned over to us. "Asenav is Eman's first Magister. She has served him the longest."

We all gaped at the Magister. No wonder Ophidian wanted to destroy her mind. How much knowledge did Asenav have that could end him?

"Yes," she confirmed, lifting her chin. "I do know much that could end him."

I thought back to how she communicated with me upstairs. "Can you read my mind?" Was it her voice I had been hearing in my thoughts all this time?

I tried to cast a veil over my mind, causing Asenav to laugh again.

"In a way. I can sense what you feel. Whether you're

confused, lonely, conflicted, or joyous. Based on that, I make an assumption as to why. I'm usually right." She gave Silas a wink, causing him to stiffen again.

Glancing down, she opened the book and flipped through the pages. They were filled with an elegant script, but it was too small for me to read. "But, yes. I do know much about Eman, or the Mender, and his opponent. Eman and I have known each other for many years. I still remember when I was just a young Magister, trying to learn."

Tilting the book to face her, Asenav fluffed her curls before squinting at the text. "If you are to continue this journey, you need to know who and what you're up against."

My chest caved as dread clouded my thoughts, but I nodded. She was right. Silas reached over and placed his hand over mine, giving it a gentle squeeze of encouragement. My skin tingled beneath his touch, and I scooted my blush-pink chair closer to him. Asenav noted our hands, then focused back on the book.

"Eman wasn't always the only one of his kind. Many millennia ago, those who mended hearts were abundant in all the realms. Each of the Lands of Decim, as well as the surrounding realms, were thriving and at peace with one another. It was a glorious time."

She paused before threading her fingers through her thick ringlets. After a moment, she produced a pair of round spectacles. "There you are," she beamed, securing them on the tip of her nose.

Clearing her throat, Asenav continued, "There were two menders who were favored: Eman and Pulchar. Not only were they the best of the heartmenders, but they were also the best of friends.

"The Twelve Lands of Decim and the seven realms surrounding them were at peace like never before, but something changed. One day, while Pulchar was in Necto's Library, he came upon a prophecy: In the darkest of times, a warrior will rise among them. Braided with the Sword and the Mallet, the Staff will complete the trio of almes, reigning light over dark."

I laced my fingers through Silas's, remembering reading that same prophecy when I was in Ramni. After pushing her spectacles up the bridge of her nose, Asenav twirled a blonde ringlet around her finger and read on.

"Since all the realms were at peace, Pulchar thought the prophecy was nonsense and discarded it as nothing to be worried about. But the One who sent the prophecy noticed Pulchar's denial of what was to come."

"What do you mean 'the One who sent the prophecy'?" Claire cut in, clutching the green book to her chest, fully engrossed in Asenav's story.

Asenav glanced up, her eyes three times bigger behind the magnified glass. "He is the One who controls all time and dimensions, weaving them into what they are. But that's a tale for another time."

Focusing back on the page, she explained, "The prophecy revealed itself to Eman next. Always trying to listen to the texts in Necto's Library, Eman set forth to find the other two almes required to defeat the darkness in the coming days.

"As Eman tried to explain this to his friend, Pulchar became irate, believing his longtime friend a fool for putting his faith in the words of an old book. Eman tried to convince Pulchar to go with him, and together they would find the staff and the sword, but Pulchar refused.

"Once Eman left on his journey, Pulchar started to change. He refused to mend hearts, believing he had a greater, more powerful purpose. Each night, he would seethe over his comrade's stupidity for leaving on nothing but a belief. It was gradual, but soon his own pure heart transformed. At first, it was only a shade darker than before. But as Pulchar continued his hate and refusal of what he was instructed to do, his heart darkened until it was blacker than the night sky."

"No," Claire gasped, biting her nails. James gently patted her knee.

"The One who sent the prophecy would not allow one of such evil in the realm of healing. So, he cast him out, forcing Pulchar to leave everything he knew. The bitterness and hate continued to grow in Pulchar's heart until there was nothing but a black heart. With his hardened heart, Pulchar changed his name to the one you know now: Ophidian, meaning heart of darkness. Ever since the day he was banished, Ophidian has been plotting against the One who banished him. He believes that if he can obtain immortality, he will have the power and strength to defeat the Weaver of Time and take his place.

"Regno is where Ophidian first entered into Decim, and it's where he began poisoning all the Lands of Decim with his darkness."

Asenav paused and glanced up, blinking. The room was silent, no one daring to move as we waited for her to continue.

Straightening in her gilded chair, she focused back on the book. "Eman's own heart broke when the news traveled to him. He wept for days, unable to believe his friend's betrayal. But in his heart, Eman knew it was true. He who was once his friend was now his enemy.

Claire sniffed, and I turned to find her wiping her eyes. "What?" she growled. "It's sad."

Asenav cleared her throat, and we both straightened before focusing back on her. She gave us a stern look over her spectacles, like Headmaster Clive, then read on. "Pulchar's revenge began abruptly. He hated who he used to be and wanted to rid his mind of any memories of his former life. Hundreds of heartmenders were slaughtered by his creatures with red eyes in the Beginning Battle. It was a mass genocide throughout the realms.

"Eman refused to kill his friend and escaped before the creatures descended on him. He cloaked his realm of healing from their red eyes, sealing himself away from the other realms.

"It wasn't until the beating of a pure heart sounded so strongly that Eman was able to break his seal to find its owner. That was when he faced his friend once again. It had been many years since he last saw Pulchar, and Eman kept his hope alive that his friend would return to his former self. But as he studied the dark figure in front of him, cloaked in hatred and rage, Eman made an iuram with the Weaver of Time to end Pulchar and stop his revenge, whatever the cost."

Asenav closed her book. Claire was leaning so far forward in her seat, she was practically on the floor. Silas was stiffer than stone, his knuckles white as they grasped my hand. And Damien, who woke up halfway through the story, blinked rapidly, looking around Asenav's cottage with confusion. James leaned back in his chair, face somber.

"So," Asenav said, placing her spectacles back in her hair, "your task goes much further back in time than you thought." She rose from her seat and returned the book to its place on the shelf.

My fingers twitched in Silas's hand, palms clammy. How was *I* supposed to end this feud from centuries ago?

"Don't fret, young Bellata," Asenav said, prying my hand from Silas's before leading me in front of her. "You are more powerful than you believe."

Releasing my hands, Asenav turned her palms to the ceiling, summoning a bright light. Within seconds, the flanged mace that had almost killed me before appeared in her grasp. The blades were silver, each one giving off a deadly shimmer as she wrapped her delicate fingers around the sturdy metal handle.

I gawked at the brutal weapon in amazement, thanking the Heavens Asenav hadn't struck me earlier.

Asenav grinned widely. "The more you know, the more you need to protect yourself." Kneeling, she pointed the mace to the ceiling. "I, Asenav Mirab, Magister of Valde, swear on my alme to fight with you until there is no life left within me."

Reaching out, I grasped the handle of the mace, allowing its light to twist around me and infuse my heart with the iuram's power until we were connected. As the light dissipated into the air, Asenav closed her palms, and the mace disappeared.

"She may seem kind and gentle, but you'll think differently once you watch her wield that thing," James said, standing slowly from the corner. He stretched out his leg a few times before wobbling toward us.

"Oh, I know," I muttered.

Asenav laughed as she held her hand out to James. He quickly took it.

"I truly am thankful that you are with us again, Dimitte. We need all Twelve to defeat the darkness. If we are not united, we will fail."

James looked over at me with a proud smile. "I would have made my iuram to my granddaughter, whether all Twelve unite or not."

I grinned back at him, realizing how thankful I was that he was here with me. Without James, I wasn't sure how we would have made it this far.

senav offered her home for us to stay in for the night. Though the earlier events made us hesitant at first, we all slept soundly.

The next morning, Asenav gave Claire the green book to keep and showed her a special salve that would help James's knee before checking Damien's wound one last time. Though her magic had healed his injury, he hardly remembered getting bitten by one of the rabid. Thankfully, he didn't ask too many questions as we exited the cottage.

Before we crossed the front door threshold, James peeked outside to find that the number of townspeople had grown. The once rabid people hugged each other with tears of joy streaming down their cheeks.

"Since you destroyed the doors, my people didn't have to be separated any longer," Asenav explained, her eyes twinkling as she took in the joyful Valdeans. "My spell dividing them was broken, and they're now reunited with their loved ones once more."

James's gaze bounced between all the villagers before he stood in front of our group, cautiously leading Silas, Claire, and Damien around the edge of the village. They each gave quick good-byes and hurried away toward the plain. I turned to tell Asenav thank you only to find she was already there.

"Do not be wary of your journey ahead, Bellata." She gently touched my forehead. "Eman is with you. He will do what is right."

I nodded, unsure of her meaning. "Thank you, Asenav. For everything."

She gave a small bow before releasing my hands, motioning to the satchel. "Your sacrifices as the Bellata are only beginning. Do not lose what you created from the destruction of the doors. When surrounded by darkness, there is always a glimmer of light."

I remembered the golden leaf that had appeared after the doors had exploded. After stuffing it in my satchel, I had almost forgotten about it. Before I could ask for a further explanation, Asenav pushed me toward the group.

"Don't start the battle without me!" she yelled, waving from her doorway.

James laughed, but the rest of us were silent. Asenav's story of Eman and Ophidian kept playing through my thoughts. Ophidian would stop at nothing until he became immortal, and I feared that when we did fight the Beast, we may not return.

CHAPTER 24

As we returned to the grassy plains, I pushed our future battle to the back of my mind. What mattered now was finding the next Magister. Adjusting my satchel, I grasped the book. When I opened the cover, the map had disappeared, replaced with the phrase:

Probar se Duodecim forti resurge

"A warrior will rise to prove herself to the Twelve," I read aloud. When I scanned the phrase again, the word Twelve had shifted to Eight. I straightened my stance, giddiness filling my steps. Four of the Twelve Magisters had joined my side.

James and Silas took the lead, giving me time to flip through the pages of the book. I expected to find it drawing a map of where we were to go next. But after I made it halfway through, and nothing happened, anxiety pricked my thoughts. What if Ophidian's army had broken through Eman's defenses and had taken over Ramni? What if Ophidian had somehow cursed this book, stopping it from helping me any further? Frantic, I turned the pages faster, causing everyone to stop.

"Calm down, Addie," a familiar voice said.

My head jolted up. "Did you say something?" I asked. Silas shook his head. I turned to Claire. "Did you?"

She snorted. "You would've known if I had said something."

I spun to James and Damien. "Did either of you?" They both shook their heads.

"Addie, down here."

Looking down, I saw Lyle's face smiling up at me. I gasped and dropped the book, flattening the tall grass at my feet.

Silas took a step toward the book. "Was that—"

"That was Lyle!" Claire cried as she elbowed Silas in the stomach to get to the book. Kneeling on the ground, she quickly flipped it open and began filing through the pages so fast the book almost shrieked.

"Easy, Claire, you're going to rip my face off." Lyle chuckled.

Claire squealed as she smoothed out the pages with Lyle's face on them. Excitement burbled in my chest as I joined her in her crouched position.

"There she is!" Lyle exclaimed with lifted hands. His eyes were bright behind his dark-rimmed spectacles.

"Hey," I said hesitantly, unsure how to handle talking to my brother through a book. "Sorry for dropping you."

Lyle laughed, bringing joy to my weary spirit. "No worries. I wasn't sure if I could make the connection at first, but Eman has been teaching me so much. Ever since you left, we've been trying to lift the curse on that book you found."

"Any luck?" I asked as Silas, James, and Damien gathered around us.

Lyle shook his head, sending his dark curls sprawling across his forehead. "None yet. Like I said, I've been learning other things, like contacting you through a book!"

Claire and I both giggled.

Focusing on Claire, Lyle placed a hand over his heart. "I miss you."

Claire imitated him. "I miss you, too."

Damien scoffed. Without missing a beat, Claire reared back and jabbed his shin with her elbow.

Damien stumbled back, cursing under his breath.

"There's something you need to know, Claire," Lyle said with a serious tone.

"What is it?"

"It's about Doct—your dad."

I leaned away from the book. Doctor Magnum. I had completely forgotten about him *and* about telling Claire we had brought him to Ramni. I held my breath. It was too late to tell her now.

Keeping more *secrets from your friends?*

I didn't keep it from her on purpose. There's been a lot going on. I waited for the voice to respond, but it stayed silent.

Claire tilted forward, her freckled nose almost touching Lyle's face. "What? Did something happen to him? Is he all right?"

Lyle gave a concerned frown before he continued. "Don't worry, he's okay. He's actually better than okay … he's here, in Ramni with all the others from Barracks."

Claire sat back. "What?" She shot me a glare. "That would've been nice to know earlier."

"I'm sorry," I mouthed while lifting my shoulders sheepishly.

"After you all left, he woke up," Lyle continued, glancing over at something, then back at us. "He wanted to see you, but I told him that you were on a quest."

Silas snorted. "A quest, indeed."

"Shh!" I said, slapping his foot.

"What did he say?" Claire asked.

"That he missed you and wanted to see you."

"Oh."

A few moments of silence passed as we waited for one of them to say something. Finally, Lyle asked, "Do you want to see him?"

Hesitating, Claire drummed her fingers on her thigh before nodding. It had been years since she'd spoken to her father. After he had left her in Ophidian's clutches, I wouldn't be surprised if she never wanted to talk to him.

Lyle motioned someone over, then stepped out of view, allowing Doctor Magnum to take his place. The heart extractor still held onto his youth and appeared more at peace than the last time I'd seen him.

"Claire," he breathed.

Claire swallowed again, tears rimming her eyes. "Hi, Dad."

Doctor Magnum's lips quivered as he reached out to Claire. Claire hesitantly placed her hand on the pages.

"Claire, I'm so sorry." He bowed his head, his shoulders shuddering. "I was such a fool. A coward. I didn't know what your mother had done, or what to do about it, when *he* came."

"It's okay, Dad," Claire replied, blinking away the tears, her face a mask of calm. "At least you're safe."

"And he's been a big help," Lyle's voice chimed in from behind him. Soon, he and Doctor Magnum were sharing the space on the pages of the book. "He's been trying to help Eman and me lift the curse."

"That's great," Claire said, her voice straining as she summoned a weak smile. I placed a hand on her trembling fists, and her eyes pleaded for help. Moving closer to the book, I changed the subject.

"Lyle, do you know anything about a blonde woman named Dacenda?" I asked. I wasn't sure why, but something was probing me that she was involved with our parents.

Lyle shot a worried glance at Claire, then focused on me. "Who's Dacenda?"

I gave Claire a small nudge to push her out of Lyle's

view. Holding back her sobs at seeing her father, Claire crawled into the thick grass.

I gestured at Silas to go to her, but he shook his head in refusal. What was wrong with him now? Pursing my lips, I motioned to James, who quickly found Claire and offered words of comfort.

"She's this woman who's been tracking us," I explained, remembering how Damien discovered that someone was following us. The lord stood silently as he straightened his knives. "She can control the malum, so she definitely works for Ophidian, but I didn't know if you knew anything else."

"Hmmm." Lyle placed a hand over his chin, his eyes shifting back and forth as if filing through all the books he had read. He furrowed his brows in thought before they jumped up. Nodding, Lyle picked up a different book. He rifled through the pages, then stopped, his lips turning down. "Yes, I actually do know something."

"What? What is it?" I asked, gripping my knees.

Lyle's eyes darted across the pages before he took off his spectacles and rubbed his eyes. "I think she's the one who killed our parents."

Nausea boiled in my stomach, and my heart wrenched in two. I curled my fingers into fists, hot tears burning in the corners of my eyes.

"What?"

"It's all right here," Lyle said softly, holding up the book.

Sunlit pages welcomed me as a group of people walked

across the page. They were jovial, smiles adorning their faces as they conversed with one another.

Then the pages changed. The people ran, the background of the pages shifting from bright white to a dark gray. The group was half of what it had been in the previous scene. Their faces were cloaked in fear as they disappeared off the other page.

The pages then turned to black. There were only two people from the group left: a man with blond hair and a woman with dark curls. Recognition pulled at my memory before the scene changed again. The man and the woman ran to the right page, glancing over their shoulders. A woman with long, blonde hair came into view, stalking behind them as if they were her prey.

Everything within me stilled.

The couple tried to retreat off the page but were pushed back by a group of black figures. When the singular red eye appeared on each of the black creatures, I instantly recognized the malum.

Dacenda stalked toward the couple, but they refused to back down. The man sent streams of white light from his hands, while the woman sent out bright orange ones. Dacenda easily deflected their attempts and countered an attack. Ice-blue bolts shot out of her hands, immediately knocking the man down. The woman crouched beside him, and though there was no sound, her shuddering shoulders exemplified her cries.

Pain stabbed my chest. I clawed the area, trying to subdue the agony of my breaking heart. A large hand gently gripped my shoulder, but I couldn't tell if it belonged to Silas or Damien.

Dacenda sauntered toward the woman with dark curls and grabbed a fistful of her hair, yanking her off the man. She sneered at the woman before dragging her along the ground, disappearing off the page. The images from the pages flickered, then disappeared, returning to their original cream color.

I tried to breathe, but my breaths came out as sobs.

You're not the only one keeping secrets, the voice mocked in my thoughts.

"Why didn't you tell me sooner?" I gasped through tears, slamming my fist on the book. Thick droplets fell to the page, absorbing into the parchment.

"Because," Lyle said, his face fallen with grief as he shut the text. "I didn't know who she was. The name and description you gave me matched the story perfectly. So, I have to assume she's the one. She's the murderer."

"But why did she kill them?" I questioned, fighting the tears.

"Because they were the last ones in their time to follow Eman's ways."

I forced myself to face James. He had stepped away from Claire, who had her head buried in her hands. James placed a hand over his eyes, bowing his head.

"Did you know?" I asked through clenched teeth. "Did you know my parents worked with Eman? Did you know Dacenda killed them?"

James's entire posture slumped forward as if he couldn't bear to hold himself up.

Betrayal whirred inside me. "Why didn't you tell me?"

My grandfather started to speak when Lyle interjected. "Addie, it wasn't only James who knew. Eman was the one who told him, but not us. When I found this book, he told me the whole story, explaining that the time was now right for us to know."

"But why wait? Why didn't *you* tell me when you knew?" I exclaimed, distrust churning in my thoughts as I pointed to James.

He didn't tell you he was your grandfather either, remember?

"Or *you*?" I spun around and picked up the book, glaring at Lyle.

All this time, Eman, James, *and* Lyle knew what had happened to my parents. I had been hoping for more information, praying for Lyle to get his memories back so we could find out more. But he didn't need his memories to find their story. Eman had known all along.

And you still trust the heartmender?

"I just found out her name, Addie," Lyle replied, setting his glasses on his nose. "And I really wanted to tell you as soon as I found out, but I only just learned the entire story, and you had to leave so quickly, and we didn't have the time to talk ..."

I wanted to throw up. I wanted to hide. I wanted to run.

I threw the book down, turning away from Lyle's babbling.

"Addie." Silas cautiously placed his hand on my arm. I shoved it off and stalked away from them.

"Addie, wait!" Lyle's voice rang through the grass. "There's something you need to know. Something about Eman. Please, listen!"

Heat built in my chest. I took in deep breaths, trying to calm the rapid palpitations of my heart, but my thoughts couldn't move past the deception and betrayal. Balling my hands into fists, I did what I hadn't done since this journey began: I ran away.

CHAPTER 25

I ran hard and fast. I didn't look back.

I sprinted until my knees grew weak. Every breath I took seared my lungs. Tears stained my cheeks as I crashed to the ground, falling into white sand instead of green grass. Bottles and vials spewed from my satchel as I curled into a ball and cried.

My parents gave their lives for a man who chose not to tell me about their deaths. I let out a wail, placing a hand over my heart as pain jabbed my chest. Had my heart cracked again?

I laid in the sandy grass for what seemed like hours, not caring about my fate. What did it matter about the Magisters or Ophidian anymore?

"Addie!" My name echoed in the distance.

I blinked a few times, lifting my head to hear the voice.

"Addie, where are you?"

I wanted to shout back, but I was too broken to speak. Instead, I raised my arm in the air, hoping he would find me. In a matter of moments, rushed footsteps approached me before Silas joined me on the ground. I was soon swept up into two strong arms. The pulse of his half-heart comforted my own as Silas cradled me to his chest, and I cried.

"It'll be okay," Silas said, wiping the granules of sand from my cheeks.

"How could it be okay?" I said into his shirt through sobs, clutching the plaid fabric. "He knew. They all knew!" I lapsed into another fit of sobs before continuing, "And they kept it from me. Not once did Lyle try to contact me when he found out. Not once did James mention why my parents died. Not once did Eman explain what happened to them. If I hadn't asked about Dacenda, I would've never known!"

"I don't think so," Silas said calmly, moving a strand of hair out of my eyes. "Eman may not say everything at once, but he's always been truthful. Maybe he wanted to tell you at the right time, to make sure you would be ready when it came."

I scoffed. "This was the right time? When I'm trying to gather forces for *him?*"

Silas sighed before cradling my face in his hands, bringing me back to the days when we were only a little girl and young man trying to figure out the realm.

"Eman knows what he's doing. You have to trust him."

I turned away and sniffed.

Silas gently tugged my face back to him before placing his forehead on mine. "Sometimes, we keep things from those we love the most to protect their hearts from breaking."

I pulled away, ready to demand an explanation for that statement, but instead, Silas's hands cupped my neck, threading his fingers through my hair, and brought his lips to mine. I paused before melting into him. All thoughts of demands and heartbreak fled my mind.

Silas wrapped his strong arms around my waist. Warmth coursed through my body, filling the empty hole as I drank him in, savoring the saltiness on his lips. Our hearts galloped faster as we embraced one another.

Silas's kisses were different than the ones we shared before. While those were passionate and hungry, these were desperate and pleading, as if he never wanted them to end. Like they were the last ones we'd share.

I broke away and rubbed my thumb along the tears that had rolled down his cheeks. Pain seared my chest at the sight. Silas cast his eyes downward, refusing to meet my gaze.

"What's wrong, Silas?"

My fingers grazed the thick blond hairs growing from his jaw before they met the scars from the siti. Silas had received those scars while protecting Nana. He was always looking out for my family and me.

Silas worked his jaw. "There's just so much ..." Footsteps came from behind me. Silas peered over my head before he quickly placed a kiss on my palm. "Looks like they found us," he muttered before standing up.

Reaching down, he offered me his hand. I hesitated. If I stood, this moment would be lost forever. I would never understand what was going on with Silas. I so badly wanted to get inside his head and figure out what was happening. I needed to make sure he was okay and that he would always be by my side.

Claire, James, and Damien trudged up to us at once, and I knew the time had passed. I wiped the remaining tears from my face before I gripped Silas's hand and stood to face the others. Claire hugged the book to her chest, a few sniffles escaping from her. Damien scowled as he flipped his cloak over his shoulders, while James's eyes burned red as if he had been crying, too. We stared at each other for a moment until James cleared his throat.

"I believe I have some explaining to do."

I nodded quickly, not tempting my tears by speaking.

James sighed, rubbing his chin before beginning. "Long before Lyle or you were born, Decim was a different place. Things were all around better. Your mother and father had just gotten married and were ready to start their life together. That's when they met Eman. It was a few years after their Heart Reign. They both decided to keep their hearts instead of trading them away." I opened my mouth to protest, but James put up a hand. "This was before the law of forcible trade." He cracked a small smile. "Actually, I believe your parents were the reason *why* the law was made."

I closed my mouth, my curiosity growing.

"Your Nana's heart was the purest Barracks had seen. But that was before your mother and father. Once they met Eman, they discovered the purity of their own hearts and the power they held within them. It was then that Eman asked them to follow him—to learn his ways and become Magisters for Barracks since the previous Magister had disappeared." James studied his boots as he wiped a hand across his mouth.

Damien cleared his throat, stepping between James and me. "I know this is a pressing issue," he offered, his voice soft as he interrupted. "But since we know we're being followed, and Adelaide decided to wander off course, shouldn't we figure out where we are?

"That's a good point," Silas agreed.

Scooping up the scattered items, I placed them in my satchel and slung it onto my shoulder. I wondered why Silas was agreeing with Damien. They never agreed on anything.

As I brought my attention back to James, I noted his sagging shoulders and the pronouncement of gray growing from his chin. He looked exhausted, as if each word coming from his lips stretched him thinner and thinner.

James's ice-blue eyes filled with sorrow. "I know I should have told you before, but Eman Band I didn't think you were ready for the truth. I do wonder if Eman allowed Lyle to know before you so that you could hear it from your brother."

I wrapped my arms around my stomach and nodded, now understanding what Silas had said before.

James shuffled over and grasped me in a tight hug. "Your parents loved you and Lyle very much. The reason they sacrificed themselves was because they believed in Eman. They knew he would make Decim safe for their children."

I hugged him back, the betrayal dissipating from my thoughts. I still wasn't happy with Eman for keeping something so important from me. But I understood why he did it. And James had taken care of all of us on this journey. He wouldn't have kept this from me to harm me.

"Thank you for telling me," I said, releasing him. "I hope one day I can know the rest of their story and yours."

Silas came up behind me and placed his hand on my shoulder. "We really should continue." He turned to Claire, who was still clutching the brown book to her chest. "I apologize about before. Is there any way we can try to reach Lyle again?"

Claire pulled the book away from her body, inspecting it. She opened the pages, thumbing through them quickly. "I don't think so. I think only he can contact us. And after little miss feisty pants over there threw him on the ground, again, I don't think he'll be calling anytime soon."

"Sorry," I said. Lyle was in the middle of saying something about Eman that I probably should have listened to. Hopefully, it wasn't too important. "I'm also sorry for not telling you about Doctor Magnum."

Claire slammed the book shut, and I jumped. "As much

as I would've liked to know before, there's nothing I can do about it now. He's safe with Eman; that's all that matters."

I studied my friend. How could she forgive me so easily?

"But"—she narrowed her eyes as she pointed the corner of the book at me—"if you keep anything else from me, I may not heal you the next time you decide to be stupid."

CHAPTER 26

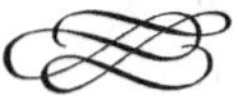

As I took the book from Claire, white grains of sand tumbled from the brown cover, joining the granules covering my boots. I shook my foot, trying to force the scratchy grains from entering the melted hole on the side of my shoe.

Damien's question regarding where we were resurfaced in my thoughts, and I opened the text to find out. Once the pages flattened, the invisible quill drew a bold blue line on the parchment. Grass and sand formed, but the line continued, sketching soft blue waves at the edge of the page. I turned around, and the book glowed, assuring me of the direction we were to take.

"This way," I said, not breaking my focus from the pages. The steady crunch of my feet pressing into the sand soothed my churning thoughts as everyone plodded through the sparkling snow-white grains and tufts of tall grass behind me.

We continued until the sound of calming waves gliding in and out flowed through the air. Dusk coated the sky with alluring shades of pink and orange. Closing the book, I admired the beautiful sight. The sun was a work of art against the serene waves of the evening ocean. For just a moment, I forgot about everything. This journey, Ophidian, my parents. All that mattered was watching the intricate masterpiece. I didn't blink, not wanting to miss a moment.

"I've never seen anything so beautiful before," Damien said, staring at the sunset. Like me, he seemed to be trying not to blink, but soon his eyes watered, and he shut them for a few seconds.

"Got something in my eye," he said gruffly before turning away. He quickly stalked to the shoreline and began collecting pieces of driftwood.

I laughed before Silas came next to me, taking my hand in his own and giving it a kiss. I loved my small hand in his. Leaning into his chest, I relished his strength. I was protected, safe.

"I've missed your laugh," he said with a crooked grin.

I ruffled his hair with my hand. "I like your smile."

"Oh, will you two quit it!" Claire called from behind us. She and James had joined Damien in gathering pieces of grass and driftwood that had washed ashore. "I'm going to vomit if I have to hear any more."

Silas planted a kiss on my cheek, and Claire pretended to throw up.

"Speaking of vomiting," he said, "we need to find something to eat before getting some rest."

As if an answer to our prayers, two men carrying a canoe and a fishing net appeared in the distance. Besides their skin, which had been bronzed by the sun, they could have been Silas's twins. Both had shaggy golden hair with chestnut brown eyes. But it wasn't just that. Their long, steady strides—and the way they favored their left sides when they stood—were just like Silas's.

The men dropped the canoe near the water and strode up the beach toward us. The one on the left raised an arm and waved excitedly at us with a welcoming grin. Though not as crooked, his grin definitely resembled Silas's.

"Hello!" he called cheerily. The other man's stance stiffened as he leaned over and grumbled something, causing the first to shrug and wave again. "Welcome!" he said when they reached us.

"Oh, please don't," Claire said, shuddering. "I don't want to hear another 'welcome' ever again."

The young man scratched his chin, confused, before turning back to us. He was a few years younger than his counterpart and stood a couple of inches shorter. "We saw you come out of the grasses and thought you looked like you needed assistance."

"Clearly, they don't," the other said, pointing to the fire that James and Damien had just finished. "Come on, Brand. We can't miss another order."

As the grumpy one reached out for his friend's arm,

the cheerful one, Brand, swerved out of the way, escaping his grasp.

"So," Brand said, flipping his shaggy strands out of his eyes before leaning toward Claire. "Where are you guys from?" He then surveyed her thick red sweater and black pants. "Obviously, not from around here."

I wriggled my toes, realizing we were all still dressed in what we wore in Barracks. Thick pants with sweaters were the everyday outfit in our cold wasteland of a home. But this place was different. It wasn't cold and bitter, but warm and comforting.

The two men wore nothing but dark cut-off pants, exposing more leg than I'd ever seen and flowing cream shirts.

Instead of answering his question, I asked my own. "Where are we?"

"You don't know where you are?" the grumpy one asked skeptically.

"We're on our way to visit family." Silas glided closer, wrapping an arm around my waist. "We just want to make sure we're heading in the right direction."

"Hmm," the grumpy one narrowed his gaze at Silas with suspicion. Silas lifted his chin and glared back in challenge.

Was I the only one who saw the resemblance between them?

After a few testosterone-filled moments, the grumpy one broke his gaze and turned toward the ocean. "You're in Ratcha, home of all things nautical."

"We've been traveling for quite some time," Silas said, not missing a beat. "I'd be willing to help you fish if you agree to allow us some of the catch." He gestured to the canoe and net at the shore.

The grumpy one started to protest, but Brand cut him off, pushing more hair out of his eyes as he extended his hand to Claire. "We can always use more hands. Especially yours."

Claire snorted. "I don't fish."

Brand took a step closer, giving her a dashing grin. "You don't have to fish. I'd just enjoy your company."

Claire gave Brand a once over before a mischievous glint twinkled in her eyes. "Little boy, you're not my type."

Brand beamed in challenge as the grumpy one scoffed and took off down the beach toward the canoe.

"Don't worry about Gaius," Brand said, waving behind him nonchalantly, keeping his attention on Claire. "He's always opposed to anything new. He's been a stick-in-the-mud ever since we were kids." He wriggled his brows at Claire. "Unlike me. I'm always fun."

Claire rolled her eyes before joining James.

"So, he's your brother?" I asked.

Brand nodded with a sigh. "Sadly, yes. We've always been so different, so I don't know how we're related." Shrugging, he motioned to Silas. "All right, you want to eat, you have to work." Brand cupped his hands around his mouth. "I'll be back soon, my lady!"

"I don't care!" Claire shouted back.

I gave Silas's hand a squeeze of thanks before he

headed off with Brand, looking like the perfect piece to an incomplete puzzle.

"I'm going, too," Damien announced, stalking after the blond trio.

Silas whipped around, clearly annoyed. I lifted a shoulder, then waved. Damien had proven himself useful more than once during our journey. I'm sure he would do so again. And it would be nice for him and Silas to try to get along. I just hoped Brand and Gaius had another canoe.

I joined Claire and James by the fire, where we swapped stories of adventures, failures, and successes until the rumbling of laughter echoed in the distance. Four figures strode confidently against the horizon, two of them holding huge bundles of fish. As they trekked closer, the fire's light reflected off three golden heads and Damien's dark locks. The group marched toward us with giant grins.

"Did everything go okay?" I asked, glancing at their exhausted faces.

"We haven't had a catch like that in ages!" Brand said, plopping down by the fire next to Claire. He ran a hand through his shaggy mane, then shook it out, spraying water everywhere.

"Ugh," Claire said, scooting away as she covered her nose. "You reek of fish."

"You don't like it?" he replied, sticking out his bottom lip in a pout.

Claire grabbed a nearby stick and whacked Brand in the head before relocating to the opposite side of the fire.

"Brand," Gaius chastised as he carefully sat next to his brother, smoothing the wrinkles from his pants. "Try to be somewhat civilized."

Ignoring Gaius, Brand rubbed his head before pointing at Damien. "And you! No offense, but just looking at you, I thought you were nothing but a pretty boy who had never worked a day in his life. You sure proved me wrong!"

Damien reached for a knife on his belt, passing it between his hands as he nervously chuckled.

Silas was the last to sit, unloading another sack on the ground as he dropped next to me. He wrapped his arm around my shoulder and pulled me in for a quick hug. My stomach jumped as I breathed in the salty scent of the ocean.

"You've got yourself a fine fisherman there," Gaius said, nodding toward Silas. "I've not seen a man work harder than him in a long time."

"Hey!" Brand said, throwing a small piece of driftwood at his brother. "I work hard!"

Gaius dodged the stick. "Napping in the canoe while I haul fish is not working hard."

Silas laughed, bringing warmth to my heart. I couldn't help but give him a kiss.

Claire groaned and started reaching for the sack. "Are we going to just sit around and talk, or are we going to eat?"

"I like a woman who knows what she wants," Brand said.

"Good. I don't want you. Leave me alone," Claire replied, stabbing a fish onto her stick.

In a few moments, we skewered several fish and cooked over the flames before we feasted. The roasted fish melted in my mouth. Besides the few items Eman and James had packed and what Damien had foraged along the way, we had barely eaten anything since our journey began. Within an hour, we had made up for lost time.

After we stuffed ourselves, Gaius neatly wiped his lips with a cloth and asked, "So, where did you two learn how to fish?"

Silas motioned to Damien, offering for him to share first, but Damien ignored Silas and continued to filet his fish with a thin knife.

Rubbing the back of his neck, Silas answered, "I'm not really sure. I've always loved the water, but there was never any where I grew up. I guess I was just figuring it out as I went along."

Brand belched before letting out a laugh of disbelief. "Are you serious? You could've fooled me."

"Brand," Gaius scolded. "What about you?" he asked Damien.

Glancing up, Damien gripped his knife. "My father wasn't around while I was growing up. He always sent me away to different places, so he could spend more time with his wives." His lips curled deviously. "I also wasn't the most obedient child. But one time, he sent me to an old fisherman, probably somewhere around here." He waved the knife, gesturing to the beach around us. "I hated it and him. It was hot, and he smelled like rotting fish. But every day, he tried to convince me of the wonders of fishing until I reluctantly agreed. After I did it one time, I couldn't get enough."

"Really?" Claire asked. "You don't seem the fishy type."

Damien snorted but couldn't cover his grin.

All this time, we thought he had been spoiled and condescending, growing up with luxuries none of us had.

Yet Damien's story weighed on me. His parents didn't want him. Although my parents died when I was young, at least I had Nana, and now a wonderful grandfather who protected and kept me safe. Maybe Damien's arrogance and snide comments were just a front. Maybe he wasn't as rude as he made himself out to be. But then again, there was his harem of women. I wasn't sure what to think of that now.

"So, none of you know what's going on in Ratcha?" Brand asked, his gaze bouncing between us. At our silence, Brand's face filled with grief.

Gaius gripped his knees with his slender fingers, blowing out a heavy breath.

"What is it?" Silas asked, leaning forward.

The brothers shared a look. "That's why we fish. We have to supply food for the champions of Obesque and Ratcha. We're trying to prevent a war."

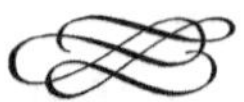

CHAPTER 27

Claire spat out the piece of fish she was chewing on. "A war? With who?"

Brand fidgeted with his pants, seeking Gauis's guidance. The elder brother rubbed his temples. My chewing came to a stop as I studied their exchange, anticipating an answer. Divad had said that some of the other Lands had been engaged in a long period of battle. Is this what he meant?

Finally, Gaius took a stick and drew in the sand.

"As you all probably know, there are twelve Lands in Decim." He drew semi-circles in the sand, symbolizing waves. "This is Ratcha." He tapped the stick on his drawing before poking deep holes in the sand next to Ratcha. "And this is our lovely neighbor to the north, Obesque." His voice dripped with sarcasm as he threw the stick into the fire when he completed his picture.

Silas cupped his hands over his mouth as he focused on Gaius, completely absorbed.

"Have Obesque and Ratcha always been enemies?" I asked, placing my cleaned fish bones aside.

Gaius frowned. "Not always. But I can't remember the last time we've had a pleasant encounter with an Obesquean."

Brand groaned, gathering his wet strands into a ponytail before tying them with a strip of leather. "This 'combat of champions' has been going on for ages. It's been, what, seven, eight years? Most of my life, I've been hauling fish so those brutes can eat." He pointed to his ponytail. "Do you like this look better? I can shave it all off, too."

"I don't like blonds," Claire retorted before turning to Silas. "No offense."

"None taken," Silas replied then turned to Gaius. "Now, you fish for Ratcha for the champions? Why?"

"We don't have a choice, and it's better than being sent into Perda Forum," Gaius muttered.

"What did you say?" I asked, the name tickling the back of my mind.

"Perda Forum," Gaius repeated with a raised brow. "The Market of Thieves? That's where the combat of champions has always been held."

"Please forgive our questions," James said with a gentle smile. "But we only just found out your two Lands were not at peace."

"Of course," Gaius replied. "The competition between

Ratcha and Obesque is unlike any other battle. While there are still soldiers, things are settled in a different way."

"What do you mean?" Silas asked.

Brand glanced at Gaius, grabbed the partially filled sacks, and stood. "We'll take you there." Silas quickly joined them.

"What?" Claire and I gasped simultaneously as if the same thought passed through our minds.

"I haven't made it all this way to be killed by some greedy thieves," Claire said.

"Agreed," I added. I didn't want to go waltzing through the Market of Thieves in the middle of the night.

Silas subtly sunk back down onto the sand, trying to hide his excitement.

"No need to worry, my lady. I'll protect you." Brand puffed out his chest.

Claire poked him in the ribs, and Brand deflated.

"Brand, they've been traveling all day and are probably tired," Gaius said, placing a hand on his brother's shoulder. "We'll come back for you in the morning. Then all your questions will be answered."

"I'd be happy to stay the night and lead you there first thing." Brand started toward Claire before James blocked him.

"I think we'll be okay for tonight, son. Thank you for the offer."

Before Brand could muster a reply, Gaius yanked Brand's shirt collar and dragged him back to their canoe.

We watched silently as they waved before picking up the canoe and disappearing into the night.

Claire wiped her forehead. "Well, he was annoying. Thanks, Grandpa." She then flopped down next to Damien, giving his arm a playful punch. "So, who knew you were a fisherman at heart?"

"I suppose so," he replied, trying to sound annoyed, but instead, he sounded tired.

"I have a question," Silas said quietly, his head bowed.

Everyone turned. The stillness of Silas's body made me nervous.

Slowly lifting his head, Silas's eyes became slits as they focused on Damien. "What happened to all the girls?"

"What girls?" James asked, turning to me for an explanation.

Silas's shoulders tensed. "The girls' hearts you took."

Nausea rolled in my stomach. How many women did he have now? Five, six? Silas and I would always bet on who would trade their heart to be in Lord Farmount's harem each year at Heart Reign. But that game ended when I had received an invitation from the lord. Though he couldn't emote then, Silas made it clear he wasn't happy about the invite.

I gave Silas a wary look.

"You're still doing that?" Claire gasped. "Like your dad?"

Damien stiffened at the question. "I'm nothing like my father," he growled as he slowly stood, not taking his focus off Silas. "You would like to know that, wouldn't you, hero?"

Silas met his challenge, and the fish soured in my stomach. This wasn't going to end well.

Damien's hands were at his sides, but his arms tensed, ready to grab his knives. Silas was the same, his fingers twitching above the hilt of his blade.

"Silas," I said cautiously.

"Stay out of this, Addie," he snapped.

I jerked back before a thick charcoal cloud replaced Silas's beautiful eyes, reminding me of the siti in Ophidian's Realm.

With the skill of a warrior, Silas unsheathed his sword and lunged at Damien. Quicker than light speed, the lord grasped two knives and flung them at Silas. Silas batted the blades away as if they were nothing but bugs on a summer day. In a blink, Damien threw two more. This time the knives pierced Silas's right shoulder. A rumbling roar rolled from Silas's throat as he launched at Damien.

Claire scrambled out of the way, retreating to where James and I were.

"What's the matter with you, Silas?" she screamed.

Silas growled and lunged again, aiming his blade at Damien, this time hitting his mark. Damien gasped as bright-red blood dripped from his side onto the fire-lit sand below.

Panicking, I yanked Damien out of the way. Claire ran to him with her satchel and started working on the wound.

I held out my hands, using myself as a shield to protect them. "Silas, stop, it's me. It's Addie."

My chest tightened with each breath as his black eyes stared back at me. Sweat trickled from my brow. "Whatever is going on, you need to fight it. This isn't you."

Are you sure? This may be who the real Silas is.

Silas's chest heaved before he shoved me out of the way. My boots tangled in the thick sand before I stumbled to the ground.

"Addie!" James yelled as I landed inches from the burning fire.

The clang of metal rang through the once peaceful night. James had intercepted Silas's attack.

Sitting up with a groan, I shook my head before my gaze darted to James. Though he was older, I finally saw James's experience. With each attack Silas made, James blocked it and returned with his own attack without once harming Silas.

And Silas. Though I had seen him fight off siti before, I had never seen him against another skilled opponent. It had been years since he'd fought with a sword. But the way he parried and jabbed was incredible. It was like a dance he had unknowingly memorized the steps to.

I sat there with my mouth agape until Claire shouted, "Addie! Stop sitting there and do something!"

"Right!" I said, scrambling to think of some way to help.

"Don't worry, Addie," James said with a focused grin,

sweat gleaming from his forehead. "I got him right where I want him."

James dodged a jab before pounding Silas's head with the flat side of his axe. Silas blinked, his sword held out mid-swing before his eyes rolled back. Grains of sand bunched around him as his body smacked into the ground.

We all hesitated before crowding around him.

"Are you all right?" I asked James.

"Yep," he said. He wiped his brow with his sleeve, taking in a few deep breaths, but his ice-blue eyes were bright with excitement. "I hadn't fought like that in years. That boy is something else."

"What happened?" Claire asked, helping Damien stand next to her.

I shook my head. "I'm not sure." I turned to the lord. "Are you okay?"

Damien grunted but said nothing as he placed a hand on his bandaged side.

No one responded for a while, not sure of what to say.

After the long silence, James stretched his back and lowered himself to the ground.

"I suggest we all try to sleep. Silas is going to be a bear with that lump I gave him." Lines of worry creased his bright-blue eyes. "And we should all pray that this doesn't happen again."

I nodded before rolling Silas on his back and sitting next to him, waiting to see if anything unusual happened.

The wound Damien had inflicted had already healed, leaving nothing but a small hole in Silas's shirt.

Damien scoffed at Silas before stalking away. Claire gave him an apologetic look before she sat on the other side of Silas.

She grabbed his sword and held it tight. "Just in case he wakes up crazy again." She added a forced smile.

"I can't believe that just happened," I exclaimed, digging my palms into my eyes. "He never acted like that before."

Claire shrugged. "He didn't have his heart before."

See?

"Do you think that's it? That his heart is making him do this? Is this what Silas is really like?" The questions kept tumbling out of my mouth before Claire held up a hand.

"Whoa, Addie, calm down."

"What do you think is going on with him?"

Claire blew out a breath, bringing her knees to her chin. "I have no idea, but I never want to see that side of him again." She paused, gazing at the ocean. "Although, it does smell like Ophidian."

I hugged my arms around my stomach. "What are you thinking?"

"Doesn't it seem a little too coincidental? The Silas you saw in Ophidian's Realm was crazy, and now the Silas *outside* of Ophidian's Realm is crazy, too?" She tightened her grip around her legs. "I did learn one thing in my years of captivity: The Beast doesn't change his tactics if he doesn't have to."

Realization hit me like a boulder. Everything Claire said was true. But the question was, how? How was Silas being influenced by Ophidian? And who was it intended for? Just him or all of us?

And how much of it is actually his own doing?

I chewed on my lip. Claire was on the right track. "I bet you're right. But I don't know what we can do about it."

"Me, either." She shrugged. "Let's just hope we can fend him off long enough until we figure it out. Without James, I'm not sure what would have happened."

As if in response, steady snoring tumbled from James as he slept soundly.

"Is Damien okay?" I asked. The lord hadn't moved since he retreated to the far end of the fire. "Is his wound bad?"

Claire stretched out her legs, pressing her weight on her hands as she leaned back. "Nah, it's not too bad. Luckily, he had me to help him." She faked a grin that soon fell from her lips. "But I'm not sure how good tonight was for group bonding."

"No," I agreed, focusing back on the rolling waves. "It was definitely a step backward."

Claire snorted. "More like a giant leap."

My lips twitched, wanting to laugh.

Changing the subject, I said, "I'm sorry about losing

the connection with Lyle. And about Doctor Magnum, again."

Claire brushed her strand of brown hair away from her face. "It's okay, Addie. It was tough talking to my dad; I needed an excuse to get away. Besides" —she waved her hand in the air— "I already spent six months with Lyle. He's your brother that you fought so hard to have back, and you've barely seen him at all."

I placed my chin on my curled knees, wishing I had Lyle's sweater to comfort me. I did miss my brother and prayed that this would be over soon so we could be a family again. The evening breeze rustled against the waves, blowing Silas's hair across his brow. I gently pushed it away, yearning for his warmth, too, but I couldn't have that either.

"Yes, but I'm happy Lyle had you," I replied.

A blush came to Claire's cheeks before we sat in silence. Silas's face was a picture of peace as his chest moved with even breaths. What made him think of Damien's women? I'd never seen Silas so quick to violence. What would happen if we couldn't fight him? Would he kill us all? I dismissed the thought. I couldn't think that way. Eman wanted Silas to come on this journey. He wouldn't have sent him if he were going to kill us, right?

Are you sure?

"What is it?" Claire asked.

I pulled the string holding my hair, freeing my curls in the wind. "Nothing. I'm excited to go back and see Lyle when this is all over." Combing my fingers through the thick strands, I thought about my mother. How would she handle everything? The Magisters? Silas? Damien? I wish I had her guidance.

As I untangled the knots, I continued, "But, for now, I made an iuram with Eman that I would find the Twelve Magisters, and I intend to keep it."

"And I will be with you until you do," Claire said, rising to her feet as she dusted off her pants. Pursing her lips, she cocked her hip to the side and added, "I don't need to make some fancy magical promise with you to prove that now, do I?"

"No," I laughed. "I trust your word."

"Well, just don't be stupid."

I laughed and wished her a good night before unfolding my blanket and lying on the sand to admire the starry sky. Different twinkling constellations blinked at me, reminding me of the ones I had seen in Ramni. The vibrations of the waves rumbled beneath my fingertips as my pulse beat along with them. How could I protect all of us and Silas when I didn't know what Ophidian was up to?

My lids began to droop, heavy from the long journey. Soon, sleep overtook me, and I pushed my worries to tomorrow.

CHAPTER 28

The bright sun blazed through my eyelids. Morning had come too soon. I tried to shift my weight, only to find something pinning me to the ground. Gasping, I rolled out from under the heavy weight and jumped up.

A groan escaped from Silas's lips in response to my quick movements. He flipped onto his back, using one arm to shield his face from the morning sun. My cheeks instantly grew hot. Silas had wrapped his arm around me as we slept.

"What's the matter with you?" I scolded, glaring down at him as I placed my hands on my hips.

He lowered his arm and sat up. Rubbing his head, he squeezed his lids shut. "What are you talking about? And why does my head feel like it was trampled on?"

Fury boiled in my chest. "You stabbed Damien!"

Silas squinted up at me, shielding his eyes from the

sun. "Damien? Oh, right. Lord Farmount. What about him?"

Did Silas not remember what had happened? Was Ophidian taking his memories? I turned away from him, too angry to say any more.

James stretched his arms and stood. As he leaned back, a large crack sounded from his spine before he rubbed his sides. "I'm getting too old for this."

"James, please tell Silas what happened last night." I motioned to Silas, hoping someone else could help.

James brushed the sand off his shoulders. "Well, son, you went a little cuckoo last night and tried to give the grumpy lord a beating."

"What?" Silas asked, sitting up quickly. "What happened?"

"You said something about the lord's women," Claire yawned, stretching her arms in front of her. "Then you attacked him." She pointed to Damien, who was awake as well but kept his lips shut.

"No," Silas whispered, backing away from all of us. "I couldn't have. I don't remember anything." He held his face in his hands. "This can't be happening."

"What's happening, Silas?" I asked. "Talk to me."

He lifted his head, tears gathering in his eyes. "Addie, I don't—"

"Hello, over there!"

We turned to find Gaius and Brand approaching in their canoe from the sparkling waves. Cupping my hand over my eyes, I watched the brothers paddle to shore. My shoulders deflated. I really needed to talk to Silas about what had happened, why it happened. But I didn't want to address it in front of Brand and Gaius.

The brothers left their canoe at the shore as they jogged toward us, each grasping a large stick with spikes protruding from the top. As they headed closer, their faces were furrowed in concentration.

Before we could greet them, Gaius targeted Silas. "Come. We must be quick."

Silas jumped up, his gaze unwavering from mine. "I swear, Addie, I didn't know what I was doing." He started toward me, but I backed away.

"I don't know, Silas." I rubbed my hip where I had landed last night. "I can't." I hurried to where the others were, feeling Silas's gaze burn into the back of my head.

As we gathered up the rest of our supplies, James handed Silas his sword.

"Guard your heart, Silas," he cautioned.

"Should we give that back to him?" Claire asked under her breath.

"I'm not sure," I replied as Damien rolled his eyes and stomped away.

We strode to where Gaius and Brand stood. Planting their sticks through the ground, they waded through the sand, away from the waves. Silas curled his hands into fists before walking in step with Damien.

"I want to apologize about last night. I'm not sure what came over me. It won't happen again." He held out his hand.

Damien's eyes narrowed to slits as he grasped Silas's forearm. "It better not."

Silas's lips thinned, but he dipped his head. He jogged to the front of the group, giving my hand a quick brush as he walked by.

I curled my fingers. I wanted to believe him. I wanted to think that he wasn't aware of what was happening, but how many more things like this were going to happen? How many more people were going to get hurt? Was I going to get hurt?

We trekked through the sandy grass until all traces of foliage were gone. Brand, Gaius, and Silas led our group, conversing in hushed tones. James stayed in the back, always wanting to make sure we were protected from all sides, leaving Claire, Damien, and me in the middle.

After an hour of walking, my boots were heavy with blazing hot sand. I was sure my feet were raw from the scratchy grains. Before us laid miles and miles of golden dunes, whipping in the desert wind. I glanced at the ground. A thick white line separated the white grains of the Land of Ratcha, from the golden sand of the Land of Obesque.

Raising his spiked stick, Brand pointed it across the desert. "Continue in that direction until you come to Perda Forum."

"How will we know if we're in the right place?" Claire asked.

Brand bowed. "I would guide you there myself if I were allowed, my lady."

"You're not coming with us?" I asked, disappointed to be leaving the kind brothers and having more people to stop Silas in case he attacked again.

Gaius shook his head. "We dare not cross the border unless instructed by Sirhc. The last time someone crossed without permission …"

Brand rose and grabbed Claire's hands before she could object. "Be wary of Sirhc and Bocaj," he interjected, his hair whipping in the dry wind. "They began this competition years ago, and it's because of them, it's continued. I will pray to the Heavens that you can pass through unscathed, my lady, and that we will be reunited again."

Claire ripped her hands out of Brand's and shoved him back. Brand stumbled but caught himself before blowing Claire a kiss.

Silas gazed into Obesque, keeping his distance from the rest of us. I understood that he was worried about our safety, especially because of last night, but my heart tugged toward the Market of Thieves. I didn't need to check the book to make sure I was right. If Schism's cursed doors were anywhere, they would be there, right in the middle of chaos.

I glided past Silas toward the two brothers. "Thank you for your help. I hope we meet again soon."

"Sooner than you'd think," Brand mumbled, ogling at Claire before Gaius elbowed him in the ribs.

I cocked my head at the remark before Gaius pulled

my attention back to him. "We were happy to help." The brothers bowed in unison.

As we said farewell to Gaius and Brand, my confidence waned. I couldn't help but think things were about to get a lot worse.

〜

The golden sand reflected the sweltering sun back in my face. Sweat collected on my brow and neck from the intense heat. I pushed up the sleeves of my long shirt, allowing the breeze to cool my skin. Though I no longer had Lyle's sweater, I still wished it was with me to give me some comfort.

We trudged through the hot sand until the tops of large, square rocks reached our sight. As we neared the horizon, the rocks transformed into various stone buildings of a city. Some were tall and thin, others were short and fat, but they all held the same dark gray color.

A series of cheers erupted from the stone city as we traveled closer. Silas tensed beside me and grasped his sword, ready for an attack.

We craned our necks up as we approached the entrance. While the buildings were minuscule from afar, they were huge up close.

A narrow dirt path separated the buildings, turning a few feet to the right after the entrance. "Tu solve vos sumo," was chiseled into the side of one of the buildings, underlined in a dark substance I didn't want to think about.

"What does that mean?" I asked James.

"'You pay, you choose,'" James replied. His hands shimmered before his hooked axe appeared in his hands. He adjusted his grip on the weapon. "Sounds like we're in the right place."

A series of yells came from inside the city, but this time they weren't cheers of victory, but screams of anger. Goosebumps ran along my arms, but I was positive this was where our next destination lay.

"Well," I said, taking a step onto the narrow path. "It's now or never."

Before I could complete my step, an arrow flew from the right.

"Addie!" Silas cried before shielding me with his body. The arrow sunk into the ground at our feet.

Another arrow soared from the left. Silas unsheathed his sword and sliced it in half before it reached the sand below.

Pushing me behind him, Silas cut through the arrows coming at us.

I ducked, watching the arrow halves flutter to the ground. How could he move so fast?

"Go," he grunted. "Find someplace to hide."

"Come on!" James yelled, holding up his axe. The metal dinged as he deflected a few arrows before motioning for us to follow him. Claire held up her satchel as a shield and sprinted past us into the winding streets of the Market of Thieves.

Sweat dripped down Silas's neck as he fended off the attack.

"Please, Addie," he said in a strained voice. "I couldn't live with myself if anything happened to you."

I laid my hand on his back, sending a prayer to the Heavens that Silas would be protected before Damien stepped next to him.

"Go," Damien said, knives in hand. "I'll help Silas. We'll find you later." Rearing back, he threw a knife in the direction of the arrows. A wail bounded off the stone buildings before a body sailed off a ledge. I winced at the sounds of the skull cracking against the hard ground. In seconds, a new archer appeared, and twice the number of arrows rained on us.

"Go!" Damien commanded, flinging knives at the hidden archers.

With one last glance at Silas, I turned and sprinted to catch up with James and Claire.

The whooshes of arrows died down as we crept through the twisted street of the market. The narrow dirt path reminded me of the corridors in the Seven Choices. I gripped the satchel strap, hoping that was the only similarity between these two places.

Abandoned vendor booths hunched on some of the buildings' steps. Their decorations and wares were absent, leaving the booths empty as husks. A few more booths lined a wider street we passed, but other than that and the defense at the front, the Market of Thieves was deserted.

The cheers and screams we heard from before vibrated against the stone walls. As we turned the next corner, I collided with the rock-hard back of a hairy, shirtless man. I backed up slowly, praying he didn't feel anything. Within a few moments, the man bellowed a passionate cheer. I clamped my hand over my nose as he flailed his arms, releasing a sweaty stench. Crushed between his thick fingers was a small, black sack, jingling with coins.

Moving away from the man, I stood on my tiptoes, trying to find the reason for their cheers. But rows and rows of cheering, sweaty men obstructed my view.

Using his axe, James marked the outside of a building with a circle, then drew an X through it before he grabbed Claire's and my hands, dragging us into the stone space.

As soon as the splintered door shut, I turned to Claire and James. "Did you guys find anything about the Magisters?"

They both shook their heads before we poked around the room. It was mostly empty, save for a few broken tables and chairs. James padded toward one of the windows covered by a piece of tattered scarlet cloth, carefully lifting one of the corners as he peered out.

The cracked door of the building quietly creaked open. James had his weapon ready while Claire and I stood like stone. Could it be an attacker from the entrance? Or had Dacenda found us again?

Silas stumbled inside, his face coated in sweat, blood, and sand.

"Found you," he gasped as he fell to his knees.

"Silas," I cried, rushing to catch him. "Claire, help me."

Claire ran to my side, and we carefully laid Silas on the ground.

"Addie," she said, holding Silas's arm up. "I think you need to see this."

Black veins pulsed angrily from beneath Silas's creamy skin.

My breath hitched. "What's happening to him?" I turned to my friend for an answer, but she only shook her head.

James crouched next to Silas. Creating white light with his hand, James positioned his palm on Silas's forehead. "He needs to rest."

"James, what's happening to him? Please tell me," I cried. But James kept his lips tight.

More secrets.

"This may help," Claire said, placing a drop of silver liquid on Silas's wrist.

The shining drop dissolved into his skin, and the black in his veins faded to a more natural blue. Silas's breaths evened out as I brushed the damp hair from his clammy forehead.

"Thank you, Claire," I said.

She gave a quick nod before placing the vial back in her satchel.

"Where's Damien?" Claire asked, standing. She strode

over to the window and lifted the cloth to peek out.

"He was right behind me," Silas breathed, wincing as he tried to sit up. "I just saw him."

"Rest, Silas," James said, gently pushing him back down. "Or you won't be able to continue your journey."

"I don't blame him for running off," Claire muttered before exploring the room's perimeter.

"We need to get a better look at what's going on," James said, changing the subject.

I grabbed Silas's hand. "James, what's happening to him?" I asked again. "I know this is Ophidian, but what is he doing to Silas?"

James worked his jaw. "Something dark, Addie. That's all I can say."

I placed Silas's hand back down. How was Ophidian torturing Silas? And why couldn't James say more?

"I know the Magisters of Ratcha and Obesque, and the doors are here," I said, standing. "Why else would two of the Lands continuously battle one another? It has to be the work of Ophidian and Schism's doors."

"Hey, guys!" Claire shouted. James and I ran to the window, and then searched around the room but couldn't find her.

"Guys!" she said again, then popped up from a door hidden in the ground. We jumped in surprise, and Claire laughed. "I think I found where we need to go." She disappeared beneath the floor.

I hesitated before James waved his hand and said, "Go. I'll stay with Silas."

"No," Silas grunted, slowly opening his lids. "I'm okay. I can go."

"Silas, you need to rest," I said, unable to look away from the black veins snaking up his arm again.

"I'm okay, Addie." He sat up with a weak smile. His skin was pale, contrasting with the dark circles beneath his eyes.

"Silas—" I started, but James stood and offered Silas a hand.

"Even a strong man needs help sometimes."

Relief flooded Silas's features as he accepted James's offer.

"Go on, Addie," James said. "Silas and I will be right behind you."

A narrow staircase only wide enough for one person to fit on at a time descended into the building's cellar. Claire went first, then me, then Silas, and James.

I couldn't stop thinking about Damien's disappearance as I eased through the narrow stairwell. I understood why he left. I wouldn't have stayed if Silas had attacked me, but it still made me worry.

As we took each step, the cheers and screams grew louder. A bloodcurdling cry reverberated through the building, and I stifled a gasp. My pulse hammered, sensing the growing danger.

The stairs ended, opening into a large room filled with the same glistening men. With their bodies so exposed, a variety of colors of skin and hair filled the open arena. They were all screaming while waving small bags in the air. Though we were slightly higher than the crowd, it was still difficult to see what was going on.

"We need to get a better look," I whispered, motioning to a ledge next to us.

Moving as quickly and quietly as we could, the four of us gathered onto the stone ledge.

Two men stood across from one another. One was short but muscular with bronzed skin and long, blond hair. A wide cut, oozing blood, extended from his shoulder blade across his back. Several more cuts and bruises lined his arms and legs.

The other man was tall and lean with short, black hair. While he didn't have a large cut, his fingers jutted in all the wrong directions. As I peered closer, I saw that his body was covered in large, red lines.

The men growled at each other, holding their weapons steady. The muscular, short one gripped a long whip, snapping it before it snaked around the lean man's leg. The lean man fell to the ground. One section of the crowd cheered for the stout man. I curled my fingers into fists, remembering the whip Schism used in the window of the Shadow realm.

The lean man wielded a spiked stick, much like the ones Brand and Gaius were using before. He freed himself from the whip before he charged toward his opponent. The other section of the crowd erupted into cheers.

I brought a hand to my mouth as each man attacked. The crowd continued to cheer and scream until there was silence. The man with the whip had the cord wrapped tightly around the lean man's throat. My mouth dropped as the life seeped from the lean man's eyes before he fell to the ground.

Disgust churned in my gut as half of the crowd cheered again. I glanced over to find Silas's and James's jaws clenched tight with Claire looking just as sick as me.

The crowd continued to yell as a dark-skinned man glided into the arena where the muscular man stood triumphantly over the lean man. Shirtless like all the others, the man strode around the edge of the fighting area. The large, gray cloth wrapped around his waist moved fluidly as he silenced the crowd with a raised arm. Long, black braids cascaded from his head, each tied off with a golden band. A matching golden band defined his muscular bicep, twinkling as he passed by.

He turned to address the crowd, and I jerked back. On his chest was the mark of a Magister.

James shook his head, his eyes downcast.

A cold sweat dripped down my neck, my pulse quickening at the thought of approaching this Magister.

With a large grin, the Magister held up the hand of the short, muscular man. "Ratcha is victorious!" The crowd responded with a mixture of cheers and shouts.

The Magister grinned at the crowd, relishing the bloodlust. This wasn't right. No Magister would allow this to happen. When he turned, I saw the crimson shade covering his irises and the large white circle on the ground. Frost covered my thoughts. Ira's Vindicae had come to Decim.

CHAPTER 29

"Who's next?" the dark-skinned Magister yelled, motioning toward the arena around him. "Who will leave Ira's Vindicae unscathed?"

The crowd grew silent. The leather bags stopped mid-air, as well as my pulse. How could Ira's Vindicae be here? Were there more horrors from the Seven Choices seeping into Decim?

As the crowd retreated, the white line of Ira's Vindicae taunted me. Schism and his horrid creature form flooded my memory from the Third Choice.

"You know the rules," another voice shouted, thick with a rich Obesquean accent.

From the opposite side of the crowd, another shirtless man stepped forward. His pale skin and shaved head were a contrast to the dark-skinned Magister. A black braided beard descended from his chin, matching the black swirls branded into his thick arms. Like the others, a cloth circled his waist, though decidedly shorter than the other Magister's. My hope vanished when I saw the Magister's mark and blood-red eyes on this man, as well.

"Bocaj," the dark-skinned Magister said, stepping aside.

"Sirhc." Bocaj lifted his chin before facing the crowd. "You pay, you choose," Bocaj continued, his deep voice ricocheting through the arena. "Who is willing to pay for the next warrior?"

"I will."

Out of the crowd stepped a middle-aged man clad in leather armor with cropped walnut waves and black gloves. His golden eyes shimmered as he stalked toward the center of Ira's Vindicae. A dark trimmed beard grew from his cheeks, accentuating his stern lips.

The man strode slowly but with confidence. Two blades gleamed from behind his back as he held out a blue bag. The dark-skinned Magister opened his palm, and the man poured a series of glittering crystals into it. I sucked in a breath, my stomach twisting into knots. Those were my crystals. The ones the thief had stolen from me in the night.

"Aren't those from Neural?" James questioned quietly, giving me a side-long glance.

"Why does that guy have them?" Claire pointed at the thief.

"Who is he, Addie?" Silas glowered at the man.

Rage bubbled in my chest as I ignored my friends' confusion and disbelief. I dug my fingertips into the ledge until they turned white. How dare he use my crystals for this barbaric competition?

"Excellent," the dark-skinned Magister said with a devious grin, closing his hand around the jewels. "Who do you choose for your warrior? And for whose side?"

"I choose that warrior," the thief said. "The side I choose is my own."

All heads of the crowd turned toward the ledge as the thief's finger pointed steadily at me.

The eyes of the gambling men fixated on our position, and panic sliced through my body. After a moment's pause, a huge bellow of laughter rose from the Magister with the long, braided beard.

"What's this? The great thief, Romen, has decided to finally enter the competition?" He looked at the thief with mocking disbelief. "And he has chosen a *woman*, no less!" The Magister bellowed again, holding his stomach. The men in the arena howled with laughter, as well. "This will be a fight to remember!" The Magister turned and motioned toward the lifeless body from the previous fight with disgust. "Take his heart and give it to the arenam."

I held my breath as one of the men dragged the lifeless body out of the circle and discarded it in front of a thin, gangly man. The thin man held the same circular tube Doctor Magnum had used for extractions. But while Doctor Magnum's instrument was shiny and pristine, this device was rusted with chunks of metal falling off of it. Placing the tube over the dead man's chest, the thin man extracted a black heart from the man's lifeless body. Two other men dragged the heartless body through the dirt until it was lost in the crowds.

The thief lowered his hand, his glowing golden gaze searing my skin. He tipped his chin up, challenging me to accept his bet.

The men continued to double over with laughter. Heat swirled in my chest before the power of my rage seeped into my fingertips, igniting them with orange light. If only they knew that this *woman* had already triumphed through Ira's Vindicae before. Just barely, but still triumphed. Insulted, I rose from the ledge.

"What are you doing?" Claire shrieked, placing her hands on her head.

"I don't think this is a good idea," James added, starting to stand as well.

"Who is that guy, Addie? And why does he have our crystals?" Silas hissed.

The darkness in his veins had returned in force. With each pulse of Silas's half-heart, the black blood traveled up his arm to his neck. The look in his eyes wasn't compassionate like it was outside of Perda Forum but held anger. "Why aren't you answering any of our questions?"

My gaze cut to Silas. "He was going to kill all of you before, but he didn't because of me."

Silas began to rise. "What? When? Why didn't you say anything?"

I jerked out of his grasp. *I* protected everyone from the thief by giving him the crystals, not Silas. I was strong, and I was going to prove it.

The Magister with long, dark braids silenced the crowd with an outstretched hand. "Man or woman, it does not matter. The rules are the same. The thief, Romen, has paid more than any of you and has chosen his warrior." He turned toward Romen. "You have not chosen Ratcha or Obesque to battle for, but your own side. Tell me, what is it you fight for?"

Romen's lips twitched as if he had heard an amusing joke. "When my warrior wins, I will tell you my stakes, Sirhc."

The dark-skinned Magister, Sirhc, nodded. He hadn't laughed once since Romen declared me his warrior. And for that, I liked him far better than the brutish Magister.

"That is wonderful, Romen," the bearded Magister bellowed once more, slapping the thief on the shoulder. "You are so confident your little woman will win. Since you haven't chosen one of our Lands, I will choose her opponent for you. She will fight me."

Ice raced down my spine. What had I gotten myself into? Not only was this man muscular beyond belief, but he was huge. At more than a foot taller than me, this Magister could easily destroy me during a fight. Maybe I could still back out. I ran my hand along the satchel, hoping I'd feel the book shaking, telling me I was in danger. But not even a quiver came from the bag.

Below, one side of the crowd jumped up and down, raising their arms in the air as they supported the Magister, while the other side looked disappointed, as if they had wanted to fight me instead.

"And, by some miracle, if she does win, I will give her this!" The Magister turned his palms to the ceiling.

White light flowed from the Magister's hands. Before I could blink, the black handle of a spiked flail appeared, and I took a step back. The Magister lifted it up, twirled it in the air, then slammed the shining spiked ball to the ground. Vibrations traveled to the ledge, shaking the foundation of the arena. I stumbled forward, falling to my knees. Sharp pebbles cut into my palms as I braced myself against the ground. When I looked back up, a satisfied grin laid on the Magister's lips.

Rage and pride fueled the power igniting my hands. He thought I was nothing but a useless fool. I wasn't sure why the thief from the forest had chosen me, but I was ready to prove this smug Magister wrong. I wasn't useless. Bright orange flames blazed from my fingertips, ready to be unleashed.

Squaring my shoulders, I threw the satchel off and started to climb down the ledge when Silas's hand whipped out and grabbed my wrist.

"What are you doing? You're going to get killed."

I yanked my hand away. "At least it won't be by you," I snapped before I could stop myself.

Silas's mouth dropped open as his hand fell to his side.

"Addie," Claire whispered, her eyes wide.

I shot her a glare, silencing any more protests. James only clucked his tongue, keeping his eyes focused on the Magisters.

Gripping the stone wall, I completed my descent and

landed feet-first on the ground below, ready to face my opponent.

I tilted my chin up, and the perspiring men parted. Some pulled gold coins from their bags, passing them to different men in the crowd while snickering under their breaths. I growled. I hadn't even gotten to the circle, and they were already betting against me.

I stopped at the edge of Ira's Vindicae. The white line encouraged me to dive into my fury and enter its ring of death. Memories of Schism's mocks, Ophidian's threats, Eman's silence, and Silas's episodes flooded my mind, building the fire in my chest. But I had learned what this rage wanted. It wanted to consume me, control me, and, ultimately, destroy me. I was overrun by Ira's Vindicae once before, and I wouldn't allow it to happen again.

The thief, Romen, and the Magister, Sirhc, watched me with interest. When I didn't move, an impressed grin came to Sirhc's face.

"Ah, your warrior is more than what she seems. Obviously, she knows the rules of Ira's Vindicae: once you enter, only one leaves."

"I won't enter unless I'm allowed a weapon of my choice," I demanded, finding my confidence.

It wasn't until Silas's sword had come to me that I stood a fighting chance. But now that it was gone, I had nothing. If I had to fight in this circle again, I would defend myself.

Sirhc slapped Romen on the back like the other Magister had. But Romen never moved, his stance stayed unwavering and tense. Since I had climbed from the ledge, his blazing golden eyes hadn't left my face.

"You've chosen a wise warrior, Romen." Sirhc turned to me. "Of course, you will be given a weapon, my lady." He gave a deep bow that I couldn't tell was genuine or mocking. When he stood, Sirhc motioned toward the crowd. The men parted once again to reveal the same gangly man who had extracted the dead man's heart. Only now, instead of the extraction instrument, he carried a variety of weapons.

The gaunt man looked as if a single gust of wind would scare him out of his skin. He laid the bundle out before me. I immediately noticed the weapons all had one thing in common: each was caked with dried blood. I clenched my jaw shut.

The first weapon was a sword. After wielding Silas's sword, this one seemed inferior, so I moved on. The next was the whip the warrior from Ratcha used. The vivid memory of him choking the life out of his opponent was still too fresh. And I also would never want to use the same weapon as Schism. Shaking my head, I studied the next weapon. It was a spiked flail like the bearded Magister had.

The air was thick and hot with anticipation. Wiping the sweat from my upper lip, I glanced up to find all eyes on me. I assumed an experienced opponent would pick the same weapon, some sort of fight fire with fire concept.

Yet as I looked back down, the spiked flail just didn't

seem right; too barbaric for me. Hoping to get some sort of help, I surveyed the collection some more until my eyes landed on the last weapon, if you could call it that. It wasn't a weapon at all, but a black rod.

Recognition tugged at the back of my mind, and I crouched down to examine the long cylinder. There was something familiar about it. As I got closer, my heart pulsed with confirmation. I had definitely seen this rod before, but where? I searched the corners of my mind until I found the memory. This was Claire's rod, the one she had in Ophidian's Realm to defend against the siti. But how had it gotten here?

As I reached toward the rod, a cool surge of power seeped from it, beckoning me to choose it. The strength between my heart and the weapon was unlike anything I had ever experienced before. Silas's sword was powerful. But this force was beyond the power of his sword.

With my hand only inches from grasping the black rod, the faintest voice spoke in my mind.

You are more powerful than you believe.

Eman's crisp, soothing voice was nothing like the slick, slithering voice that had invaded my thoughts. Though I was still peeved at his silence about my parents, if Eman was speaking to me now, this weapon was the right one to choose.

Reaching out, I fully grasped the rod. A chilling wave of energy flowed through my veins as orange light poured from my palm around the rod. The ground quaked as I grasped the weapon with both hands, trying to absorb the power. The energy within me locked into place, awakening a new strength. Panting, I gripped the rod and stood. I had finally found my alme.

Gasps and stunned silence filled the battle arena. It wasn't until I stepped into Ira's Vindicae that I realized what they saw. A long, blue tunic trimmed with golden leaves and brown leggings replaced my former Barracks clothing. Brown leather armor laid over the tunic, covering my chest, shoulders, and back. Matching brown leather gloves wrapped around my hands, my skin beneath writhing with power ready to be unleashed.

I grasped my alme tight, watching the mark of the Mender burn itself into it. The circle with the slash through it matched the mark on my chest, branding this alme as my own. My heart and the power of the rod beat as one, the rod's cool texture calming the fire burning inside me. I strode confidently toward the center of the circle, finally complete. Sirhc watched with wide eyes, the red draining from them.

Romen stalked toward me, and I squared my shoulders in defiance.

"That was quite a show," his deep voice said.

Ignoring his remark, I asked, "Why did you use *my* jewels to choose me?"

He glanced at the anticipating crowd, then back to me. Before I could react, he unsheathed one of the swords from his back, grabbed my free palm, and dragged the blade across it, slicing through my new leather glove.

I cried out and yanked my hand away. "What are you doing?"

Clutching my hand, I watched him do the same to his palm. Quickly, he grabbed my hand again and pressed his bloody palm on mine.

"What are you doing?" I asked again, panicked at the level of power surging between our hands.

I tried to wrench away, but he held our hands firm. Orange and golden light swirled between our palms, twisting around one another until they were perfectly entwined. Finally, he released them. I spun away and examined my hand. Rubbing my fingers against my palm, I saw that the cut was no longer there, and my glove had been repaired.

"What did you do?" I narrowed my eyes at him.

"A blood oath," he said nonchalantly, wiping his blade on his pant leg. "You are bound to my cause. And I am bound to yours."

"If you're done trying to woo the lady," the bearded Magister bellowed, arousing snickers and hoots from the crowd, "I would like to kill her now." He lifted his flail and charged.

"Wait!" Sirhc cried, his irises fully drained of the bloodlust. With his arms outstretched, he tried to stop the sprinting Magister. "Bocaj, wait! She's—"

Before he could finish, Ira's Vindicae launched Romen and Sirhc out of the circle, leaving me with a deadly Magister, completely alone.

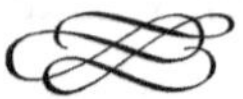

I surveyed the awestruck faces of the gambling men. There were no cheers. No screams. No longer was the crowd disgusted but completely transfixed on what was happening in the deathly white circle.

Taking a step back, my foot hit the barrier, and my mind flashed back to the Third Choice. Only one warrior survived. But when I had fought Schism, we both exited the circle. So, there had to be a way for both Bocaj and me to leave Ira's Vindicae alive.

A bellowing battle cry and the whooshing of the flail interrupted my thoughts. I scrambled out of the way just in time. Bocaj's weapon lodged into the ground, cracking the dirt where I had just stood.

"Come now," he said with a wolfish grin. "I'll only hurt you a little." He flung the flail back with a roar, launching its spiked end at me.

Crouching to the ground, I rolled out of the way, gripping the rod with both hands. This was my alme. Everything in me connected with it. But I had no idea how to use it.

Barely escaping the flail again, I retreated to the edge of the circle. Bocaj snarled at me, his mocking arrogance gone. No longer were his irises glazed with red but shrouded in black, like Silas's had been the night before. The sweat dripping down my back turned cold. If I didn't defeat the Magister soon, I'd be fighting something much worse.

I sucked in a breath before my gaze darted over Bocaj's head. Claire, Silas, and James were huddled together on the ledge. Their eyes were wide with fear, their faces white as snow.

I shouldn't have snapped at Silas. I may never see him again. Or James and Claire.

It was at that moment I realized what I needed to focus on. Not on my fear of death or my anger and pride of being underestimated, but my love for those I cared about. Just like in Ophidian's Realm, when I switched my focus from my hate and anger of Schism to my love and care for those who had been abused by him, I had the upper hand.

My heart infused with energizing power, and I guided it into the rod. Instantly, the metal glowed, transforming from its black color to a solid white. My mouth fell open as two blades extended from the ends, shining bright orange.

Every part of my body infused with power, vibrating with adrenaline. I bowed my head and laughed. Ophidian thought he had already won, that I was a nuisance and would soon meet my end. But he was wrong. I had found my alme and was ready to use it to defeat him.

Allowing my newfound power to surge through my being, I readied my stance toward the Magister before me. He was no longer the man Eman chose to follow his ways. He had been possessed by the Beast, stolen from his true path, and I intended to free him.

Bocaj barreled toward me, twirling the flail above his head. Planting my feet, I swung my alme, slicing his stomach. Blood trickled from the wound as Bocaj's animalistic roar filled the circle. He quickly recovered and lunged at me. I attempted to roll out of the way again, but the flail's sharp ends pierced my side. I let out a cry and fell into the grime. The pain intensified as Bocaj extracted the flail. I covered my wounds with my hand, wincing as my fingers brushed the large gashes and broken skin. Fresh blood seeped from the cuts, staining my beautiful tunic.

Straining, I heaved my weight onto my alme and stood. Blood dripped from my side and onto the dirt. The droplets mixed with Bocaj's blood before flowing into the white circle around us. Our barrier shifted from white to crimson, as if Ira's Vindicae was feeding off the life we were losing.

My limbs trembled, and my vision spun, but I fought through my exhaustion. The cool power of my alme rejuvenated my strength and quenched the throbbing wound on my side.

Straightening, I scanned the circle before I located my

target. The Magister twirled his flail in the air, a malicious smirk on his lips as he waited for me to attack. Holding my alme in front of me, I charged at Bocaj. The Magister swung his flail back, ready to impale me again, but I dodged, striking him on the head before pulling back and stabbing his shoulder. The Magister roared again, but, this time, stayed in his place. I retreated as far as the circle would allow me, panting as I watched him closely. The brute of a man stood, his arms twitching at his sides. Was the real Bocaj trying to fight the monster that had overtaken him, as well?

Rolling the rod between my palms, I allowed all the power, love, and injustice in my heart to pour into my alme. My powerful pulse vibrated in my hands as the two became one. The orange flames coating the two blades on the ends intensified, ready to consume everything in their path.

My arms quaked with power as I sprinted at Bocaj, spinning the rod in the air, before lunging to pierce his right bicep. He screamed again, trying to move, but another force caused him to resist. I moved faster, hoping the other Bocaj, the real Bocaj, could fight the darkness consuming him a little longer.

Reacting on instinct, I stabbed my alme into the ground, using it as a force to swing around and kick him where I had first cut his stomach. My body whipped around the rod before I landed, detaching my alme from the dirt. Bocaj fell to his knees, his hands grasping at the flail that had fallen from his grip. With the alme as my guide, I rushed at him once more, using the speared end to slice his stomach again and create an X. The monster within roared, then snatched the flail and threw it with full force in my direction.

I slid to the ground, barely escaping the flail flying too close past my head. Catching my breath, I glanced up to find Bocaj's irises shifting from black to light blue. I scrambled over to where the flail had landed and grabbed it.

Enraged by my theft, Bocaj turned toward me, eyes black as night while the monster regained power. Bocaj raced toward me, snarling. My heart roared with my alme's power, directing me to the next and final step of this fight. Waiting until he was inches from my reach, I reared back, swinging the flail as hard as I could, before lodging the spiked ball into Bocaj's bleeding chest. Time within the circle froze. Bocaj slowly looked down at his own weapon protruding from his body.

I swallowed hard, beads of sweat rolling down my temples. My entire body tensed. Had I just killed a Magister?

But then, the unexpected happened.

A relieved smile formed on Bocaj's lips as his eyes transformed to their original blue. He fell to his knees and said, "Thank you, Bellata," before falling to his back, motionless.

The flaming spears retracted into the white rod before my alme returned to its normal charcoal color. My heart rammed against my rib cage as I ran to the Magister's side. The red ring around Ira's Vindicae faded to white, then disappeared completely. Footsteps rushed in all directions as the men gathered around us.

"Move. Now," a deep voice said, and the men shuffled away.

The thief, Romen, crouched beside me while Sirhc, now gowned in a light-blue cloak lined with white leaves, knelt next to Bocaj. I watched as the Magister extracted the flail from Bocaj's stomach, expecting blood to gush out. Instead, the blood retreated into his body. The wounds I had inflicted disappeared as his skin knitted together.

Sirhc glanced up at me with a gentle smile. "You are a fierce warrior, Bellata. No one has ever taken down Bocaj."

I blinked at him, surprised.

Sirhc laughed. "You didn't kill him, Bellata. We, Magisters—especially brutes like Bocaj—can't be killed by our own alme. He'll wake in a few moments, with his pride hurt, no doubt." He scratched his temple. "Given that you struck him with his weapon, I thought you knew."

I shook my head quickly. I had no idea what I was doing. My alme had guided my attacks; I had only followed.

"Well," he said, standing from his crouched position with a light chuckle. "That was lucky." He turned to Romen. "Your stakes, great thief."

"End this competition, Sirhc," Romen said. "There are darker things ahead that need to be defeated."

Nodding, Sirhc turned to face the crowd of men who were now confused as to what was happening. Murmurs bounced between them.

"My friends," Sirhc announced, opening his arms wide. The crowd went silent. "We have led you astray in what we have allowed to happen between our Lands these past years."

All the men turned to one another, then back to Sirhc, their eyes wide, anticipating his next words.

"We have been deceived and possessed by another force. An evil but powerful force. Though Ratcha and Obesque have not seen eye to eye for years, we've been at peace before and will be at peace again. Go back to your homes and rest while you can. A different war is on the horizon."

The men were silent, apart from a few disgruntled groans before the cheers started. Another wide grin came to Sirhc's face as the men patted one another on the back and shook hands while they filed out of the battle arena.

"Bellata," Sirhc said, kneeling before me. "You have done a great service for the Land of Ratcha, and for that, I owe you my life. It was eight years ago when bloodlust and rage ravaged our Lands. Sadly, the rage spread to Obesque, consuming not only Bocaj but myself, as well." He motioned to Bocaj, still on the ground. "I'm surprised we're still alive. But when I saw the bright light coming from you, it seemed as if Eman was speaking to me, telling me of the evil that was consuming my mind, heart, and people." He bowed his head, his ebony braids spilling around his shoulders. "I'm ashamed for having not fulfilled the duty Eman has given me."

I placed a hand on Sirhc's shoulder. "Eman knew of the evil you faced. That's why he sent me. He requires your aid in defeating the darkness."

Sirhc lifted his head. "And I will aid him until my death." Turning his palms to the sky, he waited as a large, metal rod with spikes protruding from the top laid in his hands. I reached out and held fast to the alme as he vowed, "I, Sirhc Prolod, Magister of Ratcha, swear on my alme to fight with you until there is no life left within me."

Sirhc's light, blissful power pranced around my heart, the iuram binding us together, and I released the weapon. Another Magister's power locked into place.

"Bellata," a bellowing voice said. Bocaj stood behind Sirhc with his spiked flail in his hand. Though he was still huge, he performed a graceful bow, making him slightly less intimidating.

Kneeling next to Sirhc, Bocaj's loud laugh echoed against the walls of the vacant arena. "If all women fought like you, I would have been happily married a long time ago." A few men that were still left in the arena laughed along with him, and I couldn't help but grin.

"Because we are near the gates of the Beast, our Lands have been heavily exposed to the wrath of his evil," Bocaj explained, glowering at the weapon in his hands. "Though I don't know the state of the Lands to the north, I fear they have been under his darkness years longer than any of the southern Lands." He bowed his head as Sirhc did. "I, as well, am ashamed of not fulfilling what Eman intended for me to do."

Before I could respond, he lifted his flail. "Even if I didn't want to, I already agreed to give you my weapon if you defeated me." Another wide grin broke through his dark facial hair. "Although I hate to admit it, you are a fearless warrior, Bellata. I would follow you into battle any day."

Holding out his flail, he vowed, "I, Bocaj Samor, Magister of Obesque, swear on my alme to fight with you until there is no life left within me."

As I wrapped my fingers around the weapon, Bocaj's heavy, thundering energy shook me to the core. His power soared through my veins before braiding around my heart. Half of the Twelve Magisters had agreed to fight against Ophidian. I only needed six more.

"Addie!"

The crowd parted to allow Silas, Claire, and James through. Running toward me, Claire and James enveloped me in their arms.

"You stupid, stupid girl," Claire said as she held me tight.

"Careful," I cried.

Claire jerked back and immediately saw the oozing cut on my side.

Opening her satchel, she murmured, "I shouldn't even help you anymore, but I know you wouldn't survive without me."

I grinned and turned so she could bandage the wound.

I expected the cool salve to chill my skin when Claire gasped, dropping her bottle to the ground.

"What?" I asked, twisting to look at my side. The wound was gone, all traces of blood vanishing from my tunic.

"An alme heals its holder," James explained, planting a kiss on my forehead.

I ran my finger across my side. Nothing was there but soft fibers of fabric. So, that's why Silas left battles unscathed. The gashes had stopped hurting almost immediately after I received the wound earlier. And my tunic had been repaired, as well. I studied the black rod. An alme was pretty useful.

"I'm so proud of you, Addie," James exclaimed, handing me my satchel. "You found your alme." Placing a hand on his chin, he shook his head. "Although, I think I'll spare your nana the details on how you found it."

"Dimitte!" Bocaj bellowed, wrapping his arms around James and pulling him up for a hug. "Glad you're back!"

"Me, too," James said weakly.

"How did you do that?" Claire asked, examining my side before poking me in the ribs. I slapped her hand away, but she poked again. "And this warrior armor. I haven't seen anything like it." She prodded the leather surrounding my arms.

"I'm not sure—"

"It was amazing!" she cut me off, throwing her arms in the air. "If you would've fought like that in Ophidian's realm, you wouldn't have been nearly as hurt as you were.

I would've saved more of my supplies, too. And, my siti stick was your alme!" She scratched her temple. "That probably would've helped you out more, too."

I snorted, suppressing a laugh. "Thanks, Claire."

Silas stood far away from the rest of us, his eyes downcast.

"You've proven yourself, Bellata," the thief said, pulling my attention away from Silas.

"Who are you, and why did you make her do that?" Silas called out from where he stood.

Roman lifted a brow. "That was nothing compared to the battle that is to come. She was to prove herself a warrior, and she did."

"Prove herself to who?" Silas growled, taking a solitary step forward.

Romen's lips formed a grin, revealing a set of perfectly straight teeth. "Me."

Silas growled as he unsheathed his sword. Romen held up a hand. "Don't try to start a fight with me, boy. You'll lose."

"Wait," I said, stepping between them. "I was unwillingly bound to your cause, which I assume was ending the competition between Obesque and Ratcha. Am I right?" The thief nodded. "And you're bound to my cause, which is defeating Ophidian." He nodded again. "If we're to work with one another, we need to know we can trust one another."

"You're wise, Bellata, but are you sure you want to put your trust in a thief?" Romen questioned.

I eyed him, remembering Eman's friend among the thieves. Could this be him? "I don't have any other choice, do I?"

Chuckling, the thief patted a pocket on his chest before pulling out a long pipe. He stuffed some herbs into the top before leaning toward Sirhc. The Magister sighed as he lit his hand and ignited the herbs.

"I thought you were giving that up," Sirhc said. "You know it confuses your weaving."

Romen ignored Sirhc as he sucked in a breath, his shoulders relaxing.

What were they talking about? What weaving? Before I could ask, Bocaj shouted as he trudged toward the exit.

"Bellata! We must discuss what has happened to our Lands these long, terrible years." We hesitated before Bocaj bellowed again. "Come!" he repeated, causing us to jump before scrambling toward the Magister.

The men who were once thirsty for blood had exited from the arena, leaving James, Bocaj, and Sirhc standing where Ira's Vindicae had been. Claire shuffled behind us, while Romen marched confidently next to me, blowing hues of colored clouds from his pipe.

Tick.

Tock.

Tick.

Tock.

The ticking mimicked the beat of our steps, stomping along the ground. My pulse matched the rhythm, ramming against my ribs. The clock had gotten louder and harsher since I had first heard it, vibrating my bones with each sound. I winced as each tick pinched my nerves. Squeezing the satchel strap, I tried to ignore it as we followed the Magisters, but it only grew worse, blurring my vision until I could barely see.

Unable to handle the infernal noise any longer, I stopped. Placing my hands over my ears, I slammed my palms against my head to stop the clock in my mind. It only grew louder, striking my heart with harsh pangs coinciding with the ticks.

"Addie," Silas said, his voice barely audible above the ticks. "What's wrong? What's wrong with her?"

"It's getting worse," Romen replied. "She's closer to Regno."

"What does that mean?" Silas's voice grew panicked.

"Come," Sirhc directed.

His bare feet appeared in my line of sight, but his voice sounded so far away. Tears streamed down my face as the throbbing continued in my chest and my head. The pain was relentless.

I tried to move, but my foot slipped. The blood-soaked dirt beneath me came closer until there was nothing but darkness.

CHAPTER 31

"What do you mean, time is freezing?"

Silas's irritated voice pierced my thoughts, waking me from the slumber I didn't remember entering. My limbs were like rusted hinges, refusing to move. My head was heavy as if it had been wrapped in suffocating cloth.

"Not freezing," Romen's deep voice countered. "Unraveling."

I struggled to open my eyes, trying to gain some recognition of what had happened. A muted ticking unleashed at the back of my head. I squeezed my lids shut, bringing my hand to my throbbing head. Two cool hands gently placed themselves on my cheeks.

"Addie?" Claire said softly. "Addie, can you hear me?"

I slowly opened my eyes. Claire's gaze darted around my face. The ticking became louder, and I shut my lids, forcing the ticking to become muted once more.

"I can hear you," I said, my voice strained. "It just hurts to open my eyes."

A chilled sensation flowed from my temples, causing the ticking to disappear to nothing but an unwanted memory. My strength soon returned, rejuvenating my body and mind.

"How about now?" Claire asked.

Cautiously, I opened one lid to find her studying me closely. I waited to see if the ticking was truly gone until I opened the other. As I gave her a smile, relief painted over her features, and she grinned back, holding a leaf of linkslock.

"Thank you," I said.

Claire blew out a breath before standing and giving a proud smile. "I'm glad it worked."

"Yes," Silas said, leaving his conversation with Romen to kneel beside me. He reached out to me, but stopped, curling his fingers into a fist before dropping his hand. "I'm thankful you know what you're talking about, Claire."

"Of course, I know what I'm talking about," she replied while returning the linkslock to her satchel.

Silas cautiously touched my forehead. "I was so worried."

I leaned into his touch, but it soon disappeared as he retracted his arm and fled to the center of the room.

No longer were we in the spacious arena where Ira's Vindicae had been, but in a large tent. Judging by the cool temperature, this tent had been built for the dry desert.

The tan walls rippled softly from the desert wind blowing outside. Around the perimeter were large stone vases filled with countless scrolls. Some were crisp and white as if just written yesterday, while others were a muddied yellow-brown, seeming to have been around for ages.

The floor was laid with a large, circular rug. Intricate designs of gold and purple wove in and out of one another to make a beautiful floral pattern. On it stood a long, wooden table where small plates of incense burned, filling the tent with an aroma of cloves.

Sirhc and James sat at the table, their attention focused on me while Bocaj strode over to where Claire was arranging herbs. Bocaj's chest was still bare, but his Magister cloak of charcoal with red leaves was tied around his waist as he asked Claire about the herbs in his booming voice.

Silas stood as still as stone as he took his place next to James. Romen mirrored his position on the other side of the rectangular table.

"What happened?" I said, trying to stand to join them.

When I moved, my head swirled, and I placed one hand behind me for balance, where I hit a mound of colorful pillows. Sitting up slowly, I brought a scarlet pillow to my lap and wrapped my arms around it as I faced the collection of strained faces.

Silas stiffened even more as Romen turned toward me.

Sensing the rising tension, Sirhc interjected with a

forced smile, "Bellata, there are many things we don't know. But there are a few questions we would like to ask you to help us better understand what's happening."

I nodded hesitantly, bracing myself for what was coming.

Relief melted Sirhc's worrisome features as he rolled up the parchment he was reading. His long, light-blue robe swished around his bare feet as he padded toward me. Once he was a few feet away, he lowered himself to the sandy ground and crisscrossed his legs.

With a kind smile, Sirhc asked, "How long have you been hearing Time?"

Biting my lip, I tried to think back to when the ticking first started. It seemed as if centuries had passed since the infernal noise infiltrated my thoughts, but I could recollect the memory.

"When we returned to Barracks from Ramni the first time, right when we were about to enter into Wintertide. That was when I first heard the ticking."

Above Sirhc's head, Silas dropped his chin to his chest as he brought his hand to his mouth, his shoulders shuddering.

Claire closed her bag and settled by my side. She sat on the pillow next to me and held one of my hands. The kind gesture confused me, but when I saw her downturned lips, I knew something was wrong.

"So, I've been hearing Time? What does that mean? Is it bad?"

Sirhc opened his mouth to speak, but it was Bocaj that answered.

His voice wasn't overbearing and bellowing as before, but quiet, as if afraid to respond. "Obesque was the second of the Twelve Lands to be infiltrated by darkness." He clenched his fist tightly, ready to slam it on the table, but instead laid it down gently. "The first was Regno. Unlike the other Lands, the Beast came with force." Bocaj covered his face, as if ashamed. "There wasn't enough time. The darkness came, and Auso did what he had to do."

With Bocaj unable to continue, Sirhc stepped in. "Auso, the Magister of Regno, didn't want the darkness to spread to the other Lands for fear of what the Beast's control over Regno would do. Using his power, Auso broke Regno off from Decim, leaving it shrouded in the full darkness of the Beast."

"But the darkness did spread to the other Lands," Bocaj cut in. "And Obesque was the first to receive it." He stood, pacing around Romen, who was now facing us. Bocaj stroked his beard as he said, "Perda Forum was created out of Obesque's greed for treasures and power. Though it wasn't the most honorable place, the trade was still respectable. Somewhat. When citizens of the other Lands would trade away their dying hearts for other valuables or to be free of disease, the vendors would bring the dying hearts here."

I crushed the pillow to my chest, remembering what Governor Willow had said before he had transformed into a siti: *Ophidian said he would take the vendors away. But he was the one who sent them to Barracks.* I tightened my grip on the pillow, holding it close.

But Perda Forum did intrigue me. I had always wondered what happened to hearts once they were traded. The hearts that were traded to Schism were sent to Ophidian, who held onto them until their owners were ready for Eternal Knowledge and to become a malum.

But what happened to the others? The ones traded for wealth, beauty, and various other things at Heart Reign? Where did they go?

"Once the vendors brought the hearts to Perda Forum," Bocaj continued, stomping back and forth behind Sirhc, "they would trade them for all the riches and jewels the thieves of the market had collected." He stopped and turned toward Romen with a mischievous grin. "You remember the old days? The great thief, Romen, would bring the rarest treasures, procuring the best hearts to do whatever he wished with them."

All eyes turned to Romen, and, for the first time since meeting him, he actually looked nervous. Shifting his weight from one foot to the other, he didn't respond or acknowledge that he'd heard Bocaj. He only continued to face us, silently watching.

As Bocaj recounted Romen's magnificent thieving, I tried to make sense of everything he was saying. People would trade their hearts to vendors. Vendors would take the hearts to the Market of Thieves for jewels and coin. The sizes and color of the hearts probably determined the amount of riches they received. But why did the thieves want the hearts? And why would Romen give up his plunder for a specific heart? Something pulled at the back of my mind as James stood abruptly.

He hurried over to Romen and spoke in a hushed tone. Romen uncrossed his arms, placing them at his sides as he fiddled with something latched onto his belt. A rusted, flat circle flipped through his gloved fingers. The metal was dark, allowing it to blend into his clothing. He nodded steadily at James's words. Once he noticed I was watching him, he dropped the circle and returned to his statue-like stance.

Focusing back on Bocaj, I asked, "Why do thieves want dying hearts?"

Bocaj stopped his recount of the old days and gave me a curious glance. "A heart, even a dying one, still has power."

The memory of Ophidian in Ofavemore slammed into my thoughts. If the Traders never made it to the Seventh Choice, Ophidian used the power left in their hearts to fuel the power in his own mismatched one.

"Okay," I nodded, understanding. "But what do they *do* with them?"

More secrets.

"I think we've had enough reminiscing for today," Romen said flatly, not moving from where he stood.

Sirhc bobbed his head, the gold bands on his hair twinkling as the braids swayed. "As Bocaj said before, Perda Forum was a place of trade. All kinds of hearts were traded for wealth, and the thieves did what they wished with them. It wasn't honorable, but the Forum kept the balances of trade equal."

"Once the darkness spread into Ratcha, the thieves scattered, leaving Perda Forum empty of thieves, and filled with murderous men, seeking to destroy the hearts of the ones around them. The only thing keeping Bocaj and I from killing one another was the arenam."

"Sand serpents, loyal servants of the Beast," Bocaj explained, twirling his beard in his fingers.

"Wait, hold up," Claire said, throwing her hands up. "Serpents? As in literal snakes?"

"Yes." Bocaj nodded. "But bigger. Larger than Sirhc's and my height put together."

Claire's face paled as she took in the two tall Magisters.

"While I was still fighting my rage, I tried to destroy them, but couldn't," Bocaj explained. "I watched helplessly as they murdered and fed on my people."

Sirhc clasped his hands and placed them in his lap. "The arenam guard the entrance into Ophidian's lair on Regno. The only thing that keeps them away is the hearts of those who died fighting."

Nausea bubbled in my throat. "And Ira's Vindicae was provided to acquire hearts and also to allow darkness to fully enter into the Twelve Lands."

That was why there were no doors. Instead of Schism's doors injecting a disease, Ophidian allowed greed to enter Obesque before transferring Ira's Vindicae, along with its wrath, into the Land, as well. Sirhc and his people must have been lured to Perda Forum through their rage. Though everything made sense so far, something still wasn't connecting.

"What does the ticking have to do with me?"

The two Magisters shared a wary look before Sirhc explained, "Regno was always different from the other Lands of Decim."

Claire squeezed my hand.

"Those who live on Regno are blessed with a gift. One that's not given to many but has great power: the ability to weave time."

"Timeweavers have been around for many millennia, but are only known to live in Decim," Bocaj continued. "When Decim was created, the weavers decided it would be best for them to live among one another so that they could learn from each other's skills while weaving and protecting time for our Lands."

"Since darkness has fallen over Regno," Sirhc filled in, "we haven't heard from or been able to contact Auso. We fear that the Beast has gained control of the weavers' power and is beginning to unravel Decim's time."

I ran a hand through my hair, feeling grains of sand rub against the pads of my fingers. "So, I've been hearing time unravel. But why can I hear it and no one else?"

Sirhc took in a deep breath before letting it out slowly. "We believe that you're connected to Ophidian. Since he's trying to control time to undo his past, you're hearing the threads of time unravel."

"What?" I flinched and turned to Silas, then Claire,

then James. Their sagging postures and defeated faces told me enough. "How can I be connected to Ophidian?"

Sirhc started to speak, but Silas hurried toward me, silencing him.

"It's my fault," he said, falling to his knees in front of me, his head bowed.

"Silas, what are you talking about?"

He kept his head down, not willing to meet my eyes. His shoulders shook as he said, "Ophidian has half of my heart."

"Yes, I know," I said. "But what does that have to do with anything? You're not making any sense."

Claire squeezed my hand again and explained, "Because Silas gave his heart to you, you're directly connected to Ophidian."

My jaw dropped. "What?" I asked again, unable to comprehend what I was hearing. I turned to Sirhc, hoping he would tell me it wasn't true. He kept his attention on his bare feet, confirming my dread. "But can't you hear the ticking?" I asked Silas. He shook his head. "Why is it only me? Is something going to happen to me?"

Silas raised his head, tears brimming. "I didn't know this was going to happen. I didn't want this. I'm so sorry, Addie. If I could take it back, I would." He buried his face in his hands.

"What is he talking about?" I asked Sirhc.

"Silas is in possession of only half of his own heart, while darkness seeps into the other," Sirhc explained. "The connection is not as strong. Because you're of a pure heart and possess the love of another pure heart, your connection to Ophidian is stronger. With the connection between your and Silas's heart, your fate is now connected to the hearts in the Beast's chest."

Every one of my thoughts halted.

"In order to destroy the Beast," Sirhc continued, "Ophidian's heart, that's fused with Silas's, must be destroyed. With the connection between your heart and Silas's, we don't know if you'll survive."

All sounds faded around me except the low thumping of my heart. By defeating Ophidian, would Silas and I die?

CHAPTER 32

"No!" Silas yelled. He stood between Sirhc and me as if Sirhc were the one threatening me. "I won't allow anything to happen to her. This is my burden and mine alone."

Sirhc rose steadily, his dark eyes unwavering from Silas. "What has happened can't be undone. You knew this when you chose this path."

More secrets.

Silas shook his head furiously. "No, there has to be another way."

"There is," Romen said, breaking his stone-like stance as he took a step forward.

Sirhc spun to Romen, his braids flying. "Silence! If they don't know, he didn't wish for them to. You mustn't say anything."

More secrets.

Romen opened his mouth, as if to reply, but closed it

336

again. Instead, he strode over to me, extending his hand. "Dark days are coming, Bellata. You must always remember that you're not alone."

His golden eyes flashed at me, and a memory, not of my own, rushed into my mind. It was Romen who had saved Nana's heart and brought it back to Eman.

I gasped and yanked my hand out of his, flinging Romen's golden light off my fingertips. Silas and Claire rushed to my side. After assuring them I was all right, I studied Romen, seeking confirmation of my thoughts. He gave a sly grin before exiting the tent.

"What was that about?" Silas asked, following my line of sight.

As I watched the thief leave the tent, I replied, "Not everything is as it seems."

Tick.

Tock.

I tensed. The ticking had only just fled my mind. Why was it returning?

Just then, a deep moan rang through the tent, and everyone froze.

"It can't be," Bocaj said before the tent flap flew open, and a bronzed man holding a spear rushed in.

"Magister Bocaj," he breathed, his shoulders heaving as he knelt before Bocaj. "We must hurry, the gray creatures are attacking in force."

My gaze darted from the messenger to Bocaj. Gray creatures? I sucked in a breath. The siti. They were ravaging Obesque, too?

Bocaj cursed. "I thought we had rid the desert of them."

"I, too," the messenger said, standing quickly. "But we can't hold them for much longer. They're coming this way."

The moaning bellowed closer.

"Go," Sirhc commanded. "I'll be right behind you."

Bocaj summoned his flail and followed the messenger out of the tent.

Sirhc turned to us. "Take as many provisions as you need, but leave as soon as you can."

"But we can help," I said, holding my rod. I didn't want to leave the Magisters to fight the siti alone like I had to in Dunsque.

"No," Sirhc barked as he tied back his braids. His spiked stick shimmered into his grasp. "Bellata, they are here for you. To stop you at any cost from reaching the northern Lands. If you unite all Twelve, Ophidian is finished."

"He's right, Addie," James said, as he quickly threw a pouch of dried fruit into his bag. "We need to keep going."

"Take Romen with you if he allows it!" Sirhc shouted as he sped through the tent flaps.

The tent quieted, and James, Silas, and Claire waited for me to make a decision about our next move. I hesitated, hoping that Damien would've joined us by now. But the siti groans were coming closer. We had to leave.

Squaring my shoulders, I nodded. "Claire, pack as many herbs as you can find. James, continue to find food." They both nodded and hurried off. Strapping my satchel across my chest, I gripped my alme and turned to Silas. "Let's get the thief."

Silas and I rushed out of the tent. We searched all around but couldn't find Romen anywhere. Suddenly, a flash of golden light shined before us, and Romen appeared.

"I hate using my own power," he grumbled, bringing a hand to his head.

"What was that?" I questioned, raising my alme in defense.

"Where were you?" Silas asked at the same time, already wielding his sword.

"Settle down," Romen grunted as he blinked rapidly, then shook his chestnut locks.

Black siti blood caked his clothes as he sheathed his blades behind his back.

"Were you just fighting the siti?" I asked, my gaze traveling over his shoulder to find a group of siti, barely noticeable, on the horizon.

" 'Just'? No. An hour or two before? Yes. But since I'm not connected to Regno anymore, it's hard to keep the timeline straight." Romen smacked the side of his head before focusing on us. His golden eyes glowed brightly. "I cut the group down to half the size it would've been. At least they'll be able to take care of the monsters by themselves."

My lips parted to ask him to come with us before he held up his hand.

"Sirhc told you to try to get me to come with you, and

the answer is no." Romen closed one eye, then the other. "Well, not yet."

"How did you know that?" I stammered.

Romen fiddled with the black sphere on his belt before pulling out his pipe. Striking a piece of flint on a nearby rock, he lit the pipe. He sucked in a deep breath and blew out a light-blue puff. His shoulders relaxed.

"Can't tell you, but you need to get out of here." Romen sauntered to the edge of the tent and slumped down before sucking on the pipe again. Closing his eyes, he tilted his head back as a yellow cloud escaped his lips.

"You don't seem in a hurry," Silas remarked.

"Silas," I hushed before turning to Romen. "Romen, please, we really need your help."

The thief cracked open a lid, the golden glow of his iris dimming. "Not yet. But we will meet again soon." He closed it again. "Possibly."

I cocked my head as Silas started toward the tent. "Come on, Addie. He's not going to help us."

"You go ahead. I'll be right there."

Silas paused before he stomped through the flaps.

"You're going to have to talk to him," Romen said as soon as Silas left. "There's more to his story than you know, and what he's about to face is no small feat. A darkness is gnawing at him, and if he's not careful, it will consume him whole before he can fulfill his purpose. He's teetering on the edge of evil."

I stared at the spot where Silas just stood. Something bad was happening to him. All the times his eyes had turned black, his emotions were out of control, and his violence was rash. My heart throbbed. I wanted to take Silas's pain away but didn't know how. "Why won't anyone tell me how to help him? How to protect him from Ophidian?"

Romen blew one last cloud of white from the pipe before hooking it on his belt. "You can't know all your burdens at once. If you did, you wouldn't have the strength to carry them." As he stood and brushed the golden granules from his legs, I wondered how a thief could have gained so much wisdom.

With his usual hard appearance back on, Romen held the tent flap open. Claire and James hurried out, their bags stuffed with supplies while Silas stood back. His throat bobbed; the black veins were spreading further up his neck.

"If you two are finished, we're ready to head out." Silas pushed through Claire and James before stalking past me.

"Hey," Claire called after him. "You know, we've all had to deal with Ophidian at some point. That doesn't mean you have to be rude about it."

James gave a tired sigh, ushering her away from the tent before they caught up with Silas. "Come on, Addie," he said over his shoulder.

Plunking my rod into the sand, I angled toward the thief. "Are you sure you can't come now?"

Romen held the disc on his belt, rubbing his thumb over the smooth metal. "Not now. Maybe soon."

A loud siti moan pierced the air, and my gut lurched. Were Sirhc and Bocaj okay?

Romen's smirk disappeared as he unsheathed his black blades and pointed me away from the fight. "Time is running out, Bellata. You must go. Now," he commanded.

Nodding, I turned and joined the others before Romen's words hit me. All those times when the Magisters and Eman had said time was running out, I thought they were hurrying me along. Now I realized that what they were saying was the truth. Time was *literally* running out, and I had to stop it.

CHAPTER 33

The once-scorching desert air was now almost as cold as Barracks. The cutting wind chilled my skin, and I shivered, missing Lyle's sweater now more than ever.

I made my way to the front before rifling through my satchel, the golden leaf from Valde shimmering at me as I found the book.

The invisible quill sketched the Lands of Decim as it had all the previous times. As it drew the desert sand around us, I realized just how close we were to Regno.

Thinking back to everything Bocaj and Sirhc had said, I recalled that Regno was where Ophidian had first entered Decim. Because of that, it was the Land that was most overcome by darkness. I couldn't help but think about the timeweavers who lived on Regno. What would happen if Ophidian fully controlled them?

The quill continued to sketch the desert of Obesque, and then the beginnings of the Lomen River.

"What does it say?" Claire asked, joining me. By her laced fingers behind her head and easy gait, I could tell her talk with James had brightened her spirits.

I placed the book in her hands, pointing at the northern river. "We have to go that way."

She nodded, then handed it back to me. "So, Damien. It's weird to call him that, by the way. But what do you think about him leaving?"

Closing the book, I placed it back in my satchel before I rubbed my eyes. "I don't know. I was hoping he would have shown up by now, but I do understand why he left."

I assumed that when he offered to help Silas deflect the arrows from us, he had forgiven Silas for stabbing him. But I can't say I was surprised when he didn't follow Silas to find us in Perda Forum.

Claire dug through her bag and pulled out her water sack. After a long gulp, she replied, "Me, too, but I have a bad feeling."

"Yeah, so do I."

"What do you think about the thief?" she asked, offering me a handful of nuts.

I placed my rod in my other hand, taking the snack. "I'm not sure about him, either."

Romen had saved Nana's heart, so he had to be working for Eman, right? Sirhc and Bocaj seemed to trust him. I hoped I had made the right decision in trusting him, as well.

"I'm sure we have nothing to worry about," I continued, trying to change the subject to something lighter. "How's my—er—your heart holding up?"

Claire snorted, pointing to her chest. "This thing has been nothing but trouble. All I do is *feel*," she said with disgust while making exaggerated hand motions. "I *feel* sorry for the people in Decim. I *feel* worry for you. I *feel* desperation for Lyle." She scoffed, throwing her hands in the air. "I have too many emotions, and I can't control any of them!"

"You'll master them in due time," James chuckled from behind us.

"I'm not so sure, Grandpa." Claire shook her head as she slowed her steps to walk beside him.

I listened to their conversation until what Romen said about Silas resurfaced in my thoughts: he's teetering on the edge of evil. I knew Ophidian was doing something to Silas. He had to be. But *what* was the Beast doing, and how?

With the siti following us, Dacenda couldn't be far behind. I had to talk to Silas before things got worse.

I halted my steps. "James, could you lead us for a bit?" I held out the book to him.

James's ice-blue eyes studied my face before he nodded and took the text. "Of course, Addie."

He and Claire continued their conversation as they strode in front of me while I waited for Silas. Ever since I had taken the lead, he had been lagging behind.

My nerves danced in every direction as I watched him

march closer. Why was I nervous about talking to Silas? We had been together for so long; I didn't think I could get nervous around him anymore. But I knew Silas was different now. I had tried to think he was the same Silas as before, but I was beginning to realize that Silas, my Silas, was gone.

"Hey," I said, noting his quick, harsh steps as he kept his hands firm in his pockets. The sword thwacked against his thigh.

"Hey," he replied but said no more.

As we walked together, our feet crunched simultaneously through the golden sand, scattering the grains like twinkling stars as the moonlight glazed across them. The thunk of my alme sunk into the sand after every few strides, filling the heavy air between us.

My mouth went dry as I met Silas's gaze, and I focused on the edge of my tunic. The golden leaves were beautiful. And the fabric was softer than Lyle's sweater. At long last, I found my courage and began. "I wanted to apologize."

Silas didn't respond, and I didn't dare glance over at him, so I continued. "For not telling you about Romen in the woods earlier. He said he would kill you all if I didn't come with him. I didn't know if he was bluffing or not, so I went, wanting to keep you safe." I watched the sand tumble down the dunes, the cool winds whipping the granules in every direction. "I know I should've told you sooner, but it seemed like you already had so much on your mind that you wouldn't tell me," I added. "I didn't want to add any more to your load. Plus, I didn't know if Romen would come back and threaten me again."

"It's not that I won't tell you, Addie," Silas said sharply before his tone softened. "It's that I can't. I made an oath, and I can't break it. I know you're not happy about it, but it's already done. Please, let it go."

Pressing my lips into a tight line, I neither confirmed nor denied that it bothered me. Of course, I wasn't happy. Silas was happy, then he was angry, then he was confused, then he was loving. He ignored me, then he wanted to talk. How was I supposed to handle all his drastic moods?

Silas reached up and rubbed the back of his neck as he laughed nervously. "You just proved that you're not happy." His voice then turned serious. "Addie, you know how I feel about you. And I'll do whatever it takes to save you from that monster. Especially since it's my fault, you're linked to him."

My irritation flared, and I stopped. "You keep saying that, Silas, but your actions say the opposite."

Silas glared down at me with contempt. "Addie, you don't understand."

Things had been strained between us for a while now, and I had tried to patch them up, but maybe I wasn't meant to. All his outbursts and demands were wearing on me. I had tried to explain what I went through in Ophidian's Realm so he would tell me what was going on with him, but he still wouldn't confide in me. All Silas had done was take, only wanting me to give.

He doesn't want to divulge his secrets. Doesn't he trust you?

I couldn't hold back my anger and frustration any longer. "I understand that you made an oath and can't remember everything about your past." The words were rattling out of my mouth so fast I couldn't stop them. "But your reactions to everything are all over the place. You're happy one moment, angry the next. I don't know how much more I can handle." I threw my hands in the air. "Silas, you attacked Damien. What if it was Claire, or James, or me? What if you had killed him? What if you had killed me?" I pointed to myself. "I need to unite the Twelve Magisters."

After the words left my lips, I finally understood what was going on. Though I cared for Silas and wanted to be with him, I wanted to keep my heart for myself.

Silas stilled, the night wind whipping his blond strands back and forth. "And it's always about you, isn't it?"

"What did you say?" I asked. Sand crunched between my teeth as I clenched my jaw.

"It's always about you, Addie. *'I'm* the one Eman chose,'" he mocked, the black veins in his neck bulging with each word. "'This is what *I* need to do.' How many times have you said 'I' since we left Ramni? If *you're* really the one Eman chose, why do you need the rest of us?" His hands clasped into fists as he shot the accusation at me.

Fury burned in my chest, blood roaring between my ears. The voice I had been hearing all this time spoke again. I had been trying to ignore its taunts and questions, but I couldn't anymore.

Eman did choose you, my pride

encouraged. *Didn't* you *just get the allegiance of two Magister's because* you *fought in Ira's Vindicae?*

And what has Silas done besides keep secrets from you? My rage intervened. *If he really cared for you, he wouldn't have kept them from you.*

One more emotion that I hadn't realized was present, reared its ugly head. *He seems to have trusted all the Magisters with his secrets. Why not you? You're the prophesized warrior,* my envy whispered.

"You didn't have to come," I growled back, allowing myself to fully fall into the tornado of emotions, unable to control them churning in my heart. "It probably would've been better if you didn't. No one would've been hurt by your hand. Why do you think Damien left?"

Silas lowered his stance, and his eyes blackened instantaneously. He unsheathed his sword, bathed in blood-red flames, and charged at me.

I threw my satchel down. I didn't care that a darkness was consuming him. I didn't care that a darkness was consuming me. Silas may be a skilled swordsman, but I was the Bellata. He wouldn't defeat me.

My alme bled red, matching the crimson of Silas's sword. My vision swirled with jade, and my heart hardened in pride toward the man I thought I loved.

"What the—" James turned before we charged straight at each other.

An explosion of ruby light permeated the night sky, sending Claire and James flying on their backs.

The spears of the rod unleashed, clanging against the

metal of Silas's sword. I jerked back and jabbed the pointed end at him. With a snarl, he blocked my attack, returning with one of his own. I dove to the ground, barely missing the strategic move.

We engaged in a merciless fight, far more severe than the one I had endured with Bocaj. But this fight was different. Silas had always been there for me; he had always been my friend. But now he had turned into my enemy.

Lunging from the ground, I swung the rod at Silas's middle, causing him to jump back. He was too slow, and my blade sliced through the fabric of his shirt, barely scraping his chest. An animalistic roar escaped from his throat before he lashed out again. Pain sliced into my shoulder, and I cried out, my alme dropping from my grasp. The metal from the sword detached from my skin, causing fresh blood to spill to the sandy ground. I reached for my alme, but Silas kicked it further away, pinning me between his feet.

"Addie!" Claire yelled, jumping up.

Panting, I looked up at Silas, my emerald vision clearing and the rage fleeing from within me. But what stood in his place wasn't Silas, but a monster. His eyes had blackened completely. The veins throughout his entire body were stained obsidian, a plague beneath his creamy skin, poisoning his body, mind, and heart.

James and Claire's footsteps rushed closer, but I didn't move. Silas loomed over me, the tip of his sword above my mark of the Mender.

"Now," said a voice that wasn't Silas's, but the Beast's. "It's finally time to rid this realm of its Bellata." Silas swung the sword up, bringing it quickly down on my beating heart.

I squeezed my eyes shut, anticipating the pain, but the blade never came. Opening my eyes, I gasped as Silas gripped both hands over the hilt, pulling it away from my chest. His muscles bulged as he lifted it higher.

"Move, Addie." He struggled to speak, but I recognized the gentle tenor as his own.

I scampered from beneath the blade, retreating to where Claire and James stood in awe.

"I never thought Ophidian would've gotten in this far," James breathed with disbelief, placing a protective arm around me.

Sweat dripped from Silas's brow as he struggled with the sword. "You didn't defeat me before," he panted. "And you won't defeat me now." Black blood drained from the cut on his chest onto the sand. Silas plunged the sword into the black pool, unleashing an ear-piercing scream from the liquid.

We covered our ears until the noise subsided. Silas stood still, staring at the sword protruding from the ground. Nobody moved.

Tick.

Tock.

Tick.

Tock.

The clock pounded in my head.

As soon as Silas glanced up, grains of sand shifted behind him, creating ripples in the ground. A new fear pierced my heart. Something was beneath the surface. The granules rolled away from each other, creating a circle around the four of us.

I waited for the same ripples to return, but they didn't. As I leaned to the side and started to stand, a giant creature jolted from beneath the sand, sending us on our backs.

Shaking my head from the fall, I placed my hands on the ground to try to stand once more, until the earth rumbled beneath my palms. Camouflaged to blend in with the desert, an enormous snake overlooked us. It flicked out its tongue, taunting me to make a move. I stilled in my crouched position, scanning the dunes until I spotted my alme twenty feet away. The black rod was just on the other side of the snake's swaying body. My muscles screamed as I slowly faced the creature. I really wished I hadn't just battled Silas.

Sweat trickled down my temples, matting my hair to my cheeks as I slowly stood. This must be the sand serpent that guarded Ophidian's lair.

Neither the snake nor I blinked as we faced one another. If I kept eye contact, maybe it wouldn't make a move toward anyone else. Yet, as I glared into its endless ebony eyes, I understood that it would attack all of us regardless.

Directly behind the snake, Silas rose, slowly retracting

his sword from the sand, his veins now cleansed of the poisonous black blood.

Silas raised the sword above his head, ready to slice through the large reptile. As soon as his blade moved, another creature torpedoed through the surface, knocking Silas back down before it disappeared beneath the dunes. The snake facing me whipped its head around and dove back into the sand, giving me enough time to rush to my alme.

I quickly glanced over to check on Silas. He was moving slowly, but still moving.

My alme was now only a few feet away. I lunged to grab it before the snake's head crashed into my stomach. Cracks resonated throughout my body, and I cried out.

"Addie!" Claire and James yelled, rushing toward me.

James's weapon appeared in his hands. He instantly held it out in defense as Claire checked my side. Every time I took a breath, pain unleashed its fury in my chest.

"You better explain what happened with Silas later," Claire said as she gently prodded. "You also just broke some ribs." Trying to lift me up, she called to James. "We have to get out of here."

Silas limped toward us, still holding up his sword. The arenam had disappeared.

"Addie," James scolded. "These are what Bocaj was talking about. The arenam guard the passage to Ophidian's Realm on Regno. They won't rest until we're dead."

I sucked in another breath, cringing at the pain. "More of a reason to kill them, don't you think?"

Silas slumped forward, his breaths heavy as exhaustion wrapped around him. He averted his gaze from me, facing the sand around us instead. "What do you want to do, Addie?"

His voice sounded drained as his shoulders heaved. Our battle must have exhausted him, too.

The sand stopped shifting, but I was sure the arenam would return. Several feet away lay the black rod. If I wanted a chance at survival against these creatures, I was going to need my alme.

"My alme ..." I murmured, pointing to it as I leaned away from Claire. But she yanked me back, and I yelped.

"Don't move," she demanded before turning to Silas. "Silas, since you have enough energy to battle everyone in our group, go get Addie's alme." He hesitated, and Claire thrust out her hand. "Now!"

Silas sprinted to the rod and hastily placed it in my hand.

"Okay," I said as the power of my alme rushed through me.

A soothing sensation enveloped the cut and my ribs. The bones snapped back into place, and I stepped away from Claire, stretching my shoulder. Though there was still an ache, it had been muted enough for me to fight.

Thankful for the alme, I faced Claire, Silas, and James. "There are at least two of those things circling us. Silas, you take James and try to lure one away from here while Claire and I do the same to the other one."

For the first time since our duel, Silas looked at me.

Sand stuck to the sweat coating his forehead. "And if there's more than two?"

I resisted the urge to brush the grains away. "We'll deal with them, too. We have no choice."

"Ready?" Silas asked James, his voice weary.

My grandfather grunted, and the two of them ran in the opposite direction from where we stood. Within moments, the sand shifted into a line following behind them.

I sent a prayer to the Heavens for their safety and hoped for another day to talk with Silas.

Closing my eyes, I pushed the serpents from my mind, focusing on the thrum of my heart. The crisp energy surged into my veins, and I directed it into my alme. The blades extracted from the now-white staff, transforming it back into a deadly weapon.

When I opened my eyes, I saw Claire gawking at me. "What?"

She pursed her lips. "I had that stick for years, and it was never that cool."

I snorted, thankful for Claire's humor. "Come on!"

We sprinted until the sand moved beneath our feet. An arenam shot out of the grains a few feet ahead of us, scattering granules in different directions.

"I'll keep it distracted!" Claire yelled, running opposite me. "You kill it!"

Nodding, I darted around the backside of the snake while its focus was on Claire. Not wasting any time, I twirled my alme in the air and stabbed it into the arenam's neck. A loud hiss escaped its mouth before it faced me. Red liquid pooled from its black mouth, steaming holes in the sand as the venom dripped to the ground.

Claire whistled and hollered in the distance, but the snake focused on me.

Sucking in a breath, I spun my alme again and pointed it at the snake. "I'm not afraid of you or your master."

The arenam hissed loudly, sending red venom through the air. I ran backward, dodging the poisonous droplets as they scattered in the sand. Behind me, the clanging and yelling of Silas and James trying to lure the other arenam away echoed against the dunes.

As I readied myself to strike again, the sand shifted once more. In a matter of seconds, another arenam burst through the surface, pinning me between both creatures.

The arenams hissed and swayed, closing me in. When I tried to run forward, they blocked me. It was the same when I tried to escape from the side. I was trapped.

Their hissing surrounded me, muddling my concentration. Venom pooled on the ground, sizzling as it hit the sand. Smoke lifted from the granules, obstructing my view.

Silas's and James's voice rang through the desert, assuring me they were still alive and fighting. If they were still fighting, I would too.

An idea pulsed from my heart to my head, and I waited for the snakes to fully envelope me. Once their rough scales scratched my cheeks, I took the blades of my alme and simultaneously stabbed them through the sides of both arenam. The sand serpents let out a deafening scream before slithering back into the ground.

I glanced over my shoulder. Silas and James were running toward us. At first, I thought they had defeated their serpents, but when I saw their wide eyes and frantic sprint, terror coiled in my gut.

"Run, Addie!" Silas yelled, waving his arms. "Run!"

But we didn't have enough time before countless arenams bolted out of the ground, bigger and angrier than the others. Red venom dripped from their fangs as they hissed and swayed. Silas, James, and I wielded our weapons.

Claire scoffed. "Everyone else has something to kill the snakes with, and all I have is my mouth." James chuckled, then handed Claire a dagger from his pocket. She frowned at the weapon as if it were nothing but a child's toy. "This is so small. It won't do anything."

James clucked his tongue. "It doesn't matter the size of the weapon, but how you use it."

Sighing, she nodded and gripped the dagger tightly in her hand.

Silas's back pressed against mine as we faced the circle of serpents around us. I yearned for him. I wanted to go back to my Heart Reign, tell Silas about my pure heart, and together, we would figure everything out. But it was too late. Darkness was consuming Silas, and there was nothing I could do to help him.

"Addie," Silas said over his shoulder, caution in his voice.

My breath hitched. Maybe it wasn't too late. "Yes?"

"I'm sorry. About everything."

Hope fluttered in my chest. "Silas?" I breathed.

"Yeah?"

"Me, too."

We raised our weapons, ready to meet our end. Gold and orange glowed from our blades, intertwining with one another.

As we readied our stances to charge, a figure appeared in the distance. We paused, amazed as a leather-clad warrior sliced through the snakes with two black swords.

After decapitating four of the arenam in a row, Romen jumped from one of the carcasses with a grin. I gawked at him, slack-jawed. Where had he come from?

"Miss me?" He grinned while holding a black blade in each hand.

"What are you doing here?" I asked, still pointing my alme at the other snakes closing in.

"You looked like you needed me."

Before I could respond, he took off running and jumped on another snake, slicing its head clear off. Bright red blood spewed from the wound as the arenam's body writhed on the ground.

"Whoa." Claire jerked back, her eyes sparkling with admiration. "That was amazing."

Adrenaline pulsed through my veins. With a new sense of confidence from Romen, Silas and I charged at the snakes facing us, while James and Claire took the others.

In a matter of moments, headless arenam carcasses surrounded us.

"That was fun," James said, wiping his hand covered in sand and snake's blood on his pants.

"Yes, it was," I agreed.

"You are fearless, Bellata," Romen said, sheathing his swords behind his back. "For that, I'm honored to fight with you whenever you need me."

"Thank you, Romen," I said, relishing the compliment. "But it wasn't only me. Without all of us fighting, especially you, I don't know what we would've done."

A smirk came to his lips. "I'm sure you would've thought of something." He turned and started walking in the opposite direction of where we were headed.

"Wait, where are you going?"

"You no longer require me," he said over his shoulder.

"What if they come back?" Claire asked with a slight plea.

But before he could answer, a blue streak of lightning came from behind us, striking Romen in the back. He grunted, falling to the sand.

"Romen!" we all yelled before rushing toward him.

Several more bolts singed our bodies; the putrid smell of burning flesh coated the air. My friends' grunts and cries filled the night sky until a jolt of electricity paralyzed my limbs.

Numb, I fell to the ground. I landed with my body facing a woman with beautiful blonde hair and a shimmering, yellow necklace.

Dacenda had found us.

A triumphant grin adorned her lush, red lips as she toyed with the gem around her neck. But what confused me the most was the man to her right. Next to the woman who killed my parents was none other than Damien.

CHAPTER 34

Currents of electricity pulsed through my nerves as I lifted my head from the frigid sand. Dacenda grinned wildly as she sauntered across the dunes, nonchalantly stepping over the arenam corpses. Horror clenched my chest. Straining, I tried to lift my hands and legs to get away or defend myself, but my body was stiff, paralyzed by her power.

The bodies of my loved ones laid sprawled around me. James had face-planted into the sand. Claire lay as still as stone on her back, facing the night sky. Silas's sturdy shoulders sunk into the grains a few feet away. I tried to call out to him, out to any of them, but my voice was hoarse, barely above a whisper.

Dacenda approached Romen's motionless body, which was face-down in the sand. With her petite foot, she kicked him in the side with an incredible force. Frustration clogged my throat as I struggled to move again, but my limbs refused.

Dacenda sneered at Romen before rummaging through his armor. I half expected her to zap him again, but she didn't. Instead, she laughed when she found what she was searching for. In two more strides, she stood over Claire. What had she taken from Romen, and what did it have to do with Claire?

I could make out a gray object in Dacenda's manicured hand, and everything clicked into place. Eman had said he knew where Claire's heart was. Romen had found it. But now Dacenda had it.

Tears brimmed in my eyes as I strained to move and yell. But my arms stayed limp, my voice not even a whisper.

Dacenda grasped Claire's heart and squeezed. Claire's body was motionless like the others, until her limbs spasmed, her eyes wide open. Dacenda's thin brows furrowed in concentration as she tightened her grip. Claire's mouth opened slightly, the faintest scream escaping her as her body convulsed violently.

Guilt and anger raged over me as I helplessly watched my friend being killed. A slight heat tinged my fingertips, alerting me that Dacenda's bolts were beginning to wear off. Hope tweaked my heart. Maybe I could stop Dacenda and save Claire before it was too late.

Reaching within myself, I focused on grabbing the rage I was trying to forget. It was red-hot, ready to burn the second I grasped it. My anger may destroy me, but Claire was worth it.

As soon as my power wrapped around my fury, Dacenda cursed loudly. I looked up, relieved to find Claire's body still intact. Dacenda placed the heart in her pocket before summoning another blue bolt of electricity, shooting it straight into Claire. Her body jolted from the impact before her eyes rolled back.

"No!" I shouted.

The rage slipped from my grasp as Claire's body sagged, lifeless. I tried to grab the rage again to fuel my power, but tears clouded my vision, and I sobbed. My arms shook, still too weak to lift myself up. When I managed to lock my elbows, electrifying, blue heat pierced my veins. White lines dotted my vision, my back arching at Dacenda's attack before another jolt of pain paralyzed my limbs.

I slammed into the sand, the grains scratching my cheek and sticking to my tears. I wailed uncontrollably while my body laid defenseless. Footsteps crunched through the sand toward me before a large pain crashed into my head, leaving me in darkness.

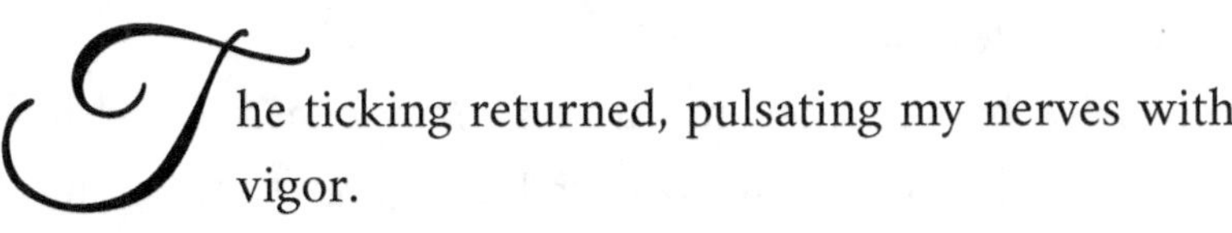

*T*he ticking returned, pulsating my nerves with vigor.

Tick.

Tock.

Tick.

Tock.

I was positive a tree had landed on my head, because it wouldn't stop throbbing. And the ticking, the merciless ticking, had returned, amplifying my pain to a new level.

My eyes refused to open as if they had been sewn shut. The last thing I remembered was the piercing energy slicing through my body and seeing Damien standing next to that witch.

Silas's words branded into my thoughts. *How many times have you said 'I' since we left Ramni?*

I swallowed the bitter truth. I had been so focused on myself and my journey. What happened to James? He had kept our group together through countless arguments and had left Nana in Ramni to protect us and guide us with his wisdom. Had I ever said thank you? Or asked if he was okay with leaving Nana?

My head sagged lower as I thought about Silas. He could always see right through me. Even when being controlled by Ophidian, Silas understood what was going on inside me, and now I had no idea where he was.

The memory of Dacenda taking Claire's heart punctured my thoughts.

Her lifeless body.

Claire had patched me up so many times, I had lost count. Had I ever thanked her? Had I ever told her how much I admired her skills and knowledge of healing?

No, not Adelaide Tye, the once burden-turned

warrior, who dismissed the people who loved her when she was nothing.

How was I going to tell Lyle? Right when they were beginning a beautiful relationship, the love of his life, murdered. Or Doctor Magnum? He and Claire had just seen one another for the first time in years.

Indignation riled in my stomach as I focused on the final person from our group. Though he had helped us before, the only way Dacenda could have known where we were was if Damien led her to us. Had he been deceiving us the entire time? Or was it only after Silas had attacked him? Regardless, I hated that I had trusted him. I hated that Claire had trusted him, and he led her straight into our enemy's hands.

My anger dwindled for a moment as I thought about the conversations Damien and I had. I thought he wanted to be friends. I believed he wanted to defeat Ophidian. But I was wrong.

I clenched my fists in frustration, but my arms fell to my sides, heavy. Finding the strength to open my eyes, I saw worn, rusted shackles tightened around my wrists. I shook my hands to try to loosen the shackles. But, of course, they were tightened to bone-crushing strength. After straining to rise from my position on the cold ground, I wished I hadn't woken up.

"Well, well, well, the Bellata is finally awake," Dacenda purred as she peered down at me through thick iron bars. She latched a torch onto the wall behind her. Her full height was shorter than I thought, but that didn't stop her from leering at me as I sat, stuck in my crouched position.

I gritted my teeth before spitting at her shined black boots. Dacenda stepped away, her lush lips curling in disgust before a terrible laugh escaped her throat. I snarled at the sound, wishing I could break out of my chains and stifle it.

She crouched down and placed her head between the bars of the cell. Condescension dripped from her voice as she asked, "Are you upset with me, Bellata? It's not because I captured you and your friends, is it? Or is it because I killed your parents? No, no, maybe it's because the man you thought was your friend was working for me the entire time." She grinned broadly, and this time, I did spit in her face.

Dacenda reared back, a choking sound escaping from her throat as she wiped the saliva from her cheek. A scowl replaced her vindictive grin, revealing the monster beneath the beautiful façade. With a flick of her hand, the bars of my cell disappeared. Before I could react, Dacenda stalked toward me and grabbed a fistful of my short curls. Pain seared my skull as she yanked my head back. I bit my tongue, not willing to give the witch the satisfaction of hearing me scream. The point of her blade rested on the tender skin on my throat.

"Rebel while you can, Bellata, but you will soon come to an end. Just like your parents, just like your friends, and just like your pathetic brother." Dacenda's cool breath crawled over my skin as she pressed the blade deeper.

"I will kill you if you touch them," I said through clenched teeth, accepting that this woman had lost her humanity long ago.

She only laughed, releasing my hair from her grasp. I jerked my head away, cursing her perfect, curvaceous figure exiting my cell. I wished my power could strike her down with one glance.

Dacenda waved her hand again, and the bars reappeared on my cell. "You should actually be thankful for your betraying friend," she said, turning back to me with a hand on her hip. "If it weren't for him, I would have already given you to my lonely warriors. They're so bored, waiting for the inevitable battle. I thought you would be some entertainment for them. But the little lord thought our master wouldn't want you tainted."

Grabbing the torch from the wall, she flipped her hair over her shoulder before she laughed again. I growled under my breath, watching her stalk into the darkness.

Once Dacenda was gone, my anger dissolved, and I bit my quivering lips. Tears burned in my eyes, but I held them back. I wouldn't allow Dacenda the satisfaction of breaking me. Sniffing, I blinked until the tears were gone.

Angling forward, I searched through the iron bars, trying to find if anyone—Silas, James, or Romen—were near. But I was once again alone.

My heart wrenched at the thought of not having any of them with me. And Claire. Tears gathered in my eyes again, but I pushed them away. She wouldn't want me to cry and babble like an idiot.

"Don't be stupid, Addie," she would say, and then tell me what to do. But she wasn't here, and I had no idea what to do.

Steadying myself, I looked through the bars again. I narrowed my eyes but could only see a black abyss. I flopped back down and discovered that I wasn't completely in a cage. The back wall was made of rock, enclosing me on three sides. The iron bars completed my confinement. Panic gripped my throat as I remembered the last time I saw cages like these. They held siti and half-transformed Traders in Ofavemore.

The shackles pinched my wrists as I gripped the iron bars. That couldn't be right. I couldn't be back in Ophidian's Realm. I wasn't sure where I was, but it wasn't as dark as Ophidian's Realm. And while this place seemed awful, Ofavemore was ten times worse.

I scooted against the back wall, defeat mocking me in every direction. My satchel was gone. My alme was gone. I had nothing. I had no one.

Fear slithered around my neck when the clomping of footsteps echoed from the shadowed corridor. It sounded like the steps of the siti-phagos hybrid from Dunsque. I pushed myself into the farthest corner of the tiny cell and hid in the darkness until the footsteps disappeared.

"How am I going to get out of here?" I whispered to myself once I was sure the creature had passed.

My question died on my lips. The bars ... they were gone.

While trapped in a cell of a place that was clearly evil, a

lot of things could happen. Giant monsters could walk by; Blondie, as Claire would say, could threaten my life. But I never thought I would witness the iron bars of my cell disappear.

"While your shock is flattering, we don't have much time," a deep voice grunted from outside the cell.

I almost cried tears of joy when Romen's irritated voice ricocheted off the cell's walls. As I tried to stand, the shackles around my wrists pinned me to the sides of the cave, holding me at a crouch.

"I can't get out. I'm chained," I whispered back.

Rowen growled, and his tall figure blocked the entrance of the cell. Without another word, he whipped out one of his dark blades, slicing through the metal chains. I jumped back, not realizing how sharp his swords were.

"How did you get out?" I whispered, rubbing my wrists.

"I'm a thief," he grumbled. "I can always get out of a cage."

I didn't question him further, but, as he turned, I noticed a glow around the flat sphere chained to his belt.

The heavy steps of the siti-phagos hybrid echoed down the corridor again.

"Where are the others?" Romen asked as we ducked into a small opening in the wall.

"I don't know."

He growled again. "You would think we would hear

that feisty friend of yours, seeing how everything echoes in this place."

"Claire," I whispered softly. "Claire's gone."

Before he spoke, Romen waited until the hybrid's footsteps echoed away from us. "No, she isn't."

"How could you say that? I watched her die."

Romen shook his head, clamping a hand on my shoulder. A wave of comfort passed through me. "Dacenda's bolts can paralyze, knock one unconscious, and even slow their pulse, but they can't kill. No matter how hard she tries. I should've seen her attack coming." He cursed. "My power alone isn't strong enough to weave the whole strand," Romen muttered to himself.

Hope lightened my chest. Claire was still alive? But that meant she was here somewhere and that we could find her.

If Dacenda's bolts couldn't kill … then my parents …

"No, Dacenda's bolts can't kill," Romen continued. "If they could, she wouldn't still be third in command. Ophidian can't have anyone close to him with power equal to his own." He removed his hand and looked down at me, his golden eyes flashing. "I don't think I need to continue." Understanding his point, I nodded.

We left the small space and crept through the corridor, pausing whenever we heard the slightest echo. I was thankful that Romen was navigating, because my mind was a hurricane of thoughts.

Claire was alive! And with this new information about Dacenda's bolts, my parents might be, too. I wasn't sure what to think about it, but I didn't have a chance before a hand grabbed my wrist, the other covering my mouth, preventing me from screaming.

The large hand yanked me backward a step before Romen slowly turned around.

"It would be wise for you to unhand the lady," Romen said, calmly. "Especially since I don't deal kindly with traitors."

Before Romen could act on his threat, the hand released me. I spun around, instantly recognizing the newly shaven face and perfectly styled coif. Balling my fist, I swung hard. Satisfaction came over me as my knuckles contacted bone, snapping it in half. A surprised groan bellowed from Damien's lips.

The darkness in the hallway receded as Damien dropped the lantern he was holding and grabbed his nose, his other hand held up in surrender.

In one fluid movement, the thief unsheathed one of his black blades, flipped it, and offered the hilt to me.

"You traitor," I spat at Damien, gripping the sword. "How dare you? We trusted you." I stalked toward him, wielding the blade before he took a few steps away, clutching his bleeding, broken nose.

"Wait, Adelaide!" His emerald eyes pleaded behind his swelling face. "Let me explain."

Before he could move, I pointed the sword at his throat until its tip nicked the skin on his neck. "Why should I listen?"

His gaze darted between Romen and me, deciding to focus on me. "I had to."

"You had to what? Betray all of us?"

"Careful," Romen breathed behind me.

Damien cowered away from the thief. "You don't understand."

I pushed the blade in, and he stiffened. "I'm waiting."

Damien's throat bobbed as he lowered his hand from his broken nose. I held back my wince at the jagged line that replaced his once beautifully straight bridge.

"When you jumped through the red doors, terrible creatures invaded Barracks. But with them came that conniving woman. She instructed those hideous monsters to kill everyone in her path, including my consorts. The only way to get close to her and seek my revenge was to trade all of you. I did try to warn you that we were being followed."

Scarlet rage tinted my vision. He betrayed us for his own revenge? My rage swirled into a heated ball, throbbing in my chest, as my hands lined with orange, ready to strike.

My heart quivered, and I paused. I needed to stop my power before I regretted killing Damien. But I wanted to kill him. He was a traitor, a liar. He deserved to die.

As I began to sink the blade into his throat, a voice spoke in my mind:

You are more powerful than you believe.

I instantly recognized the crisp voice of Eman and stopped. His voice was as gentle and soothing as it had always been. It had been ages since I'd seen him, and he was still trying to help me defeat the darkness that lingered within me.

Extracting my blade from the layers of Damien's skin, I flipped the sword around and smashed the hilt on his head. He fell to the ground, unconscious.

When I turned around, Romen shook his head.

"What?" I asked, thinking he was upset I was too weak to kill a traitor.

"It takes great strength to not kill in rage. You are a powerful warrior, Bellata."

"I would have thought rage was the only way."

"It is a way," he said, taking his sword and sheathing it behind his back. "But it's a regrettable way." Romen pressed his ear to the wall. He waited a moment before saying, "We need to move before we encounter anyone else we don't want to meet."

Caught up in the moment of being freed and not killing Damien, I realized the ticking had fled my mind. Now that the excitement was over, it returned with a powerful force. I stifled my cries as it pounded against my head.

Romen's shoulders tensed. "We're close," he muttered.

Red light streamed from a tunnel coming to the right. We crept a few more steps before turning into it, hoping to find the rest of our group. But as soon as we rounded the corner, long, clawed hands grabbed us. Romen tried to reach for his swords, but more siti descended upon him.

As I tried to struggle away, the two siti gripping my

arms pierced my sides with their claws, moaning much too close. I cried out as their claws tore through my skin, draining the life out of me.

"Didn't I say not to damage the Bellata?"

Dacenda's beautiful face contorted as she snarled at the siti. Next to her was an ebony face I had hoped never to see again.

"Little Addie," Schism said, his voice purring like a kitten's. He held out his arms in a welcoming gesture, displaying his black uniform with the silver serpents racing down his arms and pant legs. The black whip coiled around a loop on his belt.

My gut twisted at the sound of the voice that taunted me for years. Though I no longer had my nightmare, Schism's voice had burned into my mind. I glared up at him, trying to hide my fear at the sight of his stone skin.

"It's been too long." He stalked toward me and grabbed my chin.

"Not long enough," I spat back, jerking my face away.

Schism wiped his hand on his chest. "I thought when the siti tortured those two Magisters in the desert, they would've finished you, too. Pity."

My struggling halted. Sirhc, Bocaj. Was Schism telling the truth?

"What did you do to them?" I snarled, lurching forward.

"Still feistier than ever, I see," Schism chuckled, giving my cheek a hard pat. "And I so enjoyed our conversations during your journey."

"What are you talking about?"

Schism straightened his uniform. "Who do you think made you start to distrust everyone?"

The blood from my face drained to my feet. "No, not you," I whispered, trying to back away, but the siti held me firm.

Schism leaned to one side, placing a hand on the whip. "The seeds of doubt were there, but I just continuously sprinkled them with lies until they grew into that glorious battle in the desert with your beloved. How I wish that had ended with you killed." He shrugged. "Thankfully, my lord granted me enough power to play with your mind. I'm only sad that it's over." Schism pointed to the siti holding me. "You two. Bring the Bellata. There is something she must see."

"What about the thief?" Dacenda said as she leered at Romen as if he were a delicious meal.

Schism swatted his hand in the air. "Do with him what you will. He is of no importance to me."

I jerked my arms to wrench free, but the siti's grasp tightened. Straining to look over my shoulder, I tried to find Romen. At least six siti held him down. Dacenda strode toward him, her hand blazing with lightning as a lecherous grin played upon her lips.

The siti yanked me forward before Schism led us down a winding tunnel. The zapping of electrical currents echoed through the hallway. I prayed Romen would be okay.

"Here we are," Schism said joyfully, gesturing before him.

When I saw where 'here' was, I wanted to vomit. Though it wasn't the same one, an exact replica of Ophidian's throne laid in the center of a large, scarlet room. The metallic scent of blood infected the air as I analyzed the dome shape of the ceiling. There were no exits other than the one we were standing in. The black skulls framing the throne were darker than the ones from before. And on the throne sat the Beast himself.

"Adelaide," Ophidian said, interlocking his pale, thin fingers as a wide grin spread across his face. His yellow eyes glinted in the red light surrounding him, the snake tattoos adorning his cheeks slithering up and down his temples.

The siti shoved me to my knees, but I refused to take my focus off the Beast.

"I was wondering when you would visit again." He snapped his fingers, causing a black chain to appear in his hand. "A friend of yours came by, and I knew you would come along, too."

He tugged on the long chain. Appearing out of a cloud of smoke stumbled Claire, wrapped head to toe in rusted chains. Her white hair was matted with blood, her face swollen and bruised. But her head was held high, her chin up in defiance, not allowing Ophidian to break her spirit.

"Claire?" I whispered, not able to believe she was really there. "Claire! Run!"

A searing pain pierced my chest as I studied her awful state. I winced, my heart breaking further.

Her eyes widened at the sound of my voice. "Addie, get out of here!" she screamed.

Ophidian tilted his head back and chuckled. "Oh, Claire. She always has such a flair for drama." He yanked the chain, forcing Claire to his side. When she was close enough, he grasped her jaw. "Thank you, by the way, for bringing back what was mine. I hate it when one of my possessions has scurried away."

Claire lurched forward and bit Ophidian's hand. Growling, the Beast backhanded her across the face. I flinched when she landed on the ground, but as soon as she could, Claire rolled and hoisted herself back up. Ophidian may break her body, but he would never break her hardheaded spirit.

Exhaling, Ophidian lifted his hand to snap. But before he could, Claire repeated, "Addie, get out of here! He has Si—"

He snapped, and she was gone.

Torment wrenched my heart again, pain puncturing my chest. This time I screamed, and Ophidian laughed. I didn't need Claire to continue her sentence.

"The reason this whole problem began was because one insignificant little man wouldn't give me his heart." Ophidian stood, clasping his hands behind his back as he paced in front of his throne. "I didn't think I was asking for much, but apparently I was. You see, he didn't want to make a trade to me, because he wanted to give his heart to the woman he loved."

An awful grin passed over Ophidian's face as he surveyed me. "Which, just my luck, happens to be you. Not only do you bring me back my pet" —he snapped his fingers, bringing back Claire, only this time her mouth was covered with a black ring of smoke around her head, preventing her from speaking— "but you also brought me what I have sought ages for." He snapped again.

A cloud of black smoke billowed in front of Ophidian's throne before it vanished. Silas appeared on the red ground, his shirt gone, and his eyes closed. Shackles bound his wrists and ankles together.

"Silas!" I screamed, tears streaming down my face. When he didn't respond, I yelled louder. "Silas! No!" My shattering heart cracked between my ears at the sight of Silas's motionless body.

I shoved the siti off my arms and ran to his side. All my emotions of anger and frustration toward him dissolved. I couldn't let Ophidian have Silas's heart. But as soon as I got close, Ophidian snapped his fingers, and Silas disappeared.

"No! Please! Don't hurt him!" I cried, clawing at the Beast's legs. "I'll do anything. Please!"

Ophidian glared down on me, and I thought, for a moment, he would consider. But when a loud cackle burst from his lips, I knew I had made the wrong choice.

"Oh, Adelaide, those days are long gone." He kicked me away from him, but the pain was nothing compared to my breaking heart. "I told you before you would suffer the consequences of your choices. Now that time has come." He snapped, and Silas reappeared at his feet.

My heart dropped to my stomach, and I screamed, watching Ophidian's fingers extend into claws and plunge into Silas's chest.

Another crack of my crumbling heart exploded in my ears, and I cried louder than I ever had before. Screams bellowed out of my mouth as tears flooded my cheeks.

My screams only encouraged Ophidian as he dug his claws through Silas's bleeding chest, ripping out his pure half heart with a jerk. Ophidian's grin widened, his eyes bright and more snakelike than ever.

But I didn't care. I couldn't take my eyes off the gaping hole in Silas's chest. The man who had cared for me when no one else would. The man who had always been there for me. The man who I loved more than anything was gone.

The weak beating of the broken heart inside my chest sent pain coursing through my body. I couldn't think, I couldn't feel.

I watched helplessly, too weak from my heartbreak as

Ophidian dug his claws into his own chest, pulling out his black heart, still fused with the other half of Silas's pure red heart.

"One more thing," Ophidian said, holding the hearts in his hands. "In case you were wondering, all those little 'outbursts' your love had, those were caused by me." Ophidian grinned again, showcasing his sharp, grotesque teeth.

"You see," he explained as he peeled his half-black heart away from Silas's. "My heart was fused with your dearly beloved's, creating a direct connection to his other half. While you only heard Time unraveling and some encouragement from my ward, your king heard thoughts of murder, rage, and violence." Ophidian weighed the black and red heart halves in his hands. "It wasn't too difficult at times. He already had his own doubts and fears about you, and those were easily amplified until he reacted." He tossed the black heart half onto his throne. "I don't know how many times I had to tell his heart to kill you before he actually conceded. Quite the stubborn one."

I thrashed, trying to tear away from the siti who had taken hold of me again.

That was why Silas had been acting so violent and rash. Ophidian had been seeping darkness into his heart, luring him to destroy me. But Silas didn't destroy me. Even though he had his own doubts, he tried to fight Ophidian over and over again. But Silas's struggle against the Beast was hard on both of us. Still, I wished I realized sooner that we had both been frightened of what was to come.

"There was that one time he unleashed his fury on that idiot lord." The Beast barked out a laugh. "That was humorous, and the lord ended up being useful in the end."

Ophidian readied the two pure halves, his eyes big and bright with joy.

It was over. Once Ophidian had the power of Silas's pure heart, nothing could stop him. He would easily conquer all the Lands of Decim, condemning our realm to darkness as he began his immortal reign.

"This has gone on long enough, Pulchar!" a voice boomed from behind me, sending the siti fleeing like cowards.

Their sharp claws left my wrists, and I fell forward. I didn't care whether the impact of the red ground killed me or not. I would rather be dead.

But as I wished for my own demise, two strong arms wrapped around my waist, saving me from myself. Tears continued down my cheeks as I weakly lifted my head.

"Oh, Addie," Eman said, pushing a lock of hair out of my face as he held me in his arms. "You've gone through so much."

I tried to speak, but nothing came out. No words could emulate my pain. Eman nodded as if understanding what I couldn't express.

"This will be over soon," he said, seating me gently against the wall.

I blinked a few times, unsure if what I was seeing was

right. As Eman strode toward Ophidian, a white glow surrounded him. When I blinked again, it was still there.

"End this. Now," Eman boomed again, facing the Beast without the intent of backing down.

"Today is just full of surprises, isn't it?" Ophidian seethed through his serpent teeth, which had elongated. "My pet, my heart, and my dear friend have all been returned to me."

Ophidian held one half of Silas's heart, still bright and beating in one hand and the newly severed half in the other.

"There's no reason for the death of the boy," Eman said, pointing to Silas's motionless body.

My throat grew dry as I stared at Silas. The hole in his chest was growing larger in the absence of his heart. His back arched in pain as Ophidian squeezed both halves of Silas's heart. But what was worse was that Silas's eyes were wide open, as Claire's had been, suffering through every ounce of torture.

Ophidian cackled, but the menacing glint stayed in his eyes. "My dear Eman, it's so like you to continuously fend for these weak humans. Just like you did before."

"We both know there's something more you desire than the young blacksmith's heart."

Ophidian paused, obviously intrigued by Eman's comment. After a moment of consideration, he bore his sharp teeth, snapping ferociously at Eman. "I've been after this power for too long. You won't take it away again, Eman! No one will."

Ophidian curled his fingers around the halves of Silas's heart before he grasped his half-black heart from the throne. At first, I thought he was going to disintegrate it. But the other half formed in his hand, and Ophidian reattached the two together. In one fluid motion, the Beast snarled and impaled Silas's chest with his own black heart.

"Pulchar, no!" Eman screamed as he tried to stop his old friend. But it was too late.

The cavity in Silas's chest closed around the black stone, his body accepting it. His entire being shook, reacting to the darkness within it.

"What have you done?" Eman yelled, staring down at Silas's convulsing body.

Ophidian held both pure halves of Silas's heart in his hands as he grinned. "This heart will not respond to me if its owner is still alive. That fool was an annoyance from long ago. It was time to be rid of him. My heart will soon consume him, forever trapping him in darkness."

With every uneven beat of my broken heart, agony from Silas's capture pulsed through my veins. But I willed myself to focus; to do something, anything, to save Silas from this terrible fate. But as I tried to move, the pieces of my heart throbbed, sending a new wave of torture into my limbs. I cried out, landing flat on the floor.

Fighting through the pain, I glanced up to see Ophidian and Eman shouting at one another in a tongue I didn't understand. Eman was still cloaked in white, while Ophidian was blurred in black. The only break in the Beast's darkness was the faint red glow of Silas's pure heart, still beating in the palms of his clawed hands. I wondered why Eman didn't try to take it from him. But when I saw the concentration on Eman's face, and how his hands glowed brightly, I realized he was. The ground shook beneath me as their yelling intensified.

Silas released a horrible scream, his voice mixed with a creature's. His body ceased its convulsions. Terror crept down my spine as his limbs darkened to ash. My broken heart beat out another painful wave, but at that moment, I didn't care. If this was the end, I was going to be with Silas, no matter what.

Enduring as much of the pain as possible, I lifted myself on my elbows and dragged myself toward Silas. The tips of his fingers were already blacker than a starless night as the darkness crawled up his arms.

Every move I made was a struggle. Each crawl was doused in agonizing pain and seemed to take me further from Silas. Using the last ounce of strength I had left, I reached out to Silas's blackened fingertips. They were cold as ice and hard as stone.

"Silas, please," I cried. "Don't go."

I prayed for a response, a tightening of his fingers against mine, anything to reassure me that everything would be okay. Instead, the darkness traveled up his arm, making its way to his neck.

"Please, Silas," I yelled, sobbing uncontrollably. "I love you."

Silas's fingers didn't move, nor did the shadows fade from his body. But his head moved in the direction of my voice. More tears fled down my cheeks as I saw that his face was the last free place before the darkness consumed him entirely.

"Addie," he said in his own voice, barely a whisper. "I—"

A heart-shattering scream erupted from Silas's lips before the darkness covered the rest of his skin, turning his eyes completely black.

"Silas?" I said, squeezing his fingers. "Silas!" I hovered over him, cradling his cold, stone face. "Silas, please answer!"

Another loud crack resounded between my ears, and my heart shattered further. I screamed, folding forward. How many times could my heart break?

"Quiet, stupid girl," Ophidian growled.

Streams of black shadow from Ophidian lashed out at Eman, whipping him ferociously until he fell to his knees. Two siti held Eman steady as the Beast slashed his skin. Eman's white shirt draped around his limbs in strands, shredded from the attack. Ophidian looked on with delight as the shadows marked Eman's flawless bronzed chest with red lines, splitting his skin.

"Eman," I croaked, reaching toward him. Why wasn't he fighting back?

The siti then gathered around my friend, their claws ready to kill. Eman's wails smacked against the domed walls as the siti repeatedly punctured his flesh.

"No!" I shouted.

"Enough," Ophidian said, and the siti ceased, revealing

the pierced and bloodied body of Eman, hanging limp between the two creatures.

Eman's head hung between his shoulders like it was too heavy for him to carry any longer.

Ophidian held his chin high as he trampled Silas's lifeless body. He gripped the halves of Silas's pure heart and rendered them whole. A golden line spiraled around the whole heart as it thumped in the Beast's palm.

Glowering, Ophidian stood over me as his features shifted. His large teeth grew to the size of a true beast's as his eyes grew brighter and unblinking, resembling his snake form.

As he clutched Silas's heart in his claws, Ophidian laughed menacingly, vibrating the red dome.

"'Run, Addie, run,'" he mocked. "Isn't that what my old comrade told you?" He whipped around and grabbed Eman by the throat. The heartmender didn't make a sound as blood rolled down his temples from the siti punctures.

"No, please," I said, barely above a whisper. I had already lost Claire and Silas. I couldn't lose Eman, too.

Without hesitation, Ophidian smashed Silas's heart into his own chest with an animalistic roar. His thick claws elongated to the size of swords while his body grew, darkening to charcoal, as all aspects of humanity left his being. Breathing heavily before me was no longer a beast disguised as a man, but the Beast himself.

"Well, Adelaide," Ophidian said in a voiced mixed with others as his neck extended from his shoulders, taunting me as the arenam had. "There is nowhere left to run."

Ophidian sneered at Eman, whose body was slack in the monster's grip. "Sorry, old friend, you know how the prophecy goes."

Before I could plead again, the Beast held Eman in front of me as his long talons impaled the heartmender. A ground-shaking cry escaped Eman's lips as blood pooled from his chest and back. The pain in my heart reacted before my mind could. What was left of the pieces of my heart imploded in the empty cavity of my chest.

Ophidian flung Eman's body off his claws before letting out an earth-shattering roar. Fierce, midnight wings spread out from behind Ophidian's back, and he flapped them furiously before breaking through the stone ceiling of the blood-stained room.

The pieces of my heart could only beat in agony. My body stilled as shock consumed me. Silas's lifeless, shadowed body laid in one area of the room while Eman's bloodied, dying body laid in the other.

"Addie," a gentle voice croaked. Forcing myself toward Eman, I crawled to his side.

"I'm here," I said, trying not to focus on his blood-soaked shirt.

From its crimson shade, I never would have thought it was once whiter than snow. Eman had always helped me. He had always believed in me even when I didn't believe in him. There had to be some way to fix this; some way to heal him and Silas.

"Addie," he whispered, looking at me with the same kind eyes he always had. "There's nothing you can do. All of this had to happen."

"But why?" I cried, my tears bathing his shirt. "I don't understand."

"You're not meant to," he replied weakly. "But remember, you are not alone."

Before I could sob another tear, the ticking stopped. And Eman's body disintegrated into ash beneath my grasp, leaving me completely alone.

CHAPTER 36

The ground shook as if the entire realm was erupting. Instead of bracing myself against the quaking ground, I let my body crash and roll through the red room. Claire was gone. Silas was gone. Eman was gone. My heart was shattered. I was alone.

Another earthquake shook the foundation, and I landed next to Silas. Pain vibrated through my body at the sight of the darkness that claimed his limbs. Reaching out, I took hold of his hand and squeezed it tight. Tears barreled down my cheeks as I realized that he wouldn't respond. He would never respond. I would never feel his touch again. Or see his crooked smile. Or hear his laugh.

I fell upon him, not caring about the pain, and cried. "I love you, Silas. I always have. Please, please come back."

The loud moans of the siti surrounded me, but I didn't care. Let the siti come.

I tightened my grip around Silas. He had never left me; I wouldn't leave him.

The clang of metal replaced the siti moans before sturdy footsteps approached. With my strength gone and my heart bearing nothing but pain, I couldn't move. A hand gently touched my head.

"Bellata," Romen's deep voice said. "We need to leave."

"No," I whispered, too defeated to yell. "I won't leave him."

Romen sighed, but not one of irritation. This one held the heavy weight of sympathy and pity.

"I can't carry both of you."

"Take him," I said, without hesitation as I lifted my head. "I can carry myself."

His golden gaze was unconvinced, but he hoisted Silas up anyway. As the cold stone of Silas's body was pulled from beneath me, I rolled off to the trembling ground.

"We must hurry," Romen said.

Sweat drenched my body as I pushed myself to my elbows. A force within me fought against the shadows of fear and death.

I couldn't stay here. I had fought too hard and for too long. Lyle, Nana, Sana, and Doctor Magnum were still back in Ramni. And James, as far as I knew, was still alive. I still had loved ones that would die if Ophidian succeeded. I needed to be strong, if not for myself, for them.

I lifted myself from the ground, the pain and aches of a thousand grieving pieces piercing the inside of my chest.

But I would continue for Claire. I would fight for Silas. And I would live for Eman.

Wheezing, I followed Romen down the crumbling hallway. I wasn't sure how long we would be in Ophidian's lair or if we would ever escape. But when I saw the light of the sun peeking through the end of the cave, the pain in my heart receded just enough to keep me going until we reached our exit.

The sunlight warmed my skin but did nothing for the hollowness inside. I kept my eyes focused on Romen's leather boots as they crunched rapidly through the gray pebbles leading out of the cave.

As we rushed down the hill, the faint sound of water drifted through the air, caressing my throbbing eardrums. When I gazed up, the soft waves of the Patet ocean, gently beating against the charcoal ground, greeted me.

"They're around here somewhere," Romen muttered, trying to adjust Silas on his back.

"Addie!" Lyle shouted.

I strained to see my brother, tall and strong, running toward me. Two canoes, manned by Brand and Gaius, laid on the shore. The two brothers stood closely together with another figure I instantly recognized as James. My heart throbbed. He was alive. The pain overtook me again, and I fell to the ground.

"Addie!" Lyle shouted again, this time his voice laced with concern. Lyle's voice muffled with Romen's above me. "Silas," "heart," "Eman," and "Beast" were all I could make out before darkness rimmed the outer edges of my vision.

"Addie," Lyle whispered in my ear. "Addie, if you can hear me, blink once."

I blinked. A sigh of relief came from Lyle's mouth as he cradled me in his arms and carried me.

Each step Lyle took sent pain through my body, but I was too exhausted to care. I only had enough energy to watch the clouded gray sky and pretend that this would all be a bad dream when I woke up tomorrow.

He lowered me until I hit the hard floor of a canoe.

"Is she all right?" Brand whispered to Lyle.

Before he could respond, Gaius said, "No. She's not all right."

A thick blanket was draped over me, separating me from the low murmurs of Lyle, Brand, and Gaius. They spoke for only a few moments before the sound of stones scratching against wood vibrated beneath me, soon replaced by the slow bouncing of steady waves. A hand rested gently on my forehead. Slowly, I moved my swollen eyes upward to see James staring down at me. His face was badly bruised, but other than that, he seemed fine. The warmth from his hand helped soothe the throbbing in my head, and for a moment, the pain eased.

"Rest, Addie," he said softly as his hand glowed a warm white. The darkness clawing at the edges of my vision didn't need much convincing to fully lure me into sleep.

ges seemed to pass as I slept, only a dark abyss filling my dreams. But soon, the darkness shifted, swirling and changing into the red light of Ophidian's lair, bringing me back to that same horrid scene. I screamed when Ophidian impaled Silas's chest. I thrashed and wailed as I watched Eman's body whipped to shreds. My heart broke over and over again, exploding in my chest. Every moment was torture. And I was always helpless to save them.

A hand grabbed my shoulder roughly, shaking me.

"Addie, wake up!" Lyle shouted. When I opened my eyes, my brother's face stared down at me, his brows knitted together. He fell back in his chair. "Good. You're okay."

With my vision still blurry, and my chest still aching, I blinked a few times before searching around. "Where am I?"

Lyle fixed his spectacles. "You're back in Ramni."

The posts of the elegant bed and the streaming waterfall came into view. Intricate braided vines wrapped around the bedposts, sprouting buds of white and gold. Relieved to be safe within the healing realm of Ramni, I relaxed into the rose-scented sheets.

I turned to Lyle, whose face shifted to concern. "What happened?"

"I was afraid you would ask that," he said. When I gave him a blank look, he sighed. "I'll be right back."

Lyle quickly stood and left the room. In a matter of

moments, he returned with a gray book in his hands. I immediately recognized it as the cursed text from his bedroom.

"Is that ..."

He nodded. "Doctor Magnum and I have been working for a while to break the enchantment." Lyle opened the book and flipped through it until he got to a specific page. He glanced up at me with sorrowful eyes. "It was me who stole the book from Ramni and put the curse on it."

"But why?"

Lyle shook his head, unable or unwilling to say any more. Instead, he focused on the book. "After reading through it again, I now know why Ophidian wanted this book so bad. There's a legend, a prophecy, of who will defeat him."

"Yes, I've read it," I said quickly.

"No," Lyle replied. "You've read part of it."

"There's more?"

He bobbed his head. "The prophecy you know says, 'In the darkest of times, a warrior will rise among them. Braided with the Sword and the Mallet, the Staff will complete the trio of almes, reigning light over dark.' But there is a prophecy for each thread of the braid, as well."

"What?" I asked, reaching for the book. "Where does it say that?"

Lyle snatched the book away before opening it. "The warrior who wields the Staff will endure heartbreaking pain, but their heart will be rendered once again." He placed his hand on my knee. "You'll make it through this."

I wrapped my fingers in the plush, purple blanket, trying to block the images of Silas's body consumed by darkness, and the blood dripping from Eman's chest. How could I ever heal from this heartbreak?

Lyle cleared his throat and turned back to the book. "The healer, who wields the Mallet, will sacrifice himself for the throne ..."

"What?" I screamed.

Lyle looked up, his spectacles sliding down his nose. "What?"

Eman's words echoed in my thoughts. *There is nothing you can do. All of this had to happen.*

"Is that why?" I shook my fist at the rustling leaves forming the ceiling. "Is that why you barely fought back?"

"Addie," Lyle said softly. "Eman knew what he was doing. He had to sacrifice himself so that the rightful heir to the throne of Lignum could ..."

"I don't care about Lignum or the Rexus!" I shouted. The pain in my chest intensified as tears of fury streamed down my face. "I've lost everything!" I clenched my fists until the skin of my palms broke beneath my nails. Why would I care about the Rexus, especially when Eman sacrificed himself for him?

Lyle's fingers gently grasped my fist. "You haven't lost me."

Guilt fell on me as I wrapped my arms around my

brother's neck and cried. He held me close, protecting me like he always had when we were young.

After I had cried enough to soak the entire shoulder of his shirt, Lyle snorted. "After you hear the last prophecy, you may reconsider your feelings for the Rexus."

Detaching myself from his shoulder, I sunk into the giant floral pillows on the bed. Taking a shuddering breath, I wiped away my tears.

Lyle adjusted his spectacles and cleared his throat. "'The king, who wields the Sword, will not suffer heartbreak or sacrifice, but a test. If he succeeds, all evil will rest. But if he shall fail, all will be forever in darkness.'"

Lyle waited for a response, but I was too awestruck by what I had just heard. I had always thought Silas's sword was the one spoken of in the prophecy, but that meant …

"A king?" I said before I could stop my thoughts.

Lyle nodded.

"The Rexus?"

"Mhmm," he replied, bouncing his leg up and down.

"Eman sacrificed himself so that …"

"Silas could prove himself as the Rexus and the rightful heir to the throne of Lignum," Lyle finished with a triumphant look, throwing his fist in the air. "Silas is meant to rule over all the realms."

I mulled over Lyle's statement before asking, "Why would Eman give his life for one person?"

Lyle smiled. "One person matters."

"So, Silas is still alive?" I asked, not wanting to be too hopeful. Lyle drummed his fingers on the page, hesitating.

The hope that had built in the pieces of my heart dwindled.

"From what I've read, he's neither dead nor alive, but in a middle state until he's passed or failed his test."

"What's the test?"

Lyle shrugged his shoulders as he shook his head. "I don't know. But I do know that Silas knew about this and had known about it for a while. That's the only way those two guys with the canoe would have known to wait on the shores of Regno. Without them, I don't know what would've happened."

Thinking back, I remembered all the hushed conversations Silas had with James and the Magisters. How he would never tell me what was going on or why he was so burdened. This was why.

"I wish he would've tried to tell me."

"Would you have let him go through with it if he did?"

I didn't respond.

Closing the book, Lyle laid it on the bed. "Trust Silas, that he knew what was right. Trust Eman, that he knew what was right, and trust yourself, that you know what is right."

An entirely different man than the one I grew up with sat in front of me. This one wasn't angry or bitter, but content and strong. Yet dread still weighed my chest.

"Ophidian still has Claire," I said quietly, unable to meet his gaze.

A sadness layered in Lyle's eyes as he ran a hand

through his dark curls. "I know. But Claire is strong. She'll be okay."

"How do you know?"

Lyle placed a hand over his chest. "I feel it. I feel her spirit still fighting and her heart still alive."

A small smile was finally able to come to my lips. "When did you become so wise?"

Lyle laughed. "I've been reading a lot of books."

CHAPTER 37

"Come on," Lyle said, offering his arm. "I need to show you something."

Grabbing his arms, I completely relied on him to stand. As the white sheets fell away, I saw that a light-green dress embroidered with golden leaves had replaced my torn and bloodstained armor.

"Sana was here earlier. She's working on mending your clothes now. Though she's confused as to why you keep destroying everything you put on."

I chuckled before my laughter died on my lips. "Does she know about Eman?"

Lyle wrapped an arm around my waist, helping me shuffle toward the open door. "I think she always knew. When Eman left, we didn't see Sana for days."

As we hobbled through the doorway, I wondered how Sana was faring through the loss of Eman. Was her heart shattered like mine?

But I didn't have much time to wonder, because Sana appeared in front of us, a kind smile on her face.

"Welcome back, Bellata." Shadows circled beneath her tear-stained eyes.

The pieces of my heart trembled. "Sana, I'm so sorry."

"Apologies are unnecessary, Bellata," she said, her delicate bronzed hand covering my own. "I know Eman did what he had to."

"Addie!" another voice shouted from the moss-covered hallway. I peered over Sana's head to find Nana and James running toward me with Doctor Magnum by their side. Tears misted my eyes when Nana wrapped her arms around me, gripping me so tight it hurt.

"I thought I lost you again," she said as she caressed my curls.

I leaned my forehead against hers, then took Doctor Magnum's hand. His grip was soft and gentle.

"I'm so sorry." My voice wavered. "We'll get her back."

Clearing his throat, the doctor patted my hand before excusing himself.

After a few moments of hugging, Sana stepped toward me. "There is someone you must see."

Nana gave my cheek a gentle pat before releasing me. James kissed my forehead before placing his arm around Nana's shoulders. Lyle rewrapped his arm around my waist as we followed Sana down the mossy hallway into the main one. Sana's fluttering footsteps barely echoed against the walls as we padded to Eman's mending room.

We passed by several rooms that held a variety of creatures I'd never seen before. When I turned to Lyle for an explanation, he only shrugged.

Sana padded into Eman's room while I prepared myself for who was in there.

"Are you ready?" Lyle asked after a few moments. I gave him a nod, and we headed in.

Sucking in a breath, I tried to stifle the pain in my broken heart as I focused on Silas's ebony body lying on Eman's mending table. A white liquid covered the gashes on his chest from Ophidian's claws.

"It won't save him, but it will heal the wound within," Sana said to my unspoken question.

I studied Silas's face. His mouth was held open in a scream while his eyes were squeezed shut. He was frozen in pain from when the darkness fully consumed him. Steadying myself next to the table, I reached out and caressed Silas's cheek.

"We'll give you some time," Sana said quickly as she ushered Lyle out of the room.

Once they had left, I pushed Eman's wooden chair closer and sat down. I grabbed Silas's hand, leaning forward to kiss his fingers.

"Is this how you felt when I jumped through Schism's doors?" I asked him. "It's just like you to do to me what I did to you. It's not very nice." I sucked in a shuddering breath before continuing. "But there's one thing that I don't understand." I brushed his palm. "Ophidian said he needed to destroy your body so that your heart would respond to him. But you're not the owner of your heart. I am."

"And that's why he's the Rexus," a deep voice said from behind me.

Still holding Silas's hand, I glanced over my shoulder.

"You see," Romen said, striding into the room. He placed the brown book from Eman on a round table to his left. "This boy had either known this was going to happen or was very, *very* lucky."

"What do you mean?"

Romen crossed his arms over his chest as he scanned Silas's motionless body. "The heart Ophidian holds will only obey his wishes for so long. It desires to be bonded with its true owner. One way or another, Silas has begun the destruction of the Beast."

I pressed my hand on Silas's chest, too stunned to respond. Lyle had also said Silas knew this would happen. But how could he have known? I thought back to when we first came to Ramni when Eman mended Silas's heart. Eman had to have told Silas then. My broken heart quivered, realizing the weight of the burden Silas had to carry during our journey.

"So, what now, Bellata?" Romen said, breaking me from my thoughts. I watched as he pulled my alme from behind his back. "Are we to hide here and wait for our untimely end? Or are we to meet it head-on and make the darkness quake with fear?" The glint of his golden irises shimmered with mischief as he held out the black rod to me.

I blinked at it in surprise. "How did you get that?"

He smiled smugly. "Thief."

I snorted, unable to stop my grin.

Regardless of the owner of Silas's heart, Ophidian was still out there, ready to destroy Decim, along with the other realms. He still had control over Regno and was trying to gain control of the Time Weaver's power.

We had gained only six of the Twelve Magisters' allegiances to Eman. Though he was no longer here, I was still going to keep the iuram I made to him.

Turning back to Silas, I squeezed his hand and pressed my lips to his forehead. I didn't know what test he had to endure, but I knew he would triumph.

Standing tall, I grasped the cool metal of my alme. The power instantly fueled my weary bones. The green dress of healing transformed into my warrior's uniform of strength. My black rod was no longer a staff but a weapon ready to fight and defend. And though my heart was still broken, and I was still weak, I would continue to fight until darkness fell.

ACKNOWLEDGMENTS

Jesus, my Savior: Thank you for Your continued guidance and assurance. You always provide!

David: Thank you for being my best friend and biggest fan. I'm so thankful for a husband who loves to talk about plots and character development on evening walks.

Matthew: I love you so much!

Nana, Paw Paw, Lauren, Tyler, Jake, and Steph: Thank you for always cheering me on from the sidelines and being the best babysitters so I can shoot for the stars. I couldn't have made it this far without all of you!

Esther, Randy, Paul, Courtney, John, Kaitlyn, Lydia, Ben, Rachel, William, and Clarissa: Thank you for supporting my endeavors and attending all my events!

Chris, Lauren, and Rachael: Thank you for geeking out with me and loving my stories and characters before they were lovable.

Lydia: Thank you for your countless hours of work on edits and STILL loving every character and version of my stories.

Mrs. Zeek: Thank you again for all those lessons in Twelfth grade English!

A BIG thank you to my amazing readers and book community! I enjoy your excitement and love for my characters and their stories. I hope to bring you many more adventurous books in the future.

ABOUT THE AUTHOR

V. Romas Burton grew up bouncing up and down the East Coast where she wrote her first story about magical ponies at age seven. Years later, after studying government and earning an M.A. in Theological Studies, V. Romas Burton realized something even bigger was calling out to her--stories that contained great adventures and encouraging messages. Because she couldn't find exactly what she was looking for, V. Romas Burton decided to write her own great adventure. She is now the award-winning author of Heartmender. When she's not writing, she spends time reading as many books as she can, watching YouTube videos and taking care of her adorable son. You can visit her online at www.vromasburton.com.

9 781957 899138